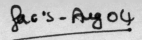
Jac's - Aug 04

Anne McCaffrey, a multiple Hugo and Nebula Award winner, is one of the world's most beloved and bestselling s~~cience fiction and fantasy~~ writers. She is the au~~thor of the successful~~ *Dragonriders of P*~~ern series. She lives in~~ a castle in Ireland.

Elizabeth Ann ~~Scarborough is the author~~ of *Channeling Cleopatra* and the Nebula Award-winning *The Healer's War*, as well as more than twenty science fiction and fantasy novels. She lives in the Puget Sound area of Washington State.

Anne McCaffrey's books can be read individually or as series. However, for greatest enjoyment the following sequences are recommended:

ACORNA'S REBELS

ANNE MCCAFFREY
& ELIZABETH ANN SCARBOROUGH

CORGI BOOKS

ACORNA'S REBELS
A CORGI BOOK : 0 552 151351

First publication in Great Britain

PRINTING HISTORY
Corgi edition published 2003

1 3 5 7 9 10 8 6 4 2

Set in 11/12pt Palatino by
Phoenix Typesetting, Burley-in-Wharfedale, West Yorkshire.

Corgi Books are published by Transworld Publishers,
61–63 Uxbridge Road, London W5 5SA,
a division of The Random House Group Ltd,
in Australia by Random House Australia (Pty) Ltd,
20 Alfred Street, Milsons Point, Sydney, NSW 2061, Australia,
in New Zealand by Random House New Zealand Ltd,
18 Poland Road, Glenfield, Auckland 10, New Zealand
and in South Africa by Random House (Pty) Ltd,
Endulini, 5a Jubilee Road, Parktown 2193, South Africa.

Printed and bound in Great Britain by
Cox & Wyman Ltd, Reading, Berkshire.

Papers used by Transworld Publishers are natural, recyclable
products made from wood grown in sustainable forests. The
manufacturing processes conform to the environmental regulations
of the country of origin.

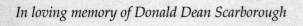

In loving memory of Donald Dean Scarborough

Acknowledgments

Thanks again to Rick Reaser for science, salvage, and cultural consultation regarding Linyaari birth disks. Thanks also to Martin H. Greenberg for his support of the Acorna books, and to Denise Little, our editor at Teknobooks, for her careful editing and suggestions. Thanks also to Diana Gill, our editor at HarperCollins, for her suggestions on how to improve the book.

ACORNA'S
REBELS

ONE

The mountains were still not right. Oh, the peaks soared majestically enough. Gaali, a huge crest translucent with snow and deep blue glaciers, loomed above the purple-blue cone of Zaami, which nestled between it and the rugged, sharp-edged icy summit of Kaahi, the only one of the three massive slopes ever to have been scaled.

These peaks had an almost mystical significance to Acorna's people, the Linyaari. They were the top of the world, and Our Star's progress from one side of Gaali's peak to the other had once divided a Linyaari day as the rising of moons did on other planets. The sight of the rugged mountains against the horizon had meant home to the Linyaari – until their world was invaded by an alien race, the Khleevi. The Khleevi had destroyed everything in their path, even the highest mountains on Vhiliinyar, the native planet of the Linyaari.

Many of the Linyaari recovery teams working on their ravaged homeworld had recently seen their mountains again, beautiful and whole. Caught up in the alien machinery of a long-buried ancient city there, they had been trapped and snatched into their planet's past. Returning time travelers brought back sketches, notes, specimens, even vids of the peaks, but Acorna could not reconcile any of their images perfectly with the holo program that would form the basis for the re-formation of the peaks.

'You've redone that range twenty times if you've done it once, Princess. Give it a rest,' said Jonas Becker, CEO of Becker Interplanetary Recycling and Salvage Enterprises Ltd., and captain of the firm's flag and only ship, the *Condor*.

'It's as if every person who has seen those mountains has seen different ones, Captain,' Acorna said. 'No matter how we build them, someone will be disappointed or think there is something we have left out.'

'We'll just put all the controversial stuff at the top of the high one, then.' He shrugged. 'That way if they want to nitpick they'll have to either climb it or land on it to find fault.'

'Maybe. But they are already rebuilding our home more slowly than most people truly wish because of Aari and me. I want everything to be just right when each feature of old Vhiliinyar is reinstated.'

'You are really something,' Becker said, shaking his head. 'You look like you haven't finished high school, yet you're trying to push mountain ranges around and tell forests how to grow because you also think you can tell people what to see when they look at them? Give it up, Princess. It wasn't just because of Aari that your people decided to take the more conservative approach to re-terraforming Vhiliinyar. Expense

14

entered into it, and truly owning their home, and all that other stuff Kaalmi Vroniiyi and the Ancestors talked about at the last Council meeting. It's time for you to let go a little. You have to do something besides work and hang out at the time machine in case Aari pops up.'

'I do other things!' Acorna said with a little jut of her lower lip. 'I go for long walks. I talk with the Ancestors and the Elders. I make notes of how the environment is trying to heal itself from the Khleevi damage.'

At that moment a piece of debris flew between them on an ill-tempered breeze blowing through the ancient city. Though the breeze was nothing like the high roaring winds that plagued Vhiliinyar's barren surface these days, it carried blades of ice in it nonetheless. The debris was pounced on and subdued immediately by Becker's first mate, a Makahomian Temple cat Becker called Roadkill, or RK. Being the second in command on a salvage ship, RK was a highly skilled professional when it came to collecting junk. However, in this case, once he had pounced on the object, which turned out to be a crumpled list of specimens collected by *aagroni* Iirtyi in different eras of Vhiliinyar history, the paper's lack of resistance bored the cat.

Abandoning his prey, RK strolled over to greet Acorna, leaped onto her shoulder, and walked across her chest. Purring madly, he rubbed his face against the tablet she held. She finally released it and rubbed his chops, which had been his master plan all along, she suspected.

Becker continued his own blandishments.

'Going for a walk isn't like really *going* anywhere. You haven't even visited MOO in over six weeks. Hafiz has summoned RK and me to visit him there, and we're about to board the *Condor* now. Come on with us. Mac would love to see you. Besides, if there's salvage to haul, we'll be short-handed without Aari. We could really use your help. My back has been acting up lately.' The very able-bodied veteran spacefarer rubbed the small of his back and groaned, while watching her from slitted eyes to see if she was looking sympathetic.

She laughed. 'Oh, very well, Captain. I take it that you are not employing your acting skills because you wish me to heal your "bad back," but because you're so flatteringly desperate for my company, such as it is these days. Let me tell Maati and the others I'm going, leave a few notes for them on how to continue my work here, get some things together, and I'll be right with you.'

As soon as they were back in space Acorna realized that Becker had been right to lure her away from the planet. Back on Vhiliinyar, no matter how hard she worked, she always kept one part of her focus on the people around her, secretly waiting for someone to say they'd seen him – coming out of the lake or near the time device or . . . somewhere.

Here on the *Condor*, with Becker, Mac, and the cat, it was almost like the impossibly recent good old days when they had all been together. Except now there was someone definitely missing. Aari's absence was still all too painful to her.

One nice thing about the *Condor* was that, since Becker was continually patching it up with salvaged parts and pieces, it never actually looked the same, outside or in, two trips in a row. Something always needed to be repaired or replaced, and Becker had a particular talent for integrating the mechanical and electronic equipment of far-flung alien cultures so that it blended together into the intergalactic hash that was his vessel.

On this trip she recognized some hull modifications made with bits of salvaged Linyaari ships – the gaily painted and gilded loops and flowers made the skin of the *Condor* resemble a patchwork quilt. Becker seemed to have had a bit of trouble with the control panel, too. A part of the current module had been salvaged from a Khleevi vessel. The Khleevi controls were designed to be manipulated by widely spaced pincers and were sized for a very large being, instead of human or Linyaari hands. Becker had rigged sticks with pulleys that operated pincers at the ends of them for performing certain functions at the control panel. Acorna wasn't sure she wanted to know what those functions were.

As the ship approached MOO, she felt her anxiety rising about being so far away from Vhiliinyar and the time machine again. What if Aari returned while she was gone?

'Captain, could we hail Maati?'

'Sure, honey, but don't you think she'd have hailed us if anything had happened? Look, Acorna, I know this has to be rough for you, but Aari loves you. It doesn't matter how much it seems like the guy went out for a packet of chickweed and was gone for six months; if there's a way for him to get back, he'll be back. And you're going to be the first person he looks for. You know I'm right.'

'Actually, Captain, I just wanted to see if Maati had a message for her parents. They're back on MOO now finishing up some research.'

Though he raised a doubting eyebrow at her, Becker did as she asked. It took some time for Maati to reach a com console and report back, but when she did, she looked more excited than Acorna had seen her look since Aari's disappearance.

'Khornya, I'm so glad to hear from you! The *aagroni* Iirtye is back from his latest time voyage. He's been collecting specimens again, you know, but he found out something really strange on this trip. Apparently he couldn't find any *pahaantiyirs* on Vhiliinyar, no matter where he looked, and he looked right up until a generation or two before the older Linyaari among us were born. Of course, he couldn't continue his search any farther because of the space-time continuum problem, but he didn't find any ancestors of the *pahaantiyirs* on our planet at all.'

Acorna was hard pressed to understand her young friend's fascination with this discovery. Maati had never seen the species the older Linyaari remembered from Vhiliinyar before the Khleevi invasion. The Linyaari Elders claimed that RK looked incredibly like those beloved feline creatures, however.

'The species must not have been indigenous

to Vhiliinyar, then,' Acorna said. 'Probably they came from one of the trading planets.'

'Nobody remembers which one, if they did,' Maati said. 'It's kind of a mystery, really.'

'More of a mystery to me is the fact that, if they were so highly thought of, why didn't our people bring *pahaantiyirs* with them from Vhiliinyar when they fled?'

'It's funny about that,' Maati said. 'Everybody I've talked to said they just suddenly couldn't find their furry friends when the time came to go. Like the *pahaantiyirs* had already disappeared. The evidence from our recent explorations seems to bear that out. At least we haven't found any feline bones in the rubble out on the surface. That's good, don't you think?'

'I suppose. Maybe the *pahaantiyirs* all found the secret city and have been hunting vermin down there. Maybe we'll run into their offspring, fat and happy, when we explore the city further.'

'I hope so,' Maati said. 'But meanwhile, the *aagroni* would like to know if Captain Becker would ask Commander Kando if she knows anything that might connect RK's fellow Temple cats and our *pahaantiyirs*.'

'Be glad to,' Becker said. 'Nadhari doesn't talk about the old homeworld much, but maybe we just need to ask her.'

Acorna heard something unsettling in Becker's tone when he spoke of Nadhari Kando, the security chief for Hafiz Harakamian's Moon of Opportunity, and a very formidable woman. 'Is there something wrong with Nadhari, Captain?' she asked. She could read him, of course, but that would have been a breach of good manners, and besides, Becker was very good at expressing himself verbally.

'Yeah,' he said. 'I think so.'

'Is it because you are no longer mates?'

'No. I mean, it's not just me. Seem to me like she's shutting down emotionally – and with everybody. At first I thought maybe it *was* just me, because she was mad at me and wanted to be with that Federation soldier, but then she dumped him after a couple of months. And she doesn't mind that I was seeing Andina. She likes her, says she's better for me than she was. That's not like Nadhari – trust me. Nadhari and me – well, we're still friendly, and yeah, I still care about her. But something smells funny to me – though we haven't had a real conversation since I came back from collecting the salvage on narhii-Vhiliinyar, so I'm not exactly sure what's on her mind.'

'But you have an idea?' Acorna prompted.

He nodded, eyes down, lips compressed, shoulders hunched forward a little. 'Yeah. I think she's still stirred up inside about what happened to her when Edacki Ganoosh and General Ikwaskwan doped her up and turned her into a torture machine to use against your people.'

'But surely she knows that was not her fault,' Acorna said. 'And my people, as soon as they were able, healed her of her wounds, both physical and psychic. Didn't they?'

Suddenly she felt guilty. She had been so preoccupied with her own problems – her lifemate Aari's disappearance, initially due to a temporal accident caused by Vhiliinyar's systematic destruction by the Khleevi, and later exacerbated by her own attempts to find him and bring him back – that her worries had caused *her* to shut down in a way. She'd somehow forgotten that other people had problems, too, problems they might not want to share with her for fear of adding to her burden. But the truth was that it was a relief to think of someone else's troubles now. For the time being, she had gone as far as she could with her own.

Becker shrugged. 'Sure, *they* forgave her for the harm she did to them, and healed her of the drugs and her wounds, but did she forgive herself? For someone like Nadhari, someone used to being in charge of her own destiny, to being the meanest, baddest, toughest thing walking – what those guys did to her must have messed with her spirit in a real fundamental way. I think she distracted herself for a while with MOO, the Harakamians, me, the Federation guy, but I don't think she's over it. I don't think anyone else *can* cure someone of something like that. I think she has to figure it out for herself, and she just isn't doing it. Instead, she's cutting herself off from everybody who cares about her. The only one she really seems to be normal with is RK, but she doesn't want me to leave him with her. I offered. Hell, *he* offered, but it's like she doesn't trust herself not to hurt him or something.'

'Oh, Captain, I had no idea. I am very sorry for her pain. Do you want me to try to read her? To see if I can do some deeper healing? It sounds to me as if her . . . condition is somewhat similar to Aari's.'

'Yeah, it is. Except, I think, Aari wasn't forced to do anything against his own nature. Even though he was tortured and everything, he stayed a Linyaari. The Khleevi took his horn and broke his bones and nearly killed him, but they didn't make him hurt anyone else. He endured pain, but he didn't inflict it. Ganoosh and Ikwaskwan turned Nadhari inside out, let loose that bad dog she always keeps on a tight leash, and turned her into what she hates the most. She has that monster side to her and she knows it, but she controls it rigidly because at heart she's a protector, Princess. A natural-born hero, a defender of the weak. And Ganoosh and his goons doped her up and turned her loose on the weak to maim and destroy them. Think what that must have been like for her – to get turned against her will into the very monster she's always fought against. It's no wonder she's a little messed up right now. She needs *something*, but she doesn't know what it is, and I don't know what it is, but I don't think it's anything you Linyaari can supply that you haven't already.'

Unable to say anything to help, Acorna fell silent for most of the remainder of the short hop to MOO. She and Becker each thought their respective thoughts while RK lay between them on the console, his tail waving lazily back and forth.

Hafiz Harakamian, a wily, wealthy intergalactic businessman and her adopted uncle, greeted Acorna warmly when they arrived on the Moon Of Opportunity, but he kept a sympathetic reserve. Acorna could see many unasked questions in his eyes. Just as well he didn't ask. No, Aari had not shown up or been located. Everyone in the galaxy would know when he turned up – she would be so happy she'd broadcast that far and wide.

For Becker, Hafiz had a mission in mind.

'I am told you can communicate with these persons,' Hafiz said, gesturing grandly toward the perpetually suspicious and usually filthy forms of Wat and Wat, the Terran unicorn hunters who had accidentally been transported from ancient times to Vhiliinyar along with the Ancestors. The nearest anyone could figure, Wat and Wat, once their presence was discovered by the Ancestral Hosts, had been sent to an ancient period in Vhiliinyar's history where they could do no harm to sentients. However, when the ruination of Vhiliinyar's surface caused fractures in the time apparatus, the two hirsute Earthmen had suddenly reappeared and began hunting Linyaari as if no interruption in their activities had ever occurred.

'No one else can make themselves understood to these ruffians,' Hafiz said. 'They annoy my guests and they have the deportment of goats. They speak to you; therefore they are your responsibility.' Hafiz crossed his wide brocade sleeves across his chest. He had spoken.

'Hey, that's not my fault! What am I supposed to do with them?' Becker asked, scratching his head.

'Must I think for everyone?' Hafiz demanded. 'I don't know. Take them back to Terra, sell them to a slaver, but somehow or other you must' – he gave his hand a graceful twirl – 'recycle them out of here. The red one had the audacity to make unseemly advances to my Karina. He advanced so rapidly, in truth, that had my wife's screams not alerted me and had I not rushed to her rescue immediately, accompanied by Commander Kando . . .' His voice dropped dramatically as he shook his head to indicate his shock and grief at what he had witnessed. 'Well. It is only due to great speed on my part and great forcefulness on Commander Kando's that my delicate flower will not be bearing a barbarian baby in a few months.'

Karina, wafting toward them, had caught Hafiz's remarks and did not fail to capitalize on her victimization. 'So . . . coarse,' she breathed, 'and smelly. And thought patterns of an extremely rude and crude sort.'

Nadhari Kando, just behind her, grinned. 'Sounds to me as if they are perfect for your crew, Jonas.'

'Sounds to *me* like *you* should put them through boot camp, Commander. Doesn't seem like it should take these boys that long to get religion if you put your mind to the task. Not to mention respect for the fair sex.'

'You do me much credit, dear,' Nadhari said. 'And in fact they are warriors and might do well to train as such.'

'I don't think it's a real good idea to arm them, since their idea of an enemy is the Linyaari,' Becker pointed out. 'And they can't come with us, since I already asked Acorna if she'd help us out while we're shorthanded.'

Acorna was about to object when she picked up thoughts blaring from one of the Wats. (Go home. Back to our lord Bjorn. Away from these bewitched animals who walk like men and women. Away before they spit us on their horns and roast us like oxen.)

(We are vegetarians,) Acorna reassured them mind to mind. (Why would we do a thing like that?)

Both Wats looked at her as if she had hit them on their heads with an axe. Their brains were working on the concept of 'vegetarians.' She gave them a mental image of a rabbit eating leaves, a sheep eating grass, herself and her friends grazing along with them.

'We don't eat meat of any kind, especially not Wats,' she told them aloud in a rough approximation of their language. 'And your old master is many years dead by now. You have been brought forward in time. You must bring your ideas up-to-date, too. My people and I are descendants of the unicorns you once wrongfully hunted. We will look for a new home for you now, somewhere that may feel somewhat familiar to you. What is it like, your home?'

Asked a question, they resolutely folded their arms across their broad chests, now clad in ship suits instead of armor, and clamped their beards tight to their mustaches. Their beards and mustaches were now much shorter and far more neatly groomed than they had been when the Wats first appeared. Becker had, in the not-too-distant past, forcibly washed and barbered the Wats as a conversation opener.

But as steadfastly as they refused to verbalize their memories of their homes, their thoughts betrayed them. Acorna got images of vast dark forests of gigantic trees, rolling storm-tossed seas, and great smoky fortresses filled with clanking, clomping humans clad in metal and heavy leather garments. On their heads some of the men wore helmets embellished with a set of horns.

She smiled at the Wats, baring her teeth in an expression that was friendly for a Terran and hostile for a Linyaari – and just right for the emotion she felt toward these two misguided and misplaced human beings. 'I think I know where they might feel at home, at least temporarily,' she said.

'Indeed?' Hafiz asked.

'Yes. The Niriians are in need of help in rebuilding their planet since the Khleevi invasion. Their two-horned appearance very closely resembles some of the totems these people apparently used to worship. Perhaps these fellows could work off some of their aggressions by helping the Niriians rebuild their planet. And there is something about these men that reminds me a bit of Toroona and her mate, too, don't you agree?'

The Niriians were Linyaari trading partners of long standing, a peaceful, industrious, and sometimes overly conscientious bovine race. When the ravenous insectoid Khleevi attacked Nirii, Toroona and her mate had escaped their home-world in time to seek help from Hafiz and the Linyaari. Thanks to their actions, Nirii had not suffered anything like the degree of devastation the Linyaari planets, Vhiliinyar and narhii-Vhiliinyar, had. Before the Khleevi could destroy Nirii, Acorna and her friends had devised a strategy to lure the buglike aliens away from Nirii to another place. That plan had eventually resulted in an end to all Khleevi destructiveness forever.

'Good idea, Princess,' Becker approved. 'The cowboys and cowgirls will know what to do with these guys. And they're not fragile, graceful people like you Linyaari. These fellas give them any trouble, the Niriians will sit on 'em till they holler "calf-rope." '

'Ye-es,' Hafiz said. 'Yes, indeed. I like it. Acorna, my dear girl, as usual you have devised a solution that is both convenient and kind. In this case, far kinder than these lecherous barbarians deserve. But . . . convenient. Captain, there is the solution to our problems. You and Acorna will deliver these two troglodytes to the Niriians. If they decline to accept our gracious gift of manpower, remind them please that they are deeply in our debt.'

'No,' Becker said.

'No?' Hafiz seemed puzzled by the word, as if it had no meaning for him and was spoken in a language he did not understand. The head (emeritus) of the fabulously wealthy House Harakamian did not often hear such a word. At least not in public.

'No. Acorna shouldn't have to put up with that stuff. I told you. These guys hunt unicorns.'

Hafiz waved his objections away. 'My dear Becker, you speak of our niece as if she were *any*

27

Linyaari, or *any* female, for that matter. As you can plainly tell, she has already established even better communication with these barbarians than you yourself have, has read their minds, and has determined an agreeable and humane disposition for their offensive persons. They are like lambs with their shepherd. They would do her no harm. Think you that I would allow the daughter of my heart to be endangered? Besides, she has you and the estimable Mac to protect her should she require such protection!'

'Your faith in me is touching, Uncle,' Acorna said dryly. It was amazing how competent people became in Uncle Hafiz's estimation when there was something unpleasant he wanted them to cope with because he didn't want to be bothered with it himself. 'But I can't go that far. I only came for a short visit. As soon as I have seen Kaarlye and Miiri and some of my other friends, just as I have seen you and Karina, I must return to Vhiliinyar. We all have a world to rebuild there, after all.'

Hafiz gave her a look. She knew it was meant to make her realize that they were able to rebuild it only because of his financing. But he had picked a fine time to nudge her – blackmail her, actually – into doing his will, when it involved a prolonged absence from Vhiliinyar, the time machine and possibly Aari. She didn't *want* to leave Vhiliinyar. But Hafiz was so besotted with *his* love he would do anything to spare Karina trouble.

Suddenly a pair of comforting hands landed on her shoulders and she turned to see Miiri, Maati's and Aari's mother, standing behind her.

(There, there, dear,) Miiri said to her in the mind-to-mind communication all adult Linyaari shared. (Uncle Hafiz is the soul of kindness, as we have good reason to know, but he is used to being spoiled and served by those around him, which has made him extremely self-centered. I imagine he has convinced himself that the solution to his problem will in some way ease your own troubled heart.)

Becker, however, struck a pugnacious pose, sticking his lower jaw out and glaring at the old despot. 'Look, Hafiz, Acorna doesn't need to be hassled right now.'

'Oh, no, my estimable Becker, that is very true. And naturally I would not suggest it if I thought it would, as you so colorfully express, hassle her.

'As for rebuilding Vhiliinyar, well, it occurs to me that the Niriians, as old and trusted trading partners indebted to the Linyaari for their continued existence, have resources and goods that may be useful to the Linyaari in the rebuilding of their worlds – both Vhiliinyar and narhii-Vhiliinyar.

'Under their current circumstances, the Niriians may be inclined to have a bit of a fire sale, and such items as our Linyaari friends find desirable might be exceedingly cheap at this time – free even, to the dear friends who saved the Niriian home.

'But some kind soul, someone who would perhaps be willing to collect or trade damaged goods, to salvage them, shall we say, must first confront the Niriians with a Linyaari ambassador to whom they may express their gratitude and eagerness to do business. And it comes to me that they will be more eager yet to reward such a person with low prices for high value. That is, if you – or any wise salvage merchant who seizes this once-in-a-lifetime opportunity – and a Linyaari ambassador should arrive at this time bringing news of the Linyaari plight. Not to mention the gift of two louts with strong backs to assist in the manual labor of restoration.'

Hafiz shrugged ingenously. 'It was a little idea I had, nothing more. Please do not let this humble and useless old man impose upon your other pressing plans.'

The red-haired Wat, bored with the unfathomable exchange of words going on around him, let his eye wander to Karina. He made a flirtatious but forceful gesture in her direction, no doubt intending to charm her with his 'wit.'

Karina looked thoroughly revolted and alarmed. Her eyes rolling upward, she half swooned into her husband's arms. 'Oooooooh, I am having one of my visions. Yes, yes, I see clearly now. Hold me, my protective pasha, while I clear my channels.'

With one arm she clung to Hafiz's neck – the side of his neck farthest from the Wats – while with the other she batted at the air as if being attacked by miniature Khleevi.

She made an odd puffing sound as she performed this ritual. Karina knew that the Linyaari were genuine psychics, and she knew in her innermost mind that she was not psychic, or at least mostly was not, no matter what she publicly claimed.

This in no way prevented her from carrying on the periodic charades with which she hoped to impress others with her 'powers.'

On the other hand, when Hafiz had wavered when it came time to inconvenience himself on behalf of the Linyaari, Karina had persuaded him, not with a vision, but with the threat of performing the necessary manual labor herself. There was much to like in such a person.

(Indeed there is, Son's Beloved,) Miiri agreed with Acorna's estimation. (Some of us have tried to communicate with her mentally, to touch her mind and school it in nonverbal communication, to encourage the psychic powers she seems so desperately to desire. But try as we will, we cannot affect her. Poor Karina is absolutely the least receptive being any of us have ever encountered when it comes to reliable day-to-day thought transfer.)

'Oh, yes! Yes!' Karina cried, waving the billowing lavender sleeve of her robe about before touching the back of her plump beringed hand to her forehead. 'Oh, I will tell her. Be sure that I will tell her.'

Her eyelids had been fluttering like butterfly wings above the whites of her upturned eyes, and now she opened them all the way and stared full at Acorna. 'You must undertake this journey, not for itself but for where it will lead you, Acorna. What you seek is not on Vhiliinyar. It is not near. It is very far. You are meant to take this journey.'

Acorna had not been reading the likable but slightly ridiculous wife of her 'uncle.' Her own sensitivity, which had been rubbed raw by the loss of her lifemate so soon after they were joined, was outraged with the presumption of this person she considered a friend. To so blatantly try to manipulate her, and in that fashion . . .

(On the other hand . . .) Miiri continued, her voice full of grudging admiration (there are times when not even Karina knows that it is happening when she is wide open. At such times, totally unexpected and uncanny things issue from her.)

Acorna turned to look Aari's mother full in the face. 'You mean, you felt that she was genuinely in touch with something just then?'

'Oh, yes, I felt it myself as she spoke.'

It occurred to Acorna that Hafiz was not the only one who was self-absorbed. Once more she realized that the pain of her loss was blunting her perception of other people's problems – and in this case, abilities. Aari's parents had told him that during the time he was imprisoned by the Khleevi, his mother, a powerful empath, had experienced the pain of his torture sessions to such a degree that she was violently ill most of the time. It took all of the healing strength of their people to help her bring his little sister Maati into the world. Karina might lightly fake such a message, but Miiri would never lightly endorse it.

(Do you – should you and Kaarlye or Maati come, too?) Acorna asked. She knew that if it had been one of them who received such a clear message and she was not asked, she would insist on being included.

Miiri read that thought and smiled. (No, Khornya. The message really was for you.)

(Was it from Aari? Is he all right? Will he show me how to find him?)

(Sweet child, you know nothing is so direct as that. No, I do not think it was from Aari. I can't actually say where it came from. But I know it was genuine, and it was meant for you. You still don't realize, do you, that though you are Linyaari like the rest of us, you have special abilities and qualities that make you better suited for some missions than others of us? Perhaps it is your unusual upbringing. I don't know. I can tell you that if Aari were in serious pain, or . . . no longer lived, I would know and I would tell you. You know, too, that Kaarlye, Aari's father, is as powerful a transmitter as I am an empath. If we have word of our son while you are gone, we will get a message to you, no matter where you are.)

(I know. I know.) Acorna was trying to be reasonable, sensible.

Miiri reached inside the neck of her tunic and pulled from it a silvery chain Acorna had often noticed glinting at her neckline. Three small silvery disks jingled together upon it. Miiri lifted the necklace over her head, undid the catch, removed two of the disks and slipped them into her tunic, then ceremoniously placed the chain and the remaining disk around Acorna's neck.

(This is Aari's birth disk,) Miiri told her. (I had been meaning to give it to you anyway.)

(Birth disk?)

(Yes. When a baby is born to our people, it is customary for the artisans to make a disk like this with the exact position of the stars overhead inscribed upon it, as well as his unique personal code. It is a gift for the mother at her birthing. When the child reaches maturity, generally the mother gives it to him on his birthday. When he takes a lifemate, it becomes what you would call a wedding gift. I was going to give this to Aari, but then you two became lifemates, and I thought perhaps I would give it to you when we were all together. Now I think you must have it, as a token of the love you share with my eldest. I can get another chain for Maati's and Laarye's disks.)

Acorna examined the little disk, which shimmered in her hand with a shine that was not silver, but more like the opalescent fire of a healthy Linyaari horn. She recognized the constellation from the night sky – Hronii's Book, the source of knowledge of the universe.

She clutched it for a moment, her emotions so strong that she was unable even to thank Miiri. Then she kissed the little disk and tucked it into her tunic.

Miiri enfolded Acorna in an embrace that was the most comforting thing Acorna had felt since Aari was lost. When Acorna finally released Miiri, she turned, ready to face Hafiz and Becker and agree to what they asked of her.

Becker barely glanced at her, nodded, and turned to Hafiz. 'Tell you what, HH. You send Nadhari along with us to protect Acorna from the Wats, and you got yourself a deal.'

TWO

'You didn't need me, Jonas,' Nadhari said once they were well away from MOO. 'MacKenZ is strong enough to subdue our hairy friends, or you could have tied them up and locked them in an inner cargo hold.'

'Yes, sweetie, but I *wanted* you to come,' Becker said, twirling the ends of his mustache. 'You know how much more secure I feel when you're here to protect me. I just used Acorna as a smoke screen so nobody else would know what a wuss I am.'

Acorna added, 'Nadhari has a point, Captain. Mac fought the Wats when they attacked Thariinye, Maati, and me. They regard Mac as a superior warrior. Him and RK both.'

RK was draped across Nadhari's shoulders like a fur stole, his tail describing lazy Js against the insignia sewn to the sleeve covering her left arm. The cat's face, framed by its furry mane, was so large it looked as if Nadhari had two heads.

'Our Temple cats are ferocious fighters,' the woman warrior said, running a finger along the cat's curl of tail.

'I believe it, having seen RK in action,' Acorna

agreed. 'However, he doesn't have Mac's facility for alien languages. I think, Captain, that since Mac mastered the Khleevi utterances well enough to fool their ships, he could certainly pick up the tongue the Wats are speaking among themselves.

'Our people have tried using the LAANYE on their language, but those two don't seem to carry on normal conversations and the only words that consistently appear in their thoughts when faced with most of us are, "Maim, kill, destroy, rend," and that sort of thing. Most of my people find that too disturbing to pursue, not to mention it being too limited a sample to build a language base from. If Mac can communicate with them consistently, then perhaps we can start teaching them current languages and manners. It must be very frightening for them to suddenly be among us. We should try to help them assimilate so they can continue their lives in this time in a somewhat normal way.'

'If you say so,' Becker said. 'Personally, I think we should just send them back to whenever it was the old-timers had banished them to.' He grinned at Nadhari. 'At least they were a bargaining chip for me to get Hafiz's security chief off MOO for a while.'

Acorna watched attraction spark between the captain and Nadhari like static from RK's fur. The two humans still cared for each other, that was clear. With a sigh, Acorna turned to go speak to Mac.

The android readily agreed to her proposal. 'You mean you want me to modify the Wats in the same way you modified me? An upgrade of their memory banks?'

'Yes, sort of. Though they are very backward and superstitious.'

'What is superstitious?' Mac wanted to know.

'Hmm, some people would say it means to believe in any sort of magical charms at all, but I think it is more the belief in false magical charms that presuppose a cause-and-effect relationship between events or incidents that are actually unrelated.'

'Then there are true magical charms as well as false ones?' Mac asked.

'I don't know. I suppose that depends on the definition used for magic. In some places, the ability my people have to read minds, or the way that I can discern, from a distance, the mineral content of planetary bodies throughout their mass, would be considered magic. We cannot actually explain these abilities yet, and some people consider all unexplained events as magic. Many phenomena for which we now have scientific explanations were considered to be magic before we learned those explanations. There were no scientists that we know of in the time Wat and Wat came from, so all events and phenomena must seem magical to them.'

'Ah,' Mac said, 'that may explain their hostility to you and your people. Is it possible that they wish to kill your people because they believe you are magicians with evil powers?'

'No, they kill us because they want to steal our horns. Their leaders believe that our horns have the power to make them more virile, to keep them from being poisoned, all that sort of thing. It's even true, but what they don't understand is that if they'd befriended our Ancestors and asked for help nicely instead of killing every horn-bearer they saw, things would have worked out better on both sides. As it was, their ruthless pursuit of "magic horns" back on Old Terra meant that soon there were no more "magic horns" to pursue.'

She and Mac worked as a team, spending hours on end with the Wats. She read their thoughts and supplied the images to Mac, who asked questions in their guttural language, which he understood very quickly. 'It is, as Captain Becker discovered, a very early version of Standard, with some Teuton and old Norse mixed in. Many sentences are actually not very different from those spoken by Captain Becker and other Terrans, but the inflection and accent make the words sound foreign.'

Acorna had already noticed this, and was picking up on the similarities and learning the accent, but since the Wats were the ones who would have to assimilate to the dominant cultures around them now, it was more important for them to learn modern languages than for her to learn ancient Wat.

Now that the Wats were actually in a mood to communicate, thanks to Acorna's telepathic skills, Mac made rapid headway teaching them words and concepts. The android tried to explain to them that they were flying through space in a spaceship. They asked him in awed tones if the

Thunder God had his hand on the *Condor*, guiding the vessel across the heavens.

'Did you explain it to them?' Acorna asked, amused.

'I tried, but in the end I said no, it was more as if we were riding the Thunder God's lightning bolt. They seemed not only satisfied with that explanation, but impressed and proud.'

Though neither Wat had as yet directly addressed her, Acorna felt that great progress was being made in their socialization. She had no idea at what point in their temporal incarceration the time rupture had released them, but they were still relatively young men.

The red-haired one with the amorous intentions toward Karina was taller than his companion and was heavily muscled through the chest, shoulders, and arms. He had a blue-eyed stare that at some times was direct and at others seemed to be looking back into his past and asking many questions. Reading his thoughts, Acorna saw that he had several mates and many children in scattered villages.

The other Wat had sandy hair and blue eyes as well, and was more of a warrior by disposition. His glance was suspicious and his questions were sly, as if he thought to catch his captors out in a lie. He kept alert to escape opportunities.

Acorna cautioned Mac to watch that man. Though his outward behavior was less aggressive than that of the red-haired Wat, he was the more dangerous and less civilized of the two.

What they had taken for the red-haired Wat's crudeness was simply a healthy lust that had stood him in good stead in his homeland while siring his dynasties. He also had a certain sort of gregariousness, a willingness to found new dynasties no matter where his circumstances took him. Hafiz, with some justification, considered the man a barbarian rapist, but of the two Wats, he was actually far less hostile and more amenable to learning. Even his actions toward Karina would, in his own culture, have been a compliment. Acorna had deduced that the Wats' world had some remarkable differences from modern human society.

The personality and character differences between the Wats caused the men to argue among themselves a bit, which gave Mac opportunities to learn more of their language, and – once he'd deciphered what they meant – give them further instruction in modern Basic.

Acorna became sure they'd reached a turning point with the barbarians one day when she walked, on her way to turn in for some much-needed rest, through the cabin to which the Wats' lessons had been moved. Becker had hoped providing a civilized environment would speed the barbarians' education. Mac had a replicator salvaged from a merchant ship and was serving the men tea and cakes, though they would have much preferred beer and little salted fishes. Indeed, the blond Wat had developed quite a sweet tooth. The red-haired Wat looked up at her, and for the first time, his blue eyes focused. 'Female' was the word that registered with him, and a broad grin – the baring of teeth the Linyaari considered so hostile – lit his face.

Acorna kept her face carefully grave, though she wanted to laugh and smile back. This one would cheerfully misinterpret friendliness for . . . uh . . . passion. Even in another species. He was starting to remind her a bit of Thariinye that way.

Acorna hurried out of that room as quickly as good manners and the Wats would let her.

She wasn't required on the bridge much on this trip. With the *Condor*'s new Khleevi control panel modifications, Becker and Mac were able to manipulate the controls much better than she was. She hoped that Becker would wear out this particular configuration before Aari returned. She doubted her lifemate would really appreciate the ironic humor in the use of Khleevi technology aboard the *Condor*. He was more likely to decline to board the ship while it was in place.

As she settled in for a sleep cycle, she pondered how to break it to Becker that the ship's current configuration was not one of his more successful ones.

She fell asleep at once and dreamed of Aari, as always, but also, and primarily, she dreamed of cats. At first they were very large cats, as big as Aari. Then Aari began shrinking in size until his size in relation to the cats around him was the reverse of how it really should be. A lot of the dream was just about the daily life among the cats – the birth of kittens, hunting and eating, building. There were humans there, too, and they and the cats sometimes fought together. The dream became long and involved and increasingly catty, until Aari was not even in it. And the cats were crying, mewling, scratching, begging for something.

She awoke to the realization that the sounds were real. RK was setting up a horrible ruckus outside her quarters, scratching at the door, crying as if his heart was broken.

When she opened the hatch, RK rushed in, while from the bridge came roars from Becker. 'Fragitall, RK, you know better than to play with the controls!'

'To what do I owe this honor?' she asked the cat, closing the hatch. 'Could it be that you're looking for sanctuary?' She lay down again on her bunk, cradling her friend in her arms.

RK growled softly and burrowed his face into her hand.

Then the ship lurched and she was catapulted from her berth. The cat laid tracks on her flesh right through her shipsuit as he shot out into the room and bounced off the far wall. The ship bucked again. The artificial gravity on board fluctuated wildly once more from Federation standard to zero G and back again. Acorna's first impulse was to head for the bridge and see what the trouble was, but until things were a bit more stable, that didn't seem to be wise. Rolling down the corridors and ricocheting from the ceiling would hardly be helpful. She lay back down on her bunk and strapped herself in, searching for Becker's thoughts. The process didn't involve much mind reading at the moment. The captain's mental voice was very loud when he was upset.

(Fraggin' Khleevi piece of decomposing roach manure, who would have thought they'd put the warp drive where the brakes ought to be? Fraggin' cat playing fraggin' Tarzan with the fraggin' levers.)

The ship's gravity failed again. RK levitated from the place where he landed during the first lurch. He swam expertly to the hatch, bumped against it, and when it did not give, roared his complaint. He wanted out and he wanted out now, with the same intensity he had formerly exhibited expressing his desire to come in.

The *Condor* lurched and shuddered. Acorna could only imagine what was happening to the ship. It felt roughly like it did when Captain Becker took the *Condor* through a patch of what he called 'black water,' where space was full of wormholes and pleats that either offered short-cuts to their original destination or landed them somewhere far removed from where they entered.

Cautiously, Acorna unfastened her berth strap, moved hand over hand along the wall to the storage locker, found her gravity boots, and did a few somersaults while pulling them on, fastening them, and activating them. It was a bit tricky making sure her feet were pointed at a place that would not endanger the rest of her when they grabbed hold of the surface. Her quarters were small and, while not as cluttered as they had been during Becker's 'bachelor' days, when the *Condor*'s crew consisted solely of him and RK, they were still barely large enough for Acorna to stretch out full-length. RK continued to howl and claw at the steel door hatch. Acorna opened it and the cat swam out like a newly launched torpedo.

Becker's thoughts were still thoroughly profane. Nadhari was attempting to soothe him, but being soothing was not a natural role for her.

Hearing panicked bellows and pounding noises, Acorna made her way to the hold where the Wats were incarcerated. Through the viewport, she saw the two hirsute men floating and flailing, their faces distorted with terror and their mental state much too confused to make any sense of the thoughts she was trying to read.

Mac must be on the bridge, helping Becker, she decided.

Unlocking the hatch, she ducked between the airborne Wats and found the storage locker there. She pulled out gravity boots for them. Snagging one of the struggling Wats by the arm, she tugged at him. His arm shot out and caught her on the side of the head and his hand tangled itself in her mane. Shaking her head to loosen his grip, she reached for his foot.

'The Thunder God is dropping us!' he was screaming.

'Calm yourselves,' she mentally commanded both of them in their own language. It was the first time she had actually spoken to them since she read them back on MOO. 'The thunder god has nothing to do with this. This is simply a navigational difficulty, such as you would have with one of your ships. The captain has it under control.' The *Condor* lurched again. 'Almost under control. Put these boots on and you will regain control of the . . . the air, which will once more stay properly above your heads while you keep your feet on this . . . deck.'

'You speak sooth?' asked the red-haired one, who was not the one she had grabbed to begin with.

Acorna was having some success radiating calm and courage at them, reminding them mentally that they were warriors on a more perilous journey than any of their kind had ever dared. Why, if they were back where they came from, the deeds they had done and the tales they could tell would be beyond belief, but if such stories were believed, would elevate them high above their former liege lord in the estimation of their fellows.

Acorna was frankly winging it in these assurances, for she had only the most shadowy idea of what their society must have been like. She would have to find some vids and books about Old Terra, she thought, and realized she should have done this sooner.

But her glorification of their adventures – which carefully omitted the part about their being terrified and completely at the mercy of people they considered mortal enemies or prey – served its purpose. The Wats' bellowing stopped, their breathing slowed, and their muscles relaxed. Then Acorna read a thought going through the head of the sandy-haired one – that now would be an opportune time to overpower her and take her horn.

She recoiled, calling mentally to Nadhari as she did so. 'You are incorrigible!' she shouted at him, aloud this time, and quickly translated her sentiments into the closest approximation in his own tongue, an idiomatic expression rustic at best.

'What good would that do you? We are about to make a forced landing on an unknown – no, not a star, a world. If we landed on a star we would burn up. My horn is of the greatest possible use to you now firmly attached to my head, where it belongs. As we told you before, the liege lord you wish to impress has been dead for several thousand years. You are the last of your kind. We are trying to rehabilitate you enough so you will have a place in our universe, but you will not impress the authorities – who are known as the Federation – by butchering a Linyaari ambassador, which is what I am. You really must stop thinking of your old mission and switch gears. Oars. Whatever!'

The red-haired one pried his friend, who had one boot on and one boot off, away from Acorna, putting himself between them, and said, 'She is no beast, but a lady. The lady goddess herself now, I am thinking. If we displease her, well, you know what she will do to us. We will be turned into swine. Perhaps we do not realize it and are already swine, as she said she is trying to turn us into men who will be pleasing to the lords of this place.'

'I know no lord but Bjorn, to whom I'm sworn,' his blond friend said stubbornly.

The redhead reached out and clasped Acorna's waist with one large paw, and kicked up a large foot, currently bare. He nearly bowled himself backwards in the process, and his fingers slacked their hold on her. She grabbed his hand and extended her other arm with the boot. He got it on, and then the other one, then extracted a peace bond from his friend before helping him with his remaining boot. 'You will not harm her?'

'How can I? We are unarmed.'

'True,' his comrade agreed. 'You are safe from us, lady unicorn goddess.'

'I'm very relieved,' she told him. She thought it might be best to let them get used to all of the other new concepts that would be confronting them in the current time before officially renouncing her divinity. Just now, being a god in their eyes could come in handy. Later, if all went well, she would lose her divinity in their minds as the Wats became better oriented, and she'd never have to confront the problem directly at all. 'Now that you know you can walk, I suggest you strap yourselves into your berths. We may be making a rough landing.'

'We do not die lying down,' said Red Wat, as she was starting to think of him. 'There is no honor in that. If there is mortal danger, we will face it, and since we have no weapons, shake our fists at it.'

'Very effective, I'm sure,' she said. 'The captain does that all the time, so it's certain to be very useful.'

Becker's thoughts were calmer now and she intruded long enough to send a mental message. (Captain, the Wats wish to observe the landing. Have I permission to bring them forward?)

(Why not?) The response was weary, but she sensed that much of the danger had passed. (I was going to get them to help us unload the *Condor* so I can get to the Niriian shuttle in cargo bay four that has a control panel I can patch together. I'm going to offload all these stinkin' Khleevi parts when we make our pit stop. They're about as worthless as the bugs who made them.)

Acorna didn't reply but motioned for the Wats to follow her. In case either of them changed his mind about her divine nature and decided to attack her from behind, she kept a tight monitor on their thoughts until she stepped back and allowed them to precede her onto the bridge.

Nadhari, Becker, and Mac were all seated, their heads below the tops of their chairs, so the Wats looked straight past them out the viewport into space.

The surface of the burgeoning sphere where the *Condor* was preparing to land occupied a third of the port. The Wats gaped at it, stricken by something close to awe, then knelt as if they couldn't support themselves on their feet any longer. Their minds were literally numb.

Becker glanced back around the side of his command chair, and jerked a thumb at the open-mouthed men. 'Wot's with the Wats? They look like they got religion all of a sudden.'

'That's the least of it, I believe, Captain. I don't think they've ever been permitted to see space since they first traveled to Vhiliinyar. They're a bit overwhelmed. They've been under the impression the *Condor* is being carried through space by the Thunder God.'

'Thunderstruck, eh?' Becker asked, then held up both arms and rotated his wrists to show first the backs of his hands, then the palms. 'But you're wrong about the god! Look, Ma, no hands! We're landing under our own power – but just barely.'

Acorna got a sudden sense of the upcoming world's mineral composition. 'Captain, I don't think you'll want to linger here. This world is extremely wet and the air, while breathable, is full of sulfurous effusions.'

'Beggars can't be choosers.' The viewport was taken up with the planet's surface except for a slender halo of atmosphere surrounding it. 'Strap in, folks, gravity is about to grab us.'

Acorna helped the Wats secure themselves in the auxiliary seats behind the command post and buckled in herself. The ship shuddered, and the planet blossomed to fill the entirety of the viewport, its surface becoming more and more detailed. Streamlets, rivers, lagoons, ponds, lakes, and all manner of wetlands, laced together with heavy vegetation. There didn't seem to be any seas as such, just innumerable smaller bodies of water running in and out of each other.

Finally Becker said, 'Look, Princess, there's a kind of flat plain there with a patch of grass. We'll set down in it.'

'I hope you have diving equipment, Jonas,' said Nadhari, who had been very quiet through all of this.

'Why?' Becker asked. 'Is there something you'd like to tell me, babe?'

'Well, yes, actually, but there's not enough . . .'

They splashed down rather than set down, as Becker had planned. The grass was actually a sea of tall reeds and the *Condor* was in water halfway up to the robolift. And sinking.

'. . . time,' Nadhari finished. 'Perhaps, Jonas, you could do a quick repair on the Khleevi unit

49

so it would allow us to move to a drier spot?'

He already had a torch and a screwdriver in hand. 'I wonder if there *is* a drier spot,' he grumbled. 'This whole place is one dismal swamp, from what I can tell.'

'Yes,' Nadhari said. 'And there are large, unfriendly reptilian life forms living in these waters.'

'How do you know about that?' he asked.

'Because I recognize this place. The Federation used it as a sort of boot camp for Makahomian recruits, to see if we qualified for the Corps. It is near enough to Makahomia that those who didn't make it through the training could be returned – dead or alive.'

'Do tell?' Becker asked, scratching his chin. 'Hmmm. We seem to have gone a little out of our way.'

'I don't want to be rude, Captain,' Acorna said. 'But did you maybe detect some small differences in the functions of Khleevi navigational equipment as compared to that of other cultures whose salvage you have adapted to the *Condor*?'

Becker harrumphed and looked at the strange array he had installed, waving at it casually. 'You mean this? Well, Princess, when you've been in the salvage business as long as I have you learn that there are just so many functions a ship is going to perform and that they are to some extent interchangeable. If it wasn't for that blasted' – he looked at Nadhari and RK, who were both eying him through slitted eyes, and revised his adjective – 'holy cat swinging from the toggles and playing leapfrog across the buttons . . .'

Acorna and Nadhari looked meaningfully at the watery landscape outside the viewport. The tops of the tall reeds were beginning to tickle the belly of the *Condor* by now.

'You suppose that's it?' he asked with a pained and apologetic grimace as he worked on the control panel. 'The Khleevi warp drive is maybe a little juicier than what I'm used to?'

'Since we are now in a totally different quadrant of space than we planned to be, it would seem as if Khornya has justification for her assumption, Captain,' Mac said. 'If I may make a suggestion, sirs and ladies?'

'Sure, Mac, what is it?'

'Are the ship's communication devices still functional?'

'Seem to be,' Becker said, checking them.

'Then I suggest we send a Mayday message, sir, and promptly. I do not believe the *Condor* has the appropriate modifications for supporting our lives for the rest of eternity under the sludge into which we are sinking.'

'I was just about to do that little thing,' Becker told him. 'No need to state the obvious, Mac. In fact,' he said, turning to Nadhari, 'if we're close to your homeworld, babe, why don't you do the honors?'

Before she had finished her opening hail in her own language, RK had planted himself in front of her face. Becker plucked him out of the way, and with help from Acorna, they wrestled the cat into a harness that tethered him to one of the bridge seats. Afterward, Acorna doctored Becker's scratches and puncture wounds.

The Wats did not seem to entirely understand the danger they were currently in and Acorna saw no need to enlighten them for the time being. The two men stared out the viewport and seemed lost in the scenery. From the snatches of their thoughts Acorna caught while Nadhari made repeated hails in her native tongue, the Wats seemed to think sinking into an alien marsh was just another of the strange things their current captors did. They weren't sure if it was a function of battle, a form of transportation, a demonstration of power, or possibly some kind of strange courtship ritual, but Acorna's previous reassurances had gained their confidence and they saw no reason to lose it now.

Sooner than any of them had imagined possible, they received a response to their Mayday. '*Condor*, this is the *Arkansas Traveler*. I don't rightly understand all that language you're speaking, but I got enough of it to know you're in trouble. I'm coming up on your position now. Could you repeat your message in Standard Galactic lingo, over?'

'Certainly, *Arkansas Traveler*,' Nadhari said smoothly in the more familiar language. 'I will turn you over to Captain Becker.'

'Uh, I don't suppose you folks could let me have a visual on you, could you? My cargo is not my own and it's always nice to know who you're dealing with. No offense.'

'None taken, *Traveler*. We'll show you ours if you'll show us yours, over,' Becker said in a tone that, in other quarters, might have implied something completely different. 'Nadhari, you're more

52

photogenic than me. Wave at the nice ship on the vid screen, will you?'

When she had done so, Becker leaned in and wiggled his fingers, too. In a moment, the handsome, friendly face of a man with green eyes and white hair grinned back at them. 'Nice to meet you folks. I'm Scaradine MacDonald. I've got a load of tractors and irrigation equipment I'm delivering, but I reckon I can stop long enough to give you a tow.'

'We'd appreciate it, Captain MacDonald,' Becker said. 'We got in a little deeper than we'd planned.'

'No problem. I've got a tractor beam on this thing that can pull you up right through the atmosphere. And hey, call me Scar. Everybody does.'

'Thanks, Scar. I'm Jonas Becker, Chief Executive Officer as well as Chief Cook and Bottle Washer of Becker Interplanetary Recycling and Salvage Enterprises, Ltd. We were en route for a planet in another sector altogether when we had an equipment failure. I thought it would be safe to land here for repairs, but it was a lot soupier than it looked. This nice lady beside me is Commander Nadhari Kando. She tells me we're pretty close to Makahomia, which is where she's from. You think you could tow us that far?'

'Sure, that's not much out of my way. I was hoping to stop and refuel there, anyway.'

Becker looked at Nadhari, who said, 'That shouldn't be a problem. I will transfer to your navigation computer the proper coordinates for our final destination.' She did so and then said,

'These are the coordinates of the Federation outpost nearest my place of origin. It has an excellent spaceport and enough landmass that the planet's various border skirmishes really don't affect the people who aren't interested in the battles.' After she'd finished the transmission, she sat back, as still as a statue.

Acorna looked at her sharply. Nadhari was clearly uncomfortable. Had she been a less disciplined and guarded individual, she might have been twitching or displaying a nervous tic, but as the highly trained peacekeeper that she was, Nadhari simply became increasingly still, outwardly calm, her face serene as a sheathed knife unless she was speaking.

At that moment the vid screen lit again. 'Okay, Captain Becker, ma'am. I'm going to turn on the tractor beam now. Hope everybody is strapped in?'

Becker reassured him on that point. 'Just about time too, buddy. The viewport is starting to get a little moist around the edges. You sure that winch of yours can pull us out of this? Want me to use my thrusters first?'

'Well, let's just crank 'er up and give 'er a go first, whatcha think?' the other captain suggested.

'Sounds good to me. Only step on it,' Becker suggested.

The tractor beam had a little problem pulling the *Condor* loose, but after a few nasty jolts and some ghastly creaking the ship began to shift, until at last the outer hull was visible again through the viewport, the landing pods choked with reeds and dripping with giant sharp-fanged eel-like reptiles.

'Ewww,' Becker said. 'Glad we didn't go out there!'

The Wats were awestricken all over again as the *Condor* pulled free from the muck with a deafening sucking noise and leaped into the air under the tow of the other ship.

When Scar's face appeared on the screen, Sandy Wat said to Red Wat, 'The face of the Thunder God as he lifts us onto his lightning bolt.' To Acorna he pointed triumphantly at the screen and said, 'You see?'

Acorna decided it was better to deal with the Wats' misconceptions later. Much later.

But Nadhari didn't move, not even when they felt the heavy pressure of acceleration as their ship was pulled out of the gravity well and into space.

'Nadhari,' Acorna said carefully, 'although we all know you and RK well, we know very little about Makahomia. Your planet has the reputation for being almost as secluded and secretive as Vhiliinyar and narhii-Vhiliinyar. Is there anything you would like to tell us about it so we can avoid embarrassing you or ourselves?'

'Like what?' Nadhari asked.

'Whatever seems pertinent right now – for instance, where exactly are we going? What is your planet like? Does the name of your planet mean something special? Answers to those questions seem like a good place to start.'

Nadhari took a deep breath, more out of

tension than the need for oxygen. Finally she said, 'The name of my home planet? Makah is our word for cat, and "hom" refers to either people or place, so we are the people or place of the cat, depending on the suffix. Makahomia, as you say, is "place of the cat." We would say "Makahomin" for place, "Makahomini" for ourselves. We'll be landing near the Federation outpost facility, which is the only place vessels like the *Condor* and the *Arkansas Traveler* can refuel on Makahomia. There is only one outpost, or at least that was the case when last I was here. It is just outside the city of Hissim, on the semi-arid Mog-Gim Plateau bordering the Great Aridimi Desert.'

'Is that where you're from, Nadhari?'

'Not originally, no, though I lived there briefly in semi-slavery before being recruited by the Federation.'

'Semi-slavery?' asked Becker, who had himself been a child slave on Kezdet. 'Does that mean they shackle you only on alternate days?'

'No,' she said. 'I was taken prisoner by the Aridimis after a battle and given to the Temple priests as an acolyte. As such, I was confined to the Temple to do menial chores. My fighting ability and my affinity for the sacred cats saved me from some of the less pleasant duties I might have been forced into otherwise.'

'That must have been terrible for you,' Acorna said sympathetically. 'No wonder you were so eager to help Mr Li free the children of Kezdet and establish the training center on Maganos.'

Nadhari raised an eyebrow and smiled a half-smile. 'Actually, it wasn't bad at all. I let myself be captured, once I had demonstrated that I could handle myself in battle. I knew our enemy was near the new Federation outpost, and I knew that the Federation recruited likely Makahomian young people and took them off-planet to train for the Corps. One of my cousins had gone and returned, which was quite unusual. He said it was wonderful, but that Makahomia needed him more than the Federation. His stories made me determine to be chosen. Mostly they didn't choose girls, but there were not many girls who could fight as I could.'

Becker had wanted Nadhari to open up, and now she was unusually garrulous. Acorna thought it was extreme nervousness, as well as being around people she trusted, that made her so talkative.

'What was your home like?' Acorna asked her. 'Now that we are here, will you be able to visit your family? Can we explore the planet with you and see where you come from?'

'I very much doubt it,' Nadhari said with a half shrug. 'It may not even be advisable to let the Federation know I'm aboard, depending on who rules Hissim these days. Also, the Federation does not allow anyone to introduce alien technologies to our people.'

'Why not?' Becker asked.

Nadhari took a deep breath. 'Because if one faction had a technological edge, it would upset the balance of power that keeps our continual wars from escalating to a bloodbath that could wipe out the population. You must understand,

Jonas, my people are at war all the time – it's part of what we do,' she told him.

'But we don't need to worry about someone shooting us down as we land?'

'Oh, no, because the Federation are the only ones who have modern weapons. Anything more advanced than a spear or a knife is considered much too dangerous to be in Makahomian hands.'

'By the Federation?' Acorna asked. 'That's very ... paternalistic, isn't it?'

'Actually, it was our priests, both the war priests and the peace priests, who jointly decided on the taboo and insisted that the Federation enforce it as a condition of their maintaining a presence on the planet. In exchange, the Federation gained the concession that it could choose likely youngsters to train for its service. Of course, when one of us was chosen to leave our world and take up fighting elsewhere, that is a different matter. As expatriates, we could learn anything they wished to teach us, including how to handle all the weapons with which they armed us. We are not allowed to take those weapons back to the indigenous areas of our homeworld with us, however. Or even to speak to our people of their existence.'

Becker snorted. 'Yeah, I can see where you could become Supreme High Pooh-Bah in a nanosecond if you had Old Betsy with you,' he said. Old Betsy was what he called Nadhari's laser rifle.

'Should I visit my planet's surface, I will be allowed to carry no weapons but the dagger I took with me from the Temple when I left,' Nadhari said.

'But on the other hand, you're saying that nobody else on your world will have anything badder,' Becker said, nodding his understanding. 'Well, that'll make things more even. But you don't need a laser rifle to do damage, babe. I've seen you in action.'

She grimaced. 'It is true I've learned much since leaving the Temple, but many of my people are at least as able in the traditional fighting skills as I was when I was chosen to leave. And though I may have had much more training and experience since, I am older now, and my reflexes are not as fast as once they were.'

'You musta been a beautiful baby,' Becker said. 'And death on wheels if you were any tougher than you are now.'

She didn't acknowledge either aspect of the intended compliment, but said seriously, 'My bloodlines on my father's side are from the Kashirian Steppes, where the best fighters come from. Kashirians, when they are not personally defending their own territory or attacking someone else's, are hired by the other peoples as mercenaries. Normally, girls are not trained as highly as boys in battle skills. However, my mother's people were Felihari, one of the Makavitian Rainforest tribes. The climate in the forests is hot and very, very wet, and fighting is done with less physical and more intellectual finesse than elsewhere on the planet. My mother was initiated as a Felihari high priestess.'

As Nadhari spoke, Acorna saw the images of

her memories quite clearly – the rubbery copper-colored foliage of the jungle, stirring sluggishly in a dripping heat, the striped and spotted creatures slithering along the ground or up and down the trees, the rainfall that came second- and third-hand after first being deposited on the tallest branches, then flowing onto the lower ones, and finally reaching the ground. The Temples draped in drowsing cats and studded with winking jewels – or were those more cats blinking back the light? Nadhari's mother, erect and proud as Nadhari herself but shorter, browner, wearing the practical dress for the climate – that is, very little dress at all. Her skin, coppery as the leaves around her, glistened with moisture. Her auburn/black hair was braided with what looked like – but couldn't be – the eyes of cats.

Nadhari was remembering one cat in particular – a sleek tawny creature with a throaty purr whose butter-soft fur turned red at ears and tail, and whose jonquil eyes always seemed uplifted to a particular young girl.

'The Felihari women hold much of the power in their culture, and since their fighting skills require more of an intelligent application of the laws of physics than brawn, the women are quite effective fighters. When my father was taken prisoner by her people, my mother thought he would make a highly desirable contribution to the tribe's bloodlines and became impregnated by him. Religiosity does not require celibacy on my home-world. The resulting child, my elder brother, was considered such a success, and I suspect my mother and father found the process so enjoyable, that they formalized their union and made me as well.'

'That's romantic,' Becker said dryly.

Acorna could tell there was much Nadhari was not saying and didn't wish to say, for reasons of her own. Perhaps the reasons were connected with the emotional problems Becker had described on the way to MOO. But until she was ready to talk about it, it did little good to press her for more information.

Instead, Acorna asked, 'Nadhari, the *aagroni* wanted some information about the Makahomian Temple cats. He believes, having seen RK, that there might be some connection between them and a species that existed on Vhiliinyar before the Khleevi attack. I would like to speak with some of the high priests about them. How much exposure have your people had to people not of their own species? Should I disguise myself, or would it be best to simply present myself as a Linyaari ambassador?'

Nadhari considered, then said, 'You will have to – in fact, any of us would have to – obtain a permit from the Federation officials to enter the cities or countryside, and especially to interact with any of our officials. Even I will have to, since I have been away so long.'

'Surely they wouldn't keep you from seeing your family?'

'I cannot be sure any of my family members still live,' Nadhari said. 'My mother was killed by a band of mercenaries unrelated to my father, who was at that time off fighting for another Makavitian tribe involved in a blood feud with

Aridimis. My brother was killed defending my mother and her Temple.' Nadhari was remembering the tawny cat, accidentally wounded with a great gash in its side, growling over her mother and brother, defending their bodies against all comers, while a little girl screamed desperate war cries and kicked and chopped until she was so exhausted her laughing opponents were able to simply scoop her up and carry her off. 'But when the mercenaries who killed them found me and learned who my father was, they ransomed me to him. He was killed in a battle soon after the one in which I was taken prisoner.'

In Nadhari's mind, Acorna saw the blood and heat of the battles, the gaping mouths of wounds and splintered bone. She smelled the stench of overheated bodies and felt the weapons slip with the sweat of hands. Heard the crunch and dull *thwuck* sound of blunt objects striking flesh, the ring of metal as it sought targets.

Becker whistled. 'You haven't had a dull life, have you? No wonder you haven't been homesick!' Acorna noted that although he appeared to understand Nadhari's motives, he was still gently probing. The concept of a settled home was more alien to him than the Linyaari were. His childhood as a Kezdet farm slave was ended by his adoption by Theophilus Becker to be son and first mate aboard the *Condor*. The ship was Becker's home more than any planet, much less any town or city.

Nadhari's rainforest memory shifted to one of hilly lands covered with riders of beasts who looked a bit like the Ancestors, without horns, and yet were not quite Terran horses. The people riding the beasts were ferocious looking, with bristling facial hair. And they gave way in Nadhari's imaginings to red-robed hairless figures, in the background, and flat-roofed houses looking out over an even flatter plain. These places had all been home briefly to the girl Nadhari had been.

Acorna began to wonder if the accident ending in the *Condor* becoming stranded near Makahomia was an accident after all. Becker was bluff and jovial with her, but also was a shrewd man, sometimes every bit as sly as Hafiz. Blaming RK was convenient, as the cat was unlikely to challenge him, at least verbally.

'It isn't only that. Without a family, as an acolyte, you become the tool of the ruling priests. Some of them are good, holy people. Others are where they are only because of their influence and family connections and because they wish to exercise power over others. Only the Temple cats,' she said, stroking RK, who slitted his eyes and purred appreciatively, 'can be trusted to be always completely honest in their reactions and judgments. They protect the Temples, the acolytes, the priests, and the people – especially those they favor. They attack, when away from the Temple, only for food or when threatened. It is a great tragedy when one is killed or injured – even for the side attacking.' She fell silent, her thoughts returning to the injured tawny red-tipped cat dying beside her mother and brother as the rain dripped onto their bodies.

'It sounds as if your cats are as revered as our

Ancestors,' Acorna said. 'And yet your people have so many wars. What do they find to fight over?'

Nadhari laughed. 'What do they not fight over? The tribes of the rainforest are wealthy, with water and growing things needed for medicines and food. Our Temples are the most elaborate, our cats the closest to the wild state, our jungles teem with wild things good for food and clothing. The people of the arid zone have no water, few plants. My father's people of the plains would perhaps be the greatest targets for attack were they not the fiercest of all fighters. They are nomadic, herding beasts from river to river, using the arable land for short-term crops when there is sufficient peace to grow them. They are often the object of attack from both the arid zones and the forest. But more often they fight for one side against the other, gaining the forest treasures for the desert folk and the sacred cat's-eye gems for the forest tribes. These are the material reasons for our warfare. We also fight for the same reasons everyone does: sport, power, love, honor, territory, revenge, loot, or slaves, or to free ourselves from slavery if we are captured.'

'Your people still keep slaves?' Acorna asked. 'And the Federation permits it?'

'They didn't interfere on Kezdet while the slavery served a purpose, did they?' Nadhari asked with a shrug. 'While we fight each other, we are not threatening those with real power out in the galaxy. Our own priests have the power that matters to them. And as long as our wars employ nothing but traditional weapons and stay confined to our planet's surface, the Federation feels that our Quaint Native Customs can be honored. I didn't realize all of this until I began to work for Delszaki Li on Kezdet and learned from him more about the uses and abuses of power. As his personal guard, I was beside him always. Mr Li was not a man to look down upon someone simply because he paid them wages. He talked to me a great deal. He taught me much of the history of the peoples who settled Kezdet. And I came to realize some of the reasons my people never found peace, although there has always been much sentimental talk of it.

'Our leaders do not actually desire peace any more than they desire annihilation. Our wars serve many purposes. They are the main business of our priests. The priests fan the conflicts to maintain a constant sense of danger and a state of emergency so people will not question their actions or motivations. The wars solidify loyalties and make simple things like starving seem trivial by comparison. The fear of death and destruction keeps the people occupied. And then there's always something for the fighters to look forward to: the thrill of acquiring loot and slaves, the joy of decreasing the population – preferably that of your enemy, of course. There are a very few cultural safeguards in all of this that have kept us from destroying the planet. Our people do not engage in wholesale slaughter of noncombatants, and we do not seek to decimate the gene pool of the opposing side by disposing of those with brains or talent when we have the opportunity. As terrible as I find the conflicts, they are not as terrible as they could be if our people followed another path.'

'But nobody else on the planet sees this the way you do?' Becker asked.

She sighed. 'I don't know. I haven't been back since I was a child. It seemed to me then that people didn't think about anything much at all. Things were as they were; allegiances shifted, but there was always an allegiance to something. There was always something to defend and something to hate and fight. Most of us have been partially raised in all three areas of the planet, sometimes as slaves, sometimes as steppe-children of the tribes we live among. We fight only each other. The Federation is here now to protect us from outside threats like the Khleevi, so we ourselves are our only enemies.'

Becker shook his head, saying, 'It still sounds weird to me. Not that I'm ethnocentric or xeno-phobic or anything.'

'If we wish it, we need know nothing of what is going on on the planet. The Federation officials may require you to fill out forms before allowing your repairs and refueling, but you need not see any two-legged Makahomians except me unless you seek to do so. If the officials permit Acorna to carry out her mission, they may arrange for the priests to come to the Federation post. It will all be very civilized. At least, if things are still as they were when I left.'

Nadhari paused, as if unsure of the wisdom of continuing. Then she went on, saying, 'You know, Jonas, when we get to my planet, it might be a good idea if you and Acorna do the talking for us while RK and I keep a very low profile, at least until we know what we're dealing with and who.'

'Why hide RK?' Becker wanted to know. 'Won't the pussycats back at your home be glad to see the big guy?'

'Taking a Temple cat from Makahomia is frowned upon,' Nadhari told him. 'Keeping him hidden could be good for your health. Such a theft is punishable by death.'

THREE

'Death? But *I* didn't steal him,' Becker protested. 'I *rescued* him. Surely they wouldn't want to kill me over that – that's killing the messenger. On the other hand, do you think they might try to keep RK there on the planet if they find out about him?'

'Probably so.'

Becker looked down at RK, still in his harness in the seat between them, and said, 'Looks like no shore leave for you, mate. I don't suppose there will be any fuzzy hussies we can smuggle aboard either. Sorry, old man.'

RK glared up at him, then dropped his chin to his paws. By this time they were well outside the atmosphere, trailing along in the wake of the *Arkansas Traveler*, floating through space in the tractor beam's embrace like a patchwork ballerina.

Acorna passed the journey to Nadhari and RK's home planet learning Makahomian with the help of her friends and the LAANYE. Since Acorna was a quick study with languages, she seldom needed to absorb them in her sleep, as most Linyaari did. By the time Captain MacDonald towed them within sight of

Makahomia, Acorna and Nadhari were con-
versing easily in the warrior woman's native
tongue.

Their first sight of the planet was impressive.
Makahomia was redder than Mars ever had been,
a rich rusty orange red, with two moons and two
suns.

'A lot of iron in your soil,' Acorna remarked to
Nadhari.

'Yes. Our iron makes excellent weapons,
especially when alloyed with some of the many
other metals so abundant on our planet.'

Even the clouds were reddish and swirled at
high speeds over the face of the planet.

Nadhari confirmed with Scar the landing zone
coordinates, and he made initial contact with the
planet, asking for landing permission and stating
that he had answered a Mayday call and had a
disabled Federation-registered ship in tow.

The *Condor*'s crew audited the exchange over
the com unit but, out of consideration for Nadhari
and RK, left the vid screen off. Nadhari nodded
to Acorna, scooped up RK, and exchanged seats
with her, moving RK's tether harness to her own
seat.

'The disabled ship will please identify itself,'
came a clipped and sober voice.

Becker gave his name, ship's name, and
registration.

'Passengers and crew?' the voice demanded.

'Yes, we have those, too,' Becker said. 'Do you
need their names and origins now?'

'That will not be necessary. Officials will be
boarding your ship when you land. We will

tight-beam immediately the list of documents you will need to show us. Please have the relevant papers ready.'

'We aren't going to stay long,' Becker said. 'Just till I can repair my ship and we can refuel.' But no one seemed to be listening to him. The resulting com silence was deafening.

'Not a friendly place you're from, Nadhari, sweetie,' he said to her after retrieving the list and scanning it.

'How surprising. After all, I am such an amiable sort myself,' she said.

'Compared to that guy, you're the life of the party,' Becker grumbled. 'But there shouldn't be any problem, should there? We've got all the papers they want. We're landing right where they said to. The place is perfectly safe, right?'

'It was when I left, yes,' Nadhari said.

Acorna punched into the com unit and leaned forward to fill the vid screen. 'Your pardon, good sirs. I am the Linyaari Ambassador Acorna Harakamian-Li. I was sent by my people to make inquiries regarding the history of a certain Makahomian life form. Could you give me the name of the ruling head of this area, so that I may address my written request for an audience with that person appropriately?'

It appeared that someone was listening, after all.

'The Federation commanding officer in charge is Lieutenant Commander Dsu Macostut,' a clipped voice answered on the com, 'and he is the one who will need to approve your request before it is passed along to the High Priest of Hissim and the Mog-Gim Plateau, Mulzar Edu Kando sach Pilau dom Mog-Gim. We will apprise the lieutenant commander of your arrival.'

'Ahhh,' Acorna said in what she hoped was an elite ambassadorial tone. 'Many thanks, good sir.'

'Edu?' Nadhari asked when the com unit was safely off. '*Edu* is in charge?'

'Glad you're on a first-name basis with the guy, sweetie,' Becker said. 'Can I just call him Ed? I can't remember the rest of that stuff.'

'No,' Nadhari said, emerging from her preoccupation long enough to touch his cheek fondly. 'Just like you can't remember the star maps from most of the known universe including uncharted wormholes, black holes, and other spatial features the regular physicists haven't named yet. You've got the best memory of anybody I know – until you hit something you don't want to remember. The name is actually very simple, Jonas. "Mulzar" is the Mog-Gimin title taken by the high priest who is also the warlord of the plateau. The current Mulzar is Edu Kando, who is what you might call my cousin – or in the local parlance, my steppe-cousin. His father was captured by my mother's sister on a raid the Felihari made before I was born. So like me, he is a Kando, of the rainforest. The "sach" indicates his paternity, usually from a captive. My father, when captured by my mother's people, became Murgad Div fron Kando, to indicate his ties to my mother's family. As he was never captured or fostered on the Plateau, he had no ardo name. I, on the other hand, am actually known here as Nadhari Kando sach Div ardo Rek.

This indicates my mother's surname, my father's clan in the steppes, where I was taken after my mother's death, and the name of the Mog-Gimin clan to whom I was sold after my capture.'

'Oh, well, sure, it's simple when you put it that way,' Becker said. 'Sach means your steppe-name, and that other word –'

'Ardo,' she supplied.

'Means your desert affiliation. But his affiliation wasn't ardo – it was some other word.'

'Dom,' she said. 'No one from the Mog-Gim Plateau captured him – he conquered the plateau.'

'Of course. I knew that,' Becker said. 'Absolutely nothing to it when you get used to it. And hey, what luck is that anyway that he's one of your family! He'll probably want to have a big ol' reunion. We can say we didn't tell the Feds about you because we wanted to surprise him or something.'

She nodded, the muscles in her jaw rippling slightly. 'He will be glad to see me,' she said tersely. Acorna looked at her sharply, but Nadhari's jaw had relaxed and a rueful smile hovered around her lips. The warrior's mind was once more opaque, but Acorna noticed that Nadhari had omitted saying whether or not *she* would be glad to see her cousin.

Becker didn't seem to notice, however. He just charged ahead at the verbal equivalent of light speed. 'Well, that's great, then. If one of your own people is in charge, we shouldn't have any problem. Otherwise, I guess we'd have to hide you or rename you and dummy up some good papers, or at least you'd need to stay aboard while we made repairs. This way, we can maybe do a little looking around while we're here, visit the garden spots, gawk at the Temples, stuff like that.'

'Yes,' Acorna said, her tone innocent but with an underlying question in it. 'If your kinsman is the high priest, perhaps he can assist me in carrying out the *aagronis*' errand to discover a possible relationship between *pahaantiyirs* and your Temple cats.'

'Yes, perhaps,' Nadhari said, though her apparent agreement was belied by her tone of voice.

Becker said anxiously, 'Maybe he'll even understand about RK, but you think maybe we should hide my buddy until we find out, huh?'

At that moment, Captain MacDonald announced that they were entering Makahomia's orbit. 'You reckon if I turn you loose now you can land under your own power, Captain Becker? Otherwise, it'll be a little tricky setting 'er down with you still wagging behind me like the tail of Mary's little lamb.'

'Of course we can land,' Becker said. 'We're not exactly invalids out here – though you couldn't prove it in that mud puddle. Turn us loose and go ahead. We'll be right behind you.'

'Jonas, we should report in to Hafiz.'

'Good idea. He'll need to know about this little detour,' Becker agreed. But when he tried to access Maganos Moonbase for relay to MOO, the com unit remained blank and dumb. 'I was afraid of that,' he said. 'Can't do the long-range stuff with the computers screwed up.'

They landed without incident, on dry ground this time. The Federation spaceport was very small. Becker set the *Condor* down beside the *Arkansas Traveler*. Both ships were instructed to have their personnel remain aboard until the Federation officials boarded their ships and inspected them.

'I just hate customs,' Becker said. 'Now we gotta play "hide the kitty."'

Acorna smiled. She had heard the plop of paws behind her, indicating the return of gravity and the departure of the cat. His harness had given him no trouble. When he chose to shed it, RK divested himself of a harness as easily as he shed hairs in warm environmental conditions.

In her time with RK, Acorna had learned that the cat understood what went on around him almost as well as Becker did. He just made a game of letting his human companions underestimate him so that he was free to follow his own agenda without interference. She did not doubt that he would hide if it suited him.

Or not.

Becker shook his head when he turned to see the empty harness. 'Well, he knows the ship like the back of his paw. He hides so well even I can't find him if he doesn't want me to.'

Nadhari nodded. 'The sacred cat will choose his own path. RK must sense where he is now.'

'Maybe,' Becker said, scratching his head. 'I don't really know for sure if RK has ever been here. When I rescued him, it was from a wrecked ship in a totally different quadrant of space. He might have been a second generation ship's cat –

you know, from a litter a Makahomian mama Temple cat had after she was smuggled off-world.'

'He knows,' Nadhari said.

'Permission to come aboard,' an unfamiliar voice hailed them from the com unit.

'Granted,' Becker grunted. 'Uh – just a minute. I have to send the robolift down for you.'

'The *what*?'

'We're a salvage vessel. Functional, not pretty. We don't have a nice door in the side of the ship for you to hook your gantry to. Just a sec.'

Becker pushed the button that activated the robolift, but though there was a groan and a clank somewhere in the workings, nothing moved. 'Sorry,' he said to the com unit. 'It may have to thaw a while. We had a little trouble with our navigation system and made a forced landing on that swampy neighbor planet of yours.' He consulted the computer and gave the coordinates. 'We were viewport-deep in water when Captain MacDonald pulled us out and saved our necks. Going back out in space dripping wet might have iced up the lift a bit. Since we're going for speed here, I'll try taking a torch and a crowbar to the seals. That should work. It's gonna be a minute before I can let you in, though. Maybe you better go see Captain MacDonald first.'

'Very well, since the timing is useful to me. Lieutenant Commander Macostut will be joining the boarding party as soon as he is able to, so that he may on this occasion personally greet the Linyaari ambassador.'

'That's very courteous of him. The ambassador

will approve. I'll let you know when I free the lift.'

Mac said, 'I will attend to it, Captain.'

'I can do it,' Becker called after him. 'It's my ship.'

Before Mac could return, however, Acorna said, 'If I may make a suggestion, Captain. These Federation officials strike me as being impressed by rank and privilege. Nadhari and I have decided to use this delay to change into more formal clothing. She has her dress uniform. Miiri packed something . . . ambassadorial . . . for me to wear to meet the Niriians, which I plan to put on before the planetary delegation arrives. Perhaps you might wish to don your most impressive uniform as well?'

He considered a moment, rubbed his chin, and sniffed at his armpits. 'I guess I could shower and shave, too, huh?'

Acorna hid her amusement and listened to the ship's sounds for a moment. 'Nadhari has just finished her shower, I believe, so there will be time for you to do those things, should you wish to.'

Acorna and Becker escorted the Wats out of the bridge and back to their quarters, where they locked them in, and continued on to their separate quarters to make themselves ready for their official visitors. By the time Mac returned to the bridge, Acorna had donned her new outfit and taken time to enhance her appearance, so that her silvery mane curled fetchingly to frame her face and grace her long neck. Her horn shone like a golden opal. Her trews were cut so that the feathers on her calves made a decorative trim, edged with small jewels that matched the beautifully embellished belt girding her flowing white tunic. Grandam Naadiina had given Acorna the belt to wear before the venerable lady's heroic death. It had been a lover's gift from Naadiina's lifemate to Naadiina, and Acorna cherished the memories it brought each time she put it on.

And now there was her new treasure, she thought with a mixture of pleasure and pain, touching the disk through her tunic. It was a gift of her lover if not actually from him. Should she wear it outside? She decided it was too precious, that she didn't want to share or explain it just yet.

Nadhari wore the dress uniform of the Red Bracelets, as she had when attending formal occasions with Mr Li. It was, not surprisingly, red, gleaming with brass trim, and made of a material that both enhanced the shape of her panther-lithe body and allowed her complete freedom of movement.

Acorna wasn't sure where Becker's uniform came from – her guess was that it was salvage from another ship. The captain wore a tailored gray outfit with silver buttons and trim, an attractive combination with the gray of Becker's mustache and the little beard he was sporting. He wore an insignia of a silver vulture rampant over a barrel, with his name and title forming a leafy silver border around the image.

He tossed Mac a plainer version of the same uniform and said, 'Go oil yourself or something, Mac, and put this on to meet the bigwigs.'

Mac's pupils dilated with pleasure. 'A uniform? I am now an official uniformed crew member! Oh, Captain! May I have a hug?'

'Hell, no, you'd crush the life out of me! Where do you *get* that stuff anyway? You've been talking to Mrs Harakamian again, haven't you?'

Mac was busy stripping and pulling on the new uniform.

'Not *here*,' Becker said. 'There are ladies present.'

'Oh,' Mac said, clearly wondering what one thing had to do with the other.

'And pick up your old stuff on your way out,' Becker grumbled. 'You want this place to look like a pigsty?'

Acorna suppressed a giggle. Only through Mac's industry had the *Condor* gained any semblance of order. Before the android had been restored, reprogrammed, and thus rehabilitated from his service under the treacherous criminal Kisla Manjari, Becker's ship had more closely resembled a junkyard than an interstellar vessel. Jonas had had salvage stored and piled in every available corner and strapped overhead. The only maneuvering room around the ship had been little more than a narrow trail from one end of the *Condor* to the other.

She supposed Becker's remark was compounded of embarrassment and the sense of captainly importance he assumed with his fancy uniform.

With the robolift cleared for action and everything shipshape, Becker hailed the Federation post again. In a short time the ship's outside monitors picked up a small group of uniformed people walking in tight formation toward the ship. Becker lowered the robolift, which worked perfectly.

After exchanging questioning glances at the unusual outfitting of the ship, the delegation followed the man in the shiniest uniform forward. Once he had stepped onto the lift, they joined him. Becker pushed the button to raise them to the lower deck. 'Ladies, we should greet our guests, don't you think?' he said.

Lieutenant Commander Dsu Macostut made his priorities clear immediately when he ignored Becker's salute and bowed instead over Acorna's hand. 'Ambassador Harakamian-Li. We have, even on this backwater posting, heard of your remarkable exploits on Kezdet and the splendid work you and your patrons have done with Maganos Moonbase. We never imagined we would have the honor to meet you.'

'You're very kind,' Acorna said, amused. Becker was chewing his mustache, highly irritated by the snub to his well-dressed authority. In his view, on a ship, the captain should always have first priority. 'Please allow me to introduce my dear friends and shipmates. This is Captain Jonas Becker, with whom I believe some of you have spoken. And here are the ship's android MacKenZ, and Commander Nadhari Kando.'

'The legendary Nadhari Kando, who left Makahomia as a humble acolyte and became one of the famous Red Bracelets? Words fail to express my delight. Your steppe-cousin often speaks of you with pride. We are great friends, you know, and he is fond of bragging about you. He says that although he now rules the Mog-Gim

Plateau, *you* did not wash out of Federation training as he did.'

Nadhari opened her mouth to protest, but Lieutenant Commander Dsu held up a restraining hand. 'Of course we are all well aware that it was his wish to serve his own people here on Makahomia that was the true cause of his refusal to accept a commission in the Corps. And I must say, in losing a soldier, the Corps has gained instead a remarkable ally. Mulzar Edu is the most progressive, enlightened ruler it has ever been the Federation's pleasure to work with on your planet. Your steppe-cousin is truly a man of vision.'

Becker did something he had rarely done before with Acorna – he aimed a thought right at her. He didn't actually have any idea that she would receive it, but he just had to comment on the Federation officer's attitude and couldn't do so aloud.

(Hallelujah,) he said, (the fan club has arrived!)

(Why, Captain, you're using telepathy!) Acorna replied mentally. The grumblings in Becker's mustache and beard turned to pleased and slightly embarrassed huffings. These turned to shock as he realized suddenly that he had read her loud and clear. He replied tentatively, but again in mind-speak, (Yeah! How about that. Look, Ma, no mouth! Hey, is this mind-reading stuff catching?) he asked, clearly enjoying having a secret with her from everyone else.

(Not unless you can hear what I or others are thinking when we are not consciously sending to you,) Acorna said. (But if you address your thoughts to me, I will certainly do my best to read them and respond in kind.)

Becker's eyes sparkled. (That's great. I like this. Let's do it more often.) He looked as pleased as a three-year-old boy with a new land-skimmer sled.

She smiled at him – no teeth showing, of course – and would have hugged him had they not been in the company of strangers.

Macostut was still speaking, after a spate of fulsome compliments to Nadhari. 'Perhaps you illustrious ladies would care to come ashore while my men and the captain go over the inventory of this vessel? Our accommodations are spartan and humble, but are, I am told, somewhat more luxurious than those of the average – er – salvage vessel.'

'That's very kind of you, Lieutenant Commander, but I'm afraid that I must refuse your kind offer for the time being. Captain Becker has a large and varied inventory, with which we are both familiar,' Acorna said. 'As my close personal friend, he has granted me the use of his vessel as my traveling embassy with no cost to myself or to the planetary government I represent in exchange for my help as a crew member when needed. Captain Becker has saved my life and the lives of my people many, many times.'

'That is true for me as well,' Nadhari said gravely. 'I owe him my life many times over. Captain Becker and his vessel were crucial in successfully defeating multiple Khleevi invasions and in saving me from equally terrible enemies.'

Macostut tried to look impressed and more

cordial toward Becker, but Acorna sensed resentment radiating from him. The Federation officer clearly wanted Nadhari and her to himself. His thoughts seemed to indicate that he felt another male officer would cramp his style. 'And these – what did you call them? Khleevi? They needed defeating?'

'Oh, I suppose that the news of the rest of the universe doesn't reach you often here, as isolated as you are,' Nadhari said. 'Or you would have at least heard of the invasion of the Federation planet Rushima by the Khleevi, which was foiled by a massive combined force of Federation, mercenary, and private ships only after Acorna's relatives came to warn her of the impending attack and enabled the Federation and its allies to surprise the invading Khleevi. It was quite a battle. I was there.'

'But *he* – the captain, I mean – wasn't in on that one?'

'That was before we met,' Becker said shortly. 'If we're going to inventory *my* cargo, we'd best get this show on the road, ladies and gentlemen, or we'll be here a month before we're officially allowed to disembark.'

'Oh, no, Captain. A quick look will suffice, I think, since you come so highly recommended by a local celebrity as well as a foreign ambassador. And we must be well done with this before second setting, when you must all dine with me. I insist.'

'You mean real food?' Becker said.

'Exactly. There have been a few shortages recently on Makahomia, but we are well enough

82

supplied here. I will leave you now in order to finalize the preparations while you and your . . . crew . . . escort my officers on their inspection tour. They in turn will then escort you to our guest quarters and on to the officers' mess. You and your crew and Captain MacDonald will of course be our guests.'

'I will be so pleased for the opportunity to thank Captain MacDonald properly,' Nadhari said. 'We would probably be looking out the *Condor*'s submerged viewport at those repulsive reptilian life forms and breathing our last were it not for him answering our Mayday so quickly and effectively.'

'Lieutenant Commander Macostut,' Acorna said, 'speaking of Captain MacDonald, I would like to ask him to relay a message to our headquarters about our mishap. I wish to inform my uncle of our safe arrival. May we provide Uncle Hafiz with your outpost coordinates in case he wishes to contact us?'

'That's not a problem, Ambassador. However, I should mention to all of you that in order to avoid cultural contamination of the Makahomians, no technology that is in excess of what could be produced locally with indigenous resources is permitted beyond the official boundaries of this spaceport. The only gate from this compound, which opens into the city, contains a very sensitive scanner to make sure that no one carrying any off-world devices can pass through undetected. All communications emanating from our post are monitored. There is a dampening field around the post that will obliterate, scramble, or otherwise impede the signals from any ship attempting to contact another com unit in the civilian sector, should such a unit find its way there despite our precautions.'

Becker whistled. 'Seems pretty restrictive.'

Macostut regarded him coldly. 'Not at all, Captain. The Federation believes these measures are preferable to overflying Makahomia ourselves, causing yet more cultural contamination. We take our responsibility here very seriously.' He turned back to Acorna, all smiles. 'That said, we would be more than happy to relay your message to Mr Harakamian through Federation channels if you wish, Ambassador.'

'That's very kind of you, but Captain MacDonald has already offered to do that,' Acorna replied. He hadn't, but she felt certain he would be amenable. Just to tie up loose ends, she quickly returned to the bridge and hailed him. She didn't want to explain to Macostut or any other official that she not only wished to inform Hafiz of the *Condor*'s change of route but also wanted to learn if any messages for her had been relayed from the Moon of Opportunity through Maganos Moonbase. It would be just her luck if Aari had returned to Vhiliinyar and no one knew how to reach her!

FOUR

The officers' mess was filled with fragrant candles. Their soft glow lit the room, but the scent of their melting wax did not mask the succulent odors of cooking food that made Becker's nostrils twitch. The group from the *Condor* were all very hungry and tired, since the inspection had taken much longer than that 'little walk-through' Macostut had promised them.

Though the inspection crew did not find RK, they did find the Wats and asked to see their papers. The Wats didn't have any papers. Paper, much less *papers*, hadn't been around when they were born on Old Terra. The Wats did not have files to speak of, either, and even if they had, the ship's computers were still not working properly after their little adventure with Khleevi hardware. Becker had finally gotten the bureaucrats to leave by blaming the lack of documentation on the malfunctioning computers.

The inspection team had also wondered about Mac. Kisla Manjari's name came up when they verified the android's records. That certainly seemed to worry the Federation inspectors, who were familiar with the Manjari name. But the android had happily assured them of his complete rehabilitation. Since one of the team, a female chief petty officer, showed polite interest, Mac showed her his original model number. He then explained in detail about his various non-factory-authorized upgrades and reprogramming at Becker's hands, up to and including his new promotion to uniformed crew member. Mac could be exhaustingly thorough sometimes. In the end, the team had cleared the android, probably in self-defense.

But by the time they were ready to disembark, Acorna had her answer from Captain MacDonald – no message about Aari was waiting for her on the *Arkansas Traveler* from Maganos or MOO. The only message from either place was a short list Hafiz Harakamian had sent, naming things Acorna should let it be known she was in the market for while they were on Makahomia.

She saw one of these items – or rather, several specimens of one of them – as soon as Becker, Nadhari, and she were seated across the table from their host. Seated at dinner with them were a few Federation officers, two men in what appeared to be the local priestly raiment, and a young girl similarly clad. That raiment was what caught Acorna's eye. The attire was red, woolen, and long-sleeved. One priest's clothing was trimmed around the neckline and sleeves with a two-inch-wide ornate band of multicolored embroidery depicting cats, beautifully embellished with cat's-eye stones. The other priest's robe featured a plain stripe of gold embroidery around his sleeves and neckline, and the girl's robe was unornamented. The man in the most elaborate robe had thick dark hair and a luxuriant beard and mustache, in contrast to the other man, who was as bald and clean-shaven as the first man was hirsute. The girl's braided hair was so dark an auburn as to appear black, but the red highlights in it shot back reflections of the candlelight the same color as her robe.

Each of the three Makahomians wore a single striking jewel – a large cat's-eye stone. The ornately dressed man's was round, approximately four centimeters in diameter, and hung from a thick rose-gold chain around his neck. The stone was golden in color, with a deep velvety black cleft down its center. The second man's cat's-eye jewel was half the size of the first, dark green in color, and strung on a leather thong as a pendant. The girl's stone, pale green in color and much smaller than her companions' jewels, was also suspended on a leather thong, but was worn on her wrist.

Acorna had been raised by human asteroid miners. Growing up, she had demonstrated a special psychic gift that had proved very useful to them. She was able to determine the mineral content of any given object without the aid of equipment or computers, simply by using the powers of her mind. As a result of that upbringing and her gift, Acorna was acutely aware of minerals and gemstones of all sorts. The cat's-eye stones the local people were wearing – which were more properly called chrysoberyls – were not only beautiful and sacred, according to Nadhari's lesson on Makahomian culture, but also very useful in the mining and terraforming industries across the universe. Acorna wondered if it would be culturally inappropriate to dicker to purchase a few on behalf of Hafiz, since they were on his shopping list.

All of this she noticed in the blink of . . . well, a cat's eye . . . while beside her, Nadhari tensed and then smiled at the man in the embroidered robe as he rose and reached across the table to take both of her hands in his.

'Nadhari – cousin, you've come home to us. Dare I hope you've come to stay?' The man's eyes were large and brown and melting with sincerity. Nadhari flinched. The man noticed it, which Acorna thought was unusually sensitive of him. Most human men, in her experience, would have missed that small movement. 'Sorry. Of course I know that cannot be the case,' he continued. 'Dsu has already explained to me that you've arrived with your friends unexpectedly and in the course of business travels elsewhere.'

He started to turn to Acorna. Macostut, evidently feeling the introductions were going too fast and were proceeding without him, said, 'Oh, please, Mulzar, allow me to introduce all of our guests to you. Your cousin, of course, you have already met. The Linyaari Ambassador Lady Acorna Harakamian-Li, is on her right, Captain Jonas Becker on her left.'

'Yes,' Becker said jovially. 'Acorna's the one with the horn. I'm the alien-looking one.' Acorna smiled at the jest, reflecting that, like many of the planets under Federation protection, this one seemed to be populated with people of Terran stock. She had learned in her studies of galactic history that this was because, since ancient times, Old Terra kept overpopulating itself.

To remedy the problem, Terra had established space colonies, which soon developed the same problem. Those Terrans who were excess or simply adventurous were sent to colonize still other planets. By the time the old planet had worn itself completely out, Terrans had a vast web of colonies throughout their sector of space. They were the dominant, if not the only, sentient species on every planet and moon they could make habitable for their own kind throughout their galaxy and beyond. Through his jest, Acorna knew Becker was trying, however awkwardly, to show his support of her and his solidarity with her.

But Kando laughed as if the jest truly amused him. Acorna considered the possibility that he was more sheltered than she might have supposed, or else, contrary to her experience else-where, old jokes were not truly universal here on Makahomia.

'And this is Captain Scaradine MacDonald, who rescued all of them when their ship foundered on Praxos.'

Kando shuddered exaggeratedly. 'Ah, yes, Praxos. How well I remember our Federation training there – eh, Nadhari? You must have gone through it, too. I wouldn't wish that on anyone! Thank you so much, Captain MacDonald, for bringing my beloved kinswoman and her friends safely home to us. How did you happen to be nearby at the proper moment?'

'It's on my regular route, uh—'

'Forgive me! Forgive me!' Macostut interrupted jovially. 'I didn't complete my introductions. Mulzar Edu Kando sach Pilau dom Mog-Gim is the High Priest and Temporal Ruler of the City of Hissim and the Mog-Gim Plateau, Captain MacDonald, and these are his companions, Brother Bulaybub Felidar sach Pilau ardo Agorah and Little Sister Miw-Sher, a Keeper of the sacred Temple cats.'

Acorna had already sensed that all was not well with Little Sister Miw-Sher, who glanced around looking a bit desperate when she thought no one was looking, and who seemed to long to leave. Her eyes were almost as red as her robe, as if she had been crying. Acorna instinctively wished to comfort her and sent an inquiring probe before she was quite aware that she had done so. The girl's green eyes widened as she stared back at Acorna, though she didn't seem to know what to think.

When everyone finished exchanging greetings, Kando looked back to MacDonald, clearly prompting him to answer the question he'd been working on before Macostut had decided to butt in.

'So you're a high priest?' Scaradine MacDonald hedged. 'Well, now, that's real nice, Preacher. I'm a Methodist myself, or used to be when I had a church to go to. I hope you won't hold it against me.'

Kando looked a little confused, but prompted the ship's captain again. 'Is it your Method to linger near swampy planetoids so that you may rescue other ships?'

'Oh, that. No, sir. That's got nothing to do with religion. I'm a tech rep for agricultural supply and equipment companies. I sell and repair all manner of implements and machinery, plus seeds and chemicals and such. I have a regular route for my repair schedule, and part of it takes me within range of where I heard the *Condor*'s distress signal. I've never actually stopped in this neck of space before, though I go through it pretty often. I understand you people don't hold with – uh – my way of doing things.' Acorna knew he'd started to say 'new' or 'modern,' and then politely changed his wording.

Brother Bulaybub studied Kando's face as they waited for his reply. Acorna felt a certain emanation from him, as she did not from the girl.

(Nadhari,) she asked silently, (are your people telepathic?)

(Not as a rule, no,) Nadhari replied, rather startled by the sudden mind-touch, but remembering just in time not to look at Acorna. (It would probably be wise not to let them know that you are a strong mind-speaker, at least until we get our bearings.)

(It may be too late already,) Acorna replied, thinking of Miw-Sher's startled face, (but I'll see what I can do.) She watched Kando, who seemed to be trying to drink in MacDonald's words with senses other than his ears. (Is your cousin, the Mulzar, among the few telepaths here?)

(No more than any other good manipulator of people,) Nadhari replied, with a bite to her thoughts.

'That was the original arrangement, yes,'

Kando said in answer to Captain MacDonald's comment. 'But I think there are times – such as the ones we now find ourselves enduring – when change is mandated. I know Dsu agrees with me on this.'

Little Sister Miw-Sher made a small, strangled noise and looked with wild hope into Captain MacDonald's face and back to Kando's. The poor child seemed desperate to say something and at the same time, desperate to flee the hall.

'What's the matter, honey?' Captain MacDonald asked her. 'Cat got your tongue?'

Acorna got the feeling that Kando was not happy to have the captain's attention diverted from himself, but the priest smiled and said, 'You may ask what you are longing to ask him, Miw-Sher.'

The girl gulped. 'Please, sir, do you know how to doctor animals? That is, do you know anything about how to cure cats?'

'Something is wrong with the sacred cats?' Nadhari asked sharply.

The girl suddenly looked startled and guilty. Kando consciously assumed an expression of concern, and Brother Bulaybub looked down at his lap as if to dissociate himself from the proceedings.

'Yes, ma'am,' the girl replied quickly, before her permission to speak was rescinded. 'The cats under my care have been sick and dying for over a week now. We have only four left and they have not taken nourishment for at least two days. They may well be – be –'

'Calm yourself, little sister,' Bulaybub instructed her.

'. . . gone when we return.' The young girl valiantly swallowed her tears.

'She is such a tenderhearted child,' Kando said, reaching across Bulaybub to stroke the girl's cheek with a long brown finger. 'So concerned for her charges.'

'As she should be,' Nadhari said. 'This is terrible news.' She turned to look imploringly at Acorna. Sensing a chance of rescue, Miw-Sher stopped wiping her eyes and shrinking miserably into herself and turned her face toward Acorna as well.

Kando said, 'Dear Nadhari, for one who has lived so long away from those who cherish her, you are such a traditionalist. I almost feel that it is the plight of our poor pusses that has brought you back to us – as if they reached out over the vastness of space to draw you toward them, to comfort them as they diminish and die.'

His face bore tender sympathy as he looked at her, and in a possessive aside said to the others, 'She is such a devout girl. She's always been like that.'

The food arrived.

'Oh, yeah, very pious,' Becker agreed, pulling a slab of meat Acorna could have sworn was previously dehydrated, onto his plate. 'Righteous, even.'

He filled his dish with other foods that were also likely to have been reconstituted, which Acorna thought was odd fare to serve high-ranking guests, especially on a planet that prided itself on its agricultural products. It implied serious problems – problems that nobody here had touched upon yet. But Becker seemed so fascinated with the byplay between Nadhari and her cousin that the bad news – both the sickness being discussed and the disaster implied by the food before them – had not registered with him.

Acorna, however, was alarmed. 'A plague, you say, sir? Your wonderful felines, of whom Nadhari has told me so much, are actually dying? But that is terrible!'

Captain MacDonald was the one who responded. 'It's a darn shame, and I can tell this poor little girl is broken-hearted about her kitties. But it's even worse than that. Those fellas who inspected my ship tell me it's not just her pussy-cats involved. They say a lot of the animals here have got the same disease.' His cheery expression and bantering tone were gone. His head was lowered, as in deep thought – or remembrance – and his shoulders slumped. He appeared to be personally stricken somehow by the misfortune of the Makahomians.

He wasn't the only one. Panic hit Acorna, too, at the thought of RK catching the disease. Acorna launched a mental search for her friend. She received a clear image of RK walking though the city. The little rascal had probably left the *Condor* as soon as the robolift was freed, even before the inspection team had arrived.

(RK, since you are off the ship, you should know that there is some sort of contagious illness among your kind,) she told the cat in direct thought-speak, which she had never quite used with him before. (You should return to the ship to avoid catching it.)

She was more surprised than she should have been to receive an immediate answer in clear Standard thought-forms expressed with a slight feline accent and a strong dose of feline imperiousness. (I know. Why do you think I brought us here? Would you and my other people please stop eating and get to work? My fellow holy cats are in sad shape. I could hear them mewling their hearts out clear back on Vhiliinyar. I'm trying to calm them down, telling them you're coming and you'll help them, so please don't make me look bad here, Acorna.)

She didn't bother asking why the cat chose now to communicate directly with her. She and RK had been in peril as bad or worse than this together before, and she'd never gotten anything like this from him. But like all cats, RK did things his own way and in his own time. Perhaps the cat's sudden communicativeness had to do with him being on his world of origin. Or perhaps he was just getting around to experimenting with thought-speak because he felt like it. Or maybe RK had finally found something he considered to be worth talking to her about. Reading minds didn't actually help one understand cats any more than it helped one understand any other life form. And cats – certainly RK, at least – could be rather coy about providing context for their decisions and thoughts. (Since you brought us here, RK, you know the dangers better than we do. Don't *you* allow yourself to be seen, if you can avoid it. And don't get near enough to the sick ones to catch the disease, please. We all love you.)

(I know you do. That's why I'm not afraid. If I

catch it, you'll just heal me again, right? Now, please, will you all stop jabbering and get to work?)

'Ambassador, I believe you wished to ask something of Mulzar Edu?' Macostut said. His tone, which was very polite but quite insistent, indicated that he had given her previous cues that she'd been too preoccupied to hear while she'd been communicating with RK.

'Oh, yes. Yes, I did. But your new revelation about the disease has distracted me, I'm afraid,' she said, making eye contact with the Mulzar. 'Somehow I suppose I had the idea the Temple cats were immortal.' She had not, but thought such a naive comment might elicit more information.

Edu Kando laughed and smiled at Nadhari. 'Did my cousin tell you that?'

'Why, no. I just assumed from the ancient myths that I have heard concerning them that they must be.'

'Well, pampered as they are with the best of everything, they live lives longer than many who walk on two legs, but then, our – shall I say lifestyle? – here on Makahomia isn't always conducive to longevity. Our oldest cats until recently were eighty and seventy-five years old.'

'So very young,' Acorna murmured.

'Young?' Edu Kando asked. Miw-Sher was looking down at her plate, moving the food around without interest or appetite. Bulaybub also pretended extreme interest in his food.

'My people live quite a long time, into a very healthy old age, sir,' she said. She could tell that despite their kinship, Nadhari did not care for Edu. Acorna knew her friend must have a very good reason for her dislike of her cousin. Fighting was Nadhari's business. She did not waste her hostility carelessly.

'Oh? Do they?'

'Yes, mainly because my people possess great knowledge of medicine and healing. Like most of my kind, I have some skill at such things. I would be happy to look at your cats and other animals and see what I can do for them. I will attend to it, with your permission, as soon as possible. The matter I mentioned upon our arrival that I wished to inquire about involves research and interviews with a number of your priests, I believe. At the moment, I am too distressed about the ill health of your legendary cats and the other creatures to conduct that other business. Perhaps, with your permission, we can discuss it later. I will not be able to rest until I have seen if I can help the stricken among your charges. I hope that will not present a problem?' She remembered to smile charmingly at Dsu Macostut. 'I understand the Federation's permission is necessary. I trust under the circumstances . . .'

'There are forms to be filled out,' Macostut began.

Mulzar Kando evidently enjoyed considerable power here, for he easily brushed aside the post commander's objections. 'I believe we could waive that, Dsu, can't we, in view of the fact that these people have brought my dear cousin Nadhari back to us again? And of course, if the ambassador can truly help our sacred cats, then we must make all haste to bring her to them. The glory of our Temple and the faith of our people depend upon it. Perhaps you can bundle up some of the forms for our guests. Then when the ambassador has dealt with the current emergency, she can fill them out at her leisure.'

Becker and MacDonald both cleared their throats. 'As can these gentlemen, of course. And all of you will be our guests here. You must come and stay with us as long as you like at our Temple. Dsu has made provisions here on the Federation base for you, I know, but the post offers only the simple comforts afforded high-ranking military personnel. Our quarters, though they lack the technological amenities the Federation can provide, are far more comfortable. Our people are very conscientious in their worship. All of the best that Makahomia has to offer belongs to the Temple.'

'Since that would bring me closest to your sick cats, it would suit me admirably,' Acorna said with a gracious ambassadorial inclination of her head.

'I wouldn't mind having a look at your critters and at what they're eating, where they're sleeping, Preacher,' Captain MacDonald said. Kando smiled at the form of address, apparently finding it amusing that this rustic man equated him with someone of similar position in his own culture. 'My skills are in agriculture. I know that on other planets, it's sometimes been the case that diseases in animals have been traced to contaminants in their feed or elsewhere in their environment. I could maybe do a few tests and see if I can find something that is contributing to your problem.'

'Remember,' Macostut chided, wagging his finger at them, 'no alien technology is allowed beyond the Federation outpost. The application of any necessary medical knowledge to heal the all-important cats is permissible, but nothing beyond that, including mechanical technology. You do understand you will not be allowed to take with you off-post any of those amenities the Mulzar speaks of?'

'How about a couple of tin cans and some string? Could we phone home that way?' Becker joked.

Macostut gave him a pained smile. 'Tin cans are also a product of off-planet technology, however antiquated. I know you were joking, but this is not a laughing matter. Not only is there the dampening field and the gate scanner, but our monitors are manned at all times. Any attempt by you or anyone else to circumvent these rules will lead to your immediate expulsion from this planet and or a strict fine, including possible impoundment of your vessel and imprisonment. Perhaps the treaty is a bit overly restrictive, but so long as it is in force, my command will do its duty and enforce it. We mustn't be a bad influence eh, Edu?'

'By their tails, no,' Kando agreed, then gave Acorna a charming smile. 'However, if we can avail ourselves of a skilled physician, we must certainly do so and try to save our sacred guardians.'

Acorna stood. 'I find I have no appetite when I think of those poor sick cats, Lieutenant

Commander Macostut. Please forgive me, but I wonder if perhaps Mulzar Kando might provide an escort to take me to them so I may begin treating them at once.'

Miw-Sher jumped and scooted her chair back from the table, but Acorna saw Bulaybub tap the air with one finger, cautioning patience.

'If you are certain you do not wish to eat?' Macostut said in a tone that was both disappointed and surprised.

Acorna looked at the foods that had been placed on the table – various platters of meats, breads, and sweets, none of them particularly appetizing to her friends either, if she was reading her human companions well. As a vegetarian with a strong preference for uncooked greens, she wasn't qualified to judge. The aromas were synthetically produced, the food itself clearly reconstituted or heavily processed. Under the circumstances, this was not surprising. If the planet's animals were suffering from some type of plague, meat from any beast that could possibly be harboring such illnesses could not be served.

Acorna shook her head apologetically. 'While I thank you for offering this bounty, my people are grazers, sir. We eat only grasses, vegetables, and occasionally fruits. The foods here would not agree with my digestion, I fear.'

'I could provide—' Macostut began, genuinely distressed to have failed to take her diet into account when planning his dinner. She was an *alien* ambassador, after all.

Acorna smiled gently and placed her hand on

his shoulder when he started to rise. 'Please don't bother. You have been an excellent host, but all of my instincts are telling me I must go now to my patients. Please continue eating in my absence. I have a little hydroponics garden aboard our ship. Perhaps if your local diet does not include food such as I've described, Captain Becker and Nadhari would be good enough to harvest a small meal for me from my garden later before coming to the Temple?'

'Oh, we have grasses and vegetables here,' Nadhari's cousin assured her. 'Of a poor quality this season, to be sure, but we can provide food for you of the best sort at the Temple.' He clapped his hands and Miw-Sher almost knocked her chair over in her haste to escape it, while Bulaybub stood up with a smile, patting his mouth with a napkin he then laid upon his plate.

Kando said, 'You see, Little Sister, you have your wish. The ambassador has graciously offered her help. Now you must escort her to the Temple and the infirmary where our sacred ones are being treated.'

'Your Holiness, I beg your permission to accompany Miw-Sher and the honored ambassador so that I may oversee preparations for the arrival of our guests this evening,' Bulaybub said. Acorna received the distinct impression that he was as glad as Miw-Sher to leave the table, though not for the same reasons.

'Very considerate of you to anticipate my wishes as always, Brother Bulaybub. You have my leave.'

Both acolytes bowed from the waist. When

Kando turned away to the table again, the girl shot Acorna a quick, intense glance under heavy lashes. The sprinkle of freckles across her nose and cheeks seemed much too frivolous to match the red-rimmed green eyes above them.

In those eyes Acorna saw despair turn to a tentative hope. Miw-Sher's hands were clenched so tightly Acorna thought they might bleed, but her stride was purposeful as she led the way from the hall. The girl was having trouble containing herself enough to keep from running.

The force of her personality reminded Acorna of Maati. Thoughts of Maati brought thoughts of Maati's brother and a fresh stab of pain to Acorna's heart. Almost involuntarily, her fingers flew to the neck of her tunic, beneath which was Aari's birth disk.

The guards nodded to Brother Bulaybub and Miw-Sher and allowed them to pass through the gate, but they asked Acorna to show them her authorization to leave the post, which Macostut had provided. They pointedly did not look at her horn, even though she distinctly caught the thought (What kind of an alien *is* this, anyway?) before the other guard, with a roll of his eyes at his comrade's lack of worldliness, then directed her to pass slowly through the gate, which as Macostut had promised, contained a scanner for forbidden devices.

A red-draped box on wheels waited outside the Federation post and spaceport, hitched to two hornless beasts that bore a striking resemblance to Linyaari Ancestors.

'We should take the carriage,' Miw-Sher urged, heading for it.

'His Eminence did not grant us permission to do so,' Bulaybub replied, and Acorna again received the impression that he was trying to temper his tone.

'It would save time,' the girl pointed out. 'She might save a sacred one by its use.'

'Perhaps,' Bulaybub said reasonably, 'but the Mulzar is aware of this concern and yet did not suggest that we had his permission to use his conveyance. If he chooses to leave and we have taken the carriage without permission, the ambassador will not be able to save *us.*'

Acorna didn't think he was entirely serious about the consequences of taking the wagon, but he was senior to Miw-Sher in rank and he clearly did not want to take the carriage. He shot a glance into the twilit streets of the city, as if looking for something or sensing something. Acorna reached out to see if she could sense a bit about his thoughts – that would be very rude, and not honorable, without asking his permission. She sensed that he was waiting, expecting something . . . someone. And it had nothing to do with their mission. Her probe was not mind reading exactly, just ordinary sensitivity to the movements of body and eye and the expressions of other people. She considered asking him about it, but rejected the thought.

Whatever he was up to could not be nearly as important as the lives of the Temple cats, who needed her so badly that RK had diverted the

Condor to get her here. And RK wasn't the only one worried. Miw-Sher was beside herself with impatience. Acorna said lightly, 'I'm quite a swift runner. Lead the way at your fastest pace, please.'

'If you are indeed swift of foot, there is no need for me to lead you,' Miw-Sher replied eagerly. 'You can see the Temple very clearly from here. It is not far.' She pointed. The Temple was three stories high, and above the highest floor of the Temple rose a spire, a dome, and two conical towers. The structure dwarfed the low homes, shacks, and shops of the city. 'Let's go!' Then they were all sprinting toward the Temple.

The Linyaari ambassador, like other Linyaari, was an extremely fast runner, so she paced herself so she would not outrun her guide. However, Miw-Sher was so swift that Acorna needed to slow only slightly to stay behind her. The run through the city was exhilarating after being cooped up on the *Condor* for so long. It also kept her from absorbing too quickly the noise of this strange place full of unshielded mouths and minds which otherwise could have overwhelmed her senses. Thousands of conversations, laughing, weeping, screaming, soothing, screaming again – she blocked it all out, focusing on her run and preparing herself for the task ahead.

The girl's heels flashed before her. Brother Bulaybub's trudging footfalls fell behind quickly, fading so completely into the general din that it was as if the priest had taken a different direction.

Rounding a corner, Acorna found herself facing the Temple's main gate, where the girl stood beckoning impatiently. Now the building's uppermost embellishments made sense. The Temple was in the shape of a gigantic cat with one paw raised aloft. The dome was the head of the cat, and the conical towers rising from it the ears. The open mouth of the muzzle formed a covered balcony. The main part of the building was molded to resemble a cat's haunches; the outer protective wall, the tail. RK would probably want to fight the whole building when he saw it.

Darkness was closing in now, the third sun setting, but it was still very hot. Once she ran into the open gate, Acorna saw that the courtyard was positioned to catch the most sun possible. The building's outer walls were a good six feet thick. Between the first and second story, they were laced with thin planks leading into holes in the walls.

Up the cat's chest a similarly flimsy pair of ladders rose on either side to the balcony in the muzzle. Long galleries of columns supported a shaded cloister inside the tail and along the lower body of the Temple. Though the main structure of the Temple was of a red and brown stone, the columns supporting the cloisters were white and oddly striped down their length.

'This way,' the girl said, and led Acorna inside the Temple, pausing for a few words with a sentry who allowed them to pass, though with a long wondering glance at the alien stranger.

'Back here,' the girl called over her shoulder. They came at last to a room lit by a gaseous light. The interior, although it looked clean, stank of illness, of the pungency of male cats, of blood, urine, and dead fish.

Five people looked up when the girl entered.

'Miw-Sher, you've returned too late,' a woman the right age to be the girl's mother said. 'Grimla has left us. She went into convulsions a few minutes ago. She was so weak her dear body could not sustain them.'

'No!' the girl cried. 'Where are the others? I've brought a doctor, someone from off-planet who can help them.'

'I can cure your cats,' Acorna said, praying it was true. 'If I may I examine them now, please?'

Two feeble squeaks intended to be mews issued from very thin, bony-looking cats no more than half RK's own splendid size. The one with the jaundiced-looking yellow coat wobbled forward on trembling paws and stared at her. His eyes were half clouded with the third eyelid.

She walked to him, and his caretaker stepped in front of him. 'No alien hands will touch my Pash,' the man declared stoutly. As Acorna started to muster an argument, the man suddenly said, 'Aiee!' He jumped wildly, then rubbed his behind.

Miw-Sher said, 'Pash seems to think otherwise. Step aside. Let the doctor work.'

The man reluctantly stepped aside.

'First I must reassure the cat and let him get to know me,' Acorna said, to explain why she picked up Pash. The poor animal felt like bones webbed together with silk, and he smelled as if he had turned himself inside out just recently. But he stroked his face against her hands.

With great care, Acorna stroked and petted him, held him up to her face, rubbing her cheek

106

in his fur and urging him silently to touch her horn. He did, grabbing it with paws still velvet to lever himself upward and rub his jaw against it. The frail shudders running through his skeletal body took a while to be recognizable as purrs, but that's what they were.

She continued to stroke him.

(Don't take forever.)

She glanced up. Two coin-bright eyes stared down at her from one of the holes above her head. RK glared down at her. (There are three others that I can see, besides the dead queen. Can't you revive her? These other toms aren't going to do me a bit of good.)

Acorna tried to release Pash, but he clung to her with all his claws. She sent him a message to desist, but he snuggled his great head deeper under her armpit.

RK made some low sounds that could have come from any of the cats and Pash abruptly disengaged, hopped onto the counter, and with a flip of his tail, went to his personal food dish to see what was in it. Satisfied crunching and slurping sounds came from the direction of the dish as Acorna moved on to the next stricken cat.

'It's a miracle!' one of the priests cried.

'The Star Cat has sent us a miracle!' another agreed.

The third said, 'This stranger is a great doctor indeed, Miw-Sher. Where did you get her?'

Acorna didn't listen to the answer. She was busy communing with a lovely golden-and-rust-colored fellow who appeared to be huge and fluffy. When she lifted him, however, he was as

107

light as if he were in zero G. She cooed and crooned the most awful drivel to him, but he didn't seem to mind. In fact he seemed to like it.

'What is his name?' she asked Miw-Sher, who was bending over another of the cats.

'Haji,' the girl said in a voice unsteady with weeping.

Haji was very weak. Like Pash, his eyes were only half open. Drool dribbled from his mouth and raw sores pierced the pink of his gums. The cat did not even have the strength to reach for her. He lay limp as a discarded velvet scarf against her shoulder. She lay her cheek in his fur, bringing the horn into contact with him almost as if by accident. 'Poor Haji, where does it hurt, darling boy?'

(Ugh. I think I'm going to be sick myself now,) RK said. He accompanied his statement with a mental image involving a hairball.

(Shhh,) Acorna said to him mentally, then turned the thought into a 'Shush, shush, poor little kitty, poor dear boy, are you beginning to notice, hmmm? It doesn't hurt anymore, does it?'

She inclined her head to stare into his face and brought her horn in contact with his mouth. The sores disappeared. The nictating membranes of the third eyelid retracted so that his eyes were fully open and bright as the highest caliber peridots.

With a voice rusty from disuse, Haji suddenly said, 'Ryow!' and flew out of Acorna's arms as if hurricane winds blew in the direction of his food dish.

Miw-Sher's tear-ravaged face was both frightened and hopeful as she advanced toward Acorna with a limp and spiky-furred tortoiseshell cat in her arms. 'This is our Grimla. She is still warm, Doctor Ambassador. Not stiff. M-maybe I feel a little breath. M-maybe she is not entirely gone yet. J-just very tired? Could you please just look at her?'

Acorna stroked the fur and felt a very faint sigh of breath beneath it. Grimla hadn't used up all of her lives yet, but it was fortunate for her that the *Condor* had arrived as soon as it had or she would have been lost. The life in the old queen was faint and flickering, but life nevertheless lingered. Acorna could see the essence of it trying to flee, clinging only to the tips of the cat's whiskers, the very ends of her fur, moving them very slightly.

'Poor sweet girl,' Acorna said, and bent to stroke the once-beautiful cat while she lay still against Miw-Sher's chest. The acolyte's own heart was beating hard, as if trying to encourage the cat's.

Again, as if by accident, Acorna touched the Temple cat with her horn while seeming to examine her elsewhere. Grimla gave a deep sigh and a cough, and blinked twice. Then she stretched.

'You were faking, weren't you?' Acorna teased. 'You scared your friend very badly, you naughty cat!'

As she said these silly words, she waggled her lowered head, encouraging Grimla to play with her horn. Instead, with another sigh, the old queen stretched up and put the velvets of her paws carefully, one behind the other, on the top of Acorna's horn, then stretched up and with a dry and raspy tongue, licked the tip once, and started down. Acorna caught her and kissed the top of her head. Then the cat took her leave of both Acorna and Miw-Sher to seek her own food dish. But she paused once and looked back at them with a serene expression. They could hear her purr from three feet away. Turning a contentedly waving tail on them, she stuck her nose in her dish.

After Acorna had cured Sher-Paw, the last of the remaining Temple cats, she said, 'This room should be cleaned. I suggest that you discard everything that can't be washed in disinfectant and very hot water, then wipe down all of the scrubbable surfaces. Though your sacred cats are cured, the disease could still be spread by vectors from the sick cats.'

'Vectors? What are these, Doctor?' asked the male priest. 'Tell me what this is that has killed so many of our guardian felines and I will slay it with my bare hands. My revered companion, Pedibastet, was the first of the holy creatures to succumb. Are these vector beasts demons, or perhaps some evil magic spell cast by the shaman of an enemy clan?'

'I was thinking more in terms of mutant nano-viruses.' The people around her looked even more bewildered than before. She tried to explain. 'I don't actually know what causes this illness, but the causes of most sicknesses are organisms rather like animals but very, very small, too small to see. They are so small that they can go right inside a person or beast without anyone noticing, and attack healthy beings and make them sick. If you want to keep from spreading the sickness or getting the cats re-infected, you should do as I suggest. Clean everything thoroughly, including rugs, pillows, countertops, walkways, and the insides of those holes your cats climb through. If they become reinfected or if perhaps new cats are introduced to this group and become infected by organisms still living in the environment, I will not be here to cure them.'

'Aiee,' Miw-Sher said, 'I could not bear this again. Is there no medicine you could leave us, none of your knowledge or spells?'

Acorna pondered this. Even if she sacrificed a slice of her horn, as she had once done on Rushima, it could not serve all of the stricken for all of their illnesses. For that reason and many others, the Linyaari tried not to allow others to realize that it was their horns that healed and purified water and air. But until she analyzed the causative agent of the disease that had decimated Temple cats all over Makahomia, she couldn't hope to vanquish the illness merely by curing these few victims of it.

'I will do what I can before I leave,' she said finally. 'Meanwhile, introduce no other cats—'

At that point, RK half jumped, half fell among them. At first Acorna thought the big fellow was faking it to gain access to Grimla, but he did not spring back up when he landed, even though Pash was growling menacingly at him. He gave the smallest, saddest mew Acorna had ever heard him utter. In case she hadn't got the point, he sent her a feeble transmission, along with a pitiful vocalized mew.

(I don't feel so good,) he said.

(I did warn you,) she told him silently. By now the other cats hopped up to surround him.

'What Temple is guarded by this one?' Miw-Sher asked. 'Is he from the steppes?'

'No,' Acorna said, lifting RK's considerable bulk. Since he had acquired the disease apparently between one breath and the next, he had had no time to lose weight and was his usual hefty self. She didn't elaborate. She didn't wish to have anyone seek to execute her or Becker or anyone else for being in RK's company. 'He is my friend and Captain Becker's, who came with us on our spaceship. Not a very wise cat, but a friend nevertheless.'

Rubbing her face against his furry sides so that her horn as well as her cheek and nose pressed against him, she murmured what sounded like coos to the other people but what she was actually saying was, (I told you so! I knew you would catch this disease, you stubborn beast.)

RK wriggled free and with a smug purr and eyes wide and bright again, said, (And I told you that you would heal me if I did.)

'He certainly looks like a Temple cat to *me*,' one of the priests who seemed unaffiliated with any particular feline said. 'In fact he looks more like the real thing than any of ours at the moment, tatty as they are from undereating and all of that noisy puking they've been doing.'

'With all respect, Your Reverence, the ambassador is not only our guest, she has laid

112

healing hands upon our sacred guardians and saved them from certain death,' the woman in the priestly robes said. 'I think we must give her the benefit of the doubt.'

'Oh, of course,' the man said with false joviality. 'No offense meant, Your Excellency.' But his smile was oily and his eyes were shifty. Acorna imagined he would be giving a report to Nadhari's cousin before long, and would not neglect to mention RK's entrance.

'None taken,' Acorna said lightly. 'But now, if you'll forgive me, the healing process is very draining to me. I need to rest.'

'You're welcome to leave your guardian here with ours if you wish, Excellency,' the woman grooming Sher-Paw said with genuine concern.

RK had been doing reconnaissance among the Temple cats, but apparently found them still too weak to be stimulating companions. He hopped up on Acorna's shoulders and made himself comfortable around her neck, letting his head and front paws drape to her waist on her left side, while his back paws dangled on her right side to the middle of her arm.

Acorna laughed. 'I believe he has spoken.'

'I will show you to our guest quarters,' Miw-Sher said, leading them from the room. As the girl began to turn down a hallway that appeared to penetrate deeper into the Temple's interior, Acorna said, 'Please tell your high priest that RK and I must return to our vessel. I can examine the tiny animals that cause this illness there, and perhaps discover a means to combat the sickness. If I am successful, I will be able to leave with you a medicine you can use in case of further out-breaks of the disease. I may also be able to teach your people how to prepare this medicine them-selves.'

Acorna thought she might be able to prepare a vaccine for the illness using a blood sample from RK, but the Temple would lack the necessary laboratory facilities to purify and test it. And, given the Federation proscription on introducing new technology to these people, she'd better do any research she wanted to do aboard ship.

Miw-Sher said, 'Perhaps your friend should stay aboard your vessel until you go. I fear he may not be allowed to return with you unless you keep him out of sight. Especially with the number of our own guardians so sadly depleted. You may find him missing when you are ready to leave.'

That provided Acorna with an opening to dis-cuss her ambassadorial role with someone she felt instinctively was trustworthy.

'This cat is very important to my people.' That would give her a further justification for RK's presence with her. 'You must understand that my people have had their world destroyed twice just within my lifetime and have already suffered many losses.'

The girl nodded as if they were discussing the weather. 'Makahomia wasn't destroyed, but my family and home have been,' she said. 'We allied ourselves with the Kandos and sent warriors to fight beside them. So when our village was attacked, our men were away fighting for *them*, and no one was around to protect us from our enemies. My mother and brothers were all slain and I alone of all my family remained to greet our allies when they finally arrived. Among them was Brother Bulaybub, who is my mother's steppe-cousin, and he persuaded the Mulzar that I would be good with the cats, particularly Grimla, whose special friend was killed in the battle. But I'm interrupting you!' the girl said, her hand flying to her mouth as if to shush herself. 'I'm sorry. I'm very rude. Please go on.'

Acorna continued. 'During the first attack, my people left their original homeworld. They took what they could with them in one great evacuation. They intended to take with them cats they called *pahaantiyirs*. I know this only through the stories of my people. I myself was not born on our homeworld, but was orphaned in space. I've only just returned to my people recently.'

'You have? But I thought you must be from an important family, and very well known to have achieved your high office so young!' She saw that Acorna was patiently waiting, and once more her knuckles flew to her lips. 'Oh, there I go doing it again. Pardon me, please, and continue.'

Acorna smiled. 'You could say my status has something to do with having been adopted by an important family – several of them, in fact.' There were Gil, Calum, and Rafik, the asteroid miners who were her original adoptive fathers. Then there was Rafik's uncle, the wily and wealthy Hafiz, who had adopted her instead of collecting her when he learned she was part of an alien race and not a freak of human physiology.

And there was her dear friend, Mr Li, who had also adopted her and helped her rid the planet

Kezdet of child slavery and prostitution before he finally succumbed to the illness that had crippled his body for so many years.

Then she had been found by her mother's sister, Neeva, and returned to narhii-Vhiliinyar, where she was adopted by Grandam Naadiina and Maati.

Captain Becker, too, had been like another uncle to her, and had saved the life of her beloved Aari. Finally there was Aari himself, her lifemate and other self – well, there was Aari for a short time at least, before he disappeared during the exploration of Vhiliinyar. In the meantime, she had the support and love of his family – his mother Miiri, his father Kaarlye, and his sister, Maati.

She had to admit upon reflection that even though she did not have Aari's company at present, she had been very lucky in her adoptive families.

'At any rate, I am told that when the time came for my people to evacuate, their *pahaantiyirs* were nowhere to be found. They disappeared entirely and have not been seen, alive or dead, since. They all say RK bears an incredible resemblance to the *pahaantiyirs*. Nadhari Kando, who as you saw is with us, tells us that RK also looks very much like a Makahomian Temple cat. So my mission is, now that I'm here, to learn if there is kinship between these two species, and if so, how close that kinship might be.'

Miw-Sher looked thoughtful, staring first at RK, then back to Acorna's face. 'It is possible, though I know little of worlds beyond our own.

You're not likely to learn much here. His Holiness is very good at . . . delegating . . . matters of doctrine and history to others. But please, we have tarried here too long. The others will be coming soon and somehow I feel your plans may not meet with His Holiness's approval.'

'Then I would rather not meet His Holiness right now. It sounds as if this may be my best opportunity to return to the ship. Is there a back way out of here?'

'There *is* another way,' the girl said, hesitating, then saying, as if arguing with herself, 'It can be frightening – but then, you must be very brave to have come so far from home through space. And you have a guardian with you. Just remember he will protect you, and do not be afraid, no matter what.'

'I won't,' Acorna promised.

Miw-Sher made up her mind and motioned Acorna to follow her. 'Come quickly, then, and I will show you the way.'

They passed through a maze of corridors and back out of the main Temple building, across a much narrower courtyard. This contained a lush garden, a central well, and enough fountains to make Hafiz happy. Rows of cloisters enclosed the garden. Miw-Sher pulled Acorna and RK back between the columns and the wall. As they came to the join where the tail-shaped wing of the building met the body, Miw-Sher pressed her finger against a stone in the wall and it opened. The opening was not nearly tall enough for Acorna, and even Miw-Sher had to stoop to show her the way. 'Just keep going straight through here. It's only about sixteen feet to the end of the passage. It opens into an abandoned dwelling. Be careful not to be seen as you leave or someone may misunderstand. You'd best cover your head as you go. You are – conspicuous.' Miw-Sher gave Acorna a large scarf such as some of the Temple's inhabitants wore for a head covering.

'Yes,' Acorna said, 'I will return as soon as I can.'

'Remember,' Miw-Sher said, 'don't be afraid. Nothing can hurt you, and even if it could, your guardian will protect you.'

Acorna ducked low into the wall. Once she was past the entrance, the opening grew taller so she could walk upright. Miw-Sher waved from the opening, then started. 'Someone is coming. Safe journey.'

With that the door shut behind her, the darkness deepened, and the sounds of the courtyard were snuffed out like a candle flame. RK stiffened in her arms. His fur bristled and his claws pricked her arm. When she touched his head to quiet him, his ears were laid back. A low growl leaked through his teeth.

And then she heard it, too. Coming from inside the surrounding walls, there was a whisper like blowing sand or a serpent's hissing. As she listened more intently, the whisper rose to a mumble and she thought she could make out separate words.

She stroked RK soothingly and listened with her mind as well as her ears. The words were incomprehensible but the feelings behind them were anxious, angry, frustrated, and also afraid.

The emotional storm they created enveloped her and RK. The cat's tail switched back and forth, back and forth, faster and harder. He puffed to twice his size, but Acorna was the only recipient of his bared claws.

His growl grew in his throat, and as it grew, a corresponding growl entered the words until they ended in a hollow, reverberating roar Acorna was sure would bring everyone running. Just as she stepped forward, however, the roar was replaced by a calmer sound, a deep and throaty purr. RK's tail no longer switched, and his ears, when she touched them, were pricked forward, alert but calm. The hair on the cat's back gradually settled down sleekly along his spine. RK was sending no thoughts at that point for her to receive, nor had he from the beginning, but now the cat settled into a relieved purr that seemed to be echoed by whatever it was that lived inside the walls of this Temple.

Miw-Sher's skin twitched as she listened to the noise within the wall. Grimla mewed plaintively. Miw-Sher was glad the occasion had arisen to introduce Acorna to the wall's resident. There was so much to explain, so much to ask, but she sensed a firm ally in Acorna if only she could enlist the ambassador's help without alerting her enemies.

When the roar came, Miw-Sher had already reached the cattery and deposited Grimla within it. Her beloved friend could not help just now. The cat needed to gain strength. Miw-Sher was loath to leave Grimla and the other cats, even for a short time, but she could not stay inside the Temple without knowing what was happening. When she was once more in the darkness of the back courtyard, she changed quickly and leaped to the top of the wall and over.

FIVE

The grub wasn't nearly as good as advertised, Becker thought, but to give him credit, Macostut, after a bite or two of his own meal, apologized for it. 'Usually our facility can offer excellent fresh meat and vegetables to our guests, and I automatically promised that when I invited you. The truth is, the disease the Mulzar mentioned has caused the Makahomians to quarantine the meat animals and forbid their slaughter for food. Since, as you mentioned, Captain MacDonald, diseases such as this may be caused by some problem in the food or soil, we have also had to process our fresh vegetables until they are no longer in their most edible condition.'

Becker was gracious. 'It's better than cat food,' he said incautiously.

'I beg your pardon?' Mulzar Kando replied.

Nadhari began damage control. 'Captain Becker is a thrifty and resourceful man. He accepts many commodities in trade for his salvage. One of his regular customers gives him large quantities of cat food. There have been times during his more perilous journeys when he sustained himself by eating that when other rations were unavailable.'

Kando looked interested. 'Hmmm, perhaps, if we have something you would like to trade for, we could take some of the cat food off your hands? If the diet of our Temple cats is indeed responsible for the disease that has decimated them, some alternative food may provide relief until we can bring the problem under control.'

Becker thought for a moment. 'Maybe. I had the impression you folks don't use a lot of machinery.'

'That has always been true in the past, certainly,' Kando said.

'You got any hard-copy books, maybe? I could trade for some of those.'

'No, I fear not. Our writing tends toward sacred subjects and is usually inscribed upon monuments.'

'Is that so? Seems like you'd have to write down your laws and rulings on things, your history, that kind of thing.'

Kando appeared genuinely grieved. 'Alas, I fear that being always at war has undermined our ability to retain such ephemeral documents. Battles are recorded only by the bards of the winners. The possessions of the losers that are not looted are burned in the victory bonfires.'

'I can see where that might present a problem,' Becker said. 'How about those stones in your necklaces? Got any of those you're willing to trade?'

Everybody but him and Scar laughed as if he was being intentionally funny.

'No, I'm serious,' Becker said, holding up his hands for silence. He explained. 'As a gemstone, they're not considered to be worth a lot – I mean, at least not elsewhere – but they have other uses.'

'He's right,' MacDonald said. 'They've used them a lot in spot terrestoration.'

'We're only laughing, Jonas,' Nadhari said, 'because no matter what was offered for one of the sacred eyes, we would never trade or sell it. The stones are religious items, you see. They are believed to have been given to us by the earliest deities of our people.'

'Oh, well, no offense meant,' Becker said. 'Just tryin' to drum up a little business. Didn't mean to interfere with anybody's religion. But they're used for a special kind of particle beam—'

'Ah-ah, Captain Becker,' Macostut said, waving his finger in warning. 'Such things are not relevant to the Mulzar's culture.'

'Oh, of course, sorry,' Becker said again, and wished himself back on the *Condor*, where he was not so socially inept.

The Mulzar waved both of his hands as if to blow away the smoke of embarrassment. 'Nothing to be sorry for at all, Captain Becker. Dsu forgets sometimes that while my culture may be more or less uncontaminated, I myself was contaminated at an early age by no lesser agent than the Federation itself. I was well aware at the time that stones similar to our sacred ones were used as particle beam accelerators to produce blade-like laser beams for mining. We have very fine stones here, and I am sure you will be extremely sorry when you see them that my people will not

123

allow me to trade any of them for your cat food.'

This time the laughter was unanimous. Becker thought Kando was probably an okay guy after all. And he was Nadhari's cousin. If anyone had an insight into how to bring his former lover out of her funk, Cousin Edu and the old folks at home might be the ones.

Whatever else was affected by the planet's current difficulties, the wine was fine, if undistinguished, and everyone was enjoying it and becoming quite relaxed under its influence.

Captain MacDonald told some amusing stories about farming and tractor repair on some of the planets where he visited, and Becker chimed in with a couple of tales of his own, as well as relating a thrilling account of the battle against the Khleevi. He was hoping this might stimulate a war story or two from Kando. And that might also open the door for Nadhari to talk about what was bugging her.

Instead, Kando said simply, 'Thank you, Captain Becker, for reminding us how fortunate we are that the Federation shields us from these truly terrible threats. The Federation, that is, and heroes like you and my cousin. Most of my people are unaware that such dangers exist, but my friendship with Dsu and my own experience while training for the Corps have given me different insights. It is because of this other reality that I differ from my predecessors, who considered constant war a way to keep the economy lively and the power in balance. I have come to feel strongly that these wars divide us against each other to no good purpose. They weaken our planet's voice in the Federation. They retard the progress of our civilization, destroy valuable individuals, and drain our resources, both natural and cultural.

'We don't need to be at war constantly, fighting over the same thing. We need roads and bridges both physical and cultural that will connect us, not divide us. Better schools. Better medical care. And we won't get those things until Makahomia is united. Only then can we hope for more than our present impoverished level of existence.'

Becker wasn't sure whether he was supposed to applaud or head right out to the polls and place an illegal (since he was not Makahomian) but enthusiastic vote for Kando for Mulzar.

The speech did stimulate Nadhari. She smiled one of her slow and dangerous smiles and said, 'And who do you suppose could unite our planet and how, Edu, hmmmm?'

Kando reached over and took her hand, his voice practically throbbing with sincerity as he said, 'I was hoping you might help me answer that question, Nadhari, now that you are home again.'

Then the Mulzar started in on a narrative about Nadhari's childhood. She kept protesting what he was saying, and he lapsed into one of the Makahomian dialects, one that Macostut apparently understood, too. Occasionally one of them tried to translate the conversation, but this seemed to be an in-joke kind of session and the Mulzar's Standard wasn't up to it, especially as his wine goblet emptied more and more often while he joked.

Becker and MacDonald looked at each other and shrugged. Then MacDonald sat back in his chair and patted his uniform tunic with satisfaction. 'So, Jonas,' he said, 'that young lady you're with, the one with the horn. I heard about someone like her back on Rushima, last time I stopped over there to repair some of their tractors and give their people a few lessons. They were telling me about a tall young girl with a horn in the middle of her forehead who brought them a special tool that cleaned up their mucky water in no time flat. I looked that tool over and I couldn't find anything but a little slice of something that looks a little like this girl's horn.'

Becker was nodding, grinning, as if he knew all about it, and thinking fast. If he knew Acorna, it *was* a slice of her horn. Since he and Aari were practically blood brothers, and Acorna sort of a blood sister-in-law, that made him practically Linyaari himself, he figured, and he had to protect their secrets.

'Oh, yeah,' he said, broadening his grin and going into a riff that was very much like his spiel at the nano-bug markets where he sold some of his salvage cargo. 'Aren't those slick? Linyaari nano-technology is something else. I can't believe what those people can fit into one of their little devices. The thing you saw is really just a kind of trigger for the machine. That coating on it is to make it look like the horn is their trademark. They have this whole class of people who take things other people invented and refine them and give them a style that's all Linyaari.'

'Do tell!' MacDonald said. 'Well, those folks are

okay with the people on Rushima, I can tell you.'

'Oh, yeah, they're wonderful people. And Acorna is probably the best of them all. She'll probably have all those guardian pussycats healed and eating out of her hand by the time we get there.'

Kando suddenly tuned into him and dropped the Makahomian to ask in Standard, 'Then she really can do as she claims, the ambassador?'

'Of course she can. Your pussycats got nothing to worry about,' Becker told him.

'Oh, yes,' Nadhari said, also in Standard. 'Ambassador Acorna is a wonderful physician.' Now it was her turn to elaborate. 'Her healing techniques are being taught to the more gifted children on Maganos Moonbase. You may have heard of it, Lieutenant Commander?' The inference in her tone was that Kando, being in the Makahomian backwater, was *un*likely to have heard of it. 'My former employer, Mr Li, helped Acorna rid Kezdet of child slavery.'

'Why would he do such a thing?' Kando asked.

Nadhari smiled innocently at her cousin. 'I forgot. Do you still practice slavery here, Edu? It's considered a very primitive practice elsewhere. I'm surprised the Federation allows it. On Kezdet it was only because the leaders of the slave industry had many low friends in high places.'

Macostut sputtered and hurried to defend himself. 'We try not to be ethnocentric when dealing with the inhabitants of our member worlds, Lady Nadhari.'

Lady Nadhari? Becker looked from the official to his former girlfriend with surprise. Well, she

127

was from the ruling family, after all. Maybe this gave her a rank she didn't claim or hadn't been aware of. From the look on her face it was also one that didn't impress her much.

The man continued. 'We try to respect their customs, religion, and cultural mores.'

'Cultural mores change in a healthy culture,' Nadhari told him.

'Yes,' Kando said, 'they do. And should. That has been my position since I became Mulzar. If our ways do not change with the times, the culture becomes stagnant. So does a faith when it is not renewed so that the trappings no longer necessary drop away while the essence remains.'

'I take it when you say "trappings" you're not referring to the priesthood, Edu?' Nadhari said, pretending to tease. 'Or to your own position?'

Becker turned to MacDonald and drew a number 1 in the air with his forefinger. 'Chalk one up for Nadhari,' he mouthed. MacDonald nodded sagely.

'You're joking with me now, aren't you, cousin? You always did like to keep me off balance,' Kando replied. To Becker he said, 'She is such a tease.'

Becker began at that point to wonder if this man had any insight into Nadhari's psyche after all.

SIX

'What could that *possibly* have been?'

RK stopped purring, laid his ears back, and opened his eyes to annoyed slits. His paws kept kneading in time to the low grumbling noise, which was now barely audible to Acorna.

(Were we going somewhere or did you just want to stand here to find out if cats can really see in the dark?) RK asked in a quite normal thought pattern.

(Yes,) Acorna said. (Let's go. You can explain what that was all about when we're out of here.)

Whoever or whatever was within the wall, it continued its noise on a very low level but no longer sent emotional messages. Acorna felt like rapping on the wall and asking, 'Excuse me, is everything all right in there? We couldn't help noticing you roared.'

However, RK squirmed out of her arms and dropped to the ground, then scratched impatiently at something just ahead of them.

She would question both the cat and Miw-Sher more thoroughly later. She walked two more steps and caught up with RK, touching his flank with her foot.

He did not have to thought-speak to tell her he was at the door she was supposed to open. Standard cat/biped nonverbal communication was eloquent enough. She had to give the door a hard shove that nearly spilled her into a dark space where dust tickled her nose and cobwebs brushed her face, snagged on her horn, and dangled before her eyes to further confuse what little vision she retained in the dark surroundings.

By the time she reached the street, she wouldn't need the scarf, she thought. She would look like a woman-shaped cocoon, totally wrapped in silken webbing.

'I wish Mac was here with the flashlight attachment in his arm,' she whispered to the cat.

(Why?) RK, apparently feeling sociable again, asked in thought-talk. (I can see perfectly well. My eyes are much better than yours, but there's not much to see. I'll bet the mice around here are starving. This place is empty. If I weren't convalescing from my recent illness I'd jump down and chase some of those sassy spiders.)

(I'd much rather you'd find us another door – preferably one that doesn't open right onto the street,) she told him.

(On your left. Just reach out with those long arms and clever fingers of yours. Although I am, of course, the perfect life form just as I am, I rather wish I could have come with those as optional attachments. I could open anything!)

(You'd lose out on the fun of getting others to do it for you,) Acorna told the cat, grasping the door latch and pulling. Hot air assailed her nostrils. A lash of a breeze blew fresh oxygen into her face. She closed the door, which led into an alleyway between the building and the one adjacent to it.

Through the crack between the buildings she saw the moons quite distinctly. She drew the scarf over her head. RK climbed up on her shoulders and said, (Now cover the kitty. That's a good girl.) He purred to give her positive reinforcement for doing as she was told. Not that she hadn't intended to anyway. His desires were distinct enough without the verbalizations. Being privy to the specific meaning of opinions the cat had formerly expressed by body language would take some getting used to.

Once they were in the street, RK leaped down from her shoulders and streaked ahead of her, sprinting from shadow to shadow.

With her scarf draped low over her forehead to cover her horn, Acorna aroused no interest in the locals. Indeed, there was no one to be interested. The streets were lined with low, flat-roofed dwellings, each with a single small window near the door. Otherwise, they were occupied only by a pungent haze of smoke. She supposed the lack of windows in the thick red-clay walls served to keep the heat as well as the light out. However, this night was cool, and may have even felt chilly to people accustomed to a semidesert climate. She vaguely remembered, on her sprint from space-port to Temple, seeing a few people sitting on their rooftops, watching the last of the suns setting in the west while waiting for the first glimmer of the first of the moons to rise in the east. Both moons were up now, crescent shapes floating through the night sky.

She supposed people might sleep up on the roofs sometimes, but no one appeared to be doing so tonight. The rooftops were inhabited only by shadows, or so she thought until suddenly RK halted directly in front of her, growling, tail lashing, staring at something above him on the far side of the street. She followed his gaze and saw it, just briefly.

At first she thought it was a person, for it moved more like a biped running in a stooped position than a true quadruped. But she glimpsed ears rotating back to catch RK's growl, saw the claws and muzzle silhouetted in the moonlight and what appeared to be a clubbed tail, lashing like RK's.

It leaped and was gone as if it had been no more than a cat fancy, one of those things that cats alone can see. Acorna had seen it, however. Perhaps because she was linked to RK's consciousness, but more likely because it had been there.

At any rate, RK's fur smoothed down, his ears went up, his tail quieted, and he sat for a moment washing his paw.

(What was that?) Acorna asked. (Did it have something to do with whatever was happening inside the wall?)

RK tapped his tail twice on the pavement. (I don't know, but maybe. I never saw one like it before. Nadhari might know. Maybe it was a ritual dancer imitating one of us god-like Temple guardians. I'd chase it if I didn't have you to protect.)

(Sorry to be such a burden,) she apologized with some amusement. (I will ask Nadhari when we see her, but are you sure you wouldn't like to share with me what exactly happened before?)

RK considered. (It's a cat thing, Acorna. You wouldn't understand.)

(How so a cat thing? I am sure I heard a human voice.)

(Well, I think it was a cat priest. He lives in the wall now. Maybe he's sick. Maybe he's got the sickness and a fever and is out of his head. But before he roared, he was chanting something about the moon's eyes and the coming of the guardian guide. These people call us guardians, so between that and the roar . . .)

(It's a cat thing, I see,) she said. (You could have told me that at the time.)

(It needed sorting out. I was too caught up in the moment to translate. I would like to know what made him roar like that, though – maybe that creature we just saw?)

(Maybe,) she agreed.

She *would* ask Nadhari about it when they saw her again, and Miw-Sher as well, but for now she wanted badly to reach the *Condor* and fulfill her promise to create a vaccine for the cats. She and RK hurried onward, finally reaching the intersection of the street running perpendicular to the Federation port gate. She was three blocks further north than she had been when Miw-Sher raced her to the Temple.

A different guard stood by the gate to the compound. She threw back her scarf, announcing her name and title.

'We were told you'd be spending the night at the Temple, Ambassador,' the soldier said, though her appearance, especially her horn, left no doubt in his mind she was who she claimed to be.

'I forgot something,' she said.

'May I ask what, ma'am?' he inquired stiffly.

'My medication,' she told him. It was perfectly true, after all.

She held his eye, and from the corner of hers, she saw movement low in the shadow of the gate as RK slipped by.

For a moment she wondered how she was going to reboard the *Condor* without the controls Becker carried with him, but the robolift was already on the ground when they reached the ship. Mac greeted them cheerfully. RK sniffed the ship thoroughly, reading the scents left behind by the Federation inspectors and rubbing his face against the contaminated areas to remark his territory.

(RK, I will be needing your assistance,) Acorna said softly, bending over to stroke him as he rearranged the scent of the captain's chair to suit himself.

He sat back on his haunches and licked his paw, then blinked at her as if to say, 'Oh, you will, will you?' But did not communicate directly.

She sank into a cross-legged position on the deck and regarded him seriously. 'Yes, that's right. You heard me tell Miw-Sher and the others the danger this disease may hold for future Temple cats and kittens who may become infected by the disease after we're gone. I want to make a vaccine that will allow the people caring for the Temple guardians to protect newcomers. But to make it, I will need to take blood samples from someone who has already been cured of the disease. I can't take the syringes and needles I need off-post to draw blood from the Temple cats, nor can I bring them here. I'm afraid that leaves you. It's fortunate you chose to disregard everyone's advice and left the post and contracted the disease yourself.'

RK gave her an offended glare, his lips curling up over his fangs.

'Surely you won't mind a little needle prick? It's no sharper than the claws you have been sticking into *me* lately.'

The cat's tail jerked with agitation, but he accompanied her to the laboratory as if the whole thing was his own idea. He growled while she restrained him and drew blood from him.

When she released him, he drew blood from *her*, then strutted away, sat down at a safe distance, and preened himself as if he were waiting to accept a medal for valor.

Acorna touched her horn lightly to her scratch and said, 'Fortunately, I heal quickly.' She set to work.

When a sufficient quantity of the vaccine was ready, she prepared to return to the Temple. Mac said, 'Are you forbidden to use the flitter, Acorna? I have prepared quite a nice flitter for our use when planetside.'

'Thank you, but not this time, Mac. You heard what Nadhari said, didn't you? These people choose not to use technology readily available to

135

the rest of the universe, and the Federation wishes that their choice be respected. Given the warlike nature of the people of Makahomia, I can almost concur that the limitations make sense. By the way, speaking of warlike, how are the Wats doing? You have been keeping them fed, I hope?'

The robot looked concerned. 'Yes, Acorna. But they are restless. They had understood they were going to a new home and are . . . disappointed, I suppose . . . that this is not it.'

'Hmm,' Acorna said. 'Well, the Wats certainly pose no technological threat to the Makahomians and they are warlike people also, not remarkably different from the people here. Perhaps the Federation would give them permission to immigrate here.'

'It is possible,' Mac said. 'But I do not think they could fill out the paperwork. Lieutenant Commander Macostut had many forms sent to our computer. I filled them out to the best of my abilities and returned them, but I do not think the Wats will be able to satisfy the local inhabitants with their answers, and I have insufficient data about them to fill out many of the questions on the forms. Whether they stay here or not, I sense trouble.'

'So the Makahomians want to know who we are, including the Wats?' Acorna smiled. 'I can see where that might be a problem. Especially when it comes to formal documentation. We might have to be creative. At any rate, I'll inquire with the local authorities later and see what I can do. I must get this vaccine to the Temple now. Please make sure RK remains aboard ship.'

'Yes, Acorna.'

But as Acorna was being lowered on the robolift, suddenly a furry projectile hurtled from RK's private exit and the cat rolled onto the floor of the descending lift.

'Shall I raise the lift again, Acorna?' Mac inquired on the intercom he had installed on the robolift. 'The first mate escaped my grasp and I could not regain possession of his person without applying undue strength, which might have damaged him.'

'We can try,' Acorna said. But as soon as the lift began to ascend again, RK lightly leaped onto the ground and sat looking up at her, the scallop of his mouth broadening in a cat smile of deep satisfaction. 'Never mind, Mac,' Acorna said, laughing in spite of herself at the rebellious cat. 'The first mate knows the risks quite well and is willing to take them. Who are we to restrain him?'

SEVEN

At Kando's invitation, Becker and MacDonald followed the Mulzar out the gate of the Federation post. A sort of old-time carriage waited for them.

There was a low haze over the flat roofs of the city, and the red air smelled like smoke. When Kando knocked on the side of the vehicle's cab, a sleepy-looking monk poked his head out and scrambled up to the driver's seat.

MacDonald stroked the vaguely equine oversized goats that were hitched to the front, looked into their eyes, checked their teeth, and joined Kando, Nadhari and Becker inside. 'Looks like those critters escaped whatever it is that's been troubling you anyway, Preacher,' he said.

'In the midst of our curse, we are blessed,' Kando said piously.

Nadhari's silence hung so heavily over the carriage that nobody, not even the effusive MacDonald, said anything until they arrived at the Temple, which was shaped like a cat.

Becker was feeling a little dizzy from the wine, to which he was no longer accustomed, and the bumpy ride in the cart, not to mention trying to figure out what was really passing between Nadhari and her cousin, and the cousin and Macostut. Acorna would know that kind of thing. Personally, if it wasn't for wanting to consult with her and see how she was doing with the pussy-cats, Becker would have made his excuses and returned to the *Condor* for the night. He had to get to work on his ship's computers pretty soon. Even though Mac knew a lot, the guy's programming was hardly competent to deal with all of the ins and outs of the delicate patchwork Becker had constructed to provide the *Condor*'s control and information instrumentation. Becker wasn't sure there was a man in the galaxy capable of it . . . except him, of course.

So he was understandably peeved when they arrived at the Temple and were told Acorna had left to return to the ship on an errand.

'What errand?' Kando sternly asked the little girl – was her name Shari something? Nah, but that was close. The kid was flushed and harried-looking, hugging a tortoiseshell cat that would have been as big as RK if it wasn't so skinny.

She answered her boss in Makahomian, and Nadhari quietly translated for Becker and MacDonald.

'She said Acorna had to go to the ship so she could make a magic potion to prevent future guardians from acquiring the disease that has afflicted ours, even long after she has departed.'

'You should have detained her, Miw-Sher,' Kando said severely. The girl cringed as if she expected to be hit. Becker thought Kando was being too harsh. Becker knew it would take more than some adolescent cat priestess to keep his friend the unicorn girl from going wherever she wanted, whenever she felt like it. Of course Kando didn't know Acorna.

'I'm sorry, Your Holiness, but she said she needed to do it at once, for the future good of the guardians.'

This time, Nadhari translated both sides of the conversation tonelessly and deliberately. *Was she making some kind of point?*

'But she might have been set upon,' Kando told the girl. 'You should have gone with her, at the very least.'

'Oh, but she was safe. She had a . . .' The girl stopped, looking trapped.

'A what?'

'A way about her that none would dare trespass,' the girl finished lamely. Becker had the funniest idea she had been going to say 'guardian' or 'cat' or something that amounted to the same thing as RK, his stalwart furry first mate, who should definitely not have been seen here. But the temptations of shore leave may have overridden RK's good sense. How else was his friend going to make Makahomian Temple kittens if he didn't get out and mingle? For a supposedly unsophisticated people, the Makahomians sure had a lot of rules. They should know better than to make rules about cats. He had only one cat, and he knew better than that.

The girl stroked the cat in her arms.

Nadhari scratched the top of the cat's head and said to her cousin, 'I see our Acorna has worked her usual healing miracle. This sacred guardian should be ready to take on an army after a day or two of rest. Are you sure there's not something you'd like to trade for Becker's cat food, cousin?'

Kando's mouth spasmed, as if he was trying to smile. He probably didn't appreciate Nadhari interfering while he was dressing down the troops. But Becker was kind of surprised to see that Kando looked less than thrilled by the recovery of the Temple cats.

Miw-Sher, that was the girl's name, not Shari. Nadhari told Becker Miw-Sher meant kitten and was likely a nickname. Anyway, Miw-Sher eagerly led them back to the Temple guardians' quarters. She was partly showing off for the newcomers and partly trying to jolly her boss back into a good mood by proving to him how well everything had turned out.

The three toms were – variously – eating, drinking, and sleeping, while the female, perfectly content in the girl's arms, fell into a bonelessly limp sleep. All the cats looked bright-eyed and bushy-tailed to Becker, though they needed to put on a few pounds to get back up to fighting weight.

'Where is Bulaybub?' Kando asked the girl.

'I – I don't know, Your Holiness. He was right behind us when the ambassador and I started for the Temple.'

At that moment the slap of sandals on stone heralded the arrival of three more priests, who burst into the cats' quarters. One, breathless, said, 'Your Holiness, a city sentry came across the remains of a priest. We believe it is Brother Bulaybub.'

141

Nadhari translated this, her mouth moving only now and then while her eyes watched for more developments.

'Commander,' MacDonald said to her, 'what did that fella mean exactly by remains? You sure you got that word right?'

Nadhari listened for a moment, then nodded. 'Yes, remains,' she said firmly and catalogued, as if reciting a grocery list. 'A head, missing the face, a disemboweled trunk, and the arm bearing the tattoo of the man's order.'

'What kind of critters do you have here that did that to him?' MacDonald asked.

Kando's face was no longer warm and charming as he spoke to the child. 'You see what your negligence has caused, Miw-Sher? Our enemies have heard of the disease that weakens us and stalk the streets. Brother Bulaybub, who saved you from enslavement and brought you here, although many deemed you unworthy, may be dead because you lacked the wit to remain with him. The ambassador may have come to similar harm, for all we know. You will retrace the way you came, and if you do not find her, you will stand at the gate of the Federation compound until she is ready to return to us. All night if necessary. And the next as well. Put Grimla down. She is too weak to protect anyone. And you do not deserve protection. Go!'

'Wait,' Nadhari ordered the girl in a tone even less to be argued with than her cousin's. To Becker she said softly, 'I'm going with her.'

Becker nodded, understanding. This was what Nadhari did and she was good at it.

Kando tried to stop her and said in Standard, presumably to keep the girl from understanding the conversation, 'Cousin, please. You are my guest. You are tired from your journey. I know your kind heart urges you to keep the girl from harm, but I am exaggerating the danger to alarm her into obedience. My men will be thick on the streets now. Truly, she and the ambassador will both be safe, but the girl should learn her lesson.'

Nadhari squared her shoulders and spoke in a dialect Becker had not heard before. Amid the spate of law she laid down to the Mulzar, Becker heard her say Acorna's name and that of her former boss, the late Delszaki Li. He grinned. He knew just what she'd said. Nadhari had told Kando that he might be boss here, but she owed it to *her* late boss Mr Li to look after his adopted daughter, as she had promised, and she intended to honor that promise.

To his credit, Kando seemed to realize when he was outclassed and outgunned. With a few more sharp words to Miw-Sher, he gestured that she and the three priests who had reported the death to him should follow Nadhari.

The convalescing cats had been listening to the whole exchange with their ears cocked and their tails lashing, but when Becker looked around for them, they were gone.

Kando noticed it, too, and roared at the other priests who had been playing cat-nurse along with the girl. He pointed up to some cat-sized holes attached to rafters in the ceiling. The last puff of a tail was disappearing through one now.

MacDonald watched and shook his head.

'Somebody ought to tell him it's no good closing the barn door after all the horses – or I guess you'd have to say cats right now – have got out.'

Becker approached Kando. 'I'd like to go back to the ship myself and make sure Acorna got there safely.'

'I cannot permit any more people on the streets,' Kando said. 'Nadhari's fighting skills are a matter of record, but yours are not, Captain, and I cannot risk an incident with the Federation. Please humor me in this and remain indoors while those trained to do so handle this matter.' He gave a sudden rueful smile. 'My authority has been undermined enough for one night.'

Becker sympathized to some extent, but didn't like to hit his bunk with Acorna still missing and one of his dinner partners freshly murdered.

Kando saw the conflict in his face and said diplomatically, 'Your pardon, Captain. You are a man of action, of course, and it would not be your way to be idle while others deal with this crisis. Perhaps you and Captain MacDonald would care to assist me as I examine the late Bulaybub's mortal remains?'

Becker nodded sharply and motioned to MacDonald. The other captain wasn't saying much, for a change, but his acute green eyes missed nothing and he seemed to be weighing everything he heard and saw. The two of them followed Kando and some flunkies to a room filled with candles and torches and a group of three human-sized stone altars. One now functioned as a morgue slab and held the bloody mess that remained of the late Bulaybub.

Two priestesses arrived bearing pottery bowls full of what looked like soap and water, but Kando held up his hand and beckoned the two off-world captains forward.

As they approached, Kando picked up what remained of the head, and held it up to them. It was barely recognizable as human, so Becker didn't react to it much himself. But MacDonald drew in his breath sharply.

'Well, Preacher,' he said, 'you got yourself a real problem with this one.'

Becker, looking at the gutted torso, thought that might possibly take the cake for the understatement of the week.

MacDonald's large finger traced the long marks against the frontal portion of the skull. 'See these claw marks? Your critters are going to have worse than a disease to contend with. And you'd better keep your little pussycats in the Temple, too. These here were made by some kind of a painter.'

'Painter?' Kando asked, confused. 'I see no paint.'

'That's what we call the big cats where I come from,' MacDonald said. 'Painters, pumas, cougars, mountain lions. Maybe even a jungle lion for all I know. But you got you a really big wildcat running around loose somewhere. And judging from what it did to this fella, I'd say it was right pissed.'

As he finished speaking, Kando nodded at his people. The women began washing what was left of the body. That was when MacDonald leaned in and pointed at something caught in the neck cavity. 'What's that?' he asked. The thing was thin and long. 'I've butchered more livestock than I care to think about, and that doesn't look like anything I've ever seen in a corpse. At least not *there.*'

He had Kando's attention. The senior priest gestured for the women to wash the area where MacDonald was pointing. When a great deal of soapy water had turned pink, a long, stained string came away. It looked a bit like some of the things in the corpse, but Becker guessed whatever it came from had been dead a lot longer than the poor dismembered priest.

'Okay, Captain, I'll bite,' Becker said. 'What's the guy's shoelace doing up around where his ears should have been? Or is this an extreme fashion statement having to do with string ties?'

Of course nobody really had to tell him what the thing was. Whatever its original purpose had been, most lately it had been used as a garrote to strangle the guy. He supposed that was in case tearing out the victim's guts and face didn't kill him dead enough.

MacDonald was clearly thinking the same thing, eyeballing the neck and silently pointing to the ligature marks above the place where the head had been severed from the trunk.

'What kind of animal do you have here that strangles people before they disembowel and eat 'em, Preacher?' MacDonald asked. 'I don't believe I ever saw anybody killed quite this thoroughly before.'

Kando sighed. 'Our enemies have grown clever. Now they attack us in the guise of our myths. But the killer was a man when he used this.' He nodded toward the string as if it was the ickiest thing in the room, which it definitely wasn't, in Becker's opinion. The victim was much harder to look at than the string that had killed him.

'You'd think beheading and eviscerating the fellow would be enough to do the job without strangling him, too,' Becker said.

'My guess is he was strangled quick to keep him from yelling for help before the gory stuff started,' MacDonald said. 'It was undoubtedly a mercy.'

He didn't need to elaborate.

Becker stepped behind one of the stone altars and lost his dinner, which helped a little. One of the women gratefully abandoned the corpse to clean up the mess. Becker excused himself and went out to a fountain to wash his mouth out.

The only good thing about the whole incident, as far as Becker could see, was that Nadhari hadn't been there to watch him puke.

Nadhari followed Miw-Sher as the girl retraced the route she had taken to bring Acorna to the Temple.

Halfway there, one of the priests Edu had dispatched with them to investigate the murder said, 'You're going the wrong direction. Bulaybub's body was two streets south of here.'

'I can't help that,' Miw-Sher told him. 'The ambassador and I were hastening and he did not keep up with us. I thought he would join us at the Temple and was not concerned. We were in a great hurry to reach the guardians and save them. Perhaps Bulaybub remembered an errand elsewhere, something that took him to the place where you found him.'

'You have that story all nicely worked out, don't you?' the first priest said.

'It is no story, but the truth,' Miw-Sher said.

Nadhari said nothing – yet. The priest was being unnecessarily harsh with the girl. After all, she had been with Acorna the entire time. That was as good an alibi as anyone needed, in Nadhari's book. She distracted the girl's tormentor with a suggestion. 'If I were you, I'd post a few men on the rooftops. The attacker may have come from above.'

'From above?' the warrior priests scoffed. 'You didn't see the body, did you, lady? It was clearly a frontal attack – gutted and the face ripped off. And it had to be a wild animal that did it. Only where would you find an animal like that around here?'

Nadhari said nothing. This was not her team, she was not in charge, and she did not want to say too much in front of these men. They were potential enemies and Edu's spies. But privately she thought of the fearsome creatures that once roamed the rainforests, steppes, and deserts of the planet. There had once been plenty of likely predators out in the wild places.

The murshim, a bear-like creature that was taller than a man when standing on its back paws and had two rows of razor-like teeth on each jaw. But the murshim had been extinct since the Battle of Binda destroyed the section of forest that was their last known dwelling place. Nobody had won that fight. The Bindalari were slain by the Durg, one of the fiercest of the militant steppe-tribes. The Durg were mostly killed by the fleeing murshim, who were in turn killed by the tardy reinforcements for the slain Bindalari. No glory was had by any living thing that day.

Also there had been the rock wolves, or yowim, who prowled the remotest moorlands of the steppes, but they were already quite rare during Nadhari's post-Felihari childhood among the Div. By the time she had seen forty seasons – was ten years old by Standard reckoning – the head of the last yow was said to hang over the entrance to Binda Temple. Its body had been devoured by the Temple guardians.

Once there had been wild felines as well, but these had gradually been assimilated into the Guardian line and were now protectors of the people, not attackers.

Unless . . . could the priest have been attacked by the guardian of an enemy Temple?

The warrior priests had deserted the two women to awaken dwellers in houses between this place and the one where the priest was slain. The quiet of the night was broken for a time by their door poundings and demands, and the sleepy, frightened, or indignant responses of those so rudely awakened. Probably most of them had just returned to sleep – or tried to, after the outcry when Bulaybub's mangled body was found.

Nadhari wished she had gathered more information at the Temple before she came out here.

She looked up thoughtfully, jumped, caught the edge of the roof, and hoisted herself onto it. A ladder to the roof would stand inside the room beneath her boots, where the people of the house could use it but an outsider could not.

The girl Miw-Sher whirled, alarmed, and with a sharp lift of her head, saw Nadhari's red uniform pale against the deep maroon sky. She met Nadhari's eye and saw the finger the older woman had placed over her lips.

Nadhari gestured that Miw-Sher should continue on, and followed her, leaping from one flat roof to the next, her boots making no more sound than the furred feet of a Temple guardian.

Much of the night had been spent dining with Macostut, and now the edge of Singha, the forerunner sun, gilded the horizon. If Edu wished this girl to pay for Bulaybub's life by dying a similar death, Nadhari thought, he should have waited to send her out until the attacker had rested and grown hungry again.

Suddenly the scarlet night was split open with a scream.

Miw-Sher, with the gate in sight, froze in her tracks, but Nadhari turned and raced back across the rooftops until she was looking down upon the warrior priests and a woman who stood sobbing, pointing at the trail of blood leading from her hearth to the door and down the street.

'Something has been in my house!' she cried.

'Where were you when this happened?' the leader asked suspiciously.

'Tending my sister and her children. They've come down with the sickness. I've been gone for

150

two days. When I got here, the door was half open. Soon as I got the lamp lit, I found all this!'

'Lucky for you that you didn't come home sooner,' the guard told her. 'Murder's been done. Bloody awful mess. The murderer must have come in here to clean himself up, but by the look of it he was interrupted, probably by the hue and cry when Bulaybub's body was found. It gives us a trail to follow, anyway.'

The woman gave a little whimper.

'Fan out, men!' the leader commanded.

'Oh, excellent planning,' Nadhari said. The frightened woman yelped again when she looked up and saw a tall stranger standing on her roof and peering down at her through the darkness. Nadhari made a gesture of quiet reassurance to the woman. 'I'm here to help hunt the thing that disturbed you,' she said. She continued speaking very quietly, to the priests rather than to the woman. 'Whatever killed the priest and left this convenient trail will appreciate your thoughtfulness, Brother. It will no doubt much prefer to kill your men singly rather than as a group.'

EIGHT

The gray-and-black-brindled fur of the *Condor*'s elusive first mate blended easily with the shadows, froze into invisibility when Federation personnel passed them, and vanished out the gate while the Linyaari ambassador engaged the guard in a debate over whether or not she required a pass to come and go. They seemed to have no shortage of guards here at the Federation post. The sentry facing Acorna now was a new one, older and apparently more dogmatic about her orders.

'But the lieutenant commander already gave his consent,' Acorna insisted, 'and High Priest Kando requested that I help with the illness among the Temple cats. I am on a mission regarding that illness now.'

'I'm sorry, Ambassador, but I am not authorized to grant you random access to and from the civilian sector. Sets a dangerous precedent. These people are a lot of alien savages, though it's not diplomatic of me to say so. Why, look down the street, will you? Can you hear the ruckus? See it. They've been carrying on like that for quite some time now. And who is that woman on the roof?'

Acorna peered down the street. Two blocks over, Nadhari was outlined against the first watery rays of the first sunrise. She was looking down. Someone was weeping. 'That's Commander Kando. She came with us on this ship. But she is from here originally,' Acorna told the guard. 'It looks like she needs some help. If you don't mind, I'll just go see what's going on,' she continued, skirting around the rubbernecking guard and skipping away from her before the woman looked down again. 'I know you cannot desert your post. I'll just check to see what happened, render any needed assistance, and be back to let you know what it's about.' When the guard started toward her, clearly intending to detain her, Acorna ran up the street, calling back, 'No, no, you should stay at your post. I will be back later with the details.' The guard, torn between duty and curiosity, finally resumed her place by the gate.

If RK was ahead of her, Acorna saw no sign of him. The cat didn't respond when she sought his thoughts. Perhaps he was still put out with her over the blood drawing.

Approaching the knot of people, Acorna looked up and asked Nadhari, 'What happened here?'

The warrior priests turned on her. 'Who are you?'

'Look at it!' one of them said, pointing at her. 'It has a horrible horn in the middle of its head. It's a demon! It must have been what killed Bulaybub.'

Nadhari leaped to the ground as lightly as RK

153

might, managing to land between Acorna and the armed men. 'Steady, Brothers. This lady is not a demon or a killer. She is the ambassador from a world of wonderful peaceful beings called the Linyaari and a guest of my cousin, Edu, your high priest. She is also the doctor who healed your sacred Temple cats.'

The poor woman whose house they clustered around seemed to Acorna to be in great distress. She smelled of illness, but that didn't explain the bloody trail leading from her home.

The woman shrank from Acorna. Before Acorna could try to gain her trust and form a mental bond with her, she heard RK's thought-speech, (This blood belongs to the one I saw last night. He is not a ritual dancer. He is one of us, and yet not one of us. He is injured, and he has the sickness.)

'There is a murderer loose, Ambassador,' the head warrior priest told Acorna. 'Someone or something murdered Brother Bulaybub. We believe that the same person or thing has left this trail behind.'

'I see,' Acorna said. 'That makes sense, but why do you say thing?'

'Because what was done to our brother wasn't done by any human hand. He was clawed to death, gutted—'

Nadhari interrupted, sparing the woman householder the details. 'Were you acquainted with Brother Bulaybub?' she asked the house's inhabitant.

The woman shook her head wildly.

Acorna mentally reached out for RK, but he

shrugged off her mental touch. He was moving away rapidly.

(I am on the case, Acorna. I go now to chase the sick one down. I would bring him back to you, but he is very big.)

(He is also dangerous. He killed a man.)

(Oh, *yessss*) RK hissed, and she could see his tail lashing. (But I too can be *dangerouss*.)

She knew that. She had seen him attack the Wats when they had tried to kill Thariinye and her. But while RK was much larger than a domestic cat, he was much smaller than a tiger or a lion.

(I must take the vaccine to the Temple. Please, if you find him, hide and tell me. I will get help.)

(The first pounce is mine,) RK said fiercely.

(You've been aboard ship too long, Roadkill. Just see that you don't live up to your name. Becker would be heartbroken.)

But the intrepid animal wasn't listening. He was on the scent and stalking his prey.

NINE

The tasty tang of fresh blood, the deeply torn tracks of claws, the warmth of fresh footprints, these were a few of RK's favorite things, even if he hadn't realized it until presented with them.

He felt that his years of being first mate on the salvage vessel had all been leading up to this, his true calling, stalker in the dark of things even darker. Yes, he was in his element now. He had found his calling. Seeker after hidden truths, defender of that which was good, righteous, *his*. Destroyer of that which he didn't like.

He alone could rise to this occasion. The other felines, the Temple residents whose job this might otherwise have been, were still too weak from their long illness. Frankly, they were a bit over the hill, anyway. Becker had no liking for damaged organic things, which were not useful as salvage. Nadhari had other rats to catch. Acorna was . . . was . . . well, she *might* be useful, once RK was able to lay out the facts for her like a neatly assembled row of cleanly killed rodents, but for this kind of tracking she was not suitable. She was too conspicuous, too alien, too white and silvery and glistening, and she smelled too good. And she was too tall. She might come in handy as an assistant operative later on in the game. But this kind of job called for someone closer to the ground, someone whose heart beat with the planet's underlying rhythm.

Someone like him.

It helped too that he had actually seen what he considered to be the chief murder suspect – that roof-hopping cat impersonator. For all his poetic thoughts about being close to the ground, he soon took to the roofs instead, following the scent of his prey. This was better sport than tracking Khleevi, who were so stinking obvious even Becker could track them.

As the suns rose, more people came out of their lairs and started walking around in the streets below. RK smelled smoke, though it didn't issue from any of the roofs. He realized that he had actually been smelling it ever since he arrived on this world, but that the smoke was old and no longer had flame behind it. It hung in the air like the red dust and made his nose itch and sting. It carried an unpleasant odor made more unpleasant by the fact that what could have been the lingering scent of a cook fire was overlain with that of singed hair and the stench of rotting meat. RK wouldn't have turned his nose up at that sort of thing if he was hungry enough, but never once since Becker rescued him from a derelict ship had he ever been that hungry.

The trail had started with spurts of blood on the ground, but that smell disappeared and the scent changed, as RK followed it over the rooftops.

The traces of the killer's passing were soon augmented by another type of sign – hairs. The cat impersonator was shedding his fur. That seemed a strange thing for a cat wannabe to do, especially since the killer was shedding it a tuft here, a hair there, instead of ditching an entire hide – and RK did not even want to think how the suspect had come to possess *that*. The early discarded tufts were black, which jibed with RK's shadowy memory of the felonious feline or felinious felon – he wasn't sure which applied.

The suns rose higher until the roof tiles under RK's feet were hot enough that, had his particular paw pads not been blessed with extra fur between the toes, they might have been toast. About this time he caught other, fainter scents and found a tuft of golden fur caught between two tiles, and later three striped hairs similar to his own.

He looked around, sniffing, curling his outer lips to try to pick up a keener scent that way. Other cats had been here within the last day or two. He had received the impression that the only others of his kind in this city were the four remaining Temple cats, but that idea appeared to be wrong.

He sat and considered the roof-scape around him. Although all of the roof surfaces were flat, they were not all the same height. Second floors, little spare rooms, and other irregularities threw sharp shadows onto the broader baked-red roofs.

RK assumed his best thinking position, which was spread out to absorb the maximum warmth through his furry parts. He was now at the city's outer wall, and beyond it was the countryside, such as it was. He saw huge charred circles in the red dirt where big bonfires had been, and, being driven toward them, herds of various sorts of beasts, some of them familiar, some more distinctly alien.

Some of the beasts were already being herded into pens, and into long lines of troughs. On both sides of the troughs, men with big knives and bloody clothing stood waiting. RK felt a certain fang-thrilling fascination with all this gory slaughter, but it wasn't the particular kind of murder he had set out to investigate. He saw a small cloud of black and white hair bounce across a roof just north of the one he occupied, also abutting the city wall.

To his surprise, he found that the trail now led him in a spiral back inward toward the Temple to a rooftop only two streets away from where he started. The trail had been fresher than he thought. Had the suspect been there when the investigation began, RK knew he would have sniffed him out without the circumnavigation.

Now, within sight of the bloodied doorway, he smelled something from the deep shadow cast by a rooftop storage room. Approaching, he saw a foot – or was it a paw? No, a foot wearing a strange shoe. Perhaps even a black furry shoe with claws on. No. RK reached out a paw as far as it would stretch and touched the long pad. Paw. With a foot-shaped sole.

And this close he heard something, too. Very shallow, very fast. The exchange of oxygen and carbon dioxide by a pair of good-sized lungs.

RK jumped to the top of the storage cubicle and looked down. A man who wore his ears on top of his head, with paw-feet and paw-hands, whose belly was bare flesh streaked with blood, lay there. A yard of black tail curled around one thigh. And as RK watched, as the man/cat breathed, his tail appeared and disappeared, and his ears pricked to the top of his head and lowered to the human position. This fellow was extremely undecided about his species, RK realized. He was also badly hurt and depleted.

RK was disappointed. The guy looked more murdered than murderous. He nosed the suspect a little and almost automatically the paw turned into more of a hand and gave RK's back a feeble stroke. Okay, maybe not all murderers were *bad* murderers.

It was time to get Acorna, he realized. Of course, he could get Becker or Nadhari, but they wouldn't necessarily understand what he needed, and he'd have to explain it to them in charades, which took time. Thought-talk with Acorna was faster. Also, she could heal this creature if she arrived in time. None of the others could do that.

The man gave a groan that was half a yowl. RK knew speed was of the essence, but after all, injured parties needed encouragement to maintain their will to live. Besides, nobody was watching. Nobody would see him.

He hopped down beside the suspect, and rumbling a reassuring purr, thoroughly but quickly washed the man-cat's pain-sweaty face for him, then bounded away across the rooftops to that ridiculous cat-shaped Temple.

Acorna stared at the chief warrior priest. She wondered how to change the subject from the murder investigation to the vaccination of future Temple cats, when Miw-Sher came racing out.

'Ambassador, here you are! And you are well?'

'Very well. I brought the medicine I spoke of,' she said, handing it to the young acolyte. 'Here it is, enough for all your cats, with full instructions for its use. Now I must return to the Temple to seek transportation, or perhaps it would be better if I got maps and directions, if I am to save the cats from all the other Temples all across the planet.'

'*Other* Temples?'

'Why, yes,' Acorna said. 'I assume this Temple is not the only one on the planet, and also not the only one guarded by sacred cats. If this is a widespread problem, as seems likely, and if other cats are stricken, I must treat them, too.'

'His Holiness will never allow that,' the chief warrior priest said sternly.

'No? I find that surprising. I thought all the cats were sacred to those of your religious persuasion – regardless of affiliation. Nadhari, you never told me some cats were sacred and others should be allowed to die.'

Nadhari shrugged. 'It was not that way when I lived here, Ambassador Acorna. I'm sorry. You know how governments are. Change of policy every time you think you understand what's going on.'

161

'I really *must* speak to the Mulzar, then. Miw-Sher, perhaps you would escort me back to the Temple?'

'I'll go, too, Acorna.' Nadhari dusted her hands off, as if washing the site from them. 'The Mulzar has the investigation in hand, I believe. Miw-Sher and I came only to see that your trip last night was safe. With the murderer abroad, we feared you might have come to harm.'

'I was fine,' Acorna said. 'That poor priest must have been killed while Miw-Sher and I were with the cats.'

'Is it true that you cured our guardians, Lady?' the chief of warrior priests asked her.

'They are still underfed and weak from their illness, but they were working on remedying that themselves when last I saw them,' Acorna told him.

'Perhaps one of them will be well enough to help us track our killer,' Nadhari said. 'We should return to the Temple and see.'

When they arrived back at the Temple, they discovered that Becker had waited up for them, though Captain MacDonald had retired some time earlier, pleading that he wasn't worth much unless he'd had enough sleep.

'Girls, there you are!' Becker greeted Acorna and Nadhari, with a glance that included Miw-Sher. 'Sweet Mother Nature, but I'm glad to see you, Acorna! Where have you been?'

'I was perfectly safe, Captain, on the *Condor*. I wanted to develop a vaccine to prevent further outbreaks of the disease afflicting the cats. I had . . .' She realized that she'd been about to say that she had RK with her, but she thought better of it as Edu Kando strode into the hall. '. . . assistance.'

'There's a nasty people-eating monster out there,' Becker told her. 'But one with thumbs – it garrotes its victims first. You shoulda seen the corpse.'

'I know,' Acorna said. 'The priests and Nadhari found a trail they think is the murderer's. I ran into them as they were investigating it.'

Edu Kando was scowling as he rounded the corner, but by the time he reached them his expression had turned to benevolent concern. 'Cousin and esteemed guests, I owe you all an apology. We have offered you the hospitality of our Temple, and then we keep you up till all hours with our own petty problems. Please, you must rest. It is cool in your rooms, and I will personally guarantee it will remain quiet outside of them until you have slept. Afterward, you will no doubt be hungry again. Perhaps at that time you and I, Ambassador, can discuss your mission?'

'Yes,' Acorna said, 'thank you. I am very tired. A morning consultation is ideal for me. I have a matter of some importance to discuss with you.'

'Have a nice night, Acorna. I'm going back out to track the murderer,' Nadhari said.

'My men will deal with that, cousin,' Kando told her. 'If you are wakeful, I would love to spend time talking with you. You must learn what has happened here in your absence.'

Becker said, 'Sounds fascinating. I'd like to know all about that, too.'

Kando said smoothly, 'Alas, Captain, there are concepts my cousin and I must speak of that may be expressed only in our own language.'

'That's fine,' Becker said stubbornly. 'Nadhari can translate for me. I'm feeling really out of my depth here, Mulzar. I want to find out what's happening.'

Nadhari gave him a fond smile and a pat on the cheek. 'You look tired, Jonas. And it will be family news, very boring—'

'If you say so,' Becker agreed finally.

She gave him a light peck on the cheek and whispered, 'I'll be fine. If not, you can rescue me again. You know I love it when you do that. It's so cute.'

'I'll wait up,' Becker said, brightening. He was a little puzzled. He simply didn't want to be left out. He hadn't actually thought Nadhari needed rescuing.

Acorna watched the byplay between them, amused. Becker was, if anything, a little jealous, Acorna thought. If she was reading him correctly, he rather admired Kando. The name King Arthur kept surfacing in Becker's mind when he thought of Nadhari's cousin – that, and El Cid.

A young Temple girl Acorna hadn't seen before showed them to their rooms and brought them cool drinks. When the girl had gone, Acorna took her glass to the room across the corridor, where Becker half reclined, lifting his own glass to his lips. It was quite a beautiful vessel, its shape and design suggesting a more decorative aspect of what seemed to be an otherwise rather basic and utilitarian culture.

'Wait, Captain,' Acorna said. 'Please, hand me your glass before you drink.'

He did and she dipped her head, touching the tip of her horn to the liquid.

'You don't think it was poisoned?' Becker asked, chagrined.

'No, but I believe it may possibly have been drugged with a sleeping potion. Edu was apparently serious about ensuring our good night's rest. While I intend to sleep, I think it would be best if we both are able to awaken naturally to any stimuli that would normally pull us from sleep. We are on a strange planet. There is a murderer loose. I wish to take no chances.'

Becker shook his head admiringly. 'You're good at this palace intrigue stuff – 'scuse me, Temple intrigue stuff, Princess. Maybe you really *are* related to old Hafiz.'

Acorna smiled, dipped her horn in her own drink, and returned to the room assigned to her. She had left the door open and when she re-entered, she saw by the light of the lantern a bouquet of flowers in a wall sconce. She examined them. All of them were edible varieties of a most delicious kind. She was getting rather peckish, in spite of having grazed briefly in the hydroponics garden aboard the *Condor*. She sipped lightly at her drink, then stuck the flowers in the remainder of it so she could have a little breakfast when she awoke without troubling anyone about her dietary requirements. Putting her hoofed feet under the soft woven quilted coverlet, she felt a soft resistance. Looking down, she saw Grimla, who raised her face at Acorna's gentle touch and purred loudly.

'You are very welcome,' Acorna said, and settled down to sleep while the suns rose outside, painting Temple and city with color and shadow.

TEN

She was dying. They were all dying in misery and squalor, dying of thirst and hunger, dying of exposure and contagion, poison and plague, and she knew it was their own fault.

Dirty-faced children with crusty eyes and noses cried and clung to the legs of adults who could barely stand. The lake, the one her grandfather had called Crystal Lake, was now a turgid swamp.

When first they arrived on this planet, her grandfather said, his great-grandfather had had very little. Some small technologies were sent with them when they emigrated, to make their lives in the new place easier. But this planet, though its resources were slender, especially where she lived, was not overpopulated, and could support the making of the small machines, as Old Terra no longer could.

She had been told about all this, but she could not remember her world other than it was now.

And yet part of her was still Acorna, living inside the cracked and scaling skin of this other person, the one who lived beside the stinking lake.

That part wondered where she was and why she was here.

Then the ship landed, not near her and her people, but far away, down where the green-ness had been before it was cut into and cut out. She saw the ship in the sky and thought something like 'Linyaari?' though it wasn't quite that.

Word came that strangers had landed – two of them, both seemingly human, like her dream-self. And yet there was something funny about them. One of them had a horn in the middle of his head and the other one kept turning into a cat.

One day, without warning, the flitter arrived. Her people remembered flitters from their great-grandparents, though the word 'shuttle' came to her instead, but none of the craft had worked on this world in over a hundred years.

Two got out, one small, red-haired, and quick, one tall and white, with silvery hair and golden eyes that went straight to hers. Aari. He turned to his companion, who turned into a red-striped cat and then back to a man. The word 'Grimalkin' – was that a name? – suddenly came into her head. Was this the companion who had taken Aari from her? But no, her dream people said that *Aari* was the Companion. The red cat/man was the Star Cat. Aari smiled into her dream face as if congratulating her on her understanding.

She must have cried his name, because she heard paws thumping to the floor. But she could not awaken all the way. Aari continued to hold the gaze of her dream-self. With a meaningful flick of his eyes, as if to say, 'Watch this,' he turned to the fouled lake and knelt beside it, dipping his horn. 'And from his blessed horn came water and jewels.'

As the dream faded, she wondered how that could be, since Aari's horn was still so newly repaired and still so stunted that it would not really be capable of detoxifying such a lake. And what had happened to the cat/man? Grimalkin, wasn't that its name? He was no longer there when Aari dipped his horn in the water. But that was how dreams were. They jumped around and were not logical.

She tried to return to the dream and to Aari. Tried so hard. Wanted to see him again, wanted to feel his eyes on hers – he saw through the dream person, and knew her even in this dream.

But instead, she dreamed next of cats that were sick, dying, crying, and of cats peering out at her with gold coin eyes shining in the darkness of the little holes near the roof of the Temple cattery. She bent to heal one cat with peculiar blue and green fur, but others clawed at her legs, mewing up at her. When she bent down, their eyes shone as if they were looking into a bright light, the pupils slitted.

'Hsst!' another cat said and she opened her eyes to see a very real pair of cat eyes staring down into hers. RK stood on her chest, his nose pushed against her nose. A self-satisfied purr pumped in and out of him, and his claws prickled and sheathed, prickled and sheathed, against her collarbone,

(Come now, Linyaari Healer. I tracked, I stalked, I did what I do. Now it's your turn,) the cat told her.

(What? You stalked something?) Acorna asked, a little puzzled and still bleary from her dream.

(The murderer. Or the ssussspect. Or maybe another victim, sssince he is badly injured and needs your help.) RK's mental voice had a very distinct feline accent when he was highly excited, as he was now. (Follow me. Nyow.) His fur was electric with his nervous energy, and she reached out to smooth his fur with a stroke of her hand, soothing him so that for one brief moment his tail stopped flagellating her chest.

'Very well,' she said. He jumped to the floor as she rose. She hadn't disrobed before lying down, partly because she was too tired and partly because she knew she could be awakened without warning. If that happened, she wished to be prepared.

'Perhaps we should call the other cats to walk with us until we're clear of the Temple,' she suggested. 'You'll be less conspicuous that way.'

His whiskers twitched. (*That* again, eh?)

He paused, flipping his tail from side to side and cocking his ear to listen. (It is safe enough. Come. The Temple cats say Kando and the other high and mighty are deep in council with each other trying to figure out what to do about the – heh-heh – catastrophes that have befallen them, including you.)

'*Me?*' Acorna said. She was puzzled, but rose to follow RK. 'But I was only trying to help.'

(My entree is your '*eeek!*' and vice versa,) RK thought at her philosophically. (Cats like you. Cat servants like you. But not everybody.) He leaped up to one of the crossbars leading to a cat hole near the ceiling.

'I can't go up there,' she reminded him.

(Bipeds can be so feeble.) The cat sighed. (I suppose you'll have to leave the ordinary way. I'll meet you across the street from the Temple. Look up.)

Then he was gone. Acorna ran her fingers through her mane and stepped outside the room, where she was confronted by the Temple cats, sitting there patiently, as if waiting for her.

'Are you coming, too?' she asked them. 'This is going to be something of a parade then, isn't it?'

Well, Acorna thought, RK hadn't said to come alone. Neither had he said to bring Becker or Nadhari, so perhaps she could assume that although their mission was confidential, it was not especially dangerous. She didn't know if the Temple cats ever actually left the Temple or not, but as she walked away, they followed, so she supposed that they knew what was expected of them and could decide for themselves what they would do.

They didn't meet anyone within the Temple building, but then, her route took her only through the living quarters. She followed a path that bypassed the ceremonial chambers and opened directly onto the outer courtyard. Here people abounded, each going about their various tasks beneath the punishing suns, cooking, drawing water, building, making mud bricks, weaving, and preaching. Acorna did not look too closely into any of the activities. She tried to appear as though she was on a mission of some urgency and knew exactly where she was headed. She'd found in her past adventures that such an appearance could often take her far without causing comment. The impression she was trying to convey had the added attraction of being quite true in this case. She hoped none of the people in the Temple courtyard would look at her too closely. Drawing the scarf Miw-Sher had given her around her head to disguise her horn, she walked straight ahead, as nonchalantly as it was possible to walk when she was being trailed by four large and determined Temple cats.

She was considering what to do if the guard standing at the gate tried to stop her when Miw-Sher bounded up, swooped precious Grimla into her arms, and fell into step beside her.

'Ambassador, are you leaving us so early?' Miw-Sher asked.

'I was just going to have a look around,' Acorna told the young acolyte, continuing to move toward the Temple gate. Her tone was cautious, not because of Miw-Sher but because of the other people in the courtyard. 'I wish to learn all I can of your people and of the relationship between them and the sacred cats, as part of my mission to my own people.'

'Ah, yes,' Miw-Sher said. 'Well, it so happens I had an errand in the town today myself. I can point out the sights to you as we go. With your permission, I will accompany you.'

'How about them?' Acorna asked, indicating the three parading cats still marching along behind her. 'Are they allowed out?'

'Oh my, yes. They aren't captives – or at least

172

they never have been.' The last part of her sentence was mumbled unhappily, clearly recalling that all was not well in the Temple these days.

'It is very good of you to go with me,' Acorna said. 'And the sacred cats, too, of course, but really, I can do this on my own. I'm sure you have other duties.'

'Halt,' the guard said. He was a short, pugnacious-looking fellow with bad teeth and worse breath.

'It's all right, Brother Meyim,' Miw-Sher said, 'they're with me.'

'And who are you to have privileges, Miw-Sher?' the guard asked, spitting through the hole between two of his black teeth. 'The Mulzar has sent word that none are to pass this gate without special permission. *His* permission.'

Acorna wasn't sure this person was going to be sensitive to mental suggestion, but she tried it anyway. She directed a very light push at his mind.

He paused after the end of his last word and added, 'Except the ambassador, of course. She has diplomatic immunity.' He stumbled over the last two words.

To Acorna's surprise, Miw-Sher looked stricken. 'But I have to go, too.'

Acorna relented, not so much because of Miw-Sher's distress as out of curiosity to see what had caused this desperate desire to leave the Temple in her company. She nudged at the Temple guard's brain again.

The guard said, 'And her staff, of course.'

Sacred Pash growled. 'And the sacred cats, it goes without saying,' the guard added quickly.

Acorna added a suggestion that there was no reason why he should remember that their little party had left the confines of the Temple, should anyone inquire.

Then she looked for RK.

(Me. Ow.) RK's voice resonated in her thoughts. (I'm up here, Acorna. Here. That's right. The roof. Follow the leader. I see you've brought the Temple gang with you. Welcome, brothers and sisters. Perhaps you'd like to leap up here and I'll show you how an investigation is properly conducted?)

The Temple cats all leaped up to the roof. Acorna, not possessing the cats' abilities, guided Miw-Sher so that she and the girl were hidden by the corner of the house, out of sight of the guard, so that he would not be reminded of that which he had been persuaded to forget. They followed the cats as best they could on the ground.

RK hopped to the next rooftop, still pontificating, all puffed up in a particularly feline way. (You will notice, brothers and sisters and two-legged friends, that this rooftop where we discovered the object of our search is a mere two rooftops from the house where the alarm was originally raised.)

(You mean the place where the monk was murdered?) Acorna asked.

(*Aha*, but do we know that?) RK challenged in an insufferably superior tone. (Do we know in fact that our suspect was the actual murderer or, for that matter, that the late monk was a victim?

Possibly they were co-belligerents and the monk got the worst end of someone's claws?)

'What is happening?' Miw-Sher asked. 'Is the alien guardian cat speaking to you?'

'Yes,' Acorna said, and summarized for her RK's latest remarks.

The two females walked along beside the buildings as the cats leaped rooftops. They tried hard not to stare upwards in case passersby might follow their gaze.

Suddenly Miw-Sher ran ahead, then disappeared into the home where the woman had cried out and been answered by the guard during the night.

'This way, Acorna,' she said.

Temporarily abandoning the cats, Acorna ducked into the house and saw that Miw-Sher had set up the house ladder to the central roof hole. The girl was halfway up the ladder already and Acorna followed her, without questioning why the girl felt free to enter the home when the owners were absent. Once she was out in the open air again, however, Acorna saw that she and Miw-Sher were now exactly two rooftops away from where the cats were. The cats paid them no attention. The felines had gathered in a corner of the roof they occupied, under the sketchy protection of a makeshift shelter. But as Acorna prepared to leap across the first rooftop, RK stuck his head out and said to her, (Hurry. I don't think he has much time.)

(Distract Miw-Sher,) Acorna instructed RK.

(What? Oh, sure. You don't want her to know how you heal him with the old horn, eh? I can do

175

that. Hey, girlie, pet the nice kitty. Here I am! Pick me up! Oh, I'm so afraid! Pet me, comfort me! Man, am I bummed by this hurt guy in the corner!) He was twisting himself around the girl's ankles, clawing at her skirts, trying to jump onto her shoulder, but she ignored him with the skill of one long used to the ways of cats and managed to beat Acorna to the injured party.

The being lay, much as RK's mind picture had shown her, face up, with feet/paws and hand/paws shifting back and forth in form in time with the rhythms of his ragged, rapid breathing.

'Uncle!' Miw-Sher cried before Acorna could touch the injured cat/man. 'Oh, Uncle, what have you done?'

ELEVEN

Miw-Sher's cheek rested on the injured priest Bulaybub's chest. The cats crowded around her, so Acorna laid her horn first on his head, and then, pretending to listen to his heart, upon that. She gently shifted Miw-Sher aside to examine Bulaybub for wounds. She found one on his abdomen, a deep puncture. This she also healed, but the priest had lost a great deal of blood and had lain exposed to the elements for some time. Despite her efforts, he didn't look good.

'Will he live?' Miw-Sher asked.

Bulaybub looked at her and rolled his eyes. Through his cracked lips and parched throat he said, 'Get off me, child, and all you hot holy ones, too. The day is far too warm for your nearness to be comforting.' As he spoke, he turned completely human. His tail disappeared, his ears settled down behind his jawbone and shed their fur to become rounded and flesh-colored. His hands and feet lost their fur and claws and became dirty but bare, with broken toenails.

Even the wild animal tang in the air vanished. The priest stank as a damaged, overheated, underwashed human stank. As he transformed,

Miw-Sher draped his lower body with a scarf similar to the one she had given Acorna, to preserve his human modesty.

The cats sat back.

RK projected, (Well done, shipmate. He seems perfectly healthy now, though he's lost what looks he had.)

'Uncle, can you stand? We must get you indoors.'

The priest rose awkwardly, clutching the scarf to his middle, so that it draped down his thighs and tangled between his knees. The Temple cats took up sentinel positions on each corner of the roof. Acorna could see that they were determined to warn their human companions should anyone approach them.

Miw-Sher assisted her uncle to the ladder leading down into the house. The occupant, conveniently, was not at home, but had left the ladder to the roof in place.

Bulaybub gave his niece a conspiratorial smile, though one that was somewhat white around the lips. 'Being a mendicant monk has advantages,' he said. 'If you beg door to door often enough, you soon find out what is behind each of the doors you beg at.'

'Is that how you knew you could use the home of the woman who had gone to help her sick sister, the place where the guards found all that blood?' Acorna asked.

'Yes, and it is how I know that the family who lives here went to help their country kinfolk slaughter their infected animals and will not return for some time.' He half fell down the ladder and heaved himself onto the seat against the wall beside the cold hearth. 'Ahhhh.' He finished with a sigh as he leaned against the wall to rest.

Once the humans were safely hidden inside the house, the Temple cats followed them – flowing down the crude ladder as easily as though it was a grand staircase. They arranged themselves around the room to watch the show.

'I do believe I'm feeling better,' Bulaybub said, sounding just a bit tired. 'You are indeed the miraculous person we were told would come, Ambassador,' he said to Acorna after a moment.

'Not so miraculous as all that,' Acorna said, wondering just who had told the priest she was coming, when she hadn't known that herself until she was practically landing on the planet. She'd deal with that issue later, after she'd broached the far more urgent topic on her mind. 'I have some small talents as a healer, but it appears that in this instance, I have been able to raise the dead. I understood from the Mulzar that your corpse was throttled, nearly decapitated, and eviscerated.'

'Oh, yes. Well, obviously, the body they found was not mine. It seemed useful to let Edu and others believe it to be mine, at least for a time, however. Unfortunately, it required a great deal of rather nasty claw work postmortem to obliterate identifying characteristics.'

'Are you going to tell me whose body it was, not to mention how he came to be postmortem?' Acorna asked.

'Do you think that if I do so, I will confess how I came to be a murderer?' the priest asked with a hint of wry amusement.

'That would be truly enlightening, Brother,' a voice said from the roof, immediately followed by the lithe form of Nadhari Kando, who slithered down the ladder, her gaze never leaving Bulaybub and Miw-Sher, her grip never loosening on the deadly dagger she carried. 'And I, too, would love to hear your answer.'

Bulaybub inhaled sharply. 'Nadhari,' he said, and his voice was filled with pain, pain that clearly had nothing to do with his recent wounds. 'You must listen to me,' he said, 'I know the Mulzar is your relative, but all is not as he would have you think.'

Nadhari looked at the priest more closely, though it was hard to distinguish features in the windowless room with only the light from the roof hole to illuminate it. 'Of course it isn't. Do you think I'm a fool? But I'm a bit surprised to hear you admit Edu might be misleading us, Brother Bulaybub. I thought you were Edu's righthand man.'

From the way Nadhari and Bulaybub spoke to each other, Acorna gathered that she was not the only one in the room with secrets to keep. Everyone here, probably including the cats, obviously had agendas heretofore unshared with her.

The Temple cats lounged around and upon the various bits of furnishings and architectural irregularities in a manner designed to make a decorative display. They groomed themselves

180

while Miw-Sher, with a frightened glance at Nadhari, gave her uncle sips of water. None of the cats, however, seemed to feel that anything that was happening was especially strange or upsetting. Even RK curled up beside Bulaybub and purred.

'Wait,' Acorna said. 'Before we get into politics, Nadhari, may I ask a few basic questions? Brother Bulaybub, last night you changed from a man to a large cat, and back again. You changed up there on the roof, too. I saw it myself, and so did RK. How did that happen?'

'He did?' Nadhari asked. 'I wish I'd come earlier. I'm sorry I missed it. Go ahead, Brother. I want to hear the answer to that one.'

'I would have told you sooner or later, if only you had stayed, Nadhari,' Bulaybub told her.

'Why should I have stayed? You wouldn't see me. Your family wouldn't allow me to come near you. You weren't even talking to Edu back then. As I recall, you didn't like him in those days.'

'I didn't, I—'

'Please,' Acorna said. 'Obviously you two have a history and equally obviously it must be part of this, but it can wait. Answer my questions, Brother Bulaybub.'

'And that name!' Nadhari said, strong emotion causing her for once to override Acorna's attempts to make sense of the conversation. 'How did you come up with that one, Tagoth?'

(The plot thickens,) RK told Acorna. (I'm loving this!)

'You two are not helping matters,' Acorna said. 'Before the guards come looking for us, Brother

181

Bulaybub, or Tagoth, or whoever you are, I need answers. A lot of them. *Please* will you tell me why you turned into a cat? Who was the man who died? Did you kill him? If so, why? And what part in all this do Miw-Sher and the Temple cats play?'

Acorna looked from Nadhari to the priest, and saw their eyes locked in a battle of wills. Acorna sent a little push to each, but neither budged.

Miw-Sher sighed, set down the water jug, and said, 'About the changing. Some of us do it. From a few families – especially those who have intermarried often with certain of the rainforest tribes. It started there. It's a very rare gift these days. The families keep it a close secret when one of their children begins changing – usually there's only one in a family at any time and the trait can skip a generation, my mother said. Uncle Tagoth changes, but his brothers did not. I – I change, too. It started with my courses. With boys the changing becomes apparent later, I was told. It was later with Uncle Tagoth, wasn't it, Uncle?'

'Hmm – yes,' he said, with a meaningful deepening of his glare at Nadhari. 'Later.'

'Sometimes the gift even vanishes,' Miw-Sher said. 'If the choosing is right and just, and not tampered with by conquerors or war, the high priest is a holy person chosen by his or her blood for the position. When such a one dies in this life, in the next life, that one returns as one of the Temple guardians. All of the Temple cats here were once holy high priests and priestesses, Lady,' the acolyte told Nadhari.

'And when a guardian dies, if he or she wishes, the next lifetime may be a human one – but if so, it is to the tribes of the forest they are born, and when they are no longer children, they can resume their true form. Therefore, by our beliefs, my uncle and I have ourselves been high priests and guardians in our past lives.'

'I was not fully informed about this aspect of your religion. Is there something in your teachings to explain how some of you came to possess this power?' Acorna asked, trying to sound as if she was merely confirming the information and not as if she was incredulous. In fact, she wasn't – she had seen shape shifters before, on the Linyaari homeworld.

'It is a gift left us by the Star Cat. His own legacy of strength and agility and the ability to bond with the Temple guardians, who were also his gifts to us, as were many of the other great beasts which once roamed our world. Before the coming, we were poor and miserable, weak, barely able to survive. With his gifts, a few among us learned to live on this world, to breathe with its wind and to move like its waters. These few strong ones taught the others and saved them.'

'I was never taught that,' Nadhari said. 'My mother was a high priestess. She didn't change into a cat, and the people around me saved only themselves. If they saved others, it was to make slaves of them.'

'A woman does not change until her courses begin. And she no longer does so once life quickens inside her,' Tagoth who had been Bulaybub said almost accusingly. 'This is why a

183

rainforest tribeswoman, among her own people, is often kept untouched and unwed as long as possible. But it is not possible to keep her that way forever. Her own divinely altered self wishes to mate, and of course those men among her own people who know her secret wish her for a mate, that their children might have the power. And there is the tradition, even among the people of the steppe and those of the desert, that a rainforest woman must be bedded and bred as soon as possible. Which among our warring peoples can mean that getting the woman's consent to the bedding and breeding isn't part of the process. I have kept Miw-Sher close to me, Nadhari, and her secret I keep as if it were mine. Edu does not know, or he would use her as he has many others.'

Now, *there* was a yawning door to a whole other nest of vipers, Acorna realized. She felt that while it was very important for Nadhari and Tagoth to air their past difficulties, it was not as germane to everyone's current survival as her other question.

'Were you protecting Miw-Sher when you murdered that man?' Acorna asked. 'You did murder him, didn't you?'

'I prefer the term "terminated in self-defense" ' Tagoth said with a pained expression. 'Ambassador, your kind may be a peaceful people, but we are not. Death and the killing of enemies is a matter of routine here. Such killings are often necessary if one is to survive. Yes, I killed the man the sentries found and believed to be me. But you saw the wound he dealt me first. I had not changed then. And it was not my feline form that did the killing. Not precisely, anyway. I'll admit that had the moons not been on the rise, my strength and agility would have been less, and I would have been unable, wounded as I was, to slip behind him and use the badge of the very faith he was about to betray to destroy him.'

He touched the leather thong still around his own neck, and turned it in his hands until the cat's-eye jewel strung on it was in his hand. 'I strangled him. The thong and the jewel cut off his breath so that he ended quickly, which was fortunate, for my wound was sapping my strength, and I still had great need of what little endurance I had.'

RK made motions with his front paws as if he was digging in the cat sand and looked up inquiringly.

Tagoth laughed and placed his hand on the cat's head to stroke it. That gentle hand hardly looked capable of murder.

'Yes, sacred one. That was next. The man bore other marks of office – the special office he had trained to fill so that he might later betray all that he learned to Edu Kando.'

'What sort of marks?' Acorna asked. Tagoth and Nadhari were back in an eyelock, too busy watching each other to continue speaking unless prompted.

Miw-Sher pointed to her own forehead. 'A sacred stone embedded in the forehead, here,' she said, indicating a spot above the bridge of her nose.

Tagoth continued, finally looking away from

Nadhari. 'And on his chest and abdomen a ritual tattoo, a symbol that if read correctly is a map to the holiest of holy valleys, the lake of the stones. That was the knowledge he was bringing to Edu. I had to stop him. I did try to reason with him first, Ambassador. We were once boys together, once comrades. He attacked me rather than listen to my pleadings to keep the sacred knowledge secret, as he had vowed to the Temple. I do not kill often, and never without sufficient reason. For one in the service of Mulzar Kando I am considered mild-mannered, meek even. I told him you had come, as the prophecy foretold, and that soon we would be saved and set upon the right path, but he would not listen. He was not truly religious, and I suspect he was weary of pretending to be so. He did not believe me and I don't think he would have cared if he had. He accused me of betraying Edu, and stabbed me, as you saw. And so I did – what I did.'

'Perhaps you could explain why you think telling him of my arrival would have changed his course of action,' Acorna said. 'Our landing here was an accident. Wasn't it, Nadhari?'

Nadhari looked at RK. Acorna, remembering the cat's claim that he had brought them there, also looked at RK. RK suddenly found a dirty spot on his belly that needed washing. For his own unfathomable feline reasons, he was letting the humans sort this one out.

Tagoth glanced down at the grooming guardian of Becker's ship and nodded. 'You came when you were supposed to, whether by accident or design. As it was destined, and as it was prophesied, you are here. If the blasphemer really cared about the good of our world and its peoples, he would have realized that your arrival canceled out any previous allegiance to secular powers. You will show us the way.'

'I'm not at all sure what the way is,' Acorna said. 'Possibly I should call the guard and have them collect you. You are a murderer, after all.'

'Read him, Acorna,' Nadhari suggested. 'Tagoth, if you let her, she can tell if you are speaking the truth or not.'

Acorna considered that, then looked from RK, who flowed to his feet and began walking loudly back and forth across the room, to Nadhari and back to Tagoth. The Temple cats, who had been very quiet while their caretakers chattered, grew restive. Pash joined RK in patrolling the room, Sher-Paw took some experimental swipes at the door to try to open it, and Haji sat up stiffly and glared at all of the two-legged occupants of the room. Finally Grimla left the sanctuary of Miw-Sher's skirts, leaped back up to the roof, and stood staring down at them.

Their mental message was quite clear to Acorna. 'Perhaps your faith says something about someone like me coming right now and that gives me some authority in your mind. I don't know. I'm just visiting. Among my people, one of us killing another is unthinkable. Among humans, whole committees decide about such matters. If I have work to do on this world, it isn't anything to do with your politics. Nadhari, you are a security officer. You know law enforcement, and you know this man and this planet. You are much better qualified than I am to judge how to help him or how to thwart him, whichever is called for.'

Nadhari wore an expression quite foreign to her face, she looked genuinely abashed. 'You're right, of course, Acorna. You healed him and that's all we should have asked. But you can't heal everyone. You know you can't. You will be too weak to stand if you attempt to halt this plague all by yourself.'

'I know,' she said. 'That's why I need to speak to Captain Becker and Captain MacDonald.'

'Jonas was working on the ship's computers,' Nadhari said.

'Yes, well, I'll find him then.'

'Go with her, Miw-Sher,' Tagoth said. 'I can manage.'

'You have to hide,' the girl said. 'They'll find you here.'

'He could cover himself in blood and hide among the slaughterers,' RK suggested to Acorna, painting her a mind picture of what he had seen beyond the village.

Acorna shook her head, horrified at the image the cat sent her. (I must get to them and help them. I can't let all of this prevent me from doing what I can. Soon, RK. Soon.)

To the others she said, 'RK has sent me images of hundreds of domestic animals being slaughtered on the outskirts of the city for fear they have a disease. I must reach them if I am to heal them. And I certainly can't if I sit around here all day. So what are we going to do about this man?'

Nadhari had been searching the room and

stood up, holding a pair of rough trousers and a long-sleeved, hooded tunic that reached her own knees when she held it up. 'Tagoth, much as I like that scarf you're wearing, you're pretty obvious right now. If you want to blend in, you should put these on.'

'I will. Nadhari, I know Miw-Sher will be safe with you. I must leave and warn the priests of the Aridimi Stronghold before Edu and his men find me here. They need to know the danger they're in, and what Edu intends.' The priest pulled on the pants and slipped the robe over his head quickly, handing the scarf back to Miw-Sher when he'd finished.

'Yes, do what you must, but be on the lookout for us,' Nadhari said. 'Acorna can't accomplish what she needs to here in the city. We'll be leaving soon, too, and we could give you cover.'

Nadhari didn't sound like a police officer. Her voice was breathless and urgent, and she stood very close to the man for the first time, her eyes locking onto his.

He smiled at her, turned, and skittered up the ladder. His body must have caught on to the fact that it was healed now, and he showed no trace of clumsiness or illness as he walked up onto the roof as if he were the house's owner.

'You there, girl, you and the healer should bring the mattress up here to air it,' he said, the image of a householder ordering around his children and slaves. Acorna and Miw-Sher each took an end of the filthy sack of straw – and fleas, who were quite healthy without Acorna's help – and hauled it to the roof. Acorna was careful to keep the mattress between her and the street. Tagoth pulled the ladder up behind them and put it down again behind the house, in the narrow alley where the backs of the houses faced each other. At a nod from him, they climbed down and the cats swarmed around them.

'What about Nadhari?' Acorna asked him.

'She went out the front. Go! I'll find cover. And I thank you for the healing.'

Acorna nodded. She and Miw-Sher walked the length of the street in the garbage and filth that was stored behind the houses until they came to the end of the row. There Miw-Sher led them all to a well, drawing drinking water for the cats and wash water for her and Acorna to clean themselves with so as not to draw comment. Otherwise, anyone who saw them would wonder how they had managed to get so disheveled. Acorna was still in her dress uniform.

They walked out into the main street. It was scorching hot in the bright light of midday.

'There don't seem to be many people about,' Acorna said to Miw-Sher.

'They stay in and rest if possible while the suns are high,' Miw-Sher told her. 'We should be free to move about the city. I don't think anyone was paying attention to us. Grimla would have warned us.'

RK stood on his hind paws and sank his claws into Acorna's thigh. (Come on,) he thought.

'I must leave you here. I'm being summoned,' Acorna told Miw-Sher just as Nadhari rounded a corner.

'I'll be fine,' Miw-Sher said. 'Grimla and I look after each other.'

Acorna nodded but lingered until Nadhari was within a few feet of them. Then she followed RK's tail, which waved like a pennant ahead of her, leading her straight to the Federation post.

TWELVE

Upon reaching the *Condor*, Acorna was disappointed to see Federation vehicles parked alongside and Federation technicians riding up and down the robolift with tools in hand.

She sent a thought to the bridge. (Captain Becker, what are these people doing aboard the vessel?) She thought something might be wrong with the captain, that he might be injured or ill. He never allowed outside interference with his ship otherwise. But Becker's thoughts were positively cheerful when he answered her.

(They had a few odd scraps of this and that, even some new equipment they were never able to integrate into the old system. They're letting me have it to replace the Khleevi stuff and repair the computers. It's great, but they're everywhere! I sent Mac with the Wats over to help our friend MacDonald so they wouldn't get in the way. Mac was asking so many questions he made the federales nervous. We'll be shipshape and ready to head out again in no time, at the rate these guys are going!)

(Oh,) Acorna replied. (Good.)

Even as she sent the thought to Becker, she was

following RK's tail once more, this time to the bay where the *Arkansas Traveler* was docked.

She looked for a robolift until she noticed that this ship had a conventional entrance that could be accessed by a conventional gantry. As she registered that fact, a loading platform parked beside the scaffolding of the gantry began rising toward the hatch. Mac and Red Wat were riding the platform. Several oblong brownish objects sat at its base.

RK waited at the foot of the gantry, his tail waving patiently, for her to catch up, then hopped on her shoulders as she climbed the more conventional ladder to the hatch.

'Permission to come aboard, Captain?' she called. Mac and Red Wat had already disappeared inside the hatch by the time she and RK reached it.

'Ambassador, honey, sure, you come right on in and make yourself at home. Can I fix you something? Cuppa caf maybe or some tea?'

'No, I – may I ask what your project is?'

'Feeding the masses, honey, feeding the masses. I'm taking the Makahomian farmers some of the Metleiter boxes I prepared.'

'What are they?' Acorna asked.

'Chemical beds that grow food without the need for much water. They're not dependent on the ground soil. You left before we had the conversation, I think, but it sounded to me like this epidemic they have here might be caused by a contaminated food supply, which could be caused by contaminated soil. I can fix that – or at least show them how to fix it. If that's the problem, those boxes and others like them will keep the people in food while we figure out what to do next.'

'I see. RK – that is, I was looking over the city wall earlier, and they are slaughtering hundreds and hundreds of animals. Have you any veterinary medicines aboard which might combat the disease? I can heal some of the creatures, of course, but I'm afraid my – uh – supplies will not hold out for so many.'

'I have a couple of things that might work. I got some wagons with those tall goat-type critters to pull them coming to pick up these supplies first thing in the morning. I asked Becker if I could take the Viking guys with me for muscle. We get along pretty well using sign language, and their Standard isn't as bad as Becker said.'

'Mac and I have been working on their language skills,' Acorna told him.

'Yeah, Mac is really okay with me. I never liked androids before, but he doesn't seem much like one – more like just a really smart, strong guy. A little quirky, of course, but that's part of his charm. Anyway, I'd love to have him along. He's been a big help and he's stronger than all of us put together, but Becker says he qualifies as technological taint, and if we can't even smuggle a little radio out past the gate, we sure as hell can't take Mac.'

'Yes, I can see where that might be a problem. It is probably for the best for Mac to remain, anyway. I think Becker may need him on the *Condor*. Mac will need to familiarize himself with all the new modifications Becker is putting in.'

'Was there something special you wanted, hon? Other than meds for the animals? Somehow, I think that was just a little bitty excuse to get you up my ladder.'

'You are correct, Captain MacDonald. Becker has the ship all torn up, installing new equipment. I wish to contact our home base and my own people again, if it isn't too much trouble. We never intended to be away for so long, and I . . . am hoping for some news.'

'Thought so. Be my guest,' he said, leaving her to it.

To Acorna's relief, she was able to communicate with MOO without problems. She was so glad to hear Melireenya's voice and see her face on the com screen she almost wept.

Melireenya was effusive. 'Khornya! Oh, it is good to hear from you again. Maati has come up to the moon, and Neeva is here as well. And Hafiz will want to speak to you, and Miiri and Kaarlye and the *aagroni*. Oh, and – what is it, Thariinye? Yes, I'll tell her. Thariinye says to say hello.'

Acorna had to laugh, since she was not, after all, going to let herself weep, which would have been highly inappropriate under the circumstances. How like Thariinye to have to be in the middle of things! 'Hello to Thariinye, too, then. And to everyone. Is there any word from Aari?'

'I truly can't say. I haven't heard anything myself. Wait! Maati is here. She would know.'

Maati's face appeared on the com screen. How grown-up she looked! 'Khornya! How are you? We miss you! When will you be back?'

'Captain Becker has received assistance in repairing the *Condor* from the Federation troops stationed on this planet, and he thinks it will not be much longer before the ship is operational. But there are some problems here that may need our attention before we can return. Have you heard ... anything?'

'Well, a few anomalies have been showing up, but they don't have anything to do with Aari *exact*ly, but maybe he's closer than he was, hmmm? It's nothing much, really, but we've been wondering – oh, here's the *aagroni*.'

'Khornya, have you interviewed any Makahomian subjects about the relationship between Riidkiiyi and our *pahaantiyirs*?'

'*Aagroni*, they are having something of a crisis here. Many of the Temple cats died before we arrived. We were able to save four, and I am told others still survive, but for how long, I don't know. I – I really can say no more on this channel. I will of course learn what I can.'

'I thought the cats were held sacred by those people?' Karina Harakamian broke in.

'Yes, they are. But being held sacred is not necessarily protection against an epidemic. Other animals are dying, too. You can see that I must help.'

'Of course you must, Khornya,' said Miiri, joining the others. Each of their faces was now visible in a separate window on the com screen.

'I'll be home as soon as I can. It probably won't be too long,' Acorna said, but she felt desolate. If they were free to go soon, it would only be because they had failed in their mission to save the cats of other Temples and all the other animals in trouble. And yet she felt, seeing the faces and hearing the voices of her friends, as if she couldn't bear to wait until she could embrace each of them again. Their farewells sounded sad and concerned as she ended her transmission. Now she had worried them about her, too, and not just Aari.

And what was it Maati meant about 'little anomalies' that might indicate evidence concerning Aari?

Before returning to the Temple, Acorna asked Captain MacDonald when he would be leaving. 'Kando is sending some men and wagons over to help us load up first thing in the morning,' he replied.

That information could prove useful, she thought. While she remained determined that the former Brother Bulaybub's fate was not in her hands, it wouldn't hurt to mention to Nadhari and Miw-Sher about the wagons.

She returned to the *Condor*. The Federation technicians and their vehicles were gone. Becker apparently saw her, for the robolift descended to meet her.

'Hiya, Princess,' Becker said, meeting her at the robolift deck and slipping his arm through hers chummily. 'We are once more fully operational, you'll be glad to hear, and can leave whenever we're ready.'

'That is very good news, Captain,' Acorna said. They ascended to the bridge and folded themselves into the command chairs, turning the chairs to face each other. 'You certainly got those repairs done in record time.'

'Yeah,' Becker said, pleased. 'Apparently the Mulzar put in a word for us and Dsu Macostut couldn't send me help fast enough. These guys know what they're doing when they're using their own stuff. They – uh – had a few problems with my adaptations, but mostly they thought they were really – what was the word? – oh, yeah, inventive.'

'You are that. I wonder why the Mulzar decided to be so helpful.'

'Nadhari, maybe?' Becker frowned. 'But then, he is kinda wanting to be a kissin' cousin with her, from what I can tell, so I don't think he'd be in any hurry for us to leave and take her with us.'

'Unless her going with us isn't a part of his plan,' Acorna suggested.

'Oh, I don't think he could keep her . . . she, uh, hasn't said anything about wanting to stay, has she?'

'Not to me. Not so far,' Acorna said. 'But the Mulzar is used to ruling. Perhaps he isn't used to considering the wishes of his women.'

'Do ya think? Naaah. He's okay. In fact, I've enjoyed getting to know him a little. He's a little high-handed sometimes, but you know, he's trying to do just what the old-time high kings did – unify his world and rule it so they can get on with progress instead of everybody fighting everybody else all the time. Like King Arthur and Camelot, except Camelot wasn't cat-shaped.'

'No, I suppose not. But I wonder how united the world will stay and at what cost its unity will come. I wonder how often he will use violence and war to subdue the other peoples.'

'You gotta break some eggs when you make – uh – scrambled eggs, Acorna,' Becker told her. He sounded a little irritated with her. Acorna guessed that was because she was questioning a concept integral to the belief system of most humans – that some things had to be fought for. Perhaps because she had been raised among humans, she actually shared that belief to some degree. The Khleevi had needed fighting. They'd needed killing, in fact, and Acorna had arranged to kill them all. She'd done it gladly and would do it again in the same situation. Other humans – bad ones, like Edacki Ganoosh, were also no great loss, in her opinion. But she didn't think Edu Kando would bother sorting out the good from the bad – or that his criteria for sorting them if he did would necessarily be based on their worth as individuals or their moral value.

'You've got him wrong,' Becker said. 'He doesn't want to make war on everybody. He's sent food and supplies to the other parts of Makahomia to try to help people.'

That surprised Acorna, who had heard nothing of it.

'I'm very relieved. I was afraid he might mind when I leave the city tomorrow to try to heal some of the other animals who have been stricken by plague. RK has particular concerns about the Temple cats elsewhere on the planet.'

'He does? He told you that, did he?' Becker asked, twisting to glower up from under his eyebrows at his first mate, who was curled on the high back of his command chair.

'Yes, he did. RK is fully telepathic when he feels like it, though he appears unable or unwilling to use more than his standard forms of communication unless he's decided it's an emergency.'

'The old rascal,' Becker said, scratching the first mate's head. 'I always knew he was smarter'n most people.'

'So, from what you say, the Mulzar should be happy that I am going to help with the epidemic, even though the illness is in other lands. That is very good news indeed. Perhaps I'll get a chance to discuss it with him this evening. If so, I'd better hurry. Are you coming?'

'Not tonight. I need to wait here till Mac and the Wats return from the *Traveler*, and go over the new equipment with Mac. Besides, it's hot down there and we have central air again!'

Acorna smiled. 'So we do.'

Becker said, 'But holler at me before you go tomorrow. I don't want you going off alone.'

'Oh, I won't. I will probably start out with Captain MacDonald and the Wats. And perhaps Miw-Sher will be with me, and probably Nadhari as well. It will be slow traveling with those wagons, though. I may have to strike out alone, perhaps even with your help, if I am to be of any use to the other cats before they die.'

'Well, Kando said the cats in their Temple were the first ones to get sick. News of the others has been coming in slowly. Don't worry, Princess, you will be in time. I'm betting on it.'

THIRTEEN

When Edu Kando decided to examine the body of the murder victim a second time, and much more closely, he realized his investigators had misidentified the corpse. The dead man was not Bulaybub.

His suspicions were triggered when the surgeon asked Kando to return to the infirmary, because he had found something he didn't believe belonged to the missing priest.

But what Kando noticed immediately was the state of the corpse's skin. What there was left of it was not decomposing normally. The stench of decomposition filled the room. Kando didn't mind the stench, associating it as he did with victor's spoils, which were most often enjoyed while the former defenders of a place rotted within sight of their newly enslaved families. It was a familiar and comforting odor for him. His enemies were dead and he was not, the stench always assured him.

What concerned him was that the legs, the oddly undamaged arms, and the back of this corpse had a leatheriness usually associated with the secretive members of the Aridimi priesthood, who all but mummified themselves while they still lived.

While Kando was pointing this out to the surgeon, the man brought forth a stone.

'I found it when I examined the neck wounds, Mulzar. Its size alone told me that this was not Bulaybub's amulet stone. And when I had washed the blood from it, I was shocked. See its fine golden color and the pale yellow pupil that shines in its midsection?'

Kando held up the stone and admired it. It was finer even than his own.

'You are indeed an observant man, Dinan. Bulaybub did not possess such a treasure as this.'

What he did not say to the doctor was that he could guess who did.

Edu glanced down at the corpse, staring into the hole where the face had been, and tried to reconstruct from his memory the man who would have worn that stone. He'd have been little more than a boy when Kando had last seen him.

The top of the skull was intact. Most of the damage had been done to the soft tissue of the face. 'Wash the blood from the skull where the midsection of the forehead might have been.'

'The bone is splintered and cracked, Mulzar, and many pieces are missing.'

'Still, there may be enough left for my purposes,' Kando said.

When the woman with the washbasin had come and cleaned the bone until it shone, Kando said, 'Aha!' and pointed to the indentation in a piece that had cracked off and embedded itself deeply in the tissue. 'You see that little dent there? Who do you think would bear such a thing?'

'I – I don't know, Mulzar. Was the fracture not inflicted with the other wounds?'

'No, no. Can you not see? There is nothing fresh about this wound. I will tell you who might have such a mark, Dinan. One who has undergone initiation into the highest orders of the Aridimi priesthood.'

'Ahh,' the man said, staring from the wound to Kando and back again, still clearly puzzled.

'As part of their initiation, the skin of an Aridimi priest's forehead is opened, the bone scraped, and a holy stone is embedded there, for the skin to heal around, so that the priest's inner eye is always open thereafter.'

'Hm,' Dinan said.

'Barbaric, isn't it? Yes, I can see that you think so. The skin you see here on the body's extremities, as yet untouched by decay, is also a mark of that breed. Instead of keeping their bodily fluids flowing, these Aridimi holies purposely do without water almost up to the point of death, until they require less and less. Their skins are dried out almost as if they were salted. You see the result here.'

'I do not think I would care to be quite that pious, Mulzar, if you will forgive my heresy.'

Kando flashed one of his roguish grins. 'Although I am the high priest, I find many of these old superstitious customs extreme and unnecessary. This poor fellow may have met death happily, since he went to such painful extremes in what he called a life. Let us turn him over and see if there is anything else that might help us identify him to his fellows, since we do not now know who he is, only that he is an Aridimi priest and not our good Brother Bulaybub.'

As if they were equals, Kando helped Dinan turn the corpse to its side. There he saw the last of the proof he needed, the puckered scar from a spear wound on the man's right flank. There was no longer any doubt in Kando's mind. The corpse was all that remained of Fagad Haral sach Pilau, his steppe-brother, born among the Aridimis but captured by the nomadic warriors on the same campaign that netted Kando himself.

'Oh,' the Mulzar said as if shocked.

'What is it, Mulzar?' Dinan asked.

'This man is well known to me – from my youth. He was close to me and was no doubt murdered on his way to see how he might be of service to me now that I am Mulzar. Poor Fagad!'

'Perhaps the Mulzar should allow me to finish the examination of his friend and prepare the body for its final journey to the stars. The Mulzar does not look well.'

The Mulzar did not feel well. He felt angry and thwarted. When he first returned from his Federation training, Fagad was one of the few people besides Bulaybub who did not turn away from him. When he began winning battles and accumulating power, Kando recognized the strategic advantage of his brother's rare Aridimi heritage and sent him back to his native territory to insinuate himself into the priesthood and to learn the sect's most closely guarded secret, the knowledge of the sacred stones – how to use them best, where they came from, and how to acquire them.

Over the years, Fagad had sent infrequent messages of his progress, but Kando had counted on him as a secret resource, his most promising hope for a relatively easy conquest of the Aridimi Stronghold.

And now here he lay upon this slab. Kando was sure Fagad must have been bringing him the intelligence he most desired; indeed, this was why he was killed. Fagad had no other reason to come to this city, except to seek him out once all the Aridimi secrets had been revealed to him. Had Bulaybub seen what attacked Fagad? The missing priest must have tried to protect him. But if so, where was Bulaybub, the second most valuable resource at Kando's command, and why was he missing?

Possibly the slayer of Fagad had also killed Bulaybub in the attack – but if so, again, where was Bulaybub's body? Where indeed?

Were the death of one of Edu's greatest resources and the disappearance of the other related? They had to be.

Kando turned to the physician and said, 'What can we glean from all of this evidence, my learned Dinan?'

Dinan shrugged and looked at Kando's face for clues. It would not do for his version to be very different from the Mulzar's. 'Why, that the beast – or the man with the help of a beast – who murdered your Aridimi friend made sure its ferocious attack destroyed all signs of the victim's station in life, Mulzar. Possibly the beast ate the evidence. After the attack, perhaps the beast carried off Brother Bulaybub for later consumption.'

Kando nodded. 'Even so, Dinan. Even so. Tell me, have you often in your long career encountered wounds such as these?'

Dinan considered. 'As severe as these? Never. Nor any made with such apparent deliberation. But similar, yes. As you know, Lord, I am a Purin tribesman by birth, a man of the steppes. When my kin raided the Makavitians, as you also know, we often used stealth and traps. Solitary heroes among our people volunteered to pick off the leaders one at a time, or carry off the most desirable slaves in lieu of or preceding a direct frontal attack on a village. From time to time, one of these solitary fighters would be found in such a condition – that is, if he screamed where he could before he died. If he did not, and this was most often the case, his body was never found at all. But those few who screamed – they were less than a handful – have I laid out with these sorts of wounds, that seemed to be made by an impossibly large cat.'

'And yet, Dinan,' Edu said, 'we who walk upright on two legs are the only known predators of our kind who still live in the inhabited portion of our planet.'

'There are our Temple guardians, Lord. Though they are far too small for their claws to inflict these wounds.'

'True. When the guardians kill our kind, it

is by breaking their necks or severing crucial arteries. Still, it seems to me that this killing was done in imitation of our guardian cats, as were those others of which you speak. I, too, have seen such wounds. It has long been my belief that there is a secret cult – particularly among those born of the rainforest tribes, as I was – that worships felines with such fanatical fervor that they commit these atrocities. If one such cult is loose in our city, we must seek out these madmen and put them to death. I will have no clandestine heretical sects undermining my rule.'

'Yes, Mulzar, a very good idea. Perhaps you may still save Brother Bulaybub if you send your soldiers from house to house.'

'I think I have a better way of flushing these people out, Dinan.' He had never before favored the physician with so many confidences, but the man was known to gossip, which Kando thought would be useful to his further plans. 'If they thought I presented a danger to the remaining Temple guardians, do you think such madmen would stop at attacking me in this, the very citadel of my power and the emblem of my rule?'

'But you don't present such a danger, Lord! How could they think so?'

'I shall have to give them cause, my good Dinan. They could well be enemy agents. In murdering my brother they have dealt a blow to my own network of agents.' All factions had spies and agents, so this was not a secret. The secret was the identity of the agents.

'Ahh, I understand, my lord. A good plan. Of course you would not harm the guardians, but the cult members do not know that?'

'Exactly. But don't breathe a word of it.'

'You can count on me, my lord.'

Kando clasped the fellow's shoulder in one hand. 'I was sure I could.'

He strode away, feeling oddly incomplete without Bulaybub beside him. Bulaybub, in his own way, had been as important to Kando as Fagad, although it was possible the monk's use was of less value now than it once had been. Kando prided himself on seeing the talent, the special purpose, for which each of his underlings was created, and in using those talents in a way that would further his goals. Actually, it was Bulaybub himself who had suggested this as a leadership skill.

Bulaybub was not precisely Kando's second in command, nor the power behind the throne. He was something quite different, and only Kando seemed to realize it. Kando needed him to rule effectively. Bulaybub knew and understood the planet's history – how its peoples related to each other and why they responded as they did to certain triggers. He was deeply trained in the mysteries of the cat-ridden religion and knew how to use it to manipulate the masses if necessary. Or rather, he would advise Kando on how to do so. The monk had served as priest, master, and slave in all of the regions on the planet, had learned many occupations, and most important, had made many influential friends, who simply liked him and listened to what he had to say because there was usually substance in it.

Kando's gifts were different. Because of his Federation training and an inborn inclination for power, he was sophisticated beyond most of his people. While off-planet he soaked up sights and sounds and experiences, realizing how narrow his world had been before, but in the end he felt unappreciated out in the galaxy. His superior officers did not seem to understand that he needed their training less than he needed to fully absorb the fascinating universe around him – learn what treasures and pleasures were available out there that were not at home. He was reprimanded by old officers who had forgotten what it was to be young and who had never had his capacity for adventure. Kept down by jealous old men who probably secretly lusted after his youth and beauty, he'd failed to make rank quickly enough to suit himself and was destined for some outpost not unlike the one from which he'd come.

That being the case, he pleaded homesickness. He wished to return to Makahomia, where he'd come from, where people responded to him, where his talents, so unappreciated and lost in the vastness of the Federation's jurisdiction, could be put to use to serve his people. This service to them, he realized, he could best render as their ruler.

When he first returned as a young officer of twenty-one years, by Standard counting, his people rejected him and all he had to offer them. He thought he was better than they. He had learned alien ways and was more like a Federation overlord than one of them now. His family was dead or scattered. Those who had been his masters tried to reclaim him and might have succeeded except for the skills and contacts he had gathered off-planet.

Bulaybub, a somewhat older man originally of the Moginari tribe from the same rainforest where Kando was born, changed that attitude simply by first befriending and then following Kando. The priest sought him out, consulted him, listened to his stories, admired his style. Because Bulaybub was respected and liked, a certain . . . acceptance was transferred to Kando. He gained influence by association.

Once he was given a chance to shine, his innate kingly charisma dazzled people and led them to obey him, even when he had not conquered them. Men admired him as a brilliant and successful officer, the kind who, if they followed him into battle, was likely to lead them back out again, alive and victorious. Women were attracted to his virility and power, as if they sensed his voracious sexual appetites. Rather, *most* women were attracted to that.

But not Nadhari, with her supple, graceful body and those tilted wary eyes, that hint of mystery he found so tantalizing. Never her, though it was he who had first schooled her in the arts of battle and later had attempted to teach her some of the, if not gentler, at least more sensually pleasurable arts. But he was disappointed, on his return from space, that after the first few encounters with her, he had no further chance to lay eyes, hands, or anything else on her again before she disappeared into the Federation ship. How ironic. What was the Terran saying about ships that pass in the night? He thought he had lost her forever, his best opponent in battle and the one who had most motivated him to win and enjoy a victor's rewards.

He smiled to himself. She might pretend nothing more than a kinswoman's interest in him now, with her friends around her, but he had marked her, he could tell. There was something a bit twisted about her that he recognized as his contribution to who she was. He had taken her and taught her too young for her to have escaped being – at least in part – his creature.

He sat at the writing table in his office, which had for a window one of the eyes of the cat-Temple. He studied once more the figures Dsu Macostut had shown him, the profits to be made on a single sacred stone. Of all of his people, he was the best educated, thanks to the Federation, and he spent much of his time here, plotting his changes for his planet. Whom he could pit against whom, whom he could subvert or buy. He needed the consent – whether forced or voluntary was of no concern to the Federation, who would believe what he and Macostut told them – of the leaders of each of the tribal nations of the planet to ratify the changes in the original agreement. Half of them were accounted for with his own consent, as he controlled the Mog-Gim Plateau but had gained that control as the leader of the tribes of the Furrim Steppes. He still needed to win over the Aridimis and the Makaviti.

Bulaybub was supposed to be assisting with that, too, waxing eloquent on how wars had decimated the land and resources.

The truth was, peace was threatening to break out whether or not he wanted it. People had become, over these long years, rather homogenized, what with all of the enslavement and mercenary service back and forth among the tribes. This suited him very well, and he fostered it.

From the eye of the cat, Kando saw Nadhari striding through the gate, accompanied by Bulaybub's cat-loving little niece, clasping the tortoiseshell female guardian in her arms while the other three Temple cats trailed at her heels. Miw-Sher. Now there was a tender little morsel. What was to become of her with her uncle and protector, so far as anyone knew, dead? Nadhari seemed to have taken her under her wing for now. That might be convenient.

The truth was, much as it pained him to notice it, Nadhari was by now a bit long in the tooth. But if she was of less interest for one function, he could make use of her another way, providing he could prevent her from leaving on the salvage vessel. It would soon go back to where it came from, thanks to Macostut's intervention. Without Bulaybub to persuade the unaffiliated tribes to accept him as supreme leader, he would need a general, a war chief, an enforcer at the least. And Nadhari, from all he had learned of her extra-Makahomian career, was the best. Perhaps the vessel would not leave.

After all, it and some of her friends could be

made useful, even if their timing was exceptionally inconvenient, coming along to undo some of the impact of his little biological bomb so soon after he had planted it. However, with a carefully self-serving interpretation of the ministrations of these alien altruists – the horned ambassador's healing gifts, the farmer captain's attempt to feed the plague-ridden people – they could be turned to his advantage.

He would not ask Nadhari now.

He called Akid, the captain of his priestly guards, to him. 'Assemble the people of the city tomorrow morning. I have announcements of great magnitude to impart to them.'

'Yes, Mulzar,' Akid replied, and obeyed.

Kando turned his attention to his upcoming presentation. He glanced up once, at second setting, to see the ambassador's tall, horned, white figure walking through the gate. He blinked. Some fragment of her shadow had preceded her and flitted into the shadowed cloisters. No matter. She was an alien. He had never in fact seen one quite like her, with that intriguing horn spiraling from her head, just where an Aridimi priest's eyestone would be. There was something almost priestly about her – something as pure as her color suggested. She seemed chaste, sad, preoccupied.

He was thinking, if the opportunity presented itself, he would know how to get her undivided attention, when she walked into his office. Almost as if she had read his mind.

'Ambassador, what a pleasure.'

'I beg your pardon for my rudeness, Mulzar,

but I was told you would be here and I have an urgent matter I wish to discuss with you.'

'I can see that you are troubled, my child. Please, let me help you.'

Edu smiled.

FOURTEEN

Acorna wanted to see Kando for a number of reasons, the chief one being that she wished to form her own opinion of him. Though now she wished she had not been so scrupulous with the former Brother Bulaybub. She should have allowed him to tell her more about the plots he felt his erstwhile master had instigated. She would be better prepared for what was to come if she had. As it was, she had no idea how her self- (and RK-) appointed mission to save this planet's ailing creatures would be greeted by the Mulzar, for example, or what Edu's actions toward her might be if she let him know what she planned.

Acorna was further confused by Becker's apparent liking and admiration for Edu. Becker was usually a good judge of character, but although he was very intuitive, Becker was not precisely – or at least not always – telepathic. A charismatic and clever trickster could fool him. Especially if a profitable business deal was involved.

When Acorna entered his office, Kando sat at his massive writing table. Maps and scrolls were spread out on it. On top of the scroll he'd been working on was a large golden stone with a pale fiery stripe down the middle. Kando reached over to stroke it while she seated herself across from him. The Mulzar's thoughts were guarded carefully as he extended his seeming solicitousness toward her, but she was mildly shocked to sense an unwarranted prurient interest in her person from him. Once she picked up on that, she was aware that the atmosphere surrounding him crawled with duplicity and intrigue. Of course he was the leader of an influential section of the planet, and perhaps, if Becker was correct, would soon rule the entire planet. A certain amount of political intrigue in his mental emanations was natural.

She tried to be fair and attempted to introduce the topic in a casual manner. 'I understand you've given Captain MacDonald permission to treat your animals and instruct your people in farming methods that will feed them until the ground is safe again. I wish to go with him.'

'Do you? How kind,' Edu said with oily smoothness, picking the stone up and cradling it in his fist. 'I see no problem with that, although our primitive means of transport may not suit someone of your sophistication.'

He could not quite keep enough of his mask in place to conceal his irritation that he found it necessary to go along with MacDonald's program. He apparently was not accustomed to telepaths and had not learned how to shield against them, although his innate deviousness, which she soon discovered, served him well enough. But images flashed across his mind –

images he viewed with satisfaction – of laboratory test tubes changing hands between him and Macostut, of the contents being put into vermin traps that never sprang. The vermin partook of the tainted material, the cats caught the vermin, and cats began dying. The infected vermin spread, and their infected scat was scattered throughout the countryside. Soon enough, other creatures, including people, also died.

Until she came, and MacDonald. No, she would not seek his permission now.

'You might be surprised what suits me,' she said, and bared her teeth at him in what he would take for a friendly smile, though among the Linyaari it was a hostile challenge.

'I'd like to find out,' he said insinuatingly, stroking the stone with the pad of his thumb along the pale slash of fire in its middle.

'Well, yes, I appreciate you giving your permission. Lieutenant Commander Macostut is not so easy to deal with. Always quoting Federation rules and treaties, you know.'

'Allow me to handle *him* and the Federation as well, Ambassador Acorna. That is your given name, is it not? Acorna? It is so – exotic.' He rolled the stone down his palm with his fingertips, and when he finished saying 'exotic,' he closed his hand over it.

She bared her teeth again. 'Yes, it is, isn't it? My people even find it so.' She did not explain. She didn't want to tell any of her family history to this man.

'Acorna, I was hoping – I am speaking to my subjects tomorrow morning. I wish to recognize the work you did for our guardians. It would please me if you would come. You and Nadhari as well, of course. I know Captain MacDonald will be busy with his wagons, but as soon as I have finished, you may join him. I do hope you'll come.' He set the stone down long enough to take her hand in both of his. He stared for a moment at its three single-knuckled fingers, one fewer than he was used to, and appeared slightly nonplussed before he began stroking her palm seductively with his thumb. 'I want my people to recognize you as their – our – new friend.'

'Your wish is my command in this,' she said, because it was, of course, in this instance. She gently but firmly pulled her hand away with a strength that she could tell surprised him. Behind her, she felt him smile and pick up the stone again.

She returned to her quarters, wishing she could lock the door. She was comforted when RK dropped from the ceiling onto her bed to make himself comfortable against her side.

The events of the day revolved inside her head as if they had been poured into a centrifuge and set on Spin. Tagoth and Miw-Sher, RK and the Temple cats, all of them together, Nadhari and Tagoth, Tagoth and Mulzar Kando, Becker and Kando, MacDonald and the Wats, Kando and Acorna herself, whirled through her mind in a soup of coppery rainforest, flat red desert, cat's-eye chrysoberyl stones of many colors, and wide open steppes veined with rivers and streams. Just when she stopped recalling and started dreaming, she couldn't have said.

But all at once she realized that the reason everyone was spinning so fast was that she was flying past them, over them, and they weren't spinning at all. She was flying past the city and everything familiar to her on this world. Now there were cat-shaped Temples in the mix, poking their ears out of the trees of the rainforest, squatting beside rivers in the steppes, and reclining Sphinx-like in the desert. In fact, these Sphinx cats even had human faces. In her dream, she heard Aari's voice telling her, 'Those are not Temples you see there. They are monuments to Grimalkin. Though they call him the Star Cat, these people know well that he has a human face. He brought me here to save these people, and meanwhile, he decided to increase the population and improve the gene pool in a very personal fashion. That is how they became able to shift from human to feline. I hope you will also notice that there are no people here who resemble the Linyaari. The Companion did not see fit to pass on *his* dominant characteristics to every female in the gene pool.'

Acorna sped onward. When she reached the rainforest, she was suddenly looking down on the Temple, where hundreds of cats all lapped at a dish that bore the symbol of a skull and crossbones on the side. She jumped down and tried to shoo them away before they ate, but Captain MacDonald was there, saying, 'But they have to keep their strength up, honey.'

Then she was flying far out over the desert again, but all of a sudden the ground split open, deep and wide, the sides of the gash multicolored, and at its end the whole thing was filled with a beautiful deep lake that seemed to come from nowhere. The Temple was different, too, but before she could quite figure out how, she saw Aari down below her waving flags and pointing to a place for her to land.

But when she ran to him, an instant later in the dream, and without all of the bother of landing the craft she was flying, she saw that he was no longer a living Linyaari, but a statue of one, and she couldn't reach him because he was standing in the middle of a stream feeding into the lake.

All around him cats' eyes winked and blinked, some of them without cats behind them. 'You really can't tell,' someone said, 'until one of them decides to move to eat or fight or have sex.'

At that point she awakened. She tried to move, but could not. From the sensations in her chest and arms, it seemed as if someone had restrained her during the night, possibly even tied her up. Her arms were pinned to her sides at the elbows, and her ankles wouldn't move when she tried to rise.

She heard footsteps outside her door. A voice called, 'Ambassador?' There was a sharp 'hsst!' and the weight on her chest released as RK leaped straight up from the crouch he had assumed during the night to watch her face, apparently, for the first sign of wakefulness. He seemed almost to fly instead of jump to the catwalk, and one of the bolt-holes near the ceiling. Then he spoiled the illusion by losing a paw-hold and having to dangle his back end off the catwalk while he dug in with his front claws to force enough of him through the opening of the hole so his feet would have to follow. Pash, Haji, and Sher-Paw ran in different directions, and Acorna found her arms and legs released as well.

She'd been bound up, all right, courtesy of her cat guardians. She felt like laughing, but instead gathered her wits and composure and said, 'Yes, what is it?'

'The Mulzar's address is about to begin.'

'Thank you,' Acorna said. 'Then I'll be right along.'

'But you must refresh yourself and break your fast before you go. We were not privileged to serve you yesterday morning. We were negligent and did not attend you when you awoke. Please, may we enter now?'

Acorna sighed and reluctantly gave her assent. A string of Temple women – whether priestesses or acolytes or mere servants, Acorna could not tell – entered. One carried a ewer of water, another a basin, a third bore Acorna's clothing, cleaned and pressed and devoid of the evidence of her adventures of yesterday. Yet another woman bore a basket of fruits and vegetables of various sorts.

'Thank you. You're very kind,' Acorna told them, nibbling on something with a rubbery green texture. 'This is nice. What is it?'

'It is called sand claw, Ambassador. I removed the thorns myself.'

'A sort of cactus, then? It's very good.'

They stood around nodding and watching her chew.

'Have any of you seen Miw-Sher yet this morning?' she asked when she'd finished the cactus.

'She was searching for Grimla the last time I

saw her,' one of the women said. 'The Mulzar is most particular that all of the sacred guardians are in attendance when he speaks.'

'Oh, really?'

'Yes, Ambassador. He wishes to let the people know what wonders you have performed.'

'Does he?' This worried Acorna. If Kando had caused the cats to become ill, which he had if she read him correctly, then his seeming concern for displaying their healthy state was ominous.

After her erstwhile servants were convinced she was presentable, she was taken straight to the cat's mouth, which was open. On the tongue, a balcony looked out on not only the Temple courtyards but also the streets of the city, and beyond. Stale smoke colored by red dust hung over the city and the countryside beyond, intensifying the reddish cast the suns lent to the sky, giving the day an angry, stormy appearance.

People thronged the walls and courtyards of the Temple, but behind them the city streets were deserted and empty, except for whirlwinds of red dust that zipped and rolled drunkenly through the town like alien invaders searching for loot.

Although the wind stirred up these small cyclones, the day was scorchingly hot, and the breeze, when it came, was like the exhaust of some great antique flitter, spewing flames and fumes in its wake.

Throughout the crowd and surrounding it stood priests armed with what appeared to be some sort of circular, discus-like weapons as well as swords, daggers, and spears. Just because Nadhari's cousin was the Federationacknowledged ruler of this city didn't mean everyone who lived in the city was happy about it. Acorna read the general tone of the crowd and received the impression that people were not here because they particularly wanted to receive Edu's counsel and leadership but because they had been ordered to come. Most of them seemed to dread learning what new proclamations, taxes, laws, or restrictions Kando was about to inflict upon them.

Acorna, Nadhari, and a few other privileged people were allowed to stand on the balcony with Kando while he addressed the throng. Miw-Sher stood beside the right fang of the Temple's open mouth. When she spotted Nadhari and Acorna, the girl abandoned her toothy post to stand nearer to them.

Grimla was in her arms and the guardian cat's tail tickled the back of Acorna's hand.

Kando held up his hands and the crowd grew quiet. 'People of Hissim, I call you together to speak to you concerning the sickness that has plagued our sacred guardians and has claimed the life of many domestic beasts and some of your own kinfolk. This scourge killed, among others, Sacred Phador, Sacred Nadia, the Sacred Kits One through Forty-Two, as yet and now forever unnamed. We have reason to believe that this plague is part of a plot perpetrated on our city, our Temple, and our rule by our enemies, who will stop at nothing to overthrow us. Heretofore, no matter how desperate the battle, Temple guardians have always been exempt from retaliation, but now it has been suggested to me by my wise friends and allies of the Federation that our sacred ones were poisoned! Also spies have been sent among us, and a priest has been murdered in a brutal, ritualistic fashion. Still another priest has been abducted. All evidence points to the involvement of the secretive Aridimi sect from the deep desert, your own relations. We must redress these crimes. We will invade their lands and avenge ourselves, taking into our Temple their own sacred ones to replace those of ours that they have slain.' Edu finally stopped to take a deep breath.

'But, Your Reverence!' protested a large prosperous-looking man who wore soft white lightweight clothing and a wealth of red metal and gemstones on any part of his body that could be girded with ornamentation. 'We have heard that the sacred ones are sick and dying on all parts of the planet.'

'Ahhh,' Kando said, 'I too have heard the lies. It has even been suggested that this scourge is not a covert form of warfare, but the work of a fanatical cult that seeks to destroy all who follow the path the Star Cat chose for us. If so, they have been foiled, deprived of four of their victims, again through the intercession of my contacts in the Federation.

'However, we believe this cult idea is a fantasy, a fiction concocted by those who fear another war. In truth, it has been my greatest wish to lead you into an era of peace – or so I had hoped to, until this evil befell our Temple. Now I see that the only way to bring peace to this world is for all of it to be under a single rule. Until we find out who visited this blasphemous attack on our guardians, I believe it is for the good of all guardians that we conquer Hissim's enemies and deliver their sacred animals from servitude to people who have loosed a plague upon us. Since we know not which state is guilty, we must assume they all are, and act accordingly.'

'But why would they kill their own guardians or their own food beasts?' the prosperous man asked. 'Surely we will be able to tell who poisoned our animals by how many of their own animals survive.'

'Ah, but would they *tell* us? Would they let it be known? When our holy ones first became ill, and I heard that the other states were likewise afflicted, so deep was my grief and so aroused was my compassion that I chose slaves from each area and sent them back to their peoples bearing medicines and food. Perhaps it was my quick action that saved the others, or perhaps it was merely that we were the ones most directly attacked. I have heard that all other states were as badly stricken as we were, but what others have not heard is that of all of the Temples whose guardians fell prey to the disease, ours alone were snatched from the brink of death. This happened, we must believe, because the righteousness of our hegemony over the beings on our planet is manifest. Thus we were granted a miraculous gift and blessed with the alien doctor who healed our guardians as a sign attesting to that righteousness.'

'I heard all the guardians had died,' someone shouted.

'Three days ago, it seemed that would be true, but now the acolytes and handmaidens will show you that through divine grace, four of our guardians have been restored to health.' At his signal Miw-Sher and her fellow cat attendants brought forth Grimla, Pash, Haji, and Sher-Paw, all sleek of fur, bright of eye, and pink of nose and pads. 'Of course, this miracle, this blessing of the gods was made manifest when my Federation contacts put me in touch with the Linyaari ambassador, Lady Acorna Harakamian-Li, whose advanced medical knowledge was able to save these last precious four guardians.'

Acorna, as she understood what Kando was claiming, grew furious. Her gift of healing to the Temple cats was being perverted into a cause for war, and into something for which Kando could claim credit. She could read him as easily as if he were made of glass. He had downplayed her role in the Temple cats' recovery, being shrewd enough to realize she wanted it that way, but he'd used her actions to justify his own schemes. If he was not very specific about the nature of the help the cats received, he might even get the credit for curing them.

The people listening were pleased about the cats, she could read that, but they remained mistrustful of Kando. They quite rightly feared that they were being manipulated into something.

Acorna was thoroughly disgusted.

It took only a light touch to Nadhari's mind to read that she was no more thrilled with her cousin's speech than Acorna was.

Acorna decided Kando had enjoyed playing both ends against the middle for too long. He cared nothing for the welfare of the cats and the domestic beasts, or of the people, for that matter, or he would never have loosed the plague among them.

Acorna stepped forward, taking advantage of his slight introduction to bow graciously to the crowd, who cheered, and then to Kando, who started to say something, before she beat him to it. 'Thank you, Mulzar. I am, as you say, a healer, and in spite of being an ambassador, I am not always as diplomatic as I should be. Please forgive me that I find this talk of war and conquest under the circumstances shocking. As I mentioned to you earlier, my people do not believe in war. However, that is neither here nor there. The real point here is that this disease is spreading, is killing the guardians, creatures that all of the people of this planet hold sacred. Should not the emphasis be placed upon curing as many as possible, rather than going into a war that may – no, *will* – spread death, injury, and disease to even more two- and four-legged beings? As I look upon you, my physician's heart knows that you are weary and sick of sickness, bereft at the loss of the beloved guardians whose protective presence has always been one of your greatest securities, and impoverished and starving due to the loss of your beasts. And these feelings are shared by all the other peoples of this planet.'

'All the more reason for conquest!' one of the priest guards shouted at her.

'But what will you be conquering? Dead and

dying people with dead and dying beasts, who have no food you can use and no guardians to bring back with you. What is the point in that? I would like to propose to you, Mulzar . . .' she said, returning her attention to Kando, whose face probably looked bland from below the balcony but whose eyes showed that he was not at all amused or moved by her speech. She had not expected that he would be. She continued, '. . . is that I go among those who are normally your, um, co-belligerents and offer them the use of my skill as a physician to cure as many of their Temple cats and other beasts as I can. In this way I might at least ascertain how many of the Temple guardians have survived in various areas. If I come upon a Temple that has many, I shall ask for kittens in payment for my services and shall bring them to the Temples that have lost the most. Certainly this one falls into that – oh dear, this seems to be a pun in your language, too – category.'

The Mulzar smiled suddenly. 'You would spy for us? Truly, you are a thoughtful guest to offer to inform us who has the most of what we seek.'

Acorna felt her face grow so hot she thought her horn must be glowing with her anger, but she kept her words and tone calm and sweet. 'Oh, no, Mulzar! You mistake my meaning. If your opponents are honorable people, there will be no need for you to attack them. Some will have so few cats it would not be worth your own losses to attack them. And as for those who have escaped the epidemic with less damage, if I cure those who are ill, the priests should grant me the boon of bringing some of their kittens to the less fortunate Temples. There is no need for me to prevaricate, much less to spy. I seek only to bring aid to your whole planet during this tragic time.'

Nadhari sent her an urgent mental warning: (He's seething. Don't turn your back on him, Acorna.)

Kando said smoothly, 'It is delightful to see such idealism in someone of your station, Ambassador. But you are young, tenderhearted, and by your own admission, from a people who do not wage war. You cannot possibly understand the complications your proposed actions would cause among our planet's people. I'm quite sure the Federation would never permit you to pursue your proposed course of action.'

'I'm sure if *you* intervened, sir, your contacts there would smooth my path – I imagine that your *friend* Lieutenant Colonel Macostut would do his best to find a way to accommodate us.'

Nadhari's face was twitching as if she had some sort of nervous disorder, as she sternly suppressed laughter at her cousin's discomfiture.

The Mulzar raised his arms again to make it clear that Acorna's interruption was not going to end his speech before he was ready to end it.

'People of Hissim, while I join you in rejoicing at the survival of our guardians, it seems to me we are being tested. The gods have sent us these tribulations and this lady to determine if we have absolute trust, loyalty, and obedience to them, even as you must do to me. They have taken from us first that which we value most – our beloved guardians. And then we were given a choice in the form of the Ambassador Acorna's ability to heal our surviving sacred ones. I have had an epiphany, a revelation.'

Silence fell over the crowd. Acorna got the collective thought that they hoped the revelation would not be too bad *this* time.

'Clearly the gods have been merciful to us, but now it is our duty to show ourselves worthy and return to them something of that which they have spared us.'

Acorna caught his thought early in the sentence. So this was how he was going to reconcile his real motives with his public sentiments! She sent a mental push to Miw-Sher. 'Take Grimla and run! He's going to demand a cat sacrifice!'

However, before the thought was out of her mind, another of the *Condor*'s crew dropped down from the nose of the Temple onto the mouth, uttering a loud yowl that seemed to Acorna to translate as 'Scatter, brothers and sisters! Run for your lives! This infidel wants to waste you!'

Although there were only five Makahomian Temple cats present, counting RK, for a split-and-spitting-second the air seemed filled with pinwheeling paws, lashing tails, and slashing claws . . . particularly claws. Cats flew everywhere, leaping, bouncing, pouncing, and laying down tracks of flayed flesh wherever those lethal claws happened to touch.

Then, just as suddenly, there were no more cats. Anywhere.

However, this observation was made only by those who were still there. Acorna, Nadhari, and Miw-Sher were not.

Kando had been so caught up in the results of his own theatrics that he could do nothing but stand openmouthed for a moment, using a loose fold of his robe to stanch the flow of blood from a wound on his shoulder. The keepers of the cats, with the exception of Miw-Sher, were still present, looking around to see what had hit them. But the only remaining sign of the cats was a few stray hairs floating to the flagstones below on eddies of hot wind.

People were murmuring, exclaiming, even – though it was instantly squelched – laughing.

One of the priests whispered something to Kando and he resumed his speech. 'As you can see, people of Hissim, the cats live, but their *spirits* are in disarray because they were not *intended* to remain among us. I am sure the ambassador just realized that, which is why she disappeared. And all of you saw for yourselves the foreign cat that attacked me, no doubt a direct challenge from our enemies. The ambassador may do her best among our enemies, but we will prepare for war.'

To the priest beside him he said, 'In two days' time, when our cats have had the chance to regain their senses and have resumed their feeding stations and nests, at the second setting our precious four will travel to the gods in person to deliver our thanks.'

The wagons were loaded and ready outside the Temple. The priest driving the first of the wagons was totally taken by surprise when the rampaging RK led the four Temple cats skittering over the Temple walls and leaping onto the

231

wagon beds. Close behind them were Acorna, Nadhari, and Miw-Sher.

Captain MacDonald was at the reins in the second wagon, Red Wat in the third, Sandy Wat in the fourth. In the first was the priest who was apparently to be their guide. Nadhari shoved him off the wagon and took the reins herself. Acorna and Miw-Sher sat beside her, yelling 'Hyah! Hyah!' to the team, which broke into a respectable run. Acorna sent a mental message to Captain MacDonald: (Follow us! Quickly! We will explain later!)

He sent a startled reaction back. He'd been prepared for a peaceful mission to aid civilians, not a fast getaway from government forces. He switched mental gears quickly, nevertheless, clicked his tongue at his team, and fell in behind them. The Wats apparently relished all the excitement. They whipped their poor beasts into a lather and almost wrecked their wagons as they rattled over the rutted streets at high speed.

The city gates were open and their wagons arrived faster than any messengers telling the gatekeepers to close them. Instead of stopping to assist the local farmers engaged in slaughtering their beasts, as MacDonald had intended before this mad flight, they kept driving as far and as fast away from Hissim as they could.

'The Mulzar will send fast riders after us,' Miw-Sher said. Acorna felt the girl trembling beside her.

'I don't think so,' Acorna said. 'I think he will use our departure to his own advantage and tell the people what he wishes. And possibly try to place the blame for everything on RK and me.'

'Of course he will,' Nadhari said. 'And Jonas and Captain MacDonald as well. Since the people of Hissim only know what Edu chooses to tell them about the outside world, they will be persuaded easily enough that we are all evil. He will tell people that we must be guilty of something; otherwise, why would we have run?'

Acorna told her, 'Maybe it would have been better timing to wait until he'd tipped his hand about killing the Temple cats. Then people would have understood that we were saving the cats. But if we'd waited for him to announce it, we couldn't have saved them at all. The guards would have had the poor things in hand, and there would have been nothing we could do.'

'We did what we had to do,' Nadhari said, negotiating a bend in the road that led past a small group of hovels. Ahead was open desert.

But as they passed the last low building a figure flung himself into the road just in front of them. Nadhari pulled back on the reins so hard that the harnessed beasts reared in their traces. Miw-Sher jumped down and ran toward the man. 'Uncle! You're safe!'

'For now. Do you suppose I could hitch a ride?'

Scar MacDonald stopped his wagon, tied off his reins, and strode forward, his face full of thunderclouds. 'That was a damn fool stunt, Commander Nadhari. You could have made us crash every wagon in this convoy into matchsticks and killed the beasts pulling us, as well as those under our protection, and then where would we be? Our speedy exit, whatever the reason for it, wouldn't have done anybody any good.' He peered around the wagon and saw Tagoth hurrying toward him. 'And who the devil is this, anyway? And what in tarnation were you doing in the road, sir? Hey – wait a minute.'

Tagoth didn't have his hat on now. MacDonald snapped his fingers. 'Brother Bulaybub? I never forget a face. But you didn't have one the last time I saw you. What's going on here?'

The first thing the Mulzar did after his speech was have the guardians' handlers taken into custody for questioning. The woman, Nekbet, was the first to break. 'Please don't sacrifice our guardians, Mulzar. It was that foreign cat who caused the trouble, the ambassador's cat.'

'She has a Temple cat? Why was I not told of this before?'

'She said he was merely their ship's cat, Mulzar, and after what she did for our guardians, we thought . . .'

'You didn't think! That cat was of *our* strain, you can tell by looking at it. You can even see from examining the claw marks on my arm. The ambassador is a spy. I knew it! Pretending to heal the guardians, she has subverted them. I must notify Lieutenant Commander Macostut of this at once and have the woman's friends taken into custody. She abducted an acolyte, as well, and the four guardians and my cousin, brought a contraband cat among us, and hijacked the wagons we graciously lent her friend to help our poor people.'

The surgeon, who was in charge of the persuas-

234

ive methods by which the captive handlers were forced to answer the Mulzar's questions, asked, 'Should we send a party after them now, Mulzar?'

Edu waved a dismissive hand. Actually, Acorna and Nadhari had done him a large favor with their rash actions. He now had a good excuse to wage the ultimate war he wanted, and locate the Aridimi Stronghold. And if it was discovered later that he had violated the taboo against Federation technology to do so, he would explain that of course he had to retrieve the Temple cats from the clutches of the foreigners. Bring them back into his own clutches. Yes, indeed. 'We have better things to do,' he said. 'We will launch a holy war on our enemies. No doubt we will sweep up the wagons and their treasonous occupants when we do so. Ready our armies.'

'The sacrifice, Mulzar?'

'Since we cannot sacrifice the guardians, we will sacrifice the handlers who were so careless as to let them escape.'

'Mulzar!' The surgeon was aghast. Only the day before the Mulzar had implied that a pretense of harming the guardians would flush out a cult. Now it seemed the Mulzar had actually intended to sacrifice the cats.

Hearing the threat of mutiny in the surgeon's voice, Kando realized his mistake. He winked at the doctor conspiratorially and saw the man relax. 'Yes, I think they will strengthen the walls of the Temple with their sacrifice. Wall them up with that other old fool. That should draw out the conspirators, eh?'

*　　*　　*

The pulling beasts were exhausted from their mad dash from the city, and all the living beings in their little convoy were thirsty. No water had been packed in the provisions MacDonald brought with him. He'd planned to load up on water outside the city at the livestock yards.

More important, Acorna thought, as she saw RK and the guardians nosing and pawing among the load, nothing a cat could eat had been packed in the wagon's cargo, either.

While Tagoth and Nadhari were sparring, and Scar MacDonald, whose questions were not being answered, contented himself with checking on and adjusting his Metleiter boxes to ride more securely in the wagon, RK hopped onto the buckboard where Acorna still sat. He walked onto her knees, looked into her face, and opened his mouth in a yowl that was silent to everyone except Acorna and the other cats.

(I want to go home *nyowwww*,) he said. (I want to go back to the *Condor*. These silly things we're riding on will never get us anywhere in time to save anybody.)

(RK, you know very well we can't just make Becker take off into space and land where we need him to. There are rules about bringing spacefaring technology out of the Federation port.)

RK yawned. (Rules? You're boring me. There're rules against poisoning cats here, too – yes, I know. I read you very well, at least as well as you read that murdering mule-whatever-he-calls-himself. Besides, you personally won't be breaking the rule. Tell Becker I want to come home. He will come and get me, and he doesn't care about rules any more than I do.)

(Hmmm,) Acorna thought. And as he punctuated his argument with his claws she added: (Ouch! Yes, you have a point. Nevertheless, that is a very obnoxious habit you've developed. That hurts, you know.)

(Tell him and stop whining, Linyaari girl! You are self-sealing.)

Grimla walked out from under Miw-Sher's strokes and nudged RK aside to give Acorna a smile with her delicately curved mouth. She was purring and suddenly she stood on her hind paws, front paws curled daintily close to her own chest, and rubbed her face against Acorna's jaw.

Pash, Haji, and Sher-Paw strolled over to see what was happening and add a few comments of their own.

Acorna laughed, scratched RK's and Grimla's ears in surrender, and transmitted as narrowly as she could, (Captain Becker, your first mate wants to come home and the rest of us could use help.)

(I read you, Princess, loud and clear, and the damned cat, too. On my way.)

(On my way.) Becker transmitted the thought to Acorna, and as he did, saw that he was not the only one heading toward his friends. At the Federation gate, a delegation of the four warrior-priests from the Temple were joined by four Federation troops. There was a hail on the com unit. 'Uh, get that, Mac, would you?' Becker asked. 'And stall for all you're worth.'

'Stall? But, Captain, we have landed and are

docked. Why should I stall, and how can I do so?'

'Keep whoever is calling, and I can practically guarantee that it will be Macostut, from stating his business and demanding to see me. Do not let on that you know where I am.'

'And where will that be, Captain?'

'I'm going to help Acorna. She just – uh – hailed me on a private channel.'

'So you *will* be trying out the flitter I readied for such an eventuality? It is an excellent flitter, of Linyaari design. I added to it several modifications usually found only on larger Linyaari crafts, such as the excellent Linyaari shielding device. I would be happy to point them out to you. Wouldn't you like me to accompany you?'

'Nope. You're going to have to hold the fort here. In fact your job's going to be much nastier than mine. Get that? Stall. Keep them off my ship.' Becker ducked out of sight.

'Yes, sir. Stalling, sir.' Mac answered the com call. 'This is Special Technician MacKenZ of the salvage ship *Condor* speaking. Please identify yourself.'

A stern face appeared on the com screen. 'This is Lieutenant Commander Dsu Macostut. I must speak with Captain Jonas Becker immediately.'

'I apologize, Lieutenant Commander Dsu Macostut, but Captain Becker is indisposed at the moment.'

'Indisposed how?'

'Oh, it is a highly interesting process, sir. You see, when Captain Becker takes on fuel to maintain adequate personal function and energy levels, not all of the fuel is acceptable to his operating system. Therefore, it is necessary that this excess fuel be ejected at some point . . .'

Becker grinned into his mustache as he heard Mac's explanation of Becker's digestive and excretory processes, while Macostut stuttered and attempted to break in to notify Becker of the arrest that was about to take place, if the look of the men marching on the *Condor* was any indication. Acorna's message of trouble plus all those marching men meant Becker's butt was going to be in a sling if he didn't get it out of there. But what was Acorna planning? How had she got the high mucky-mucks so riled up in such a short time? The last time Becker had checked in with his friends, everything had been just fine. Peachy keen, even. If they were in hot water now, the Federation had the authority to keep the *Condor* from leaving this benighted planet if necessary. If Becker brought Acorna and RK and presumably Nadhari back to the ship, they would be in even more trouble than they already were in, wouldn't they?

Then, as he was slipping into the flitter and opening the hull hatch to fly her out, he received another message from Acorna.

'Captain, RK wanted me to remind you to bring *lots* of cat food.'

Edu Kando stood beside Macostut as their combined troops closed on the *Condor*.

'I'm sorry about this, Edu,' Macostut said. 'We would never have let them come near Hissim except that your cousin was with them.'

'It doesn't matter,' Kando replied. 'And it is

right that Nadhari is here now. She will come around once she sees the breadth of my vision. Our vision. She lives in the modern universe by preference, after all. You have the chemicals?'

'Oh, yes. But you're on your own as far as getting them to this lake you told me about. If I flew you out there, it would blow my cover and I'd be replaced before our operation got off the ground.'

They watched their troops approach the strange patchworked ship. Macostut's last sentence trailed away as a flap of the *Condor*'s skin opened and something large and white with curlicues of color and swags of gilt bunting decorating its wings flew away, out over the wall protecting the port, high above the city and out toward the desert.

'What is that?' Kando demanded, pointing.

'It appears to be a flying horse,' Macostut said, shaking his head in disbelief. 'How did my people miss that during the inspection?' To his ground troops he said, 'Lock that ship down, men, along with any remaining personnel.'

But moments later they reported back, as they came out of the *Condor*. 'We are sorry, sir. Whatever personnel were aboard seem to have evacuated on the flying horse thing.'

The Makahomian troops wore thoughtful and awestruck expressions as they watched the sky.

Aboard the *Condor*, white hands burst from the soil in the hydroponics garden and Mac sat up, brushed the dirt and plants from his uniform, considerately replanted Acorna's crops, and returned to the bridge to see what he could do about breaking the just-installed locks on the new computer system without alerting any possible Federation monitors. It would be tricky, but so was he.

FIFTEEN

'Do you still think this is merely political, Ambassador?' Tagoth asked Acorna.

Acorna shook her head. 'No. I looked into the Mulzar's mind. Edu Kando started the plague himself on purpose.'

'That's terrible. Why would he do a dumb thing like that?' MacDonald asked.

Acorna said, 'The Mulzar seems to want all the things he considers modern and technologically advanced. I think he feels that if he destroys his planet's agrarian economy and undermines the people's religion by killing the sacred cats at the same time, he will force the people of this world into accepting a different way of life for Makahomia. A more galactic way of doing things. He also hopes to force the Federation to aid Makahomia by driving the planet into such a terrible condition that the Federation will have to help. By giving the people, through him, the things he thinks will help accomplish his own goals, the Mulzar hopes to set himself up as both leader and savior of this world. He even expects that all its people will be grateful to him.' She brushed the dust off of her face and clothing as she thought, then said, 'But I didn't get the sense from the crowd at the temple that he's really in touch with how the people feel. They care about their families, their animals, and the sacred cats. What they *don't* much care for is the Mulzar.'

'Then he'll want to kill us as well as our Temple cats, so no one can stand against him,' Miw-Sher said, looking up at her uncle. 'Every priest on this planet is in danger.'

Tagoth nodded.

Nadhari jumped down from the wagon and stamped a bit to stimulate the circulation to her feet, which had fallen asleep after being braced during the long, bumpy, and – by Makahomian standards – lightning-fast drive from Hissim. She said, 'I have to go back to town. I can't let Edu keep lying to the people.'

'What will you do?' Acorna asked.

Nadhari shrugged. 'Start a little coup all my own, I suppose. I've done that sort of thing before. And these are my own people. It shouldn't be that difficult.'

Miw-Sher asked, 'We've come a long way. It will be full night before you can reach the city. How well do you see in the dark?'

'Better with an infrared scope on a high-powered laser,' Nadhari replied. 'Otherwise, about average.'

'That is something worth knowing. You and the High Priest share ancestry. If you don't have the gift of night sight, then he probably lacks it as well. The ability runs strongly through family lines. I see as well in darkness as any guardian.'

'Nice for you, but I don't see what good it does me. I should have known Edu would try something like this. When he was young, he liked pulling the wings off insects. When he was a bit older, he tormented songbirds, then hawks, that sort of thing. The priests were appalled by the waste of life, but my uncle said Edu was just practicing his warrior skills. I don't think Edu has changed much. He's just more ambitious.'

'That's interesting,' Miw-Sher said, 'for I regret to inform you, Lady Nadhari, that the most recent thing that the High Priest publicly pulled off was the arms and legs of your uncle. When the old Mulim objected, the Mulzar had him walled up.'

'His was the voice I heard when I took the passage you showed me?' Acorna asked.

Miw-Sher nodded. 'A little food is passed through a slot in the wall for him – I know, because feeding the Mulim has been among my daily duties, and I often take Grimla to spend a few moments with him. There are ventilation holes on the top of the tail-wall. There were once several anchorites like the old Mulim, but they've died to this world.'

'I see,' Acorna said.

Tagoth and Nadhari were now standing very close to each other. 'Be careful, Nadhari,' Tagoth told her. 'I hope I don't have to tell you how dangerous Edu can be. I would go with you to help you, but my duty lies elsewhere. I must warn the Aridimi priesthood and help them to defend the sacred lake. My path lies deep into the desert, at the Aridimi Stronghold.'

'I've always known Edu was a sociopath,'

Nadhari said. 'I had good reason to find out quite early in life.'

'I know.' Tagoth's voice dropped almost to a whisper.

'But I am not a child any longer.' Nadhari's own voice hardened with anger. 'Edu is not the only one who is dangerous.'

Their conversation stopped suddenly as an amazing apparatus appeared overhead. Acorna recognized it at once as the flitter the Linyaari techno-artisans had been modifying with their distinctive artwork before the Khleevi attack. It was in the shape of a flying Ancestor with wings decorated in gilt, embellished with all of the colors worn in Ancestral livery and tack. Becker and Mac had salvaged it. Now it swooped down, Becker at the helm, to settle onto the sand, its wings still upraised. RK hopped down from the wagon and strolled over to the flitter, where Becker stretched out his hands to receive the first mate's paws as RK sprang from the ground onto Becker's shoulders.

'Hey, he's glad to see me. Tired of being worshipped, are you, old man?'

RK closed his eyes and purred. Miw-Sher carried Grimla, while Pash and Haji leaped from the wagon to the hull of the flitter. Sher-Paw alone approached more slowly, sniffing around and curling his lip.

Acorna said, 'I can see that your hands are full. I can take the helm, Captain.'

'Well, uh, I had to leave in kind of a hurry, Princess. Seems we've worn out our welcome back in Hissim. There's half an army sitting there,

245

waiting for our return. I'm not quite sure where we ought to go from here. And on top of that, there's only room for three of us with all this cargo I've got stuffed in here.'

'Tagoth and Nadhari won't be coming with us. They have other plans,' Acorna told him. 'Miw-Sher and the cats should come with us, I think. There is room for the cats, isn't there?'

He felt a lightness on his shoulders and looked around. All four of the Temple cats and RK were up to their hind legs in the open bag of cat food he'd brought with him.

'Yeah. Looks like it,' Becker said.

'Guess that leaves me with the Vikings to hoof it,' MacDonald said.

But as Acorna climbed into the cockpit of the flitter, the sound of an approaching mounted force thundered from beyond the dunes. A dozen riders galloped up on the Ancestor-like beasts and slid to a stop, raising a cloud of dust as they surrounded the wagons.

'Raiders?' Acorna asked Tagoth and Nadhari.

'Not necessarily,' Tagoth said. He put himself between the newcomers and the flitter and wagons, and said a few words to the riders in an unfamiliar dialect.

Then he turned back to MacDonald. 'These are the heads of families from the steppes beyond the Mog-Gim Plateau. They have heard from their relatives in the city that you have magic boxes that grow food, and that you can heal sick beasts. They want the boxes and the healing.'

MacDonald smiled amiably at them and said, 'That's what we're here for. This wagon right here is all yours, boys. Haul 'er away. As for the healing, I have a few tricks up my sleeve, but I haven't tried 'em yet, so we'll just have to see how much good I can do you on that score.'

Acorna examined the sweating, straining beasts the men were riding. She could see the signs of the plague in them. Some of these animals would not make it back where they came from again if she and her friends did not intercede. She beckoned to MacDonald and picked up Pash, carrying him with her. He purred like a buzz saw in her arms.

'Tagoth, please tell these gentlemen that Captain MacDonald and I will attempt to treat these sick beasts with the help of this sacred guardian cat,' Acorna said.

Tagoth declared their intention in priestly intonations worthy of the Mulzar at his most pompous.

'Okay, Ambassador, honey, what do we do now?' MacDonald whispered. 'I can't cure these critters on the spot, you know.'

'With the help of the sacred cat, I can.'

'If the sacred cat is so darned important, how come they needed you to cure them?'

'Oh, it's a healer's thing. Most of the time a healer cannot heal him or herself.'

'Okay, I guess I'll buy that.'

'You take that side of the beast and look clinical and busy. We'll take this other side, and I'll help Pash heal.'

'Gotcha.' And aloud he said, 'Lay on them healin' paws, O holy cat!'

Pash looked inquiringly at Acorna. She held

247

Pash up to the beast and leaned in with the cat so that her horn touched the beast's hide as she pretended to listen to Pash meow the results of this examination.

The three of them repeated this operation with each of the sick beasts until MacDonald declared them cured, dusting his hands to emphasize that the task was done.

'We have many more beasts that need curing, including our own sacred cats,' the man said. 'And we want your food boxes.'

'Okay,' MacDonald said agreeably, then turned to Acorna, 'Whatcha think, Ambassador? How do we work this?'

'You and the Wats drive a wagon behind the riders. If they will be so kind as to have one of their number lead us to their Temple, I will supervise the curing of their cats there while you demonstrate the use of the food boxes and examine their other beasts out in their fields. Then I will try to visit the rainforest Temple and heal their cats, and come back to see what I can do for the other beasts.'

'Acorna,' Becker protested, 'you're gonna wear yourself out that way.'

'Perhaps,' she said, raising and lifting a shoulder in a shrug. 'But this is an emergency. We have a planet and a species to save. What else can we do? Lead the way, Captain MacDonald. We'll be right along.'

She looked around for Tagoth and Nadhari, but they both had somehow melted into the desert without anyone seeing them leave.

She silently wished them well on their separate missions.

As MacDonald jiggled his reins and clicked his tongue at the beasts pulling the first wagon in their little convoy, he was followed by the wagons driven by Sandy Wat and Red Wat. Just as they disappeared off in the distance, another party of people arrived, this time a group of mixed sexes and on foot.

The stout woman who seemed to be their leader said to Acorna, 'I watched you on the balcony with the Mulzar. So, are you going to help us or not?' She gave a nod toward the last wagonload of boxes, the one that Nadhari had driven, which was now driverless, its beast of burden seemingly pleased to be standing still instead of moving.

'I am afraid we can't remain here to help you right now,' Acorna said. 'As I'm sure you know, the Mulzar wants to imprison us and kill the sacred cats, and we must save ourselves and them. But we can give you all the tools you need to help yourself. They are in that wagon, if you would like to have them.'

'Well, then, we'll take them with us. This thing can only slow you down and you cannot take it when you fly through the air, can you? When the Mulzar leaves to fight his battles, you and the spaceman come back and help us to use these. Fighting's all very well for the warriors who'll be able to live off *our* land, but with our beasts all gone and the drought and all, we farmers have no other options. We will starve.'

'Not if you use those boxes. We will seek other answers for you as well. We are going abroad to other lands to see how they have dealt with the sickness.'

'You do that. And keep our sacred cats safe, will you? Bring them back with those kittens you promised our people.'

The woman's face and voice were determined, but she winked at Acorna – or maybe it was Becker, since she wore a rather saucy expression as she flounced up onto the buckboard and clucked at the beasts, turned them, and waited while the rest of her party climbed aboard with the boxes before driving off again.

It seemed that the Mulzar's people had made their minds up after his balcony performance. And Acorna thought again that Edu Kando was in for a surprise when he learned who they believed and which side they were on.

'Well, I can see you've been busy,' Becker said. 'We'd better fly before anybody else shows up looking for help or a buddy to help start the revolution.'

Acorna nodded and they ascended in the flitter, accelerating until they saw the dust from the various riders and the wagons. Flying past the riders close enough above them to be seen and yet not so close as to frighten the beasts, Acorna tipped the wings of the flitter. One rider broke off from the others and rode hard to the south, waving at her to follow. Acorna allowed the man to get ahead of them, then swooped after him.

Soon they were no longer in the desert, but were sailing over broad foothills and plains, crisscrossed with rivers and streams – the landscape of the steppes she recalled from Nadhari's mental images. They saw the Temple long before their guide reached it. It sat in the middle of a green river delta. The cat whose shape this temple bore was long and hunkered down to drink – its tongue was a drawbridge, now lowered, and its tail a wall to a moat. Guardian priests stood behind its ears.

Surrounding it on the green were herds of beasts, and from the air a mile away Acorna could smell their sickness.

Acorna said, 'We should stop and help them.'

RK replied, (Cats first. Those are just ordinary food animals. What good are they compared with the lives of Grimla's and the guys' fellow holy cats?)

(You have no objection to eating those animals you disdain so much,) Acorna told the cat rather sharply.

To her surprise, RK actually considered for a moment, then said, (Hmmm, right you are. Still, cats first, then the food beasts.)

(If there are any cats still living at this Temple,) Acorna said, her voice tight at the grim thought that they might have died while she dallied in Hissim.

(Oh, most of them are still alive. I can hear that. But they are very sick and already have lost two of their number,) RK told her.

And suddenly Acorna heard them too. Thin, plaintive yowls, sick strangled coughing, and the kittens – the poor little things were as quiet and limp as damp rags. Becker said, 'You and the kid and the cats go do your thing, Princess. I'll guard the flitter and lift off in case anyone tries to hijack it.'

Acorna said, 'I don't suppose anyone here would know how to fly it anyway.'

'You never know,' Becker replied.

SIXTEEN

Miw-Sher scrambled out of the flitter before Acorna, and spoke to the crowd in her own language. Acorna was too overwhelmed with the mental pleas of the sick cats to pay much attention to her friend's words. In the courtyard, people began to gather. Most of them carried cats in their arms, all of whom were limp and listless looking. Many, many more cats had survived here than in Hissim. Miw-Sher spoke to the people quickly and urgently while the Hissim Temple cats leaped down after her and prowled among the legs of the gathering crowd.

When Acorna climbed from the flitter, a hush fell over the assembly. For a moment she stared down at the tops of bald heads, dark heads, red heads, all clothed in robes of rough scarlet cloth. In the evening sky the scarlet suns drooped one after the other, and through the mist rising from the river's surface, a pair of moons began to rise, each seeming to have a slice cut from its right side.

Acorna stepped out among them and looked at Miw-Sher. 'What did you tell them?'

'I said that you are the one prophesied to save us, and that you could heal our sacred ones. I told

253

them the healthy Temple cats who came with us were proof of your powers, but they didn't need proof. Many recognized you.'

'Recognized me? But I've never been here before,' Acorna said. She didn't wait for them to explain, however, but reached for the first sick cat. She clucked to RK to jump up on her shoulder. (You're my cover. Look useful. Like some kind of cat miracle worker. I don't want them to know how I do this.)

(Happy to oblige, but I don't think they care.)

Acorna saw that he was right. The first person she approached knelt and held up the patient, a black-and-white-spotted cat with a black nose and pads. The cat was too limp to raise his head, but RK perched on Acorna's shoulder and licked the sick cat's ear. Acorna carefully knelt, so as not to dislodge RK, and laid her face in the stricken cat's damp fur so that her horn ran along his spine.

And the cat, still held in the upraised hands of its human friend, bloomed out of his withered state, stretched all four paws out into the air, gave RK a baleful look for taking such liberties, rolled off the hands that had held it, and strolled away, presumably in the direction of a food dish. Which reminded Acorna of how the cat had probably come to be ill. 'Miw-Sher, would you catch that last patient, please? Thank you. Captain Becker, if you would be so kind as to bring some of our cat food cargo down here to share among the convalescents, we can tell these folks about the tainted food after we revive their guardians.'

By that time she had moved along to the next cat. But before she healed it, she called again to

Miw-Sher, who was poking the black nose of the black-and-white cat into the food bag Becker lowered to the ground. 'Miw-Sher, would you please sort the patients for me? Kittens and mothers should be treated first, in order of the sickest to the least affected, followed by the rest of the adults in the same order. There are so many I'm afraid we may lose some before I finish.'

Miw-Sher hurried to comply, reorganizing the handlers and cats while Acorna and RK made contact with the next patient.

This ailing party was an especially large creature with tawny spots on a black coat and tufted ears. Her coat was smooth and she was still strongly muscled beneath it. Acorna thought that this one had not been ill very long. It took only the slightest touch before the big feline raised her head and gave a lick to RK's nose and Acorna's hand. Then she adroitly flipped herself out of the grip of her handler and prowled over to investigate the food bag Becker had dragged into the Temple yard.

Before tending the next patient, Acorna called, 'Captain, I don't think we need to guard the food bag or the flitter here. You might check with one of the priests and see if relief packages containing food have recently arrived from Hissim. If so, reseal the package and keep it safe until Captain MacDonald can arrive to analyze it.'

Becker gave her a small salute and hurried off.

A priestess held out a mother cat, nearly dead, and a basket of tiny feeble kittens, blind, all but bald, and smaller than most of the mice Acorna had seen on Kezdet.

As RK extended his neck to lick, there was a sudden hiss and RK sprang away. Instantly he was replaced by Grimla, now all purrs and maternal concern. Or perhaps, considering her age, grand-maternal concern. After Acorna touched each patient with her horn, Grimla groomed them. First she groomed a kitten, then licked the mother, then groomed another kitten, until all were as normal as a new mother and very small babies could be.

RK strolled unconcernedly over to the food bag, pausing to lick his fur back into place. (She only had to say she wanted to help. No need to get huffy.)

Acorna felt his surprise as Miw-Sher knelt down to pet him, scratch his ears and whiskers, and tell him, 'Grimla meant you no disrespect, noble ship's cat. But she feels a strong responsibility for rearing our young and believes that it is too delicate a job to leave to the uncertain affections of a tom.'

RK looked up at her and gave an aggrieved 'meow' and headbutted her leg.

Three more litters of kittens and mothers, and then a basket of kittens without a mother. 'Where is she?' Acorna asked.

A youth of about fourteen with a shaved head, and bright, watery brown eyes answered in a carefully controlled voice.

'Died in delivery,' Miw-Sher answered, translating the unfamiliar dialect for Acorna. 'Before the others took sick. The mother was his special charge.'

'But then these little ones cannot have eaten the tainted food,' Acorna said.

'No, Lady. They are simply too small to do without a mother, and very hungry.'

Grimla dismounted from Acorna's shoulder and meowed from the ground, looking up at Acorna, at the basket, and at the boy holding it, then meowing again.

'She wants to adopt them,' Miw-Sher interpreted again. And to the boy she said, 'Set down the basket. My guardian lady Grimla will feed them.'

(She's too old,) RK said. (That old queen hasn't seen a decent heat in years.)

(Don't be such a sore loser,) Acorna told him. And this time she knelt to pet Grimla, touching her horn to the old cat's underside. The withered teats plumped up almost at once and Grimla, purring, accepted the orphaned kittens as Miw-Sher and the boy tenderly placed them one at a time to feed.

Many cats later, Acorna felt as though she were swimming through mud. She was so tired and so drained, she felt she could barely move.

She lowered her head to touch a particularly sick tabby and her knees buckled. Becker was at her side immediately, his arm shoring her up as she fought her way back to wakefulness. When her eyes focused again she was surprised to see that the suns were once more high in the sky, the moons long since set.

'Hey there, Princess,' Becker said. 'You're getting a little see-throughish in the old horn area. They still had a *lot* of kitties here, huh? And now they'll keep them, thanks to you.'

'Just . . . a few more,' she said.

But Miw-Sher was kneeling beside her, saying, 'No, Lady. That is all. They are all well. The food bag is empty, however. Pash, Sher-Paw, and Haji are not happy. And Grimla will need to eat soon to replenish her milk.'

'Then bring me the tainted food,' Acorna whispered hoarsely to Becker. Her neck ached from lowering it to touch the fur of the cats.

'You can't detoxify that,' Becker whispered back. 'You haven't got enough left in you. You need to eat something yourself and get some rest before you do anybody else.'

They had been speaking so urgently, with their heads close together, that when one of the priests tapped Becker on the shoulder he drew back on the man before he saw that the priest was pointing to the flitter. Its com unit was sending a signal for him to receive a transmission.

Acorna reluctantly accepted his help to half carry her back up to the flitter, and when she was seated, he toggled the unit. 'Captain,' Mac said, 'how is the flitter working out for you? Isn't it a fine one? Did you rescue our crew members?'

'Mac?' Becker said. 'Are you nuts? Or did the information escape you that the Federation monitors all transmissions, in case there are any, which there shouldn't be because they're all messed up by the dampening field.'

'Oh, that! By my count we are now in violation of perhaps fifty separate Federation directives. I thought if you had rescued everyone satisfactorily, I would just give you a hail and acquaint you with the many excellent features I installed on your little vessel.'

'A cat-food replicator would have been nice,' Becker said. 'But look, buddy, I appreciate what you've done but we can't talk now. If the Federation is listening, it's just that my friend knows how to make his voice carry really well and we aren't actually using any technology at all.'

Mac remained cheerily sanguine. 'Actually, Captain, they seem to have forgotten about us. They do not realize that I am still aboard, or that we retained special Linyaari com technology from our original communications equipment, which I repaired after the helpful technicians installing the new equipment left. You see, the Linyaari utilize technology that the Federation does not. Some of their communication systems are laser-based. Lasers will naturally penetrate the dampening fields, which are set up to prevent radio and electronic transmissions, and so we will be able to converse freely and without interference or even observance from the Makahomian spaceport. I have also installed on the flitter an excellent Linyaari scanner you had stored in the cargo bay. Of course it is not engineered for use on such a ship, and I had to make some adjustments to its function to retrofit that device to the conveyance, as well as all the other devices I mentioned earlier. But it all seems to work well enough for our current purposes.'

'That's cool, Mac.'

'And, Captain, I do not think we need to worry too much about the Federation interference. There are not many personnel remaining here anyway. The Mulzar seems to be massing an army for an attack, and all available Federation troops except for a small skeleton crew are now riding beasts or manning chariots to monitor the situation. It has been vastly entertaining.'

Becker whistled with surprise. 'Do tell? Now that is a very interesting piece of intel, good buddy. But don't call us, we'll call . . .' And with that a blast of static replaced the transmission.

'Huh,' Becker said, 'I think Mac got outfoxed this time. We'll try again later when the Federation com people have gone on their break. Maybe we better move it.'

Acorna said, 'We can't leave these cats without good food.'

'Are you kidding? Those greedy pussycats have filled up on the food we brought with us till their guts are dragging between their paws. They're not going to be hungry again for another day or two. You need to rest and recharge. Then we can see about food.'

'I'll rest on the way.'

Miw-Sher stood in the courtyard looking from the basket containing Grimla and the kittens, guarded by the boy, to the flitter and back again, clearly torn about leaving her favorite guardian behind.

(Bring the brats, too, if the old girl won't leave them,) RK said with a yawn. There was plenty of room for him and the others in the flitter's fourth space now that the food bag was gone.

Acorna wearily translated his remark to Becker, her tongue thick in her mouth and her words barely coherent.

Becker called out, 'Sheri, honey, bring the old

cat and kittens and come on. Remember those other pussycats Acorna needs to cure!'

Miw-Sher knelt beside the boy and said something, then turned to Becker. 'He cannot be separated from them. He was captured from the rainforest himself. Can he come with us, too?'

Again Acorna translated, though she was so tired she was barely able to speak. Becker looked behind him where RK and the other three Temple cats had spread themselves over all available space, the three Temple cats napping, RK regarding his shipmate somewhat cynically.

'Yeah, sure, why not? The more the merrier. At least we know he's not allergic to cats.'

After that Acorna drifted in and out of sleep, but when she roused again as the flitter banked sharply, she was aware of Miw-Sher's voice and the boy's both calling out to Becker.

The flitter was riding high above a canopy of deep copper forest, the leaves below them too thick to see the ground. However, off to the right something both coppery and smooth rose from the leaves, curling above them. Miw-Sher and the boy were pointing at this. As the flitter descended carefully, slowly, Acorna saw that the smooth thing was the curled tip of the tail of another cat Temple. The pose of the structure was a cat in a long stretch, its tail and hindquarters supported high in the air by tower-like hind legs and paws. Its front paws were outstretched and a long staircase led between them up to the cat's open mouth. Most amazing here were the eyes, which were not open or blank windows as the eyes in the other Temples had been. These were lensed with chrysoberyls the size of the *Condor*'s viewport.

Becker whistled, 'Good thing Hafiz isn't here.'

Acorna nodded. Her eyes still refused to focus clearly in the dappled jungle light, since it seemed to her that the surface of this Temple, unlike the others, was alternately rough and shining. But as they drew closer she saw that the sides were tiger-striped with rows of smaller chrysoberyl stones. Spaced here and there, high up on the sides and back of the cat, as well as on the arms and legs and sides of the face, were small platforms with dark spaces behind. Other platforms were occupied by large cats. Some of these cats were black with tawny spots, like the one on the steppes. Some were tawny with black spots and looked more like the pictures of cheetahs from Old Terra. Others were black with tawny stripes. Still others were just black or just tawny but more than the cats of Hissim or the cats of the steppes, these looked as if they had been bred from a limited gene pool. They were all much larger than RK or any of the other Temple cats Acorna had seen.

Furthermore, they all looked healthy. Ferocious too as all of them rose at once, regarding the flitter with baleful eyes brighter even than the chrysoberyls. Then the screaming began, half shrill and piercing, half a deep, rumbling roar.

The Temple cats shocked Acorna and Becker by screaming back. Even RK used a voice neither of his shipmates had ever heard before. Instead of cowering away from the awful sound, the cats plastered themselves against the viewports and shrieked, whether in challenge or greeting even Acorna couldn't say.

Because of the dense vegetation surrounding the Temple, the flitter had to pass within a few feet of the Temple walls, and a couple of the more enterprising guardians leaped onto the hatch covering with mighty thumps, and screamed again.

Fortunately, by that time the flitter had nearly landed.

'We got here in time!' Miw-Sher cried excitedly, gripping Acorna's shoulder. 'These guardians still glow with vitality and health!'

Acorna automatically translated the girl's remark for Becker, who said, 'Yeah, but will we if we try to get past them? Lookit the hooks on those beasties, will you?'

Acorna was looking into the cavernous mouth of the cat over her head as it screamed again, playfully this time, dabbing a saber-sharp claw at her.

RK immediately was on her shoulders and scratching at the top of the hatch. The other cat closed its mouth and put its nose to the glass. RK did the same.

(She's okay, just doing her job.) RK's thoughts were full of randy cat images that made Acorna giggle. He reminded her of Becker when he'd first seen Nadhari. (Her name is Haruna. Rrrrrrrowl. When do you go into heat again, beautiful?)

SEVENTEEN

Despite the first mate's desperation to have no hatch between him and the new object of his lust, Becker obstinately waited until human beings, armed and dangerous and clad in very little, poured from and around the Temple, each of them accompanied by a bevy of felines.

(We are friends,) Acorna broadcasted. (We came to warn you and to help you, if necessary.)

Having entered into their minds, she now met their eyes as they peered in at her.

Haruna and her companion apparently understood for, much to RK's disappointment, they dismounted. Then the people began talking excitedly among themselves, in a dialect new to Acorna.

'What are they saying, Miw-Sher?' Acorna asked. Miw-Sher didn't notice at first that she had been addressed, as the boy was pointing out features of the Temple to her.

'Oh,' she said when she turned back to Acorna, 'they're simply telling each other that you are the one and you have come as prophesied.'

'It's so nice that everyone but me knows about that,' Acorna said a bit crossly. She was tired of many things, including her reputation, which had so unexpectedly preceded her nearly everywhere on this planet.

'At least you can rest here, Princess,' Becker said. 'These pussycats are fine as feline fur. *You* look like you need healing more than they do.'

He raised the hatch and climbed out. Acorna and the others followed him. The sight of the boy caused one of the women to cry out and rush forward to embrace him. He was glad to see her, but disentangled himself rather quickly to show her the kittens. The Hissim Temple cats began mingling with the locals, and RK sidled up to Haruna. He was trying to get close enough to growl sweet nothings into her tufted ears, Acorna supposed.

For a few moments the locals chattered busily about everything, and Miw-Sher and the boy chattered with them. Then, as if recalling their manners, the woman, who was surely a relative of the boy's if not his mother, gestured for Becker and Acorna to ascend the steps carved between the cat Temple's outstretched front paws and up onto the tongue and into the mouth.

More stairs led them through the torso of the Temple, the interior of which was lined with beautiful murals, accented by wall sconces holding torches – currently unlit – to provide illumination when necessary. During daylight hours, as Acorna could see, the building had more than sufficient natural light because of all of the open areas leading to the exterior platforms where the Temple cats perched. If the cats wished to ascend the Temple's outer walls, they could simply leap from one platform to the next, and descend in the same manner. There were also a number of interior platforms, should the cats wish to seek shelter inside the building.

It was a bit unnerving to watch the cats leap from platform to platform right through the Temple. As Acorna and her friends walked through the building's halls, Temple cats of every color and size appeared occasionally, often seeming to shoot out of the walls and fly through the air of the passageways above their heads. But after a while even Acorna and Becker grew used to the sudden rush of air as a fully extended furry body sailed from one side of the Temple to the other, as if crossing a jungle ravine.

Although Acorna had enjoyed some rest in the flitter on the way, the climbing tired her further and her feet felt heavy and clumsy as she set them on one step and then another.

And then her feet were no longer touching the steps and she felt pressure on the backs of her thighs, knees, and upper arms as six people adroitly inserted themselves between her body and the effects of gravity on it, lifting her up onto their shoulders and bearing her among them.

'Hey,' Becker said, 'how does a person get prophesied about around here? I'm kinda tired, too, you know.'

Much to her surprise, the high priestess was not wearing robes as the priests in the other two cities did. In fact, she was wearing nothing except a coat of her own home-grown fur, pointed ears, and long elegant whiskers.

Miw-Sher gasped and Acorna caught her

thought. (She can keep her cat form during the day!)

The creature on the throne beckoned languidly and growled/purred to Acorna, 'So you are the one who He said was coming.'

Becker, who had not been in on the change in conversation and wasn't sure if the high priestess was friend or foe, stepped in front of Acorna. 'Who said she was coming and what did he say about her? Did he tell you she would heal all the sick cats? Because she did. Did he tell you she outsmarted the Mulzar of Hissim, otherwise known as the King of Everything? She did that, too.'

The cat priestess stretched out her paw-hand and ran a single claw along Becker's jaw, drawing a thin line of blood. RK suddenly reached up a paw and smacked at the hand. *'Mine!'* he said clearly in his own tongue.

The priestess snatched her hand back. 'Excuse me, little brother. I didn't realize he had a guardian. He seems to think he is one himself.'

Becker stooped down and scratched RK's ears, whispering, 'It's okay, big fella. It's not her fault. I seem to have this animal magnetism for cat ladies. You remember how Nadhari was about me when we first met.'

Acorna said, 'He's right. I don't know what has been said about me before I arrived and I would like to find out. But first, since your cats are all well, I must tell you that there is a "gift" shipment of food and medicines coming from Hissim. You mustn't accept it. It's contaminated with an organism that will kill your guardians – and

267

maybe you, too. I made a vaccine that could give you some protection, but there's not enough of it for all of these cats. The ones in Hissim all died except these few that came with us.'

The boy set the basket containing Grimla and kittens at the high priestess's feet and Pash, Haji, and Sher-Paw stepped forward as if they were characters in some feline crèche pageant.

The spotted light from the holes in the walls dappled everyone so that they resembled the large cats. The heat made the air shimmer in a way that caused Acorna to feel as if the whole thing was one of Hafiz's holograms.

The cat lady returned her attention to Acorna. 'There is something you must see. Perhaps then you will understand.'

Flowing from the throne, the high priestess stepped to one side of the platform and beckoned. 'You may use this if you wish,' she said, gesturing to a column with steps carved in a spiral around it, descending into darkness. She murmured something else Acorna didn't catch and then dove headfirst into the hole.

Miw-Sher translated. 'She said she'd take the shortcut.'

'I believe I'll use the stairs,' Acorna said.

'You're still lookin' puny, Princess,' Becker told her. 'You think you can go down that thing without getting dizzy and falling off?'

'There's a handhold,' Miw-Sher said, pointing out a groove carved into the column. It ran at about waist height and parallel to the stairs. 'And I'll go first. You can hold on to my shoulder, Ambassador, if you feel faint.'

'Thank you, Miw-Sher,' Acorna said. 'I believe I'll manage going down.'

And she did.

As she descended lower and lower, gripping the handhold with the tips of her fingers and occasionally touching Miw-Sher's shoulder for balance, she became aware that it was not entirely dark below. Thousands of gold coins with slots in the middle glittered up at her until suddenly, as the light from above grew too dim to see their feet, the space below was lit by one torch after another.

She had the sense that a few of the priests holding the torches had hastily covered their private parts, after transforming from their feline state. Of the felines large and small that lay in every imaginable attitude up and down the length of the room, she could not have said if they had declined to transform or were unable to.

Their eyes no longer glittered but blinked lazily in the light, or slitted, or in some cases showed the milky inner membrane that protected the eyes. There was no catty smell at all. In fact, it smelled fresher down here than it had in the open, with the jungle vegetation hemming the Temple so closely.

The high priestess beckoned them. 'This way,' she said, and Miw-Sher continued translating. 'We are now in the most sacred part of the Temple. Ours was the place where first the Star Cat and the Companion landed to save our people and transform them from the refugee rabble they once had been.'

Their shadows and those of the cats stretched,

danced, and gyrated ahead of them, long and deeply black.

This space felt ancient, filled with secrets sealed with the deaths of many defenders and foes for generations reaching far back into time. The feeling was far more threatening, more mysterious, than the caves of the early Ancestral Attendants on Vhiliinyar, where Acorna had uncovered part of the buried history of her own people, but all the same she was reminded of those caves.

As Acorna followed, noting that even the lay-out of these caves was similar, the high priestess turned into a side passage that narrowed until they had to stand sideways to slip through it. This was not made any easier by all the feline bodies that suddenly simply *had* to come along. Cats flowed under kneecaps and over feet, leaped upon shoulders, plastered themselves against faces, greatly impeding breathing, then passed to the other side and leaped off. In the tight quarters, it became a rather chilling sensation in spite of the cats' warm fur, until one of the furry intruders suddenly spoke inside her head: (Excuse me, pardon me, oops, sorry, coming through.)

(RK!)

(Acorna! Oh, sorry, 'scuse me, I'll just get my paw out of your ear. There. Better?)

(Much.)

(I had to come down and check out my roots, didn't I? If anybody knows, I have a feeling it's this lady. Besides, Haruna pushed me. Spirited female.)

(Yes, and big enough to eat you in one bite.)

(Well, I always think a little danger adds to the excitement of a pursuit.)

Suddenly the way widened, the air freshened, and they could walk freely again. Acorna saw something gleaming wetly in the high priestess's torchlight. As the other priests unfolded from their feline forms and stood to light torches again, she saw that the room's center contained a small, perfect lake, its dark waters glinting in the dim torchlight.

But the lake was not what the priestess had brought them to see. She flourished her torch to illuminate the walls.

Like the Ancestral caverns of Vhiliinyar, where the walls were covered with complex hieroglyphics, these caves, too, were heavily embellished, but the markings here were very different from those back on Vhiliinyar.

These cave walls were covered with crude drawings, simple boxy line figures scratched into rock, some with a few vestiges of paint still adorning them, but most were simply ghostly white lines against the dark surface. The further back in the cave the priestess walked, the fainter and more primitive the drawings became.

Finally the priestess pointed the torch at a single panel of drawings on the cave's wall. Acorna examined the images lit by its glow. A tall boxy thing with triangles on either side of it dominated the picture, but next to the tall boxy thing stood several people. The person standing to the left of the center drawing seemed to be quite tall, standing on what were clearly human feet, but wearing two triangles atop his head – cats' ears, it appeared – and something long and thin was coming out from his legs. Acorna supposed that the thing could be meant to be an exaggerated male member, but judging from the context of the image she felt that it was more probably a tail. Next to this person sat a largish but nonetheless fairly normal-looking cat, also distinguishable by its ears and tail. Next to the cat stood a stylized figure of a man the same size as the cat man, but with a round head, unadorned by pointy ears, and with no tail.

The figure on the far side of the ship was more difficult to see. Here the sacred lake's water lapped close to the side of the cave. Acorna slid her hoofed feet around the rim of floor and leaned in, gesturing to the priestess that the torch be shoved further forward, too.

When she finally was able to see the figure clearly, she realized she had been expecting something of exactly this sort. Yet the surprise that it was actually there was so great that she almost fell into the lake. As her mind reeled and her balance faltered, however, a clawed hand grabbed her arm and pulled her back upright.

The crude, dimly lit humanoid figure had one elongated triangle on its head instead of two. The triangle was located squarely in the middle of the person's head. Like a horn. The entire mural was a petroglyph of her dream.

Emerging from the underworld of the Temple was like emerging from another dream. Acorna felt as if she were awakening. She knew that the figure in the cave drawing was a Linyaari. In fact, she was sure that it was Aari. Involuntarily, her hand went to Aari's birth disk. It *was* him. That was why everyone on this planet seemed to believe that she had some special significance in their – what? History? Religion? Myth cycle?

'You okay, Princess?' Becker asked as he helped her up the last step and onto the platform beside the throne, where the cat woman was already lounging. 'You look like you've seen a ghost.'

'Very astute, Captain. I almost have. I think – no, I'm *sure* that Aari has been here.'

'When? How? Why didn't anybody say anything?'

'They *have* said something – to me. And as for when, it was a very long time ago. They just showed me an ancient petroglyph of a Linyaari. It had to be Aari – he's the only Linyaari we know of who has done a lot of traveling through time and space. And that petroglyph definitely depicted a Linyaari.'

Miw-Sher popped her head out of the hole. 'Yes, Ambassador. You saw the Companion of the Star Cat, who alone was privileged to call him by his most sacred name, Grimalkin. Tagoth says the Companion was a being like yourself, and personally foretold your coming. I saw the glyph long ago, when I was small, before my capture.'

The priestess's guards, human and feline alike, glared at the newcomers chattering away so near the throne of their ruler, and Acorna quickly led her friends down the steps to a respectful distance. The priestess had not answered Acorna's questions or offered comments of her own. She simply smiled her enigmatic, catty smile and led them back from the cavern with a 'there, you see?' air, as if the petroglyph explained everything.

Acorna was very shaken; in fact, she was worried that she might even be broadcasting her feelings. Miw-Sher put her hand on Acorna's arm and said, 'Surely you understand that this is your fate. You are the one we knew would come. Surely you knew that, too?'

'Prophecy doesn't always work that way,' Acorna told her.

The high priestess spoke then, and Miw-Sher interpreted her words for Acorna. 'Shabasta is puzzled that you are so disturbed by what she has shown you. She says that the Companion and the Star Cat foretold that you would come and save us. The prophecy was a true one, since here you are. She now asks when you are planning to save us.'

Before Acorna could think of any reply to that, a sleek tawny cat with red ears, tail, and paws came bounding up the stairs, as if on cue. Its message was simple. 'Come.'

The high priestess, no doubt for dramatic effect, gathered her legs beneath her and from her sitting position leaped over the heads of her guests and a quarter of the way down the steps. Her court, or flock, or whatever the other tribal members were considered, followed after her, as did all of the cats except Grimla and the kittens.

Acorna and her friends, except for the boy, who was gathering up his small family, trailed behind the locals.

Jungle people with spears surrounded three

priests in Hissimi garb sitting in a wagon like the ones Captain MacDonald was using. The wagon was loaded with bundles.

'Ungrateful savages,' one of the priests muttered. 'We bring them emergency food and medical relief and they treat us like enemies.'

'We are enemies, holy brother, strictly speaking,' the youngest of the three priests said in an undertone.

'Not right at this moment,' whispered the third. Then, showing his teeth to the assembly, he announced in a loud voice, 'We are friends. We come in peace from the Mulzar of Hissim. He sends lovely gifts. Food, medicine.'

'Why should we need medicine?' the high priestess said.

'There's a terrible plague on our planet that has decimated the ranks of our own Temple cats,' the man explained.

Haji, Pash, and Sher-Paw strolled forward and faced the three, their tails jerking angrily.

'By their tails!' cried the eldest.

'And their whiskers!' cried the second.

'It's our own Temple guardians. What are they doing here? We heard of no raid. How did you capture them?'

'We didn't,' the priestess said. 'They came here with these people who were seeking refuge from the murderous Mulzar of Hissim.' Seeing the priests' confusion, Miw-Sher stepped forward and translated the words for the benefit of the Mulzar's men.

'Miw-Sher! What are you doing here? You traitor!'

The high priestess stalked forward, her tail switching, her yellow-green eyes slitted and her ears laid back into her golden-brown hair/fur.

The three priests fell silent, fear apparent in their eyes.

The priestess snarled at them. The big cats moved closer and closer to the Mulzar's men.

'Well, now,' Becker said, stepping back from the wagon and pulling Acorna with him, 'we can see you're busy with your new visitors – the ones we were telling you about, ma'am. I can see you have things under control. So we'll just be going now.'

No one said a word as he and Acorna, followed after a moment of indecision by Miw-Sher and RK, returned to the flitter. The three male guardians of the Hissim Temple followed behind them, and a moment afterwards, Grimla zoomed out the door and hopped in the flitter, too. The boy they'd brought home followed close behind Grimla, carrying the basket of kittens, which he set inside the flitter. Then he retreated a short distance away, standing with his family and waving good-bye.

The flitter rose above the trees and flew away from the jungle.

Nadhari had not gone far before the wagon driven by the women caught up with her. She figured she had two choices at that moment. She could either walk back to Hissim and possibly be discovered along the way by Edu's guards searching the roads for unusual travelers, or she could blend in with these women on the road, save herself some steps, and possibly win herself some allies.

She chose the second alternative and flagged the travelers down.

'Who are you?' demanded one, but another woman caught at her sleeve.

'It's Lady Nadhari!'

'Yes,' Nadhari agreed, 'that's me.'

'What are you doing out here?'

'I had to get my friends safely out of Hissim. I have done so, but I still have unfinished business with my cousin. I was hoping you could take me back to the city with you.'

'You'd best ride up top, then.'

'Thanks. I will, just for a little while. I think it might complicate your lives if I accompanied you all the way back. I'll make my own way once we're closer to Hissim.'

'You're cutting it close if you want to find the Mulzar. I have heard it said that the Mulzar is about to leave the city with the Fed'ration man.'

'I wonder why,' Nadhari said, though she had some idea of what might be driving him.

'Don't know, Lady, but I'm sure he's leaving soon. Maybe he's going after the cats.'

'Hah! Him?' said a younger woman. 'He don't care for cats. He's got no use for creatures got more'n two legs. Him, he likes that machinery like they got at the Fed'ration post.'

The woman shot an assessing glance at Nadhari that was, in the darkness, visible only as a gleam from the whites of her eyes. If she expected Nadhari to defend her cousin the Mulzar, she could relax, Nadhari thought. Edu was far worse than the woman thought he was. Nadhari knew from long experience that the only living creature Edu had ever cared about, two-legged or otherwise, was himself.

After that exchange, they rode in silence.

The little cavalcade halted once they reached the holding of the oldest woman in the outskirts of the city. None of them could pass through the gates into the middle of town until morning, so Nadhari took the time to demonstrate how to use the Metleiter boxes to her interested audience. She only hoped she remembered all of Scar MacDonald's instructions on how to get the boxes up and running correctly.

Then all the women but her hostesses – the youngest and the oldest of the ladies, a grandmother and her granddaughter – packed up their goods and their boxes and departed for their own homes. When the time came to seek a night's rest, Nadhari was perfectly willing to sleep in her new friends' stable. It was empty now because its former occupants had been slaughtered, victims of the recent plague, but the old woman and her granddaughter wouldn't hear of letting Nadhari bunk down there. Instead, they made a pallet for her on the floor near the cooking fire. They tried to insist that Nadhari take their bed, but she declined, saying that she needed to be able to flee quickly if necessary without involving them.

Which brought up the point of how Nadhari was going to get into the city in the morning. At the urging of her hostesses, she abandoned her plan to climb the walls of the city and wing it from there. After some discussion, the ladies convinced

278

Nadhari to borrow a gown from them so that she might pass though the main gate into Hissim without attracting undue attention.

Once settled onto a prickly pile of dry grass gathered into a loose sack, Nadhari fell deeply asleep, a skill she had learned in her years as a fighter. She knew she would rouse at the lightest footfall, ready to fight or run if the need arose. But this night, at least, passed peacefully.

The next morning the farm women dressed her in one of the grandmother's ragged spare gowns. They all piled into the wagon together and drove it back to the city's main gates. There the old woman regaled the guard with a tale of finding the vehicle, clearly the Temple's property, abandoned and empty on the desert's edge. As good citizens, she told him, they were returning it, and she was sure that the guard would reward them richly for their good deed.

That did the trick. The soldier confiscated the wagon, chided them for interfering in civic matters they did not understand, and sent the women away as fast as he could – empty-handed, of course.

By the time her friends had finished loudly arguing about the injustice of the guard's behavior, attracting the attention of every person within earshot, Nadhari had quietly made her way to the wall enclosing the Federation outpost.

The post was not large, as such places went, but it covered maybe five square miles, all of it walled, rather than fenced. She doubted electronics or surveillance equipment played a part in protecting this section. It seemed to depend on height and a guard who patrolled at intervals Nadhari timed by mentally counting hippopotamuses. She made her way through town to the end of the wall farthest from dwellings and from the post gate. The guard wasn't due to return for twenty minutes or so.

Though she had never been privileged to change into a cat, as Tagoth could, the perimeter wall provided no great challenge. She was over it and on the ground well before the guard was due to return. At that point, she thought she might ambush him or her and take the uniform. With that she would return to the *Condor* and send a message to some friends of hers in high places in the Federation. They might be interested in a few of the family stories she had to relate about the Mulzar and how he'd found a soulmate in the current post commander. If they were *not* interested, she was pretty sure she could persuade Hafiz to mount an investigation. Meanwhile, she would slip back over the wall and foment revolution and dissent, not necessarily in that order.

From the shadows where she lurked, quite at home, she saw a lone Federation officer approach an apparently disabled flitter. The flitter lay abandoned in the field between the wall and where the *Condor* and the *Traveler* were docked. The large spacegoing vessels blocked the small local transport craft from the view of the Federation headquarters building. So no one would see her take out the officer and relocate, in military parlance, his or her uniform to her own person.

Unfortunately she had lacked worthy op-

ponents since she'd taken the cushy job with
Hafiz. Her reflexes and defensive instincts were
not what they once had been. She circled around
behind the officer and grabbed him as he bent
toward the flitter.

But just then she was distracted by the *Condor*'s
robolift cranking and shuddering toward the
ground. She looked toward it for just a moment,
thinking somebody ought to oil that thing. And
that, of course, was when someone attacked *her*
from behind. No low-tech scruples for this
assailant, she thought as she crumpled to the
ground with the force of the stun waves from
the gun. It was her last thought for some time.

'For a horse-and-buggy civilization, these guys
make tracks,' Becker said, sounding worried.
'This is starting to look ugly. I'm guessing the
welcome wagons with the poison goodies are
Edu's advance guard. Soften 'em up with the
disease and then send in the regular troops to
finish them off or at least subdue them. Maybe we
should have left both of the kids with the cat
queen, rather than just one. The Mulzar won't
know for quite a while that his trick didn't work
at the jungle temple.'

Acorna didn't translate verbally this time. She
just transferred Becker's ideas into Miw-Sher's
head.

'You can't leave me behind,' Miw-Sher protested, without even questioning how she
understood Becker's words. 'You need me to
show you where to go – or at least *sort* of where
to go. We need to find my uncle Tagoth. We need

281

his help. We've got to get to the Aridimi Stronghold before the Mulzar's men do. It is really hard to find. Or at least that's what Tagoth says, but he knows how to get to it. He's been there before.'

Acorna patted the girl's hand, trying to cut through the questions and feelings that were cycloning through her own mind and concentrate instead on reassuring the frightened child. They both had a job to do.

'I'm sure that we can find Tagoth if we need to,' Acorna said. 'He can't have gone too far on foot. Had I known we were going to have the use of the flitter, I would have asked him to wait for us at some hidden place, and we could have all gone there together. But why is it we need to find this stronghold, especially right now? Do the Aridimi also have many cats and other creatures who could be endangered?'

'Oh, yes,' Miw-Sher said. 'Next to the Makaviti Temple, the Aridimi one is said to be the most highly guarded on our world. You see, it is where all of our sacred stones come from. I am sure that the Mulzar will be wild to get to it. Were it not for the Aridimi location being secret and hidden, all of the tribes would have raided it long ago, Tagoth says. It is so far out in the desert that none of our armies can survive the trip. But I believe we can get there in this conveyance.'

'So what heading should I take?' Becker said.

Acorna relayed the question and Miw-Sher said, 'North, as if to Hissim, but then west toward the dunes and white hills. We call them the Serpent's Spine. That is as far as I know how to go. But I think we should be able to see Uncle Tagoth easily from this machine. The desert is vast, but it is barren, and he will be going the same direction as we are.'

Acorna passed the information to Becker as they overflew the last of the rainforest and saw the terraced steppes rising before them, wrapped with glittering ribbons of water. This close to the jungle, and far from the Temple where Edu's plague had been introduced, the fields were healthy and fertile, covered with red, green, and golden grasses waving in the wind.

'Pit stop,' Becker announced, and landed the flitter.

'Why is he stopping?' Miw-Sher asked. 'I thought everyone agreed that we need to hurry.'

Acorna wanted to know exactly the same thing. She turned to Becker and asked him.

'Well, this is as close to safe as we're likely to be for quite a while. The first wave of bad guys headed in our direction have been apprehended by the jungle cat folk, who may be making lunch of them right now. I don't think the second wave is going to be coming in the next few minutes.

'So now is as good a time as any – maybe the best time for Linyaari girls who have healed well but not always wisely to graze and get drinks of water. All of us need a break – pussycats, too. Maybe they can catch a quick mouse or something – that is, if they can move after all they ate last night. We don't know what kind of reception we're in for.'

'But the stronghold . . .' Miw-Sher protested.

Becker held up his hand to ward off her

objection. 'If this Aridimi place is so hard to find, I bet their pussycats haven't got their nice present from the Mulzar yet, and we've got a little head start here, thanks to this flitter. We need to take the time to take care of ourselves. I think we should be as ready as we can be for whatever will happen. Heck, I have to go find a handy bush myself.'

Acorna didn't translate the last part. She did realize that Becker's point was well taken. She needed to eat and drink as well as rest long enough to catch her breath, if she was to do any more mass healings. Possibly he was also correct that the cats at the Aridimi Stronghold wouldn't require her help as a healer, but if they did, she must be prepared.

The place Becker had set the flitter down was as beautiful as any Linyaari dream of the lost homeworld. A stream frothed like fine lace over rocks that glittered with as many colors as a gemstone tiara. The water's depths were the soft, clear pink of rose quartz. Still, just to be safe, Acorna dipped her horn into the running water and also cleansed the grasses of the field before she ate them.

'RK, you and the guardians should bring any prey you catch to me to purify before you eat it.'

To the disgust of the cats, however, the fields were barren of even the smallest prey, which made Acorna fear that the plague had already spread farther among the animals of the world than she had previously believed.

The grasses were delicious, though, and the water as well. She enjoyed the chance to stretch and walk about. She was feeling more like herself by the time they reboarded the flitter.

That was when she realized Becker had not been following his own advice about relaxing. 'Mac, come in. Do you hear me? *Condor*, this is your captain speaking. Give me a call if you can hear my voice.' But despite his various attempts to adjust, repair, and reset the equipment, all he received in return was static.

Had Mac been a purely organic being, he might have felt chagrin at Becker's response to his attempt to ascertain the field functionality of the flitter and to educate the crew regarding its upgraded equipment. When the *Condor*'s com receiver suddenly filled with static, Mac's initial reaction had been that Captain Becker, in one of his customary fits of gruffness, had 'hung up' on him. But then he realized that the monitoring had somehow penetrated his careful programming and those who were doing the monitoring had cut off the transmission.

He needed to do something about that, but he wasn't sure what. His programming was now quite advanced, as evidenced in his promotion to uniformed crewman, but although he was capable of independent thought, he was not actually programmed to think strategically.

He was pondering what response if any would be appropriate when he observed irregular activity in the aft view screen. Earlier in the morning a flitter had made a short hop from behind the headquarters building to the field east of the *Condor*'s docking bay. Now three figures approached it, each from a different angle. Zooming in, he recognized the person nearest the flitter as Lieutenant Commander Macostut.

And very quickly, from the litheness of her movements and some other characteristics he had stored as recognition factors, he identified the second person, coming between Macostut and the third person, as Nadhari Kando. She would be wanting to board as soon as she had spoken to Macostut, he felt sure, so he lowered the robolift. The looked up, then fell down. The third figure, one Mac did not recognize except that a certain facial resemblance to Nadhari identified him as her cousin, the ruler of this place, placed a weapon in his belt and helped Macostut bind Nadhari and load her into the flitter. Before Mac could raise the robolift again and board it to go to her assistance, the flitter was over the wall and gone.

He stood inside the robolift as it lowered.

Once the lift met the ground, Mac understood that his presence and position would now be known to any who were watching from head-quarters. Therefore, he waved in a friendly fashion in that general direction. Two men emerged from the building, looking straight at him.

It seemed as good a time as any to undo the damage they had done to his communications system. He needed to warn the captain about the Federation flitter, and to advise him of Nadhari Kando's predicament.

Mac walked nonchalantly toward the troopers, wearing his customary friendly and diffident expression. He was, however, accessing the memories he had of the time when he was 'muscle' for Kisla Manjari. There were very few of these Federation people left on the post, and only a handful in the communications area. He would reason with them first, of course, and point out that their own commander had broken their prime rule against technological contamination of this world. If they disagreed or failed in any way to be other than helpful and cordial, he, who possessed the strength of about twenty fully organic men, would be forced to modify their physical configurations.

'Captain, shall I take the helm for a while?' Acorna asked. 'It would be easier for me to do so, since the controls are built for Linyaari hands.'

'You forget I fly with all kinds of alien equipment,' Becker said proudly, forgetting that they were on Makahomia precisely because he had added Khleevi equipment to his control array. 'Besides, you need to coordinate the mental communication around here. Might be too distracting for you to do that and fly, too. While you were resting up, I familiarized myself with some of Mac's upgrades. The scanner is a little clunky, but better than you'll find in any of the antique Federation buggies they have around here.'

Acorna nodded and settled down for a quick nap. She wasn't the only one to take advantage of the opportunity. Miw-Sher was already limply sprawled under her seat harness, with cats settled beside her, on her lap and shoulders, and at her feet. RK rode up front between Becker and Acorna. Before she could fall asleep, Acorna heard RK's ruminations about his tragic parting from Haruna, and how the unfortunate feline female would never know what she had missed.

Acorna raised a solicitous hand and scratched the cat under his chin.

He climbed into her lap, put his paws on her shoulder, rubbed his face against her neck, and purred a little. (It's just that seeing those kittens makes me feel like I've missed something, Acorna, you know? I should be a daddy by now, but nooooo . . . Becker wants only one ship's cat. I want to make babies.)

Acorna laughed and scrubbed his ears. (You should know better than to try that line on me, Mr Cat. You don't care about the baby kittens at all. You just want to make time with a female cat!)

RK sat back up, since he was getting no sympathy, and licked his right front paw. (Nothing wrong with that. It's what tomcats do.)

(Yes, I understand your frustration,) Acorna said, with such fellow feeling that RK favored her once more by leaning against her face. (I know exactly what you mean. Female Linyaari long for their mates, too.)

(I know,) RK said, and rubbed against her cheek with a brief burst of a purr. (Aari was on the wall.)

Acorna felt the little disk warm against her chest. (Yes, though it wasn't what you would call a good likeness. And it could have been any Linyaari, but I have had the dreams. It's him. I know it. He's long gone, though. The way they speak of him here, he was from some very ancient time in their history.)

She hoped Aari had not returned to Vhiliinyar while she'd been off saving the world again – though this time it was RK's world. She cupped the little disk against her throat. She missed him. Aari in dreams and as an ancient historical and mythological character in the Makahomian doctrine was not at all the same thing as Aari beside her.

She sighed and settled down for another catnap. The rest, food, and drink had helped, but she still felt drained by all the healing she'd done since they'd come to this world, and from all the long sleepless nights before that she'd spent wondering when she would see Aari again. She allowed her eyelids to close, hoping to dream of him –

– And jerked awake some time later, hailed by a mental call.

(Acorna, can you hear me? It's Nadhari.)

(I can read you, Nadhari. Where are you?)

(I'm a prisoner on a Federation flitter with Macostut and Edu. We're on our way to the Aridimi Stronghold.)

Acorna relayed the information to Becker.

'What's her position?' he asked.

(Nadhari, can you see the instruments? Do you know what your position is?)

She did indeed know where she was, and relayed the coordinates to Acorna, who told Becker.

After a moment he said, 'Bingo! Tell her not to worry. Rescue's on the way.' Becker changed course and put on a burst of speed.

Miw-Sher woke with a start. 'What? Have you found Uncle Tagoth?'

'No,' Acorna said, and explained about Nadhari's capture.

'But we must find my uncle first. If the Mulzar finds him before we do, he'll know that Tagoth has betrayed him, and he will kill him.'

'I don't think so, kid,' Becker said when Acorna told him of Miw-Sher's concern. 'I bet Edu's too focused on his goal to pay any attention to a lone life form down there in all that desert. And if he does find your uncle, I bet Edu's just like us. He'll want your uncle to show him the way to this stronghold. I'm on Edu's tail now. We can see him but he can't see us, thanks to the Linyaari cloaking. If it looks like he's after your uncle, I'll take him down before he knows what hit him. He'll never lay a hand on Tagoth.'

Becker was enjoying himself now, flying low and fast, tracking Edu's flitter and keeping pace with it, following it as closely as possible without overtaking it. The Federation vehicle's signal was strong and loud. 'Remind me to promote Mac for thinking to put this scanner in,' Becker said.

'Can you find a person on the ground with it?' Acorna asked.

'Yeah, but not when the rig's set up like this,' Becker said. 'Mac adapted it from the *Condor*'s array, and it's meant to have a few more toggles in the control apparatus that this little flitter just doesn't have. To get enough focus to pick up someone on the ground, it has to be recalibrated. If I do that, I run the risk of losing "His Holiness" and Nadhari. Damn, I wish Mac had thought to install a couple of laser cannons on this thing too, but I guess that wouldn't go over big with the Linyaari.'

'Probably not,' Acorna agreed. Then she sat back and concentrated on broadcasting her thoughts to a specific mind out there on the desert floor. (Tagoth? Tagoth, this is Acorna. There's a Federation flitter with the Mulzar and Macostut aboard heading at top speed to the Aridimi Stronghold. They have taken Nadhari prisoner. Please just think of me and concentrate on an answer if you are receiving this.)

But she heard no reply, nor did she sense that her message was reaching its target. She was not too surprised. Her telepathy, though highly developed, worked best with those she knew well.

'Are you trying to contact him with your mind?' Miw-Sher asked.

'Yes. I already tried, but it's not working. I'm sorry.'

'I can do it, if I change. I can find him. But you have to land. I need to change my form and call to him – cat to cat.'

'Miw-Sher, it's a bad idea to stop. We're pretty safe here in this flitter, and we have Edu under observation. The Mulzar already has Nadhari as a prisoner. We can't give him a chance to take us captive as well. If Edu can't find the stronghold without your uncle's help, then you'd play right into his hands by giving him the opportunity to capture you to use as leverage to ensure your uncle's cooperation in finding the hidden stronghold. Can you imagine what your uncle would do if Edu and Macostut threatened to kill you?

Tagoth might be able to hold out against them if they threatened Nadhari or us, but not if they have you, too.'

'They won't get me!' Miw-Sher said. 'I can find his trail, and once I do, I can call him. Let me try. If we get to my uncle first, then perhaps the Mulzar won't ever be able to find the sacred lake.'

Acorna couldn't see how anyone in a well-equipped flitter could avoid finding an entire temple complex, but then, Miw-Sher wasn't accustomed to flying in flitters. 'He could find it,' Acorna told her.

'Maybe, but with my uncle's help, we can certainly get there ahead of him to help the Aridimi prepare some kind of defense against him. Captain Becker could keep following the Mulzar, if he wishes to, after he drops me off. He could also come to my rescue, should I be captured.'

'All right, you have a point,' Acorna said. 'We'll try it your way, but I'll go with you.'

(Hmph,) RK said, rising and stretching, (I could do with a bit of a run myself.)

Whereupon Sher-Paw, Haji, and Pash all rose and stretched as if to say that they, too, wouldn't mind a bit of healthy exercise.

Grimla mewed piteously, torn between the two competing paths her Temple guardian duties required of her. She couldn't allow her two-legged kitten to leave without her protection, but on the other hand, she had a litter of four-legged kittens to care for. What should she do? She had to stay with the youngest and most helpless of her charges. She did not think this was at all fair, but what was a mother to do?

Becker put his foot down, however. 'Nope. This situation is bad enough. I'm not gonna try herding cats all over the desert in addition to all the problems we've got already. I'm not landing, and nobody is getting out.'

'In that case,' Acorna said, 'it seems that the only alternative is to recalibrate your scanner. Excuse me, Captain. Allow me.' She did this easily. It was one of those talents she seemed to have been born with, a talent that had constantly amazed her asteroid-mining foster fathers. 'Now then. See if you can find Tagoth with the scanner.'

'What if we lose the other flitter?'

'We know roughly where they are going, so we'll catch up with them before this is over regardless of what happens. And if we can find Tagoth, we'll beat them to the Aridimi Stronghold. He's the only one among us who knows exactly where that is. So let's find Tagoth. Don't worry, I'll recalibrate the scanner for you as soon as we locate Miw-Sher's uncle.'

Becker huffed and growled into his mustache. 'You drive a hard bargain.'

The cats settled back, though Grimla left her kittens long enough to groom Miw-Sher's fingers, comforting her.

The scanner was quiet for some time as the *Condor* continued on its course, and then suddenly a small dot began to show on the perimeter of the pattern, moving away. Becker headed for it. 'I hope that's not a jackrabbit or some varmint out for a midnight run,' he said.

But as they drew nearer, a visual scan homed in on the images of a large cat bounding across the desert.

'That's him,' Miw-Sher said, leaning forward. 'It's my uncle! I'll bet the Mulzar wouldn't realize it was him if he saw him in cat form. He doesn't know Uncle can change!'

Becker didn't seem to hear her. He was happily watching the scanner. 'Doesn't that Mac do top-notch work?' Becker asked Acorna. 'Isn't this great? Your guys can't even get visuals like this with the standard scanners you have in the flitters you've got on Vhiliinyar! I knew my scanners could find salvage lightyears away, but I never tried to find a moving guy on the ground while I was moving too. Yippee!'

But finding Tagoth was one thing. Catching him was another. Although he couldn't possibly see the cloaked flitter, he seemed to sense it. He looked up, then bolted in the opposite direction. Becker headed him off again. Again the cat-man fled, this time feinting to the left but taking off again in the direction he was originally headed.

'He thinks we're the Mulzar,' Becker said.

Miw-Sher pleaded, 'Please, land. I'll chase him. I'll get him to come to us.'

'No,' Acorna told her. 'By the time we land, he'll be far away. We'd just have to load up and chase him again. If we keep this up long enough, we may wind up directly in the path of the Federation flitter ourselves, or we might chase Tagoth into their hands. I think we can find a better way to reach him. Here, link hands with me and call him – except call him as if you're speaking to me. I'll see if I can relay your thought. Maybe since we're this close to him, it will work.'

They linked arms and Acorna carefully touched her horn to the girl's forehead. Miw-Sher's eyes widened, and she whispered, surprised, 'That feels . . . nice. Not pointy and sharp or anything. It makes everything . . . feel better, even smell better.'

Acorna smiled, but knew they had a job to do. 'Shhh, concentrate. Talk to your uncle.' But before either of them could seek to make contact, the Temple cats and RK pressed in on them on every side, reinforcing the catty side of the mental conversation.

(Uncle Tagoth, it's me, Miw-Sher. I'm in a flitter flying right over you. You can't see it because we're wearing a cloak that makes us invisible to the Mulzar and the Federation commander in another flitter, but we're here and we're trying to help you!)

The cat figure in the visual scanner kept fleeing.

'We're not getting through. Keep it simple,' Acorna breathed to her. 'Just tell him it's you in the flitter this time. Think of it as a mental shout. Captain, it might help if we uncloaked for a moment.'

Becker nodded and Miw-Sher did as Acorna suggested.

This time the cat stopped and looked up at them.

'It's working,' Becker hooted, and Acorna felt the flitter begin to descend. 'I do believe he heard you, ladies. Thaaaat's right, big kitty guy, come to

295

the flitter.' The vessel landed on the sand with a thump.

Tagoth began losing his feline characteristics as he came to the grounded flitter. His ears, already flattened with alarm, seemed to melt back into his skull and re-emerge as human ears; his tail flicked once and disappeared. His muzzle shortened and his whiskers shrank to nothing and vanished, as did his claws and the fur.

'Oops,' Becker said. 'Watch it, fella, ladies present.'

Miw-Sher was already holding out her scarf, which her uncle accepted, turning it into a sort of loincloth before climbing into the flitter.

'Where to?' Becker asked Tagoth, who seemed relatively unperturbed by this sudden change in his circumstances. He settled himself in next to his niece, looked around calmly, and shared quick cheek rubs with Miw-Sher and the Hissimi Temple cats. He admired the kittens, running one finger along their tiny backs.

Acorna repeated Becker's question to Tagoth, who pointed and said, 'That way. Continue as you were going when you found me. I will say when to change course.'

Becker obliged, getting them into the air as quickly as possible.

While Becker took care of the flying, Acorna studied their new passenger. She could see the appeal of the man, understanding why Nadhari had been attracted to him. Tagoth had a quiet, concentrated magnetism. He seemed to Acorna to be a man of strong convictions, with a great sense of honor, but one who had lived for many years under the constant threat that his double life would be discovered – and that his days would be prematurely ended as a result.

Acorna sent a message to Nadhari. (We just picked up Tagoth and will be taking him to the Aridimi Stronghold. Are you all right?)

(Yeah, except for being a prisoner of a man I've hated since I was a little kid,) she replied. (But you've got trouble. Edu and Macostut spotted you just now. They're speculating as to why you just dropped off their screens again. Be careful.)

EIGHTEEN

Trying not to seem aggressive, Mac bore down on the Federation soldiers staring at him from the headquarters building. They were standing between the android and the place where he needed to go. Removing them seemed the logical solution.

'Halt!' one of them said. 'Stop right there. Who the hell are you and why were you on that ship?'

'Sirs, I have come to report a serious breach of the Federation's directives concerning this planet,' Mac said, with a good imitation of Linyaari righteous indignation. He had observed Liriili closely and drew upon this memory for the proper tone, facial expression, and body language. 'The most shocking element of this breach is that it has been committed by your own commanding officer and the present ruler of your host city.'

'What's he talking about?' the guard who had not spoken asked his comrade.

'Damned if I know. Halt! I said halt, and I meant it. Don't come any closer or I'll shoot.'

A third person appeared in the doorway. This was a young female officer Mac had encountered on the inspection team and also when loading Captain MacDonald's wagons.

'Mac!' she said pleasantly. 'What are you doing here? We assumed you were with Captain Becker on that flitter. In fact we searched your ship and didn't find you.'

'Hello, Chief Petty Officer Lea. I trust you are well and having a productive day? I was doing a bit of – uh – gardening before you arrived and shut myself down to recharge.'

'Uh-huh,' she said in a tone which, though skeptical, remained amiable. To the two men she said, 'Down, boys. Mac here is an android. I saw him lift a box of dirt weighing a ton and a half single-handed and carry it down a gantry and load it into a wagon eight times in a row. Not only will your guns fail to harm him, they just might irritate some circuits that will cause him to go berserk and profoundly assimilate us into the soil of our duty station.'

The more aggressive of the men blanched slightly but took a step backwards. 'Just so he understands our position.'

'Come on in, Mac. I presume you were planning on it anyway. Can I offer you anything? A cup of oil, a jolt of electricity, perhaps? A chip or a cookie?'

'No, Chief Petty Officer Lea, I require no sustenance or repair items at this time. However, I do need to report an irregularity, as I was telling these gentlemen when you arrived. Oh, and a kidnapping. That is a crime, is it not? Having once been a henchman of Kisla Manjari's, my moral parameters are a bit hazy and this subject confuses me. But I saw Commander Macostut and Nadhari's cousin the Mulzar stun and bind her and carry her away in a flitter. Hence the irregularity I wished to report.'

One of the men snorted. 'We never interfere in the Mulzar's love life. That's as off limits as technology beyond the gate.'

Chief Petty Officer Lea glared at him. 'Stunning, binding, and kidnapping a visiting dignitary is no part of anybody's love life, Singh. And the same rules apply to the CO as to the rest of us about what goes beyond the gate and what doesn't. That goes in spades for flying flitters while accompanied by *local* dignitaries. Come on in, Mac. Sit down, pull up a com unit and tell me all about it.'

'Thank you, Chief Petty Officer Lea. Before we carry on further discussion, I would like to send a message to my captain and warn him that another flitter is abroad and that Nadhari Kando is captive aboard it.'

'We'll see about that, Mac. We have to try to disable the dampening field because we need to contact our CO too and ask him whatever was he thinking to break such an awful lot of the very rules he's supposed to be enforcing. It's not going to be easy to disable the field, though. It's hard-wired into the system. But I'm sure Singh can figure it out if he applies himself.'

'Yes, but Commander Kando is at risk,' Mac reminded her. 'I'm sure I can easily disable your dampening device. I have, as you may guess, an affinity for such things. That is how I was able to get through once to Captain Becker. I'm sure if you will be so kind as to discontinue jamming our signal, I could do it again.'

'I'll just bet you could! We had to rig something special to jam you. Laser signals are *not* Federation approved and are *not* affected by the dampening field. But I just bet you knew that. However, once we realized you were able to communicate with your flitter, we located the signal and jammed it manually. We were going to pay you a visit later, when we had reinforcements. I figured it had to be you still aboard the ship, since the others were accounted for, being on the Most Wanted list and all.'

'I would appreciate it if you would remove the special jam, then, so that I may alert Captain Becker.'

Before she could answer, the com screen flooded with the image of another Federation officer. 'Makahomia Outpost, this is Juan Verde, with the Federation Station X2niner5foxtrot4. We have a relay for you from a ship traveling in non-Federation space. The message is being transmitted through House Harakamian channels on Maganos Moonbase. They wish to know where to locate the wormhole someone named Khornya spoke of.'

'That would be for me,' Mac said.

Acorna gave Becker Nadhari's message. He nodded grimly. She quickly recalibrated the scanner aboard the Linyaari flitter to track the other flitter's progress, but the Federation vessel showed no signs of pursuing them. Instead it just sat there, back at the place where they'd stopped to pick up Tagoth. Becker said it was as though Macostut's flitter was a hound dog, scenting the wind to try to pick up their scent, but failing. Hoping they could continue to elude the Federation ship, Becker laid in an evasive, map-of-the-land course to the secret Aridimi Stronghold. Soon the Federation flitter was so far behind them that they could not even see it on their scanners.

As they rode farther into the desert, the suns were setting in a blaze of color, leaving claw marks of gory red clouds ripped across the evening sky. Though the day had been fine and clear up to that point, unmarred by any haze or even smoke from household fires such as they were accustomed to in Hissim, suddenly a high wind arose. The first indication they had that they were facing real trouble came when the whirl-winds that continually played across the desert floor began joining together, as in a dance, into one large tidal wave of wind. This lifted vast sheets of sand with it, forming a dark, churning cloud that grew in volume until it obliterated the entire horizon, silhouetted starkly against the sunset. The gale pounded the little Linyaari craft unmercifully, howling like an angry Makahomian Temple cat. It scoured the flitter with a deafening hail of sand and pebbles, scoring the viewport and upper hatch, shrieking to get in.

'That's great,' Becker growled. 'We just lost our shielding.'

'I believe we can count ourselves fortunate if that's all we lose, Captain,' Acorna told him, her words punctuated with gasps as the craft bounced around as if it were the wind's personal juggling ball. The little ship skewed wildly back and forth and up and down, and four times spun end over end with the force of the storm. Becker increased their flying speed and altitude in the hope of rising above the tempest.

The cats did their part to try to shut out the noise of the wind. They yowled and screamed and made the most bloodcurdling noises Acorna had ever heard. Tagoth and Miw-Sher cuddled the kittens, and each also held two of the Temple cats, but their skins were being shredded as the anxiety of the felines increased with every shudder and dive the flitter took in the storm.

RK was the calmest of the cats. As Becker's longtime ship's cat, he'd seen worse. Still, he crouched low on the flitter's deck at Acorna's feet, casting a baleful eye at the hatch, now opaque from the sand. His contribution to the decibel level alternated between a menacing growl and a gradually increasing scream.

None of this had a salubrious effect on Acorna's nerves.

'*Shut up!*' Becker screamed at last, outshouting cats, sand, wind, and all. 'Everybody just shut up and stay calm and I'll drive us through this.'

Becker's hands were tight on the controls, his muscles trembling with the effort to keep the flitter in the air. Acorna could see Becker's sweating face highlighted in the soft lighting that had automatically activated inside the flitter's cabin once the suns had set. The captain's jaw was tense, and his back rigid as he bent low to survey the instrument panel.

Miw-Sher looked startled, and Tagoth grinned.

All of the adult cats except for RK looked a bit shocked and highly offended. They seemed to feel that it was their right to protest such an unseemly display on the part of the environment, or perhaps they felt it was their duty to join in the noise. But after Becker's shout, they left the screeching to the storm.

Acorna wasn't sure it would be useful, but she began broadcasting calm and soothing thoughts to one and all. She also edged over and laid her head on Becker's shoulder so that her horn touched the base of his neck. He seemed surprised by the touch at first, but it had the desired effect. His shoulders relaxed, and his hands eased a bit on the controls, while the little craft continued plowing through the sandstorm.

'I keep feeling like I have to drive this thing, and actually, it does a real good job by itself,' he told her, with a sheepish grin.

Almost more startling than the sudden storm was the sight that met them when they burst through it. The night beyond the sandstorm was still clear and bright with the striped light of the planet's two moons. They had risen during the flitter's flight through the storm, and now hung heavy in the night sky, full and round save for a stripe of shadow in the center of each.

'Ho-oh-leee cats,' Becker said. 'If we hadn't come from that sky just a couple of days ago, Acorna, I'd swear there was a big old pussycat out there looking down on us like we were inside a mouse hole.'

Tagoth and Miw-Sher began talking to each other so rapidly, while pointing through the sand-scoured hatch at the sky, that even Acorna couldn't make out what they were saying.

Tagoth finally stopped and explained. 'When our moons align themselves thusly, it is a sign of a great crisis in our world.'

'So that's a bad thing?' Becker asked.

'Not necessarily,' Miw-Sher answered the question Acorna relayed. 'While the Star Cat's eyes watch the crisis unfold, his vigilant benevolence may also serve to spare us from it, if he so wills.'

'Gee, that's nice,' Becker said when Acorna told him this. 'We'll hope the big guy is in a good mood, then.'

Tagoth tapped him on the shoulder and said, for Acorna to translate, 'Steer toward the star that appears in the center below the eyes of the Star Cat.'

Becker did so.

A range of low mountains, white as bones under the catty glare of the moons, rose before them. As the flitter flew over the ridge, its occupants could see that the white knuckle hills were not set in a line, but circled a great deep crater.

'Descend into the crater,' Tagoth instructed. 'But do not land. I will show you where to fly.'

Becker obeyed. Suddenly Tagoth said, 'Now turn back toward the desert . . . sharply, yes . . . and fly into that shadow between the inner wall of the ridge and the crater.'

This, too, Becker did. They found themselves flying right into a fissure in the side of the crater.

It looked as though hundreds of fireflies floated in the dark in front of them, their lights tiny pinpricks that were hardly enough to illuminate the darkness of the passage.

Then Tagoth said, 'Descend and land.'

Becker, who had no idea what lay beneath them, began doing so. The pinpricks of light grew larger, and flickered and drew nearer, until they were clearly visible as the flames of torches carried by a parade of people converging on the flitter. Behind them, rising almost to the ceiling of the ridge, were torches set into the face of the rock.

Tagoth said, 'Behold the Aridimi Stronghold.'

The people under the torches were armed with a glittering assortment of knives, spears, and swords. Light glinted off the coin-bright eyes of still more guardian cats. None of these cats hopped onto the hatch in curious greeting as they had back in the forest Temple. The Hissimi guardians, tired and shaken from their journey through the sandstorm, waited warily to see what would happen next.

'Have you friends here?' Acorna asked Tagoth.

'A few know me. But my journey here was long ago, and probably those young enough to defend the Temple will not remember me. Besides, there is something you should know. The highest-ranking priests speak a special secret language and I was never privileged to learn it. I was not especially trusted in my time here.'

'In that case, I'll go first,' Acorna said. Becker started to protest, but she smiled and put her hand on his shoulder. 'There should be some advantage to being the one whose coming is prophesied, after all.'

The hatch opened and immediately the torches, guardian cats, and men drew close until she could count the whiskers on the cats' faces and the hairs on the arms of the men. She stood, holding her horned head erect on a neck nearly as long as and far more slender than one of her Ancestors'.

'Hello,' she said pleasantly in the Makahomian dialect she had learned from Nadhari. 'My name is Acorna. I am the Linyaari ambassador. I believe you have met one of my race before – the one you call the Star Cat's Companion. I'm told my arrival is expected.' Becker and RK stepped outside the flitter as well and stood at attention on either side of her, ready to take on anyone who raised a hand to hurt their friend.

'Greetings, Khornya, and welcome.' The speaker – a small, shriveled figure – emerged in front of the torchbearers. 'Your arrival is indeed a cause for celebration. We are so pleased that you bring with you Joh and Riidkiiyi.' His utterances were in somewhat broken and laboriously pronounced but nonetheless unmistakable Linyaari.

Nadhari Kando was no coward, and many of the entries in her extensive resume proved her fearlessness and offered evidence of her superb fighting prowess.

It wasn't exactly fear that gripped her now as she sat bound hand and foot in the back of the flitter while Dsu Macostut drove. No, what she felt was more like revulsion for Edu, and even more for herself. Both she and Edu recognized the possibilities of this scenario, one that she thought she had long ago put behind her as she had gained in strength and fighting skill.

When he turned and grinned at her speculatively, possessively, she knew she should dismiss him as an incestuous ass and disregard his stare while she considered how to escape. But to her amazement, there was a very angry and frightened younger Nadhari inside her that wanted to hide, wanted to run away, and was something her older self hadn't been for some time – ashamed. Not ashamed for some great wrong she had committed, as she had when, under the influence of drugs, she'd been used by General Ikwaskwan and his friend Count Edacki Ganoosh as a torture machine to harm the Linyaari. No, it was the way Edu looked at her that shamed her, the way he assumed some complicity on her part had put her at his mercy this way. Probably several hundred men had made overtures to her in her life by now. More of them than she cared to admit had even been successful, but none of them had made her feel as dirty as Edu could just by looking at her.

Facing Edu on her own two feet, surrounded by her friends, she had thought she was over those feelings of shame and helplessness. But now, bound and at his mercy again, part of her felt that she was no better off than she had been at six, eight, and ten. During those times, whenever he had a chance, he had culminated victories over her in their 'fighting exercises' with fondlings, gropings, and eventually much worse indignities, things he'd told her were his right by conquest. The last, worst time for her had been just before he left to join the Federation.

The consequences had devastated her in a way that made warfare seem laughable by comparison. When she heard Edu was returning to Makahomia, she'd arranged to ship out herself.

Macostut was flying flat-out across the desert when Edu turned his chair around to face her and reached out his hand to cup her face. She pulled her chin up and back to avoid his touch. He smiled a little at her small rebellion.

'I'm so glad you came back, Nadhari. It's very good having you like this again,' he said. Edu's voice took on a cat-like purr. In fact, the only resemblance this supposed cat-priest bore to the Temple guardians was the self-satisfied rasp in his voice at such times. He reached out, gripped her hair in his fist, and dragged her head forward with one hand. With his other hand, he held her chin so tightly that it would later sport a hand-shaped bruise. Once he had her satisfactorily under his control, he gave her a grotesque parody of a lover's kiss. He did not, however, try to slip her any tongue. This disappointed Nadhari. Her teeth were very sharp and strong. She would have used them well.

Edu, as if reading her mind, pulled away long enough to begin licking her face, but not in the grooming way the guardians had. It was more like a predator tasting her in preparation for devouring her.

'Hey, what's this?' Macostut asked. 'Something just popped up behind us.'

Looking over Edu's shoulder, Nadhari recognized the shape of a Linyaari flitter against the horizon and sent a warning message to Acorna.

Knowing her friends were near strengthened her resolve to survive, to escape, to put Edu in his place. Even more beneficial, the sight of the flitter distracted Edu from his little dominance game. The Mulzar patted her cheek, mouthed 'later,' and turned around to face the screen again.

It was a funny-looking flitter, Edu Kando thought, shaped like a winged beast of some sort, but painted in bright, unnatural colors. For something that moved like a sophisticated craft, it looked like a particularly well-done piece of primitive artwork. It landed, and at that point something else in the landscape popped into view that neither the Mulzar nor Macostut had previously seen – a giant cat. It bounded toward the winged flitter, then, as the hatch opened, suddenly turned into a naked man. A familiar naked man.

Brother Bulaybub, back from the alleged grave! So he was one of the shape shifters? Just went to show you couldn't trust anyone ever, really. And that explained who clawed up the corpse of Edu's man in the Aridimi Stronghold. Which meant that Bulaybub would have seen the map on the man's skin, which meant that Bulaybub would know the way to the stronghold.

The flitter blinked out of sight as it rose, and Edu uttered a blasphemous expletive reference to the mating habits of the Temple cats.

'What's the matter?' Macostut asked.

'That creature who just climbed into the flitter and disappeared knows the way to the stronghold, and now we've lost him.'

'I'm afraid so. They're shielded.'

'Hail them and tell them we have Nadhari and will kill her if they don't surrender him at once.'

'You know I can't do that, Edu. None of the com equipment works beyond the gate. Your Makahomian rule, remember? I'll just have to head in the same direction they took and hope for the best. I tell you, we're going to find that stronghold if we have to cover every inch of the desert on this planet. We'll be able to spot it when we see it. It may be a secret to you low-tech types, but it can't stay hidden from the air.'

Edu's face wore a murderous frown for a moment; then he turned a ferocious smile on Nadhari. 'Oh dear, cousin. Apparently you're not going to have any value as a hostage. I seem to be the only one able to appreciate your charms.'

Nadhari decided that if he was going to go after her again anyway, she might as well make it interesting enough so that he didn't get any bright ideas about pursuing that flitter just now, and maybe find Tagoth and the others.

With her own purr she said to Edu, 'Better get out your stun gun again then, cousin. Because that's the only way you're going to get the best of me even now, with me all tied up. You used to fight fair, at least. I suppose your position as Mulzar has made you soft.'

'Not as soft as you can be, cousin,' he said. 'I'll give you an even chance. I'll free one of your hands. Just one, so you can put it to good use.'

'Oh, stop,' she said. 'A girl can only take so much sweet talk before caving right in. But, Edu?'

'Yes?'

'How are you planning on justifying to the Aridimi elders visiting their sacred stronghold in a bit of alien technology, in the company of a Federation official?'

'I don't have to explain anything to anyone. I am the Mulzar. I rule the high plateau and the steppes. After my gifts are delivered to all the Temples, I'll rule the rainforest as well. And the Aridimi Stronghold has made itself vulnerable by its very isolation. The priests weaken themselves with their self-imposed privations.'

'What would you know about privation, self-imposed or otherwise?' Nadhari asked.

The Mulzar smiled.

'Ummm – I have my sources, you know. My last spy among the Aridimi was murdered recently, but he was in place for years. He managed to sneak out bits of intelligence to me throughout that time using the priests' supply caravans. Without the meager contributions they bring in from the outside world to augment their supplies, you see, the priests are quite helpless. They even deprive themselves of water to avoid defiling the sacred lake any more than necessary.

'I, however, have no intention of depriving myself in any way. In fact, I plan on doing a lot of so-called defilement right away. First I'll defile you, then the lake. Then, when the priests and all of the wretched cats are purged from this world, our society will enter a new and much more progressive age than the blasted stone age we've endured for so long. The stones we've wasted as mere ornaments will be sold to mining concerns and terraforming companies and weapons manufacturers all across the universe. Their sales will provide me with a nice little war chest. It shouldn't take long, my dear, for our stones are very valuable. The size of our chrysoberyls is so rare, I am told, that their like is unknown in the universe.

'Once I have done that, we will begin training our own people to manufacture the machinery our stones will augment – particle beam accelerators and weapons. We will have a viable economy based on industry on this planet, instead of catering to all of these foolish animals. People are surely beginning to see, after my little demonstration with the recent plagues, that animals, even the cats that they so foolishly worship, are far too fragile to depend upon. The cat temples will be replaced with factories. All those cat statues, if it is not too immodest for me to say so, will be replaced with statues of me.'

'You'd make a *good* statue,' Nadhari said. Her cousin failed to understand the humor or the veiled threat behind her words.

'Thank you. You can be beside me when I take over this planet. Of course, you're a bit old for child-bearing, though there *were* rumors when I came back, rumors that our last encounter . . . ?'

He let the question hang and Nadhari willed her face not to flush. Just like Edu to count his stones before he found them. She forced herself to continue regarding him with cool amusement. She would never give him the satisfaction of knowing the pain he had caused her, and the loss.

Edu looked away. 'It doesn't matter. We will have many, many more pleasurable encounters

313

– pleasurable for me, at any rate. As my consort, you can help me persuade our people that my plan is in the best interests of this world – and of the universe. You will be the woman with whom I start an empire. Other lesser females will be good enough for my dynasty building.'

He had begun loosening his clothing and hers. Regrettably, there was plenty of room in the flitter for what he had in mind. Macostut didn't seem to mind or even notice. He sat looking out into the desert, waiting to see if anything else of interest would happen in the patch where Becker's flitter had landed.

The light inside the Federation flitter was quite dim by now – probably Edu considered it romantic. That would make sense, given his limited understanding of such things. Outside the hatch, the desert landscape no longer seemed peaceful. It looked like a storm might be blowing up out there. The flitter rocked slightly.

Nadhari was glad Acorna was the one who read minds, not Edu. He didn't know about the mind reading or about Acorna's other special powers. Those powers would have to be considered if he was to have any hope of carrying out his plans. Nor did he know about Tagoth yet. At least Tagoth was safe with her friends, as she knew from Acorna's message.

Becker, Acorna, and her Makahomian friends were all in the flitter heading on the correct course for the stronghold of the sacred lake. They would alert the Aridimi to the dangers Edu posed to them all. Nadhari would elaborate on his schemes in another message to Acorna as soon as Acorna contacted her again. Meanwhile, all she had to do was distract Edu by feeding into his schemes until the others were safely away. Perhaps, if she could just get free, she could wrest control of the ship away from him and Macostut.

'Edu?' she asked as he bent toward her.

'Yes?' His voice was gloating and bubbling with too much saliva. He liked having his prey under his control, though he enjoyed a bit of a struggle in the process. That would be the catty side of him, she supposed. Perhaps he couldn't help it.

'Did you ever think there might be a better way to accomplish these things you want?'

'Accomplish what things?'

'Your goals. You're a very talented, and some might say you are an attractive man, quite aside from your political power. Did it ever occur to you to ask a girl to dinner and a vid – oh, wait, they aren't available here – or just to watch a sunset, and then romance her into bed with you, instead of beating the shit out of her and raping her? Did you ever think of how much easier that might be for you?' She could see the shock in his face. She just knew he was going to say he didn't see where he'd find the fun in that.

She hurried on. 'Or, how about the changes you want to make on the planet? Maybe everybody else here is sick of war and farming, too. If you formed an alliance with the priests and then persuaded the people that the stones were our divine gift to help us move into a more techno-logical economy, you'd still end up ruling the planet, and you wouldn't have to kill everything in sight to do it. I know you hate the cats, but you don't need to worship them. You could just let them go be cats, and live with people who do like them.'

Edu smiled with all of his teeth. He leaned over and bit her hard on the neck. As the pain of his attack shot through her, he reached out, took out a small key, and released some of the restraints that held her captive. After he freed her right hand, he refastened her left hand to the bindings strapped to her heel, then hid the key again.

'Make me,' he challenged.

She sighed. The Linyaari would have to give her credit. She had just tried reason and persuasion, though of course she had known it was futile. Now it was time to revert to the more primitive things Edu had taught her.

Nadhari was skewed sideways against Edu. He leaned in to rip her uniform shirt from her skin.

She shrank away as if frightened, which excited him so much that he stopped for a moment, backing away a fraction to enjoy the full expression of her fear. So predictable . . . She flung her whole body forward and slammed the bridge of his nose with her head. He recoiled in surprise and pain, and the air rushed out of his lungs. He landed hard against Macostut.

The flitter lurched and jerked, but not just because of Macostut. A great wall of sand struck them suddenly, the force of it knocking the flitter this way and that until it flipped the vessel over and drove it down toward the desert floor.

Nadhari laughed out loud, feeling as if she had been given a gift.

She threw herself butt-first on top of Edu's chest and took the key to her restraints from the pocket where she'd seen him deposit it. She twisted and kicked Macostut in the head with her boots, then bounced on Edu's chest again, just in case he'd managed to take in some more air. That gave her time to free her other hand and legs.

Straddling the two men in a way that Edu could hardly find pleasurable, she took over the controls from the unconscious Macostut. She ignored Edu's pained gasps and managed to steer the flitter to a stop just before the wind and sand smashed it nose-first into the desert.

Instead of crashing and breaking up into pieces, the craft scraped to a harmless halt on its side within the wall of sand.

Nadhari had no time to congratulate herself on this, however. Edu grabbed Macostut's weapon from the unconscious man's belt.

Bracing her feet against the top of the hatch, Nadhari dug her thumbs into Edu's eye sockets. The hand with the weapon jerked to his face to try to protect his eyes while his other hand flailed and then connected with the hatch control. The hatch sprang open and all the air was immediately sucked out of the flitter into the storm, along with Nadhari, who found that it was possible to fly and be flayed alive at the same time.

NINETEEN

The elder priest and all of his retinue led Acorna
and hers into the Temple. RK prowled around,
working the crowd of Temple cats, no doubt
looking for one that was the equal of Haruna. The
Hissimi cats, with the exception of the kittens
cradled in their basket next to Miw-Sher's chest,
occupied the shoulders and arms of the other
travelers.

The Temple was extremely spartan, even on
the levels where the high priests lived. The most
luxurious items in the rooms were the quilted
pads along the walls where the Temple guardians
could stretch out and knead their claws if they
wished.

But just as Acorna thought the priests were
taking her deeper into the Temple, suddenly they
were on the other side of it, facing a long, broad
lake that looked extremely deep. The lake's
narrow shores abutted the steep cliffs of a canyon
whose sheltering sides admitted only a slice of
night large enough to allow the cat's eye moons
to shine down upon the lake and be reflected by it.

The near shores of the lake and the walls of the
Temple gleamed with stones that mirrored both

the moons and their reflections on the sacred lake. Further down the lake's length, shadowy foliage huddled in the shelter of the cliffs.

The mystical beauty of this place was overwhelming. It captivated them, enchanting the people of their little party into silence. As they saw it for the first time, not even Becker seemed able to speak. Their cats, however, had a different reaction. They grew hyperactive – playing leapfrog with each other, rolling and tumbling, running halfway up the walls of the Temple to use it as a springboard to jump down onto their companions.

Suddenly Becker yawned, as did Miw-Sher.

Acorna opened her mouth to tease them, and she yawned, too.

'You are tired from your long journey,' the high priest said to Acorna in Linyaari. 'You must all rest.'

'We haven't the time,' Acorna told him. 'We came here on a mission to warn you. Tagoth knows more details about this than I do, but the Mulzar Edu Kando is plotting to kill all of the cats of this world, and all of the members of the priesthood that he doesn't control. He killed all of the Temple cats in Hissim except for the four guardians we brought with us. He released a plague that has killed many of the farm animals around Hissim, and the wild animals of the fields and the steppes. He tried to spread the plague to the jungle and may have succeeded. One of our friends, a Terran named Captain MacDonald, has concocted a remedy and is trying to get it to all the people now. I really must get back and help him.

Also – Nadhari!' She turned to Becker. 'I haven't heard from Nadhari in hours and hours. Not since the sandstorm struck.'

Becker met her gaze. 'We had to lose them out there, or we could have brought them right where they wanted to go – into this secret stronghold.' He thought about what Nadhari could be going through, and the concern in his eyes mirrored what Acorna was feeling. 'Maybe she's fine. Maybe Edu's too busy to be giving Nadhari much trouble right now. That was a heck of a sand-storm, and the Federation flitters aren't as well able to withstand turbulence as that slick little model your people made.'

Acorna explained the problem to the high priest, who said, 'Our people will search for survivors of the storm. But we would not bring anyone we find back here. Only, perhaps, the woman who is your friend, Khornya.'

Acorna was momentarily startled by the priest's use of her Linyaari name and yet, if Aari *had* foretold her coming, that was the name he would have used.

Tagoth said, 'Holy one, I have much to tell you about the plots of the Mulzar Kando. Among the news, I must tell you that Brother Fagad was a spy for the Mulzar. I confess that I killed him before he could reveal holy secrets to the Mulzar.'

The priest's face grew grave. 'You should have reported his treachery to us, rather than killed him yourself.'

'I had no time. I had to act,' Tagoth said.

'Brother Fagad was a very holy person among our people, and we have had no indication he was other than as we knew him,' the old priest said. 'You have committed a very grave crime.' He nodded to the flock of other wizened little priests who had accompanied them. 'Please interrogate this man and report back to me.'

Acorna began to protest, but the priest patted her hand.

'If he had just cause in his actions, no harm will come to him. If he is telling the truth, then we will merely learn that which he wishes to tell us. You, Khornya, have a greater purpose in being here. I must show you something that only I, of all the priesthood, am privileged to know, and only my predecessor knew before me. This is a treasured secret of my people and ensures that a successor will always be named before the demise of the previous high priest. Come.'

Acorna looked at her friends.

Becker said, 'I think I'll bunk down in the flitter, Princess. I'll work on the com unit and see if there's anything I can do about it from this end.'

The old priest said, 'I regret, Captain, that if you choose to return to your flying animal, you will be unable to enter the Temple until morning. The crater entrance is secured and locked at night.'

'That's okay. I just want to be ready to roll in case Acorna gets any more mental messages from our missing friend.' He tapped his temple. 'You'll give me a heads-up if you get any vibes from her, right?'

'Of course, Captain,' Acorna agreed.

After Becker, the high priest, and Acorna left, Miw-Sher stood staring at the lake.

A priestess laid a gentle hand on the girl's shoulder.

'I want to look at this forever,' Miw-Sher said wonderingly.

'I have the perfect room for you. Do you see that little balcony?' the priestess asked, pointing up to the outside of the Temple, which was a bit more ornate on the lake side, studded with stones only slightly smaller than the magnificent ones these Temple priests and priestesses wore around their necks. Miw-Sher nodded. 'You may sleep there. The guardians will sleep where they choose, of course, but there is room there for the kittens and their mother, and any others who choose to stay with you. We will help you make a bed there. But first, before you rest, I think you must have something to eat. Come.'

TWENTY

Kando grabbed for Nadhari, but his fingers found only a blast of sand exploding through the open hatch. Her triumphant laughter choked off in a blast of sand.

He wasn't about to go after her in the storm. Such a dreadful waste, but it was her own doing. She'd had her chance to be his consort. Now her bones would bleach on the desert sands – and he suspected she would be scraped down to the bone in a matter of minutes in this storm.

He punched the hatch door and it closed again, but not entirely, and not before it had admitted a layer of sand over an inch deep that covered the controls. But he was able to access the controls – thank goodness he remembered that much from his Federation training – and get the flitter off the ground again before it was completely buried in the storm. Beside him, Macostut stirred and muttered. Edu dragged the man to his feet by the hair and put him in the pilot's seat. He slapped him to wake him up and get his attention.

'Get us out of here.'

'Okay, okay.' Macostut engaged the engine and the flitter lifted jerkily. 'I'll try to gain some

323

altitude. The higher we go, the less sand there will be.'

'That beats sitting here being buried forever in a sand dune,' Kando snapped. 'Let's go.'

With much bucking and creaking, the flitter gained altitude. Once Macostut tried to climb so sharply that the flitter almost flipped backwards, but an adjustment of the incline eventually took them up until the sand was little more than a sheer veil over the night sky. The turbulence diminished.

The flitter finally outdistanced the storm. As the sand cleared, the full effect of the shadow-bisected moons stared Kando and Macostut in the face.

Macostut swore. 'I never saw them do that before,' he said, his voice quivering very slightly with awe and – could that be fear? Kando grinned.

'Really, Dsu, you should have been raised here and I should have stayed in the Federation. It's just a cosmic event, probably a trick of the ring shadow that happens every hundred years or so. Or so I'm informed by the more learned among my pious brethren. It is *NOT*, however, the Star Cat or anything else supernatural.'

'Of course not,' Macostut said gruffly. 'I'm perfectly aware of that. It just took me by surprise. Must have been being kicked in the head by your *charming* cousin.'

'I'm very glad to hear that, because although it isn't supernatural, it is something else far more helpful.'

Macostut seemed to be tiring of his role as

executive officer to Kando's command. He said, 'I assume you're going to enlighten me.' He did not sound friendly.

'It is a navigational aid. If, while the moons are arranged on the horizon exactly as they are now, you head straight for the place between them, you will come in time to the Aridimi Stronghold.'

'You know this to be true?' Macostut asked.

'It says so in all of the legends and holy books,' Kando told him.

'Why haven't more people found the stronghold, then?'

'The moons are in this configuration only once in a hundred Standard years. And it takes time to follow the omens across the desert. By the time any of us made the crossing, the moons would be in some other phase. It's poetic information, but hardly useful in a primitive culture with so many restrictions. But that's no reason to suppose it's inaccurate.'

They flew toward the moons without speaking. Kando filled the time by unpacking the chemical bombs with which he intended to treat the lake. These were used in the galactic mining of the cat's-eye chrysoberyls, and should also serve to either poison the priests or drive them out of the stronghold, where they would perish in the waterless vastness of the desert. True, they were used to doing without much water, but they would not be able to survive with none at all. He wondered if the Temple would make a decent initial processing plant and packing facility.

After the flitter had continued flying for some

time, though, he began to lose faith in the moons as a navigational aid. Such directions were imprecise, after all, and fraught with the kind of mysticism that he hated.

Macostut, on the other hand, seemed to be overtaken with awe at the vastness of the desert landscape. 'Will you look at that crater!' he cried, nodding to the black hole beneath them, full of rock and little else.

Kando was delighted. 'Aha! We're near now. The stronghold is near a crater, and the lake is said to be nearby as well.'

'Maybe I should fly around a little and look for it?'

'No, keep straight between the moons,' Kando said, though he was sorely tempted by the idea of exploring the crater.

His perseverance was soon rewarded, although both he and Macostut almost missed spotting their target. As they flew over the crater and back into the Serpent's Spine ridge, the land was split between the ridge's vertebrae. The flitter was nearly past the split directly on their route when he looked directly down and saw that the space in the split gleamed in the moons' light.

'The lake!' he cried, pointing. 'There it is. Take us down there.'

The flitter passed through the crack in the ridge with barely two meters on each side of the craft to spare.

Silently it descended, and Kando gazed with wonder at the deep clear waters, within whose depths even now he could see the eyes of the chrysoberyls shining through the ripples. The moons' reflection seemed to blink in answer to his gaze as the slight turbulence from the flitter's descent ruffled the surface. Behind the flitter, the Temple was shadowed by the rocky face of the cliff, but its windows, though darkened, mirrored the water and the moons. Just beyond the flitter, stands of tall trees and grasses fluttered and waved.

'It's the most astonishingly beautiful place I've seen since I've been here,' Macostut breathed.

'Right,' said Kando, and opened the hatch to heave the first chemical bomb into the pristine waters.

Acorna followed the flickering torch carried by the old priest as he led her through the bowels of the Temple. It was very quiet now, with everyone off to bed, and all she heard was the soft shuffle of the old priest's steps, the crackle of the torch, her own footsteps and heartbeat, and the sound of running water.

The priest led her up and down stairways and through walls that seemed to contain no doorways until, as they passed through the last of these, she saw the water that had been making the sound. A broad, lively stream ran beside the narrow walkway. Acorna guessed it must feed into the lake. The Temple was built with its foundation underwater. The corridor through which she walked was inscribed with drawings as the other cave had been. It was ancient and did not appear to have been constructed. Possibly the earliest temple structure had simply made use of another lava tube like the one containing the lake.

Volcanic ranges were full of such holes, some small, but as in this case, some of great depth and volume. The one containing the lake was cracked open at the top, but at one time far back in the planet's prehistoric times, the waters would have been deep inside the mountain.

Her head began to throb with the rush of the water, the flicker of the torch, the closeness of the tunnel.

Then suddenly the priest stopped directly in front of her.

She stopped, too. He pointed the torch at a rough white column set in the middle of the stream.

Sensing that she didn't understand, he moved in closer, and now she saw the shape was not a column, but a statue set upon a pedestal with the well that was the mouth of the stream bubbling up at the foot of its base. It was very tall and white, like the stone from which the Serpent's Spine ridges were made, not the cat's-eye stone used more often in Temples for ornament. The first thing she saw was the outstretched hand. Its carved fingers bore, like her own, just one knuckle. The statue's feet were cloven hoofed, with carved feathery hairs curling up the calves, just as such feathers curled up her own calves. The statue had hair that curled around a face and the deformed and slightly stunted horn that adorned it. She recognized the statue's features and posture – all except for the eyes, into whose sockets cat's-eye stones had been set, skewing the otherwise excellent likeness of Aari. But as she faced the statue full on, she realized that these particular chrysoberyls had wider stripes in the middle than usual, giving the eyes a less feline appearance than they might have otherwise, and the face could have been that of her mate when he was lost in thought.

'Aari,' she said. Definitely Aari, just as in her dream.

The priest turned and beamed at her. 'The Companion.'

She was about to ask all of the questions in her mind when they were replaced by a rush of intense pain and an agonized cry, (Acorna! Help! Please, I escaped Edu, but he is on his way to the sacred lake to poison it, and then wipe out the Aridimi priesthood. You have to stop him.)

The feelings engendered by the cry were so intense that Acorna fell against the wall before she could regain her balance. The old priest turned, alarmed at what he saw in her face, but she was oblivious to him. (Nadhari!) she mind-called. (You're wounded. Where are you?)

(Never mind about me. You have to stop Edu and Macostut. I don't know how long I was unconscious. It may be too late already.)

(It may be too late for you if we don't get help for you. There are many people here to protect the lake.)

(He has poison, Acorna. Do something!)

(I will. But, Nadhari, I need you to concentrate now. Where are you? How long did it take you to get there? Did you happen to notice the coordinates again shortly before you left the flitter?)

(No – yes, there was a sandstorm. A terrible storm. I was sucked out into it when I tried to overpower Edu and Macostut and take over the ship. I dove into a drift of sand to escape having my skin stripped off, but I'm still pretty raw and *sooo* thirsty. The storm is over now, though, so it isn't so bad.)

(I think I have a good sense of where you are. Captain Becker can come for you. The Aridimi have searchers out, too. Someone will come to find you. Make noise if you can.)

(I can't do much,) Nadhari said regretfully. (I don't think I can speak at all, my throat is so raw.)

Acorna turned her thoughts to Becker. (Captain, I am receiving a telepathic message from Nadhari. I think she is somewhere near these coordinates. Will you please go look for her? She may die otherwise. And, Captain?)

Becker, who had been asleep when her mind prodded his own, growled, *'What?'*

(Watch out for the Mulzar's Federation flitter. Nadhari says they were also caught in the sand-storm, but they flew off after ditching her in the desert. She says Kando intends to poison the sacred lake.)

(I'll keep my eyes peeled, Princess.)

Acorna allowed the present situation to flood back into her senses. She saw the old priest bending over her, a look of excitement so great his wizened old body could hardly contain it emanating from every pore.

'Even so must it have been when the Companion came to save us. So he knew words that were not spoken, saw events that were not in front of his eyes.'

Acorna nodded. 'Yes, we do that. And, although there is so much I need to ask you about this wonderful statue – about Aari's visit here – the lake is in danger. Mulzar Kando and an accomplice intend to poison it.'

TWENTY-ONE

Splash! RK's ears twitched at the sound. He sniffed and opened an eye, trying to keep the dream he was having about Haruna safe behind his other, closed eye.

He hadn't noticed the hum of the flitter or the disturbance it made in the air. He was so used to such things, it was more noticeable to him when they were not present than when they were.

The splash woke him immediately, however. No one had mentioned fish, but it was always possible. That lake could contain fish. Real, live ones, that wiggled and swam and made wonderful sport before you slapped them silly with a blow from a mighty paw and devoured the fresh fish flesh . . . ahhh.

But his waking eye didn't catch the silver gleam of a leaping lake denizen. It saw the flitter. And it saw the second item dropping into the lake from the flitter, which preceded the second, also nonfishy, splash.

There was indeed something fishy about all of this, although not of the delicious sort.

RK sat up, staring, his tail jerking.

In the basket with the kittens, Grimla opened

both eyes wide. (What is it?) she asked calmly, quietly, so as not to alarm the little ones.

(Don't look now, but I think it's your fearless leader, the Mulzar, and that clown from the Federation.)

The kittens mewed excitedly. They were more confident now that they knew they weren't being abandoned, and one after the other asked in small, squeaky, annoying voices, 'New ma, what's a fearless?' 'New ma, what's a leader?' 'New ma, what's a Mulzar?' 'New ma, what's a clown?' 'New ma, what's a Federation?'

(I'll go with you,) Grimla said. All of the tiny mouths which had held her down were now open with questions and therefore unfastened from her person. She jumped out of the basket. (Whatever he's up to, it can hardly be worse than kittens. I'm too old for this.)

(You fought me for them,) RK reminded her.

(I thought you were going to hurt them,) she said. (Some toms do.)

(Me? Naah. It's just I never saw another cat that small before. I was curious. I am curious now.)

She rubbed her side against his as she joined him on the side of the balcony and they watched the flitter set down among the foliage on the far end of the lake. (Oh, I know better now. I can see you're an old softie. Are we going to stand around here all day or are we going to investigate? I'll have to return to feed the children again before long.) She sighed and walked back for a moment to give the nearest kitten a lick, then hopped off the balcony. (You coming?)

(As soon as I can. I'd better put this Temple's

so-called guardians and the two-leggeds on red alert.)

But as he turned to wake the other cats, he found himself hemmed in. Large, furry bodies slunk to the edge of the balcony and surrounded him, while behind them, from all ledges, balconies, door and window frames, the chrysoberyl eyes of hundreds of other guardians stared unblinkingly into the shadows.

(Acorna?) RK used his cat-to-humanoid telepathy, which here on Makahomia seemed to come not so much from his brain but up from the ground through his very paw pads. (We got trouble out here. Pass it on.)

(I know. I'm on my way.)

Miw-Sher sat up, wiping her eyes. She looked drowsily out over the canyon, then wiped her eyes again. 'The lake!'

RK didn't need her to tell him about it. He could smell it already. The lips of every cat on the Temple were curled back over the scent glands, the hackles of each cat raised, the tails bushed. Even the kittens tried to see through their closed eyes and bristled instinctively, their individual baby hairs standing up on their uncoordinated little bodies.

The waters, so clear and clean just a moment before, were boiling and steaming with an acrid stench that was worse than the combined signatures of a hundred tom cats looking for love.

RK growled low in his throat and said to the other cats near him, (Okay, troops, here's what we do. We run down the beach and some of us jump up on the ledge back there and then we drop down onto them as they come out of the flitter over in those trees and demolish them.)

The nearest cat, this one a large sleek one with midnight stripes, said, (You do that. We'll do this.)

And he and every other Temple guardian emitted ear-splitting yowls that did to the auditory senses what the polluted lake did to the olfactory ones.

But as the great yowl started, a figure emerged from the foliage. Edu Kando! When he saw the cats and heard their yowl, he turned tail, but RK, Grimla, Pash, Haji, and Sher-Paw bounded after him, only to be outsprinted by the larger, longer-legged Temple cats who guarded Aridimi. With a mighty coordinated leap, they brought him down, screaming their battle cries and – shooting sparks?

But the cats on top of Kando began falling off, lying limp, and RK realized his enemy was shooting a laser pistol.

Grimla hung onto a foot with teeth and claws. Among the roil of cats was a huge one. Miw-Sher, changed to cat form, waded into the fray. The Mulzar, freeing himself from the first ten cats to attack his body, backed up a pace, then fired at her. She crumpled. Grimla abandoned her place shredding Kando's leg and jumped away from it, running to Miw-Sher. Kando fired again and Grimla lay smoking, a bare paw's length from her friend.

Then suddenly, behind them, the flitter rose jerkily from the foliage. Federation flitters were well armed. This one opened fire. Priests had joined the cats, but both quickly fell and dropped to the ground, and in some cases, into the roiling lake waters.

RK grew very still inside, very numb, and slunk from the body of one fallen comrade to the body of another while the carnage continued. When he was behind the Mulzar, but very close, he leaped up on the arm that held the gun, hung on to it with deep sinkings of his front claws while he bit and churned his back claws with all his might.

Kando's grip loosened and RK thought that one more kick would set the laser pistol free.

And then he felt a terrible crunching pain, as if his spine had broken, as Kando's other hand crashed down upon him, and sent him flying into the foliage.

As the pain of his injuries overcame him, he saw another huge cat, Tagoth, jumping over the fallen bodies. Acorna was just behind him, supporting the old priest.

RK called out to her, but not with his mind. In fact it was just a feeble little mew, but she heard him, and looked up. Touching the old man with her horn, she steadied him before she sprinted after Tagoth into the welter of bodies. She stopped first to bend over Miw-Sher.

The Mulzar, nursing his shredded arm where RK had nailed him, didn't bring the laser pistol up in time. Tagoth landed full on top of him, disarming him.

But the flitter barked again. As Miw-Sher sat up, Tagoth's arm raised and the flitter spiraled – slowly, it seemed to RK – down to the lake.

Tagoth lowered his arm. Miw-Sher tried to rise to her feet. Acorna, clutching her throat, fell over her.

No. That couldn't be right. Acorna would *not* fall.

But she did.

Acorna fell. And lay still.

No.

RK's world crashed from night blackness to a darkness far more profound.

'Captain Becker, do you read me now?' Mac's voice woke Becker from a fitful doze.

The com unit was live again!

'Mac, funny you should mention. I was going to call you as soon as I got the com unit back up. How did you fix it anyway?' He was genuinely curious, but remembering Mac's tendency toward long-winded explanations, he decided curiosity could wait. 'Never mind. No time now. I need to recalibrate the scanner to pick up someone on the ground and I need to do it now, without having to figure it out. Run through it with me.'

'Yes, Captain, but . . .'

'I'd ask Acorna, but she has other fish to fry back at the Temple. Nadhari is somewhere out in the desert, hurt. I need to find her.'

'I am distressed to hear that, Captain, but . . .'

'No ifs, ands, or buts about it, guy. Tell me how now before I miss her and she ends up dying.'

'Very well, Captain,' Mac said. He rattled off the computations and Becker entered them quickly, his concentration narrowing to just the

337

screen. No sooner had he adjusted his instruments than he spotted something right about where he supposed Nadhari might have been ditched. 'Stay tuned, Mac. I think I got her now.'

'Oh, very good, Captain. Do you want to know . . . ?'

'Not now, Mac,' Becker said, setting the flitter down in the smoothly, even artistically drifted desert sands. The night was calm and bright with striped moonlight and seemed to be saying 'Sandstorm? What sandstorm?'

But bleeding atop one of the dunes, stripped of most of her clothing and a lot of her skin, lay a person Becker barely recognized as Nadhari.

'Hey, babe, come here often?' he called.

'Jonas, you junkman in shining armor,' Nadhari said, or tried to say. Her voice was hoarse and cracked; her hands, arms, and torso were so abraded he could see very little skin through the blood. Though she'd shielded her face pretty well, her cheeks and forehead also looked like raw hamburger.

'Oh, honeybunny, we need to get you to Acorna right away, doll. That bastard. I can't believe he dumped you out here!'

She smiled a little, painfully, and her teeth were pink outlined in red. 'I dumped him,' she rasped.

He tried to find spots on her anatomy he could hold so that he could carry her, but in the end getting her to the flitter involved him supporting and her half walking, half being pushed and dragged. She sucked in her breath a lot, but otherwise was quiet, even though that walk had to have hurt like blazes. She was a tough lady.

He would have covered her with something except he didn't want to get anything else in those wounds. He helped her arrange herself as comfortably as possible in the back of the flitter. She was half fainting from pain, loss of blood, and exhaustion.

'Mac, you still there?' he asked, toggling the com unit.

'Yes, Captain. Do you have Nadhari Kando?'

'I do and I gotta get her to Acorna right now. She's a real mess.'

'Captain, since you have been preoccupied during this transmission, I took the liberty of acquiring your position from your signal. I wish to inform you that the *wii-Balakiire* is not far from you and closing quickly.'

'The what?'

'The *wii-Balakiire*, the shuttle belonging to the Linyaari ship *Balakiire*, with crew members . . .'

'I know what the *wii-Balakiire* is. I was just wondering when and how they got here so fast.'

'They arrived only moments ago by following the same course we took, which I downloaded directly into their computer banks, correcting our coordinates so that they did not end up mired on Praxos. It saved a lot of time.'

'I'll bet it did.'

'Melireenya asked me to inquire if the crew might not be able to offer their assistance so that Nadhari would not have to suffer through the journey?'

'Sure thing. You told me how they found us, but you haven't said to what we owe the honor of their company?'

'When Acorna contacted MOO from Captain MacDonald's ship, she told her friends about the plague here. They decided to come and help.'

'Save it, Mac. Patch me through to the *wii-Balakiire* now.'

'Very well, sir. I can do that easily since Chief Petty Officer Lea removed the jamming signal she devised to interfere with the Linyaari signal, so we may all converse freely.'

'That was nice of her, whoever she is,' Becker said. 'Hurry up, will you?'

'This is Melireenya on the *wii-Balakiire*, Captain Becker. We have made visual contact with you, and if you look up and a bit to your right, you will do likewise with us.'

Becker did and saw the Linyaari shuttle berth itself in the sand. Six Linyaari waved at him through the viewport. He couldn't tell in the darkness who they were exactly, but he was glad to see them.

Opening the hatch, he stepped out and allowed two of the Linyaari to enter in his place. They immediately turned to Nadhari and began laying hands and horns tenderly upon her wounds.

'I don't suppose any of you ladies brought an extra tunic or something, did you? She might get a little chilly – you know, shock and stuff – once you put her back together.'

'Certainly, Captain,' said the one nearest him. As soon as she spoke, he recognized her as Acorna's Aunt Neeva. She blithely stripped off her tunic and handed it to him. 'She can wear mine.'

'But I – er – what will you . . .' he stammered, trying not to look.

340

'If you think it necessary that I cover myself to preserve the good opinion of Khornya's new friends, then I'm sure I'll find something. I actually felt that in such a warm climate, perhaps the attitude toward clothing was more relaxed than it is among your own people. But now you must tell me how to contact Khornya. I have been trying to reach her, but I can't seem to. Mac tells us that she is inside some sort of stronghold, so I am assuming that it has some sort of barrier to tele- pathic communication.'

'No, there's no such barrier. She contacted me that way when she was inside the stronghold and I was out in the flitter,' Becker told her.

Just then Khaari poked her head out of the hatch and said, 'Nadhari says her cousin and that crooked Federation commander were armed, and were setting out to destroy a sacred lake and kill the inhabitants.'

'How is she?' Becker asked them.

Nadhari herself answered in a strong voice. 'I'm fine, Jonas. But something is wrong at the lake. I can't get Acorna to answer me.'

'That's bad,' Becker said, adding to Khaari and Melireenya, 'You ladies better sit down or get back to your own vessel. We have to get back to the lake, and fast.'

'The location of the stronghold is a sacred secret,' Nadhari whispered.

'So is the location of the Linyaari homeworld, if you'll recall. I think we can safely guarantee that these people can keep a secret. Besides, the priests at the stronghold think Acorna is some kind of second coming. Just think how tickled they'll be to see six more folks just like her. Let's boogie, people.'

He flew right into the crater, with the *wii-Balakiire* trailing behind. The twin cat's-eye moons had set by then, and the first of the suns was rising, its pinks obscured by a squirming yellow-green fog leaking out of the mountains beyond the crater. From the readings Becker was getting, the bilious stuff was rising from the fissure above the lake. That wasn't good.

Besides, the stronghold might still be locked.

'Change of plans, folks,' he told the Linyaari escort, and flew up over the lip of the crater that contained the stronghold. On the other side, he saw the slit between the white knuckled ridges, with the fog billowing out of it. 'Hold your noses. We're going down there,' he told them, and dropped his flitter's nose through the crack emitting the steam.

He couldn't believe his eyes at first. What had been a scene of beauty and peace when he retired only a few hours earlier now looked like his worst nightmare.

The formerly clear lake was churning with stinking cloudy water, casting up stones like some filthy froth along the beach. In the middle of the mess was a Federation flitter half sunk into the water. Becker thought he could make out a body at the controls.

It wasn't the only body. As he found a place in the bushes broad enough to land, he could see through the steam to the shore, where he spied the prostrate bodies of dozens of cats and four or five priests. Miw-Sher, cradling the body of Grimla, walked through the carnage beside Tagoth, trying to tend to the fallen priests and cats.

Nadhari loped over to them as if nothing had ever been wrong with her. Embracing both of them and the cat in a single desperate hug, she cried, 'I can't believe you're all right! I felt sure you were injured.'

'I was,' Miw-Sher replied, 'but Ambass . . . Acorna . . . made me better before she was shot. Uncle Tagoth tackled the Mulzar and got the gun away from him. He shot down the flitter, but not before its guns got Acorna.'

'Got Acorna?' Nadhari asked, and the words echoed through Becker's brain like a ricocheting missile.

Kando lay further down the beach, surrounded by cats and priests. They were not trying to tend to any of his wounds. In fact they seemed to be looking for undamaged parts of him to claw, bite, or beat.

Another huddle of about ten priests crowded around something else a little farther away.

The *wii-Balakiire* found its berth beside his flitter, but before he could open the hatch, Neeva was out and running toward the huddle of priests. Melireenya and Khaari cried, 'Khornya!' together, and surged for the hatch, but Nadhari beat them to it.

They all but climbed on top of Becker's head evacuating the flitter.

Becker, feeling sick in a way that even a

Linyaari couldn't heal, followed them, stumbling over the bushes, trying to catch his breath in the stench from the lake.

His foot touched something soft and he looked down. His boot was under RK's belly. The cat was very still, and when Becker picked him up, RK's tail hung down limply over Becker's arm.

Becker tapped the nearest Linyaari on the shoulder and pointed with dumb misery to his first mate.

'Riidkiiyi!' the girl cried. 'Oh, Riidkiiyi, don't be dead.' She lay her slightly immature horn upon the cat's fur while stroking him.

After a moment, RK struggled in Becker's arms and jumped down.

'Thanks,' Becker said.

'It's Maati, Captain,' Aari's little sister told him. She'd grown so much that he hardly recognized her. She'd been on the *Balakiire* and he hadn't realized she was there. 'My father and mother and I all came with the *Balakiire* to see if we could help.'

'Thanks, Maati. Is – is that Acorna they're working on now?' he asked, trying to see through the wall of Linyaari and priestly backs.

'Yes.'

And then he felt a most welcome mental touch. Though it was weaker than usual and very tired, he knew it well. Acorna said, (Captain, I'm fine. Please persuade some of my friends to help the others.)

TWENTY-TWO

Acorna and her fellow Linyaari worked all day long treating the wounded. Had the carnage been more carefully aimed or gone untreated much longer, there would have been fatalities, too. Time was playing tricks on her. It seemed to Acorna that the carnage had gone on forever, and that after she was hit, she had laid on the beach gasping for breath for an eternity before she passed out.

In reality, once she was able to compute the time elapsed, she found to her surprise that Becker, with Nadhari and her people, had returned just after she fell and Tagoth downed the Mulzar and blew the Federation flitter into the lake.

Once people and cats were restored to health by the unconcealed application of Linyaari horns, the only human casualty untreated was Macostut, still floating in the flitter on the lake's bubbling, stinking surface. But his injuries, if he had any, were of less concern to them than the damage to the lake.

'How will we ever fix that? It's so large. All of us are depleted from healing the casualties,'

Maati sighed, tired and uncharacteristically discouraged.

The Mulzar, bound and under guard but still among the others, laughed. 'It is permanently changed. Everything is permanently changed. I have a market for those stones. The smart thing to do would be release me, fish out the Federation flitter, heal my own and Dsu's wounds as you've done those of these worthless cats and priests, and let me explain my plan for Makahomia's future to all of you.'

'You explained it to me already, Edu,' Nadhari said. 'I can't say that I cared for it. I don't think anyone else will either.'

The stronghold's high priest shook his head. 'With the lake thus defiled, Makahomia has no future. The sacred lake feeds into all rivers, all streams, all water on our world. The poison will infect everything. No one can drink the holy stones, fool and blasphemer.'

'Though I think it would be fitting punishment if we allowed Edu to try,' Tagoth said. 'Or if not the stones, perhaps a refreshing drink of lake water?'

Neeva said, 'Don't despair, everyone. We can fix it. We're simply going to need reinforcements. I know this place is sacred and secret, but I hope I may have permission to have the *Balakiire* land here as well as Captain MacDonald's flitter. *Maak* used Captain MacDonald's flitter to collect him and the barbarians.'

'I bet the Federation folks aren't going to like that,' Becker said.

'On the contrary, the outpost is nearly deserted

since the commander ordered his troops into the city to monitor and assist with the war effort. *Maak* tells me the remaining person in charge, a noncommissioned officer, has been most helpful. I have contacted her myself. She told me that so many eggs have now been broken that we may as well make a soufflé.

'I've explained to her telepathically that we will need the additional transport to deal with the emergency here at the lake. What I did not say is that once we've dealt with the lake, we will also need to disperse our people quickly to other areas to purify the other water sources.'

Acorna translated and the old priest's eyes widened and he looked as if he were about to faint from ecstasy. 'Yet *more* of the Star Cat's own sacred Companions? How have we come to be so blessed that we deserve so much pain and joy in the space of the same risings and settings?'

'That would be a yes,' Acorna said to Neeva, translating.

In less than an hour, the flitter arrived with Mac, better known as *Maak* to the Linyaari, Captain MacDonald, the Wats, and six more people from the *Balakiire:* Thariinye, Kaarlye, Miiri, *aagroni* Iirtye, Yaniriin, and – rather to Acorna's surprise – Liriili.

Kaarlye analyzed the waters. After testing it, he declared that they would not harm Linyaari horns. The Linyaari then all knelt, joined hands, took deep breaths, and ducked their horns into the filthy, bilious foam of the lake.

From the corner of her eye, Acorna saw Becker and Tagoth manhandle the Mulzar to the shore and shove *his* face as near to the lake waters as theirs were. She found it a little hard to chuckle and purify at the same time, but after what truly seemed a miraculously short interval, the sacred lake's waters were once more clear and smooth, though they seemed to be more filled than ever with the sacred stones.

Captain MacDonald, the *aagroni*, and Kaarlye and Miiri each took command of a shuttle, with one of the high priests on each vessel. Maati joined her parents in their vessel, along with Liriili and Thariinye, while Maarni and Yiitir – the Linyaari folklorist and historian husband-and-wife team – joined the *aagroni*'s vessel. Yaniriin, Neeva, Melireenya, and Khaari rode with Captain MacDonald.

Of all the Linyaari, only Acorna remained at the sacred lake. She stayed there at the insistence of the high priest.

After the last phase of the decontamination process, Aridimi priests hauled the flitter from the lake. The flitter was opened, and Macostut was pulled out. He was not actually wounded, simply shaken by the crash. The priests seemed to regret this, but did not make up for it by administering new wounds themselves.

Macostut was bound and placed next to Kando. Their priestly guards were augmented by the presence of the Wats, who thoroughly enjoyed being on the other side of the bonds for a change. They frequently gave their prisoners little blows, kicks, and intense frowns.

'You won't get away with this, you know,' Macostut said. 'The Federation will not allow you to interfere with the authority of one of its officers, to wreck a craft, to contradict the orders of the native ruler, and to interfere with standing treaties.'

Mac surprised all of them by responding. 'I believe you will find you are incorrect on all points, sir,' the android said. 'The Federation has an investigative team on the way to interview the parties you and your conspiracy with Edu Kando, the former Mulzar, injured by your actions, and particularly by misuse of Federation technology and research. Your plot to sell and personally profit from the sale of the cat's-eye chrysoberyls held sacred by the local populace is known to them.'

Macostut and the Mulzar regarded each other with suspicious slit-eyed speculation. 'How can that be?' Kando asked.

'Because the party you tried to sell them to was a subsidiary of House Harakamian enterprises, which as you may not know is run by Ambassador Acorna's foster father, Rafik Nadezda, under the occasional advisement of his uncle, Hafiz Harakamian. When the chrysoberyls, with their unique properties that would make micro-terraformation technology possible on a large scale, came to Hafiz Harakamian's attention, he recalled conversations with the ambassador and made inquiries among his – er – employees, among the Federation. It took very little research to realize that while such stones are indeed indigenous to this planet and possess the desired properties, they are not for sale and have immense religious significance to the local populace. They were very fair to you, sir, and searched the records for some evidence of a revision of treaties or rules or possibly some special permission that would allow you to collect the stones, but as you know, no such revisions or permissions exist.'

'I am ruler of half the people of this world,' the Mulzar said. 'I am making the revisions and certainly gave the permission.'

'Not anymore,' the high priest told him. 'The guardians have conferred. They know what you have tried to do to them and to the lake. Had you sought to loot us without also seeking to destroy the guardians, you might have been allowed to retain your rule. Cats, on the whole, prefer to stay out of the affairs of humans unless such affairs interfere with their comfort. But your own guardians have testified to the others on this planet. Even as a ruler by conquest, you are unfit to rule.'

'And who is fit to rule, old man? You? You are so isolated here with your sacred lake you won't drink from that you have no idea what the people need.'

'I am kept better informed than you were by the late Brother Fagad,' the priest told him.

Kando knew that yet another of his schemes had been discovered, but he couldn't seem to help himself and tried one more time, staring angrily at Tagoth. 'Fagad is late because this mutant murdered him while he was performing his sacred duty and reporting to me that which it was my right, as Mulzar, to know.' He spat at Tagoth. 'Traitor.'

Tagoth nodded. 'I deserve that. I am a traitor indeed for ever supporting you, Kando. I liked your ideas – I still like some of them. I have discussed with the priesthood ways in which the best of them might be implemented – with the consent of both our religious community and the people. If you had sincerely wished to use those ideas for the good of our planet, as you said, you would have been a great leader.'

'I did want to do it for the good of the planet,' Kando said with a ferocious passion that made Acorna feel that he was, or at least had at one time been, sincere. 'But you'll quickly learn that doing such things takes money.'

'Perhaps,' Tagoth said.

'But that doesn't mean you can just kill the guardians and all the other animals on this planet!' Miw-Sher blurted out suddenly. 'You murdered our own guardians with your germs. How could you? How *could* you? They kept us safe for years, all of our loyal friends and those poor little kittens. Some of them n-n-never even got to op-p-pen their eyes!' She was crying now. Tagoth had a hand on her shoulder, but quickly she was surrounded by the Hissimi Temple cats and many of their larger brethren from the stronghold.

'My followers will overthrow any who try to take my place,' he said. 'Under current rules, until I am bested in battle publicly, I or my descendants rule.'

The high priest regarded him ironically. 'This is not a law a progressive man such as you claim to be should invoke. However, it is the way things have always been and shall continue to be. Your descendant shall rule, but not with you to guide her. Her mother and the man who has been a guardian to her, protecting her from your incestuous lechery, will rule. She is, as you see, well loved by the guardians and has the proper love for them and concern for their welfare. Besides which, she is one of the blessed who can change in this life, as is her guardian.'

'You mean Little Sister Miw-Sher? But she's not my—'

He met Nadhari's cold, hard stare and his voice died away. 'I didn't know. You didn't tell me.'

'I wouldn't give you the satisfaction,' Nadhari said, spitting at him. 'And I couldn't stay. I was a child myself. Tagoth, whom I loved, knew about her, though not that she was yours. He followed you for my sake, never knowing how I hated you.'

'H-hated me?' Kando looked genuinely distressed. 'But you liked our little games, our secrets.'

'Hated, still hate,' she repeated. 'I will give you credit for one thing only. I learned to fight as well as I do only so that I might avoid your touch ever again. That has been what's driven me, more than life and death, to be a warrior.'

'And now she will protect those who followed you in your stead,' the priest said brightly, 'which seems entirely appropriate to me. You, of course, as an avowed religious are subject to religious law. As such, you will be walled up, to live out your life in contemplation and prayer as an anchorite. The brothers have prepared a place in our walls now. Never fear, you will not be lonely. The guardians will come to visit you at the ventilation holes in your wall.'

'Are you going to wall me up, too?' Macostut asked.

'You are not a priest or of our world. I have no authority over you,' the high priest said. 'Your own people will deal with you. I am assured by Kadi Nadhari, which is her new title as the female co-regent for Mulzarah Miw-Sher, that the star people can make the rest of your life conducive to contemplation of the error of your ways as well.'

Nadhari gave Macostut and Edu an evil grin, the toothy sort that Linyaari found especially frightening.

'Cheer up, Edu,' Tagoth told him. 'The changes you want are coming about because of you, after all.'

The prisoners were taken away – Macostut to a cell, Kando to his new home inside a wall.

The old high priest entertained his guests on the balcony where Miw-Sher had slept with the kittens. The kittens and their elders provided a floor show while Acorna and her friends ate. The high priest had ordered some bread, cheese, and fruit be brought onto the balcony for a picnic on the lake. Thanks to the Linyaari horns, even the air smelled better than it had a few hours before.

The priest told them that he was puzzled about many things contained in Mac's explanation to Macostut and Kando about how they had been found out. He wanted to know more about Acorna and her non-Makahomian friends, and particularly more about RK, who was making a determined effort to rebuild the feline population of Makahomia with any lady cat guardian he could find.

They told him much of their recent adventures, of the desolation of both planets where the Linyaari lived, of the help the isolated people had received from Acorna's friends and adopted relatives. Then of course she had to tell him about how she was found drifting in a pod in space by her three human asteroid miner fathers, and other entertaining parts of her personal history.

Becker told how he had found Aari, and how his shipmate and Acorna had become sweethearts, and how they all had fought together to finally vanquish the Khleevi.

Finally Acorna told him of the strange time aberrations they'd encountered, not sure the old man would understand such things, but knowing that mystics sometimes understood anomalies of physics long before scientists had figured them out. She told him quietly of losing Aari in time and space.

The priest nodded and rocked on his haunches, clearly thinking.

Finally he said to Acorna, 'I must share with you another thing. Please excuse us, friends. This thing is for Khornya only.'

This time their walk through the bowels of the Temple was friendlier, and where it was possible they walked side by side. As in the other Temples, there were holes high in the walls that let in light and allowed the guardians to jump in and out. At one bend in the path, RK poked his head through a hole and his body followed with a soft plop onto the path. He took a quick hop up to Acorna's shoulders. She idly tickled his tail and he flipped it under her nose.

'He is devoted to you, your guardian. I have never seen one like him.'

'Haven't you?' Acorna asked. Her heart was beating very rapidly in anticipation of what the old priest had to show her, and yet she feared to be disappointed again, to come upon another dead end and find a trace of Aari, but no way to reach him. It seemed safer to talk about cats. They enjoyed being talked about, and people who liked them always had things to say about them. 'But Captain Becker told me he found RK on a ship from your planet.'

'How can that be? We have had no space vessels since many years before the Space Cat came to us.'

'Time warp?' Acorna asked, looking thoughtfully up at RK.

He licked his paw. (Don't ask me. I don't remember anything about another ship before the *Condor*.)

They had once again reached the statue of Aari, now bathed in the reddish suns-shine pouring through the holes in the walls and ceiling.

It looks so like him. Shrugging RK off her shoulders, Acorna stepped across the water and onto the pedestal of the statue. She put her arms around the cold stone, feeling a tear that ran down her cheek cooling as it touched the statue. Then, realizing the priest was waiting for her, she stepped back across the water again. 'Sorry,' she said. 'I had to do that. I miss him so much.'

The old priest said, 'Your coming raises many questions, but it has also brought many answers. You have saved us, as was foretold.'

'Not really,' she said. 'Mostly that was my friends. And the person who was foretold in your stories could have been any of us Linyaari, as you surely see now.'

'You are modest. You are the one foretold, the beloved companion of the Companion. He knew you would come and that you would come when you were desperately needed, just as he was when he came to us. And so you have. Perhaps it is true that you could not have saved us alone, but you were not alone, for your friends and kinsmen came to help us for love of you.'

She wanted to tell him it was an accident, but she knew he wouldn't believe her. After all that had happened, she didn't really believe it herself.

'First I would show you the gift left for us by your Aari, for that was the name of the Companion in the scriptures, though it is too holy to speak of in the normal course of events.'

She giggled. 'I'm sorry. I think he would find it funny that his name is too holy to speak. Even after the Khleevi hurt him so badly, once he recovered a little he had a sense of humor – he was always dressing up in these weird outfits that concealed that he didn't have a horn. They – the Khleevi – took it from him and . . . and . . .'

Her hand closed around the little disk at her throat and she found she couldn't go on. The priest patted her shoulder and then walked behind the statue and knelt to show her something just below water level.

She in turn knelt and peered at it.

'Even when the evil men poisoned our lake, this water stayed pure because of this. If your friends had not been here to purify it, eventually the lake would have become pure again because of this. The Companion gave us this of himself so that we would never again face dying of thirst because all of our water was tainted.'

He was indicating a small piece of what could only be horn, just a sliver. For Aari to do that to himself when the Khleevi had used it as a way to torture him – his horn only recently grown . . . Acorna shuddered. Although she herself had done something similar on Rushima, her own horn had never been threatened as Aari's had. She reached out but it was too far. So she lay on her stomach and stretched out over the water to touch it. Instantly she felt not just the horn, but his arms warm and strong around her, his lips on her face, his horn against her own. She saw him in all of his favorite postures, doing all of the things she remembered so well, his face set in those beloved, wry expressions as if he were standing before her.

She didn't want to move, ever again. She just wanted to stay there where she could feel him and touch him. To stand up would not be to rejoin the universe, but to lose contact again with the most precious person in it.

The old priest's finger tapping her shoulder caused her to stare stubbornly at the horn, trying to hang on to the images of Aari the horn invoked.

But the old man was used to disturbing visionaries. His efforts were aided by RK, who yowled at Acorna and sank his claws into her hip.

Tears rolled down her face to join the artesian waters the horn purified in perpetuity. She turned back to them, pulling herself back across the watery chasm, breaking contact, losing Aari all over again.

The priest indicated something in the wall behind them, behind the statue, beyond the water. It was a huge chrysoberyl. But the priest spun it on its base and she saw that the back of it had been hollowed out. Within it lay a black box, the sort that recorded the last moments of crashed ships, the computer archives that left a record for those finding the wreckage. 'He meant this for you,' the old priest was saying, oblivious to her rebellious and angry mood. 'It isn't very pretty, but I thought it might be one of those gadgets you off-worlders like. Something that has a message?'

She clasped it to her. 'Yes, a message. Yes, oh, yes.'

Now she couldn't wait to leave this place, to return to the *Condor* or the *Balakiire*, wherever she could decode the message he'd left for her.

Fortunately, this time when she emerged from the depths of the Temple with the priest and RK, she saw a stream of people, mostly Linyaari, coming from the foliage where flitters could be docked.

'Mission accomplished, padre,' Captain MacDonald told the priest. 'We got every lake, river, stream, well, and mud puddle in the known world.'

Neeva said, 'The people who saw what we were doing asked that we thank you for thinking

358

of their welfare. They seemed surprised that someone should do so.'

Becker said, 'I guess this kinda blows the Linyaari cover about the horns not doing the healing and unpolluting.'

'No harm done,' Nadhari told him. 'My people are not a space-traveling nation who can tell others what has occurred here.'

'You say "we." I guess that means you're staying to be the queen mother, like the high priest said, doesn't it? Hafiz is going to be really pissed.'

'I know that, but I have to, Jonas. Comfort Hafiz by telling him that we will be happy to keep the Wats with us. We can always use good guards.'

'That ought to make the old man almost happy enough to make up for losing you,' Becker said, giving her a hug.

When good-byes had been said all around, the high priest made a gesture and a procession of priests bearing the largest and finest of the cat's-eye chrysoberyls began handing them to the guests and conveying them to the flitters.

'But these are your sacred stones!' Acorna said.

'They are our gifts to you,' the priest said.

'They're worth a fortune. Hafiz would buy these from you for enough funds to do anything for the planet you wanted done.'

The old priest smiled. 'You and your friends have already done what I wanted for the planet. There is not enough money in existence to repay you, but if these may be used to help rebuild the homes of your people, then take them with our blessing. The Mulzarah is in agreement, as are her regents.'

'Miw-Sher?' Acorna asked, and the girl nodded so gravely that Acorna set down the precious black box and the chrysoberyls and knelt to give her one last hug. Then Grimla needed a pat, and then the kittens had to be produced one at a time for cuddles.

By the time Acorna, the black box, all the chrysoberyls any of them could carry, Becker, Mac, and RK were back aboard the *Condor*, she was as happy to leave Makahomia as she was sorry to leave Nadhari and her new friends.

They promised that when the cat guardian population had been replenished, the Linyaari might come to them once more to claim kittens. In case the source of the elusive *pahaantiyirs*, which the *aagroni* averred were not *precisely* the same species as the Temple guardians, was never located, the Temple cats would be good substitutes.

Finally the *Condor* was heading back for MOO in a comfortable convoy with the *Balakiire* and the *Arkansas Traveler*. Captain MacDonald said he thought it likely Hafiz might be able to use a tractor or two, and joined them.

The bridge was quiet. RK was grooming Becker's hand with his tongue while Becker groomed the cat's coat with a brush. Mac was beating himself at five-dimensional computer chess.

Acorna showed Mac and Becker the box and said, 'I wish to play the message.'

Becker said, 'No can do. Not on this ship. That's

rigged for some sort of antique pre-Linyaari jobbie and I've got all Federation stuff on board now.'

This had not occurred to Acorna. She tried to keep the bitter disappointment from her voice as she said, 'Oh.'

Mac spoke up. 'I can play it, however. I have modifications that allow me to interpret the messages from such boxes.'

Acorna handed it to him.

Becker said, 'This is what the priest gave you from Aari, right?'

'Yes, Captain.'

'Come on, cat. Let's leave the young folks alone. If there's anything in it you want to share, Acorna, let me know. But I think you should be private with it.'

'Thank you, Captain.'

Mac already had the box open and inserted the modifications he had made to his right hand into the box. To Acorna's amazement, when Mac spoke again, it was in Aari's voice.

'Khornya,' he said, 'if you can hear this, then you have already come to Makahomia and fulfilled the mission you were destined for there. I know about this because I have been doing much time sliding with Grimalkin, who is one of the Friends. Unlike the others, Grimalkin is good, extremely empathetic, and uses his knowledge to help others. He began the cat race on Makahomia, and we go now to where the planet will need *pahaantiyirs*.

'I am sorry I cannot be with you right now. But in the course of all of this time sliding and traveling, Grimalkin says there will be a moment when I will be able to save Laarye from starving to death during the Khleevi invasion without damaging other lives or changing events that must occur. I have to do this if I can. I hope you understand that, and that I will return to you as soon as I can.

'I miss you very, very much, Khornya. I leave you this message so you will know that, and know that I love you and feel pain worse than the Khleevi gave me to be so far from you, to know you must be trying to find me. When I have saved Laarye, he and I will be coming home to your time and you and I can begin our life together again. Until then, my Khornya, my spirit lives with you and I will not be whole again until we are together once more.'

That was the end of the message. Mac shut off and rewound it, then asked, 'Do you want me to play it again?' in his own voice.

'Yes,' she said, still hearing Aari's voice and mulling over his words as she looked out the viewport into the vastness of space and wondered where exactly *pahaantiyirs* came from, and how long it would take to get there in the *Condor*.

GLOSSARY OF TERMS AND PROPER NAMES IN THE ACORNA UNIVERSE

aagroni – Linyaari name for a vocation that is a combination of ecologist, agriculturalist, botanist, and biologist. *Aagroni* are responsible for terraforming new planets for settlement as well as maintaining the well-being of populated planets.

Aari – a Linyaari of the Nyaarya clan, captured by the Khleevi during the invasion of Vhiliinyar, tortured, and left for dead on the abandoned planet. He's Maati's older brother. Aari survived and was rescued and restored to his people by Jonas Becker and Roadkill. But Aari's differences, the physical and psychological scars left behind by his adventures, make it difficult for him to fit in among the Linyaari.

Aarlii – a Linyaari survey team member, firstborn daughter of Captain Yaniriin.

Aarkiiyi – member of the Linyaari survey team on Vhiliinyar.

Acorna – a unicorn-like humanoid discovered as an infant by three human miners – Calum, Gill, and

Rafik. She has the power to heal and purify with her horn. Her uniqueness has already shaken up the human galaxy, especially the planet Kezdet. She's now fully grown and changing the lives of her own people as well. Among her own people, she is known as Khornya.

Ancestors – unicorn-like sentient species, precursor race to the Linyaari. Also known as *ki-lin*.

Ancestral Friends – an ancient shape-changing and spacefaring race responsible for saving the unicorns (or Ancestors) from Old Terra and using them to create the Linyaari race on Vhiliinyar.

Ancestral Hosts – *see* Ancestral Friends.

Andina – owner of the cleaning concession on MOO, and sometimes lady companion to Captain Becker.

Aridimi Desert – a vast barren desert on the Makahomian planet, site of a hidden Temple and a sacred lake.

Aridimis – people from the Makahomian Aridimi Desert.

Arkansas Traveler – freight-hauling spaceship piloted by Scaradine (Scar) MacDonald.

Attendant – Linyaari who have been selected for the task of caring for the Ancestors.

Balakiire – the Linyaari spaceship commanded by Acorna's aunt Neeva.

Basic – shorthand for Standard Galactic, the language used throughout human-settled space.

Becker – *see* Jonas Becker

Bulaybub Felidar sach Pilau ardo Agorah – a Makahomian Temple priest, better known by his real name, Tagoth. A priest who supports modernizing the Makahomian way of life, he was a favorite of Nadhari Kando before her departure from the planet. He has a close relationship with his young relative, Miw-Sher.

Calum Baird – one of three miners who discovered Acorna and raised her.

chrysoberyl – a precious cat's-eye gemstone available in large supply and great size on the planet of Makahomia, but also, very rarely and in smaller sizes, throughout the known universe. The stones are considered sacred on Makahomia, and are guarded by the priest class and the Temples. Throughout the rest of the universe, they are used in the mining and terraforming industries.

Condor – Jonas Becker's salvage ship, heavily modified to incorporate various 'found' items Becker has come across in his space voyages.

Declan 'Gill' Giloglie – one of three human miners who discovered Acorna and raised her.

Delszaki Li – once the richest man on Kezdet, opposed to child exploitation, made many political enemies. He lived his life paralyzed, floating in an antigravity chair. Clever and devious, he both hijacked and rescued Acorna and gave her a cause – saving the children of Kezdet. He became her adopted father. Li's death was a source of tremendous sadness to all but his enemies.

Dinan – Temple priest and doctor in Hissim.

Dsu Macostut – Federation officer, lieutenant commander of the Federation base on Makahomia.

Edacki Ganoosh – corrupt Kezdet count, uncle of Kisla Manjari.

enye-ghanyii – Linyaari time unit, small portion of *ghaanye*.

Fagad – Temple priest in the Aridimi Desert, who spied for Mulzar Edu Kando.

Felihari – one of the Makavitian Rainforest tribes on Makahomia.

Feriila – Acorna's mother.

Fiicki – Linyaari communications officer on Vhiliinyar expedition.

Fiirki Miilkar – a Linyaari animal specialist.

Fiiryi – a Linyaari.

fraaki – Linyaari word for fish.

Friends – also known as Ancestral Friends. A shape-changing and spacefaring race responsible for saving the unicorns from Old Terra and using them to create the Linyaari race on Vhiliinyar.

Gaali – highest peak on Vhiliinyar, never scaled by the Linyaari people. The official marker for Vhiliinyar's date line, anchoring the meridian line that sets the end of the old day and the beginning of the new day across the planet as it rotates Our Star at the center of the solar system. With nearby peaks Zaami and Kaahi, the high mountains are a mystical place for most Linyaari.

ghaanye (pl. *ghaanyi*) – a Linyaari year.

gheraalye malivii – Linyaari for Navigation Officer.

gheraalye ve-khanyii – Linyaari for Senior Communications Officer.

giirange – office of toastmaster in a Linyaari social organization.

GSS – Gravitation Stabilization System.

Haarha Liirni – Linyaari term for advanced education, usually pursued during adulthood while on sabbatical from a previous calling.

Hafiz Harakamian – Rafik's uncle, head of the interstellar financial empire of House Harakamian, a passionate collector of rarities from throughout the galaxy and a devotee of the old-fashioned sport of horse racing. Although basically crooked enough to hide behind a spiral staircase, he is genuinely fond of Rafik and Acorna.

Highmagister HaGurdy – the Ancestral Friend in charge of the Hosts on old Vhiliinyar.

Hissim – the biggest city on Makahomia, home of the largest Temple.

Hraaya – an Ancestor.

Hrronye – Melireenya's lifemate.

Hrunvrun – the first Linyaari Ancestral attendant.

Iiiliira – a Linyaari ship.

Iirtye – chief *aagroni* for narhii-Vhiliinyar.

Ikwaskwan – self-styled leader of the Kilumbembese Red Bracelets. Depending on circumstances and who he is trying to impress, he is known as either General Ikwaskwan or Admiral Ikwaskwan, though both ranks are self-administered. Entered into devious dealings with Edacki Ganoosh that led to his downfall.

Johnny Greene – an old friend of Calum, Rafik, and Gill; joined the Starfarers when he was fired after Amalgamated Mining's takeover of MME.

Jonas Becker – interplanetary salvage artist; alias space junkman. Captain of the *Condor*. CEO of

Becker Interplanetary Recycling and Salvage Enterprises Ltd. – a one-man, one-cat salvage firm Jonas inherited from his adopted father. Jonas spent his early youth on a labor farm on the planet Kezdet before he was adopted.

Judit Kendoro – assistant to psychiatrist Alton Forelle at Amalgamated Mining, saved Acorna from certain death. Later fell in love with Gill and joined with him to help care for the children employed in Delszaki Li's Maganos mining operation.

Kaahi – a high mountain peak on Vhiliinyar.

Kaalmi Vroniiyi – leader of the Linyaari Council, which made the decision to restore the ruined planet Vhiliinyar, with Hafiz's help and support, to a state that would once again support the Linyaari and all the life forms native to the planet.

Kaarlye – the father of Aari, Maati, and Laarye. A member of the Nyaarya clan, and life-bonded to Miiri.

ka-**Linyaari** – something against all Linyaari beliefs, something not Linyaari.

Karina – a plumply beautiful wannabe psychic with a small shred of actual talent and a large fondness for profit. Married to Hafiz Harakamian. This is her first marriage, his second.

Kashirian Steppes – Makahomian region that produces the best fighters.

Kashirians – Makahomians from the Kashirian Steppes.

kava – a coffee-like hot drink produced from roasted ground beans.

KEN – a line of general-purpose male androids, some with customized specializations, differentiated among their owners by number (e.g. KEN637).

Kezdet – a backwoods planet with a labor system based on child exploitation. Currently in economic turmoil because that system was broken by Delszaki Li and Acorna.

Khaari – senior Linyaari navigator on the *Balakiire*.

Khleevi – name given by Acorna's people to the space-borne enemies who have attacked them without mercy.

kii – a Linyaari time measurement roughly equivalent to an hour of Standard Time.

ki-lin – Oriental term for unicorn, also a name sometimes associated with Acorna.

Kilumbemba Empire – an entire society that raises and exports mercenaries for hire – the Red Bracelets.

Kisla Manjari – anorexic and snobbish young woman, raised as daughter of Baron Manjari; shattered when through Acorna's efforts to help the children of Kezdet her father is ruined and the truth of her lowly birth is revealed.

Kubiilikaan, the legendary first city on Vhiliinyar, founded by the Ancestral Hosts.

Kubiilikhan – capital city of narhii-Vhiliinyar, named after Kubiilikaan, the legendary first city on Vhiliinyar, founded by the Ancestral Hosts.

LAANYE – sleep-learning device invented by the Linyaari that can, from a small sample of any foreign language, teach the wearer the new language overnight.

Laarye – Maati and Aari's brother. He died on Vhiliinyar during the Khleevi invasion. He was trapped in an accident in a cave far distant from the spaceport during the evacuation, and was badly injured. Aari stayed behind to rescue and heal him, but was captured by the Khleevi and tortured before he could accomplish his mission. Laarye died before Aari could escape and return.

Laboue – the planet where Hafiz Harakamian makes his headquarters.

lilaala – a flowering vine native to Vhiliinyar used by early Linyaari to make paper.

Liriili – former *viizaar* of narhii-Vhiliinyar, member of the clan Riivye.

Linyaari – Acorna's people.

Lukia of the Lights – a protective saint, identified by some children of Kezdet with Acorna.

Ma'aowri 3 – a planet populated by cat-like beings.

Maarni – a Linyaari folklorist, mate to Yiitir.

Maati – a young Linyaari girl of the Nyaarya clan who lost most of her family during the Khleevi invasion. Aari's younger sister.

MacKenZ – also known as Mac, a very useful and adaptable unit of the KEN line of androids, now in the service of Captain Becker. The android was formerly owned by Kisla Manjari and came into the captain's service after it tried to kill him on Kisla's orders. Becker's knack for dealing with salvage enabled him to reprogram the android to make the KEN unit both loyal to him and eager to please. The reprogramming had interesting side effects on the android's personality, though, leaving Mac much quirkier than is usually the case for androids.

madigadi – a berry-like fruit whose juice is a popular beverage.

Maganos – one of the three moons of Kezdet, base for Delszaki Li's mining operation and child rehabilitation project.

Makahomia – war-torn home planet of RK and Nadhari Kando.

Makahomian Temple cat – cats on the planet Makahomia, bred from ancient Cat God stock to protect and defend the Cat God's Temples. They are – for cats – large, fiercely loyal, remarkably intelligent, and dangerous when crossed.

Makavitian Rainforest – a tropical area of the planet Makahomia, populated by various warring jungle tribes.

Manjari – a baron in the Kezdet aristocracy, and a key person in the organization and protection of Kezdet's child-labor racket, in which he was known by the code name Piper. He murdered his wife and then committed suicide when his identity was revealed and his organization destroyed.

Martin Dehoney – famous astro-architect who designed Maganos Moonbase; the coveted Dehoney Prize was named after him.

Melireenya – Linyaari communications specialist on the *Balakiire*, bonded to Hrronye.

Mercy Kendoro – younger sister of Pal and Judit Kendoro, saved from a life of bonded labor by Judit's efforts; she worked as a spy for the Child Liberation League in the offices of Kezdet Guardians of the Peace until the child labor system was destroyed.

Miiri – mother of Aari, Laarye, and Maati. A member of the Nyaarya clan, life-bonded to Kaarlye.

mitanyaakhi – generic Linyaari term meaning a very large number.

Miw-Sher – a Makahomian Keeper of the sacred Temple cats. Her name means kitten in Makahomian.

371

MME – Gill, Calum, and Rafik's original mining company. Swallowed by the ruthless, conscienceless, and bureaucratic Amalgamated Mining.

Mog-Gim Plateau – an arid area on the planet Makahomia near the Federation spaceport.

MOO, or Moon of Opportunity – Hafiz's artificial planet, and home base for the Vhiliinyar terraforming operation.

Mulzar – the Mog-Gimin title taken by the high priest who is also the warlord of the Plateau.

Mulzar Edu Kando sach Pilau dom Mog-Gim – High Priest of Hissim and the Aridimi Plateau, on the planet Makahomia.

Naadiina – also known as Grandam, one of the oldest Linyaari, host to both Maati and Acorna on narhii-Vhiliinyar; died to give her people the opportunity to save both of their planets.

Naarye – Linyaari techno-artisan in charge of final fit-out of spaceships.

Nadhari Kando – formerly Delszaki Li's personal bodyguard, rumored to have been an officer in the Red Bracelets earlier in her career, then a security officer in charge of MOO, then the guard for the leader on her home planet of Makahomia.

narhii-Vhiliinyar – the planet settled by the Linyaari after Vhiliinyar, their original homeworld, was destroyed by the Khleevi.

Neeva – Acorna's aunt and Linyaari envoy on the *Balakiire*, bonded to Virii.

Neo-Hadithian – an ultraconservative, fanatical religious sect.

Ngaen Xong Hoa – a Kieaanese scientist who invented a planetary weather control system. He sought asylum on the *Haven* because he feared the warring governments on his planet would misuse his research. A mutineer faction on the *Haven* used the system to reduce the planet Rushima to ruins. The mutineers were tossed into space, and Dr. Hoa has since restored Rushima and now works for Hafiz.

Niciirye – Grandam Naadiina's husband, dead and buried on Vhiliinyar.

Niikaavri – Acorna's grandmother, a member of the clan Geeyiinah, and a spaceship designer by trade. Also, as *Niikaavre*, the name of the spaceship used by Maati and Thariinye.

Nirii – a planetary trading partner of the Linyaari, populated by bovine-like two-horned sentients, known as Niriians, technologically advanced, able to communicate telepathically, and phlegmatic in temperament.

nyiiri – the Linyaari word for unmitigated gall, sheer effrontery, or other form of misplaced bravado.

Our Star – Linyaari name for the star that centers their solar system.

Paazo River – a major geographical feature on the Linyaari homeworld, Vhiliinyar.

pahaantiyir – a large cat-like animal once found on Vhiliinyar.

Pandora – Count Edacki Ganoosh's personal spaceship, used to track and pursue Hafiz's ship *Shahrazad* as it speeds after Acorna on her journey to narhii-Vhiliinyar. Later confiscated and used by Hafiz for his own purposes.

piiro – Linyaari word for a rowboat-like water vessel.

piiyi – a Niriian biotechnology-based information

storage and retrieval system. The biological component resembles a very rancid cheese.

Praxos – a swampy planet near Makahomia used by the Federation to train Makahomian recruits.

Rafik Nadezda – one of three miners who discovered Acorna and raised her.

Red Bracelets – Kilumbembese mercenaries; arguably the toughest and nastiest fighting force in known space.

Roadkill – otherwise known as RK. A Makahomian Temple cat, the only survivor of a space wreck, rescued and adopted by Jonas Becker, and honorary first mate of the *Condor*.

Scaradine MacDonald – captain of the *Arkansas Traveler* spaceship, and galactic freight hauler.

Shahrazad – Hafiz's personal spaceship, a luxury cruiser.

sii-**Linyaari** – a legendary race of aquatic Linyaari-like beings developed by the Ancestral Friends.

Siiaaryi Maartri – a Linyaari Survey ship.

Sita Ram – a protective goddess, identified with Acorna by the mining children on Kezdet.

Standard Galactic Basic – the language used throughout the human settled galaxy, also known simply as Basic.

stiil – Linyaari word for a pencil-like writing implement.

Taankaril – *visedhaanye ferilii* of the Gamma sector of Linyaari space.

Tagoth – *see* Bulaybub.

techno-artisan – Linyaari specialist who designs, engineers, or manufactures goods.

Thariinye – a handsome and conceited young space-faring Linyaari from clan Renyilaaghe.

Theophilus Becker – Jonas Becker's father, a salvage man and astrophysicist with a fondness for exploring uncharted wormholes.

thiilir (**pl.** *thilirii*) – small arboreal mammals of Linyaari home world.

thiilsis – grass species native to Vhiliinyar.

Toroona – a Niriian female, who sought help from Acorna and the Linyaari when her home planet was invaded by the Khleevi.

Twi Osiam – planetary site of a major financial and trade center.

twilit – small, pestiferous insect on Linyaari home planet.

Uhuru – one of the various names of the ship owned jointly by Gill, Calum, and Rafik.

Vaanye – Acorna's father.

Vhiliinyar – original home planet of the Linyaari, destroyed by Khleevi.

viizaar – a high political office in the Linyaari system, roughly equivalent to president or prime minister.

Virii – Neeva's spouse.

visedhaanye ferilii – Linyaari term corresponding roughly to 'Envoy Extraordinary.'

Vriiniia Watiir – sacred healing lake on Vhiliinyar, defiled by the Khleevi.

Wahanamoian Blossom of Sleep – poppy-like flowers whose pollen, when ground, is a very powerful sedative.

wii – a Linyaari prefix meaning small.

yaazi – Linyaari term for beloved.

Yaniriin – a Linyaari Survey Ship captain.

Yiitir – history teacher at the Linyaari academy, and Chief Keeper of the Linyaari Stories. Lifemate to Maarni.

Yukata Batsu – Uncle Hafiz's chief competitor on Laboue.

Zaami – a high mountain peak on the Linyaari home-world.

Zanegar – second-generation Starfarer.

BRIEF NOTES ON THE LINYAARI LANGUAGE

by Margaret Ball

As Anne McCaffrey's collaborator in transcribing
the first two tales of Acorna, I was delighted to
find that the second of these books provided an
opportunity to sharpen my long-unused skills in
linguistic fieldwork. Many years ago, when the
government gave out scholarships with gay
abandon and the cost of living (and attending
graduate school) was virtually nil, I got a Ph.D. in
linguistics for no better reason than that (a) the
government was willing to pay for it, (b) it gave
me an excuse to spend a couple of years doing
fieldwork in Africa, and (c) there weren't any real
jobs going for eighteen-year-old girls with a B.A.
in math and a minor in Germanic languages. (This
was back during the Upper Pleistocene era, when
the Help Wanted ads were still divided into Male
and Female.)

So there were all those years spent doing things
like transcribing tonal Oriental languages on staff
paper (the Field Methods instructor was Not
Amused) and tape-recording Swahili women at

weddings, and then I got the degree and wandered off to play with computers and never had any use for the stuff again . . . until Acorna's people appeared on the scene. It required a sharp ear and some facility for linguistic analysis to make sense of the subtle sound changes with which their language signaled syntactic changes; I quite enjoyed the challenge.

The notes appended here represent my first and necessarily tentative analysis of certain patterns in Linyaari phonemics and morphophonemics. If there is any inconsistency between this analysis and the Linyaari speech patterns recorded in the later adventures of Acorna, please remember that I was working from a very limited database and, what is perhaps worse, attempting to analyze a decidedly nonhuman language with the aid of the only paradigms I had, twentieth-century linguistic models developed exclusively from human language. The result is very likely as inaccurate as were the first attempts to describe English syntax by forcing it into the mold of Latin, if not worse. My colleague, Elizabeth Ann Scarborough, has by now added her own notes to the small corpus of Linyaari names and utterances, and it may well be that in the next decade there will be enough data available to publish a truly definitive dictionary and grammar of Linyaari, an undertaking which will surely be of inestimable value not only to those members of our race who are involved in diplomatic and trade relations with this people, but also to everyone interested in the study of language.

NOTES ON THE
LINYAARI LANGUAGE

1. A doubled vowel indicates stress: *aavi*, *abaanye*, *khleevi*.

2. Stress is used as an indicator of syntactic function: in nouns stress is on the penultimate syllable, in adjectives on the last syllable, in verbs on the first.

3. Intervocalic *n* is always palatalized.

4. Noun plurals are formed by adding a final vowel, usually *i*: one Liinyar, two Linyaari. Note that this causes a change in the stressed syllable (from LI-nyar to Li-NYA-ri) and hence a change in the pattern of doubled vowels.

   For nouns whose singular form ends in a vowel, the plural is formed by dropping the original vowel and adding *i*: ghaanye, ghaanyi. Here the number of syllables remains the same, therefore no stress/spelling change is required.

5. Adjectives can be formed from nouns by adding a final *ii* (again, dropping the original final vowel if one exists): maalive, malivii; Liinyar, Linyarii. Again, the change in stress means that the

doubled vowels in the penultimate syllable of the noun disappear.

6. For nouns denoting a class or species, such as Liinyar, the noun itself can be used as an adjective when the meaning is simply to denote a member of the class, rather than the usual adjective meaning of 'having the qualities of this class.' Thus, of the characters in *Acorna*, only Acorna herself could be described as 'a Liinyar girl,' but Judit, although human, would certainly be described as 'a Linyarii girl,' or 'a just-as-civilized-as-a-real-member-of-the-People' girl.

7. Verbs can be formed from nouns by adding a prefix constructed by [first consonant of noun] + *ii* + *nye:* faalar – grief; fiinyefalar – to grieve.

8. The participle is formed from the verb by adding a suffix *-an* or *-en:* thiinyethilel – to destroy, thiinyethilelen – destroyed. No stress change is involved because the participle is perceived as a verb form and therefore stress remains on the first syllable:

> *enye-ghanyii* – time unit, small portion of a year (ghaanye)
> *fiinyefalaran* – mourning, mourned
> *ghaanye* – a Linyaari year, equivalent to about 1⅓ earth years
> *gheraalye malivii* – Navigation Officer
> *gheraalye ve-khanyii* – Senior Communications Specialist
> *Khleevi* – originally, a small vicious carrion feeding animal with a poisonous bite; now

used by the Linyaari to denote the invaders who destroyed their homeworld.

khleevi – barbarous, uncivilized, vicious without reason

Liinyar – member of the People

Linyaari – civilized; like a Liinyar

Mitanyaakhi – large number (slang – like our 'zillions')

narhii – new

thiilir, thiliiri – small arboreal mammals of Linyaari homeworld

thiilel – destruction

visedhaanye ferilii – Envoy Extraordinary

DRAGON'S KIN
By Anne and Todd McCaffrey

Anne McCaffrey has created a complex, endlessly fascinating world uniting humans and great telepathic dragons. Millions of readers have followed book by book the evolution of one of science fiction's most popular series. Now, for the first time, Anne has invited another writer to join her in the skies of Pern, a writer with an intimate knowledge of Pern and its history: her son, Todd.

Young Kindan has no expectations other than joining his father in the mines of Camp Natalon. Mining is fraught with danger, but fortunately the camp has a watch-wher, a creature distantly related to dragons and uniquely suited to specialized work in the dark, cold mineshafts.

Then disaster strikes, leaving Kindan orphaned and the camp without a watch-wher. Grieving, Kindan is taken in by the camp's new Harper and finds a measure of solace in a burgeoning musical talent . . . and in a new friendship with the mysterious Nuella. It is Nuella who assists Kindan when he is selected to hatch and train a new watch-wher, a job that forces him to give up his dream of becoming a Harper; and it is Nuella who helps him give new meaning to his life.

Meanwhile, long-simmering tensions are dividing the camp. As warring factions threaten to explode, Nuella and Kindan begin to discover hidden talents in the watch-wher – talents that could very well save an entire Hold and which show them that even a seemingly impossible dream is never completely out of reach . . .

'Anne McCaffrey, one of the queens of science fiction, knows exactly how to give her public what it wants'
Walter Ellis, *The Times*

0 593 05287 0

NOW AVAILABLE FROM BANTAM PRESS

NIMISHA'S SHIP
by Anne McCaffrey

Nimisha Boynton-Rondymense was the body-heir of Lady Rezalla and, as such, was the heiress of one of the First Families on Vega III. But even as a child she eschewed the formalities of her aristocratic background and was happiest in her father's shipyard. By the time she was in her twenties she was the designer of the most advanced space yacht in the galaxy, and was owner of the Rondymense shipyards.

It was on a test of her Mark 5 prototype that things went wrong. In an empty space field, suitable for test runs, she was suddenly confronted with the boiling white pout of a wormhole, was sucked in, only to be thrown out into an unknown dimension of space. She was not the first. As she explored this new, unfamiliar section of the universe she found traces of ships that had been marooned over many centuries.

Not knowing if she would ever return to the world she knew, Nimisha chose to land on 'Erehwon' – fascinating, terrifying, beautiful and frightening – and inhabited not only by three survivors of a previous Vegan ship but by something else . . .

A compelling new adventure from the bestselling author of the Dragons of Pern novels.

0 552 14628 5

A LIST OF OTHER ANNE McCAFFREY
TITLES AVAILABLE FROM CORGI BOOKS
AND BANTAM PRESS

08453 0	DRAGONFLIGHT	£6.99
11635 1	DRAGONQUEST	£6.99
10661 5	DRAGONSONG	£5.99
10881 2	DRAGONSINGER: HARPER OF PERN	£5.99
11313 1	THE WHITE DRAGON	£6.99
11804 4	DRAGONDRUMS	£5.99
12499 0	MORETA: DRAGONLADY OF PERN	£6.99
12817 1	NERILKA'S STORY & THE COELURA	£5.99
13098 2	DRAGONSDAWN	£6.99
13099 0	THE RENEGADES OF PERN	£6.99
13729 4	ALL THE WEYRS OF PERN	£6.99
13913 0	THE CHRONICLES OF PERN: FIRST FALL	£5.99
14270 0	THE DOLPHINS OF PERN	£6.99
14272 7	REDSTAR RISING: THE SECOND CHRONICLES OF PERN	£6.99
14274 3	THE MASTERHARPER OF PERN	£6.99
14631 5	THE SKIES OF PERN	£6.99
05287 0	DRAGON'S KIN (with Todd McCaffrey)	£16.99
14762 1	THE CRYSTAL SINGER OMNIBUS	£8.99
14180 1	TO RIDE PEGASUS	£5.99
13728 6	PEGASUS IN FLIGHT	£6.99
14630 7	PEGASUS IN SPACE	£6.99
13763 4	THE ROWAN	£5.99
13764 2	DAMIA	£5.99
13912 2	DAMIA'S CHILDREN	£5.99
13914 9	LYON'S PRIDE	£6.99
14629 3	THE TOWER AND THE HIVE	£6.99
09115 4	THE SHIP WHO SANG	£5.99
08661 4	DECISION AT DOONA	£4.99
08344 5	RESTOREE	£5.99
10965 7	GET OFF THE UNICORN	£6.99
14436 3	THE GIRL WHO HEARD DRAGONS	£5.99
14628 5	NIMISHA'S SHIP	£6.99
52973 7	BLACK HORSES FOR THE KING	£4.99
14271 9	FREEDOM'S LANDING	£6.99
14273 5	FREEDOM'S CHOICE	£6.99
14627 7	FREEDOM'S CHALLENGE	£6.99
14909 8	FREEDOM'S RANSOM	£6.99
14099 6	POWER LINES (with Elizabeth Ann Scarborough)	£6.99
14100 3	POWER PLAY (with Elizabeth Ann Scarborough)	£6.99
14621 8	ACORNA (with Margaret Ball)	£6.99
14748 6	ACORNA'S QUEST (with Margaret Ball)	£6.99
54659 3	ACORNA'S PEOPLE (with Elizabeth Ann Scarborough)	£6.99
14749 4	ACORNA'S WORLD (with Elizabeth Ann Scarborough)	£5.99
15076 2	ACORNA'S SEARCH (with Elizabeth Ann Scarborough)	£5.99
05151 3	A GIFT OF DRAGONS	£12.99